YIWEN EDU

英语详注读物

PYGMALION

Bernard Shaw

卖花女（五幕传奇剧）

[爱尔兰] 萧伯纳 著　葛传槼 俞亢咏 注解

上海译文出版社

写在前面的话

辨认语言的正与变

朱绩崧

《卖花女》之前，我给《再会，契普斯先生》写的序通篇是忆旧抒情。本篇我想谈一点对语言学习的粗浅看法。

《再》《卖》二书乍看是没有任何联系的，但葛先生晚年读了那么多书——《英语写作》自序称所读近人著作数以千计——独独挑拣出这两本来详注的用意，在前言里说得很明白，概括起来就是一、有助于学习口语，二、学到雅俗不同的语言，三、体验名作家萧伯纳的作品。

我再浓缩一下：学习口语，分辨雅俗，亲近经典。

若还要简单，那就一个字吧——辨。

因何要辨？因为我在中国看到的是多数学习者没有“分别心”，说出的英语像念报告，从句套从句，写下的英文却很通俗，你都怀疑他中学没毕业。细究起来，其实他们对汉语也没有这方面的意识。可以说，虽然学习的是语言，而且花费的精力足令欧美教育界叹为观止，但对于语言本身的特点却茫然不知，只是一头扎在背单词、做考卷的泥潭里。

雕虫不易，雕龙尤难。辨别口语和书面语、文雅的表达和粗鄙的表达，乃至伟大的作品和平庸的作品，这些都需要下工夫才能习得。

上世纪末，《故宫博物院院刊》载有一篇《光绪帝朱批述评》，其中提到年幼的清德宗在广西巡抚奏折上朱批："知道了。你们作督抚的，务尽心民事，感召天和……"在"你们作督抚的"六字边，注有小字"尔等身膺疆寄"，显然是他的大学士师傅们在教导他如何在文字中"辨"，方不失帝主之尊。可惜，存世十八万件光绪朝朱批有多少处是帝师修改，已不得而知。否则编写文言文教材，倒是有了绝佳素材。英文方面，幸而还有《卖花女》这样一部（以我寡见，也仅此一部）真材实料造就的教材，引领我们窥见语言在教科书的模版之外，于实际生活中还有更多纷呈异彩的"变态"。

其实，整个故事大概也就是为了打破"模版至高无上、涵盖一切"的错觉而写的吧。按我愚陋的理解，萧伯纳是想说，这种自我表达的"变态"才是语言的常态、社会的常态吧——究其本质，乃天赋予人之自由是也。

前　言

"读什么?","怎样读?"　这是我们经常听到学习英语的同学提出的两个问题。学习英语，除阅读之外，当然还有听、说、写、译。这五者是相辅相成、不可偏废的，但阅读是基础。尤其在应用方面，我国极大多数从事涉外工作的人员最需要的还是阅读。阅读，对于自学者来说，更是学好外语的重要途径。

读什么?　现代英美人写的英语。作为精读材料，最好选择一些现代英美作家的作品。要新而不"怪"，就是说，语言既不陈旧，又没有很多奇怪的句子结构和俚语、方言之类；艺术表现手法新，又必须是现实主义的，既不是传统小说的平铺直叙，纯粹的讲故事，又不是"新"得出奇，变成了梦呓式的"天书"。总之，选择读物要着眼于最能起到帮助学习英美语言（进而研究英美文学）的实际效果……

怎样读?　读有精读和略读之分。两者也是相辅相成、不可偏废的，只是要求有所不同。略读从"量"来要求，广泛浏览，达到见多识广，可以容许"不求甚解"；精读则从"质"来要求，务必一词、一句都弄得清清楚楚：每个词的正确发音、它的词性、在文中的意义、色彩、搭配、用法，以及在句子中的作用；每个短语、每个从句在文中的作用和相互关系；每个句子的语法结构，有否倒装或者省略等，句型有无习惯上的特殊之处，以及句子的精确含义。这一切都弄清楚了，才能弄清每一章节的意思和各章节之间的联系。这才算是语言方面真正读懂了，才能理解全文讲的是什么，是怎样讲的，才谈得上文艺欣赏、文艺评论和翻译。

这本**注解本**是为精读而编写的，也可以说，是试图回答“怎样读”的问题的一个探索性的答案。

精读读懂以后，还希望能反复诵读，因为对于外语学习来说，懂和熟是两回事。懂而不熟，可以说并没有完成学习任务。“熟读唐诗三百首，不会吟诗也会吟。”熟读不但可以加深理解，提高阅读水平、鉴赏水平，而且直接有助于写和译，间接有助于听和说——达到全面学好英语的目的。

上面这段话是我们在合注的《再会，契普斯先生》一书“前言”中所说的。继《契普斯》之后，今又选择了萧伯纳的《卖花女》加以详注，都是试图用实例来解答“读什么？”和“怎样读？”的问题。

《契普斯》是小说，《卖花女》是剧本。这回选用一个剧本的原因是希望它在大体上帮助读者学习英语之外，还有助于学习口语。借助阅读学口语，通常采用会话书。从会话书中固然可以学到许多现成的日常口头用语，但往往比较刻板，太“规范化”，而实际生活中说的要随便得多、灵活得多。戏剧家模拟人物在实际生活中的对话，像录音一样记录成文字，比一般会话书中的对话更接近实际、更活泼。从不同人物口中，我们可以学到雅俗不同的语言，这对于听懂不同阶层的人所说的英语，也有帮助。

但是，应该强调说明，我们选用这本剧本，决不光是为供学习口语之用的。我们选用这个剧本，首先是因为萧伯纳的语言精练明快，是英国文学史上继斯威夫特（Jonathan Swift）以来第一人，而且这个剧本无论从题材还是思想性、艺术性方面来说，作为学习英语的读物都是比较理想的。

关于萧伯纳　萧伯纳 (George Bernard Shaw) 是现代爱尔兰戏剧家，鲁迅称他为“世界的文豪”，于 1856 年出生在爱尔兰都柏林一个小公务员的家庭。中学毕业后，因家贫，没有能够上大学，在一家公司里当职员。二十岁时，迁居伦敦。当时英国社会主义运动高涨，他在参加社会活动的同时，开始文艺创作，先是写小说，所著《一个脱离社会的社会主义者》(*An Unsocial Socialist*)，尖锐批判资本主义。九十年代，他受了易卜生的社会剧的影响，并鉴于英国戏剧界的萎靡不振，决心从事戏剧创作。到 1950 年萧伯纳以九十四岁的高龄逝世，半个多世纪里他写了五十一个剧本。他惯用似非而是的俏皮话，无情揭露、批判资本主义社会种种不合理现象。资本主义的政治、经济、宗教、文化无不是他抨击的对象，其影响之大，遍及全世界。然而，他本身毕竟是个改良主义者，所以始终不能指出彻底改造社会的道路。

萧伯纳曾在1933年访问我国，受到宋庆龄、鲁迅等进步人士的热情接待。鲁迅有专文记述，极言“萧的伟大”，说“我是喜欢萧的”,“他说的是真话”,“他说的是直话”(《南腔北调集》)。萧的好多作品很早就在我国有译本介绍。在1956年萧伯纳诞生一百周年时，人民文学出版社曾出版他的戏剧集，1963年又出版了《萧伯纳戏剧三种》。

萧伯纳的主要剧作有《鳏夫的房产》(*Widowers' Houses*, 1892)、《华伦夫人的职业》(*Mrs Warren's Profession*, 1893)、《武器与人》(*Arms and the Man*, 1894)、《魔鬼的门徒》(*The Devil's Disciple*, 1897)、《凯撒和克丽奥佩拉》(*Caesar and Cleopatra*, 1898)、《人与超人》(*Man and Superman*, 1903)、《巴巴拉少校》(*Major Barbara*, 1905)、《卖花女》(*Pygmalion*, 1912)、《伤心之家》(*Heartbreak House*, 1919)、《回到玛士撒拉》(*Back to Methuselah*, 1921；旧译《千岁人》)、《圣女贞德》(*Saint Joan*, 1923)、《苹果车》(*The Apple Cart*, 1928)等。

关于《卖花女》剧本原名 *Pygmalion*　Pygmalion原是希腊神话中的塞浦路斯国王，善于雕刻。他刻了一个象牙美女，名为Galatea，对她迷恋不置，祈求爱神赋予她生命，愿与她结为夫妻。爱神玉成了他的祈求，两人终成眷属。在本剧中，萧伯纳用Pygmalion比喻语言学家Higgins。Higgins用六个月的工夫训练一个满口伦敦土音的街头卖花姑娘，居然使她学会了上层社会的文雅口音、语言和风度。他带她出席大使馆的招待会，她那雍容大方的仪态使四座震惊，被疑为某国公主光临。故事的结局则与神话不同：Pygmalion 娶 Galatea 为妻，而萧伯纳却在剧中以卖花女 Eliza（即 Liza）和 Higgins 教授之间的矛盾分歧收场，并在剧本后面加上了一条小品体裁的长尾巴(sequel，本书未收入），写 Eliza 最后离开 Higgins，嫁了一个热爱她的穷小子 Freddy。

萧伯纳别出心裁地拿语言学问题作为剧本的题材，讽刺上层社会所谓文雅的语言和风度，鲜明地显示劳动人民淳朴的本质远远高于上层社会的空虚外表。Eliza不能容忍上层社会熙来攘往的浮华无聊，不能容忍 Higgins 目空一切的高傲、任性，更不能容忍自己成了一个假人。Eliza 最后离去，正表示她同上层社会的决裂。她宁愿嫁个穷小子，因为她深信，她和 Freddy 之间有真正的爱情，他们在一起可以有真正的生活。

萧伯纳在剧本序言中说，在 Higgins 身上有英国著名语言学家 Henry Sweet (1845–1912) 的影子。但这与剧情和剧本的中心思想没有多大关系。

《卖花女》写于1912年，1914年首次上演，1916年出版，是萧伯纳最有趣的一个剧本。1938 年修改，并添上了一些场景，拍摄电影，也很成功，曾在我国放映。王佐良先生在《萧伯纳戏剧三种》的“译文序”中称《卖花女》“情节有趣，发人深思。至今显得十分新鲜。”这是很恰当的评语。《剑桥英国文学史简编》(*The Concise Cambridge History of English Literature*) 也承认《卖花女》是“可喜的喜剧”，但不喜欢它的结局，这正是资产阶级的偏见。1956 年美国抒情歌曲作家 Alan Jay Lerner 把萧伯纳的这部剧本改编成音乐喜剧《窈窕淑女》(*My Fair Lady*)，把原来的结尾改成 Higgins 和 Eliza“大团圆”，并拍摄了电影，轰动一时。

关于注解　和前注《契普斯》“前言”中所说的一样，“我们是从语言角度进行注解的，力求详尽。如果你觉得有些讲解是多余的，那就说明这些你已经懂了，可以跳过去。相反，如果这样详尽讲解了，你阅读还有困难，那说明这本书也许暂时对你还太深了些，可以先读一些简易读物，作为一个阶梯。注解的详略要正好符合所有读者的要求是不可能的。我们希望读者能够看得出，我们是认认真真地做了这本书的注解工作的，煞费苦心，总想切实有助于我国的英语学习者，尤其是自学者。”

剧本因为都是对话，句子结构和所用词汇比其他体裁的文学作品简单。然而口语常有特殊的表现方法，本书的讲解在这方面特别注意，尽量指出各种惯用法和阐明有些句子比较含蓄的涵义。萧伯纳的语言是现代英国语言的典范，既如上述。剧中在模拟卖花女未受训练前的语言时，出现少数伦敦土语、土音（主要是在第一幕中），都一一注出其相应的规范英语和正规读音。另外，萧伯纳特意在拼法中把 ain't、don't、haven't 等中的撇号 (') 删去，写成 aint、dont、havnt 等；同样，把 that's、 let's、you'd、you're、it'll 写成 thats、lets、youd、youre、itll 等。但是 I'll、she'd、we'll、it's 等中的撇号不删，以免与 Ill、shed、well、its 等相混淆。I'm 中的撇号也不删，因为删了之后似应读成 [ɪm] 而不是 [aɪm] 了。对此，我们在这里作一总的说明，注中不再分散地解释了。

本剧有杨宪益先生译的英汉对照本（中国对外翻译出版社公司出版，1982）。杨译极好。如把详注对照译文研习原著，可以更加加深对原文的理解，更充分地欣赏原文、欣赏译文，学习翻译。

最后，申明一下：为了帮助读者精确了解原文，学好英语，我们的注解旨在讲清原文词义，明析原文的语法结构。注文不同于译文。翻译追求"信、达、雅"，而我们的注文常难免读来佶屈聱牙。好在没有人会把注文当作汉语规范，不会通过注文来学习汉语。但我们还是恳请读者谅解我们的苦心。

我们这样详尽的注解是否有必要，以及注解不当和错误之处，诚望英语学者和读者们予以批评指教。

葛传椝　俞亢咏

一九八五年五月

于汉光院

Pygmalion

第一幕
剧情提要

夏夜大雨。剧院散场，众人在教堂廊下避雨，一面抢着叫车子。Freddy 在纷乱中撞翻了卖花女 Liza 的花篮，Liza 要他赔钱，又缠着一位中年绅士，要他买花，说的是满口土话。语言学家 Higgins 教授背着众人在笔记本上记录 Liza 的发音。周围的人还当他是警察局的密探，以为他把她当做坏女人，要找她的麻烦，纷纷不平，引起一番争吵。后来 Higgins 才说出他是以研究语音学为职业的。他对 Liza 说，经过三个月的语音训练，他能使她冒充公爵夫人，参加外国大使的招待会，还说能使她在上等人家找到个保姆或者店员的工作。Liza 要他买花，他扔了一把钱币在她篮子里，这一把钱里不但有好些银币，还有一枚金币。

那位中年绅士 Pickering 上校是研究印度方言的。他是远道而来、专程寻访 Higgins 教授的。Higgins 对他也慕名已久。如今他们不期而遇，喜出望外。Higgins 把地址告诉了他，请他来家一叙。就是这一对独身的语言学家，闹出了一场好戏。

撞翻花篮的 Freddy 是个破落户子弟。他在这一幕里只匆匆过场，后面可成了一个意想不到的角色。

ACT I

London at 11.15 p.m. Torrents of heavy summer rain. Cab whistles blowing frantically in all directions. Pedestrians running for shelter into the market and under the portico of St. Paul's Church (not Wren's cathedral but Inigo Jones's church in Covent Garden vegetable market), among them a lady and her daughter in evening dress. All are peering out gloomily at the rain, except one man with his back turned to the rest, who seems wholly preoccupied with a notebook in which he is writing busily.

The church clock strikes the first quarter.

THE DAUGHTER [*in the space between the central pillars, close to the one on her left*] I'm getting chilled to the bone. What can Freddy be doing all this time? He's been gone twenty minutes.

THE MOTHER [*on her daughters' right*] Not so long. But he ought to have got us a cab by this.

A BYSTANDER [*on the lady's right*] He wont get no cab not until half-past eleven, missus, when they come back after drop-

---

1 **London at 11.15 p.m.** 这是名词词组构成的单部句(one element sentence),可称为名词句,后面三句同。11.15 是英国式;11:15 是美国式。 **Torrents** ['tɒrənts] **of heavy summer rain** 夏季大雨的倾注;夏雨倾盆。Torrents 作"倾注"解,用复数。 **Cab whistles** ['wɪslz] 叫车的哨子。 **Cab** Taxi-cab.

出租车（兼指出租的马车或机动车）。

2 **running for shelter** 奔去躲避。Shelter 作“掩蔽”解，是不可数名词。

3 **portico** [ˈpɔːtɪkəʊ] 有圆柱的门廊。 **St. Paul's** [sntˈpɔːlz] **church** 圣保罗教堂，即 St. Paul's Cathedral。

4 **Wren's** [renz] **cathedral** [kəˈθiːdrəl] （由）Wren（设计建造）的大教堂。Christopher [ˈkrɪstəfə] Wren (1632–1723)，英国建筑家。 **cathedral** 大教堂（内设主教法座）。 **Inigo** [ˈɪnɪgəʊ] **Jones's** [ˈdʒəʊnzɪz] **church** （由）Inigo Jones（设计建造）的教堂。Inigo Jones (1573–1652)，英国建筑家兼舞台设计师。 **Covent** [ˈkʌvənt] **Garden vegetable market** Covent Garden 在伦敦中部地区，也指那里的菜市场或剧场 the Covent Garden Theatre。

5 **among them a lady and her daughter** among them there being a lady and her daughter. 是个简略的独立结构（absolute construction）。

6 **evening dress** 晚礼服。注意：是个不可数名词，前面不用冠词，也不可用复数。

7 **turned** 过去分词，其作用等于 being turned。

10 **the first quarter** 这里指十一点钟的第一刻（的末尾），即上文所说的 11.15 p.m.。

11 **close** [kləʊz] **to the one on her left** 靠近她左边的廊柱。one = pillar.

12 **chilled to the bone** 冻得彻骨。chilled 过去分词，作表语。 **What can Freddy be doing all this time?** Freddy（去了）这么久，会在干些什么呢？这里 can 有“究竟”的意思。

13 **He's been gone** 注意有 been，指“离开此地而尚未回来”的情况。这里 gone 是形容词。

14 **Not so long** He's not been gone so long. 口语中很多用省略句。 **ought to have got us a cab by this** 到这时候应该给我们弄到一辆出租车了。ought 后接完成时不定式表示应该已经做到而没有做到。 **by this** by this time, by now.

16 **He wont get no cab not until half-past** [ˈhɑːfpɑːst] **eleven** He won't get any cab not until half-past eleven. 没受过教育的英美人常使用双重否定（double negative）；这里是用了三重否定。

17 **missus** [ˈmɪsɪz] = missis [ˈmɪsɪz]. 太太。这是没有受过教育的人的用语；正规英语称 madam [ˈmædəm]。 **when they come back after dropping their theatre fares** 在他们送掉了剧院散场的客人们以后再回来的时候。这个句子可以说是和 half-past eleven 同位，也可以说是 until 的另一个宾语。 **dropping** 使下车。

ping their theatre fares.

THE MOTHER But we must have a cab. We cant stand here until half-past eleven. It's too bad.

THE BYSTANDER Well, it aint my fault, missus.

THE DAUGHTER If Freddy had a bit of gumption, he would have got one at the theatre door.

THE MOTHER What could he have done, poor boy?

THE DAUGHTER Other people got cabs. Why couldnt he?

Freddy rushes in out of the rain from the Southampton Street side, and comes between them closing a dripping umbrella. He is a young man of twenty, in evening dress, very wet around the ankles.

THE DAUGHTER Well, havnt you got a cab?

FREDDY Theres not one to be had for love or money.

THE MOTHER Oh, Freddy, there must be one. You cant have tried.

THE DAUGHTER It's too tiresome. Do you expect us to go and get one ourselves?

FREDDY I tell you theyre all engaged. The rain was so sudden: nobody was prepared; and everybody had to take a cab. Ive been to Charing Cross one way and nearly to Ludgate Circus the other; and they were all engaged.

THE MOTHER Did you try Trafalgar Square?

---

18 **fares** 乘客。这里不作“车费”解。

20 **It's too bad** 这（在这里站到十一点半）太糟了。

21 **Well** 随口的感叹词，这里表示无可奈何。 **aint** ain't，俚语，= isn't。

22 **If Freddy had a bit of gumption** ['gʌmpʃən], **he would have got one at the theatre door.** 如果 Freddy 有点办法，他准已在剧场门口叫到一辆出租车了。had 是虚拟语气，实际是因为 Freddy 没有办法，所以车子没有叫到。不用 had had 而用 had，因为有没有办法是一个人的本领，而不是某一时刻的情况。比较：If he had had a chance, he would have got one at the theatre door.“碰到个机会”便是一时的情况。 **Freddy** ['fredi] 男子名。 **gumption** 精明能干，魄力，是口语词。

24 **What could he have done, poor boy?** 他能怎么样呢，可怜的孩子？ poor boy 与 he 同位，指 Freddy。

26 **Southampton** [saʊ'θæmptən] **Street** 伦敦一街道。

27 **comes between them** 来到他们中间。them 指 the mother 和 the daughter，即 Freddy 的母亲和姐妹。

31 **for love or money** 无论是讲交情还是讲价钱，无论如何。这是习语，只用于否定，这里上文有 not one。

32 **there must be one** 一定有一辆车的。 **You cant have tried** 你不可能已经努力（找）过。can + have + 过去分词，表示过去的可能。

33 **tiresome** 招人讨厌的，恼人的。 **expect us to go and get one** 准备让我们去叫辆车子。expect 这里是“料想，准备”的意思，不是“盼望，希望”。 **go and get** = go to get，是口语。

35 **I tell you** 我告诉你们，你们该相信我，的确是这样。 **theyre** (= they were) **all engaged** 车子都被人叫去了。 **The rain was so sudden: nobody was prepared** so sudden 后面的冒号相当于英语的连词 that 的作用。 **prepared** 有准备的，是形容词作表语。

36 **Ive been to Charing Cross** ['tʃærɪŋ 'krɒs] **one way and nearly to Ludgate** ['lʌdgeɪt] **Circus the other** 我一头到过 Charing Cross，另一头到过 Ludgate Circus。 **Ive been to** 我到过（某处）。Charing Cross 是伦敦中部地区地名；... Cross 前面不用 the。Ludgate Circus 是伦敦地名。 **circus** 英国十字路中的圆形广场；... Circus 前面不用 the。 **one way** in one direction. **the other** = the other way = in the other direction.

39 **Trafalgar** [trə'fælgə] **Square** 伦敦中区广场名；前面不用 the。

FREDDY There wasnt one at Trafalgar Square.

THE DAUGHTER Did you try?

FREDDY I tried as far as Charing Cross Station. Did you expect me to walk to Hammersmith?

THE DAUGHTER You havnt tried at all.

THE MOTHER You really are very helpless, Freddy. Go again; and dont come back until you have found a cab.

FREDDY I shall simply get soaked for nothing.

THE DAUGHTER And what about us? Are we to stay here all night in this draught, with next to nothing on? You selfish pig –

FREDDY Oh, very well: I'll go, I'll go. [*He opens his umbrella and dashes off Strandwards, but comes into collision with a flower girl who is hurrying in for shelter, knocking her basket out of her hands. A blinding flash of lightning, followed instantly by a rattling peal of thunder, orchestrates the incident.*]

THE FLOWER GIRL Nah then, Freddy: look wh' y' gowin, deah.

FREDDY Sorry. [*He rushes off.*]

THE FLOWER GIRL [*picking up her scattered flowers and replacing them in the basket*] Theres menners f' yer! Tə-oo banches o voylets trod into the mad. [*She sits down on the plinth of the column, sorting her flowers, on the lady's right. She is not at all a romantic figure. She is perhaps eighteen, perhaps twenty, hardly older. She wears a little sailor hat of black straw that has long been exposed to the dust and*

---

42 **Charing Cross Station** Charing Cross 车站；... Station 前面不用 the。

43 **Hammersmith** [ˈhæməsmɪθ] 伦敦地名，在泰晤士河北岸。

45 **helpless** 没用的，帮不上忙的；无效的。

47 **simply** 简直。 **soaked** [səʊkt] 被雨水湿透；过去分词作表语。 **for nothing** 没来由地，白白地，徒然。

48 **what about us** 我们怎么样。 **what about ...** 口语中常用，意思是"……怎么样"。 **Are we to stay** Should we stay.

49 **draught** [drɑːft] 穿堂风，风口。 **with next to nothing on** 几乎不穿衣服（极言衣着单薄）。 **next to nothing** 几乎一无所有。 **on** 被穿着。

51 **Strandwards** [ˈstrændwədz] 朝 the Strand 方向。the Strand 原指沿泰晤士河的河岸，现在是伦敦商业区（the City of London）与威斯敏斯特教堂（Westminster Abbey）之间的干道，注意用 the。 **comes into collision** [kəˈlɪʒən] **with** 和……相撞，撞着。

53 **blinding flash of lightning** [ˈlaɪtnɪŋ] 使人目眩的闪电。

54 **orchestrates** [ˈɔːkɪstreɪt] 原义是"为……配交响乐"，这里转义指"（雷电）用它的声响配合（Freddy 撞翻卖花女的花篮这一事情，即 the incident）"。

55 **Nah then, Freddy: look wh' y' gowin, deah.** = Now then, Freddy: look where you're going, dear. **Now then** 注意啊！喂！ **look where you're going** （你怎么不）看看你走到哪里去了。 **dear** 犹言"朋友"。

57 **replacing** 放回；这里不作"以……代替"解。

58 **Theres menners f' yer!** = There's manners for you! 那就是你的礼貌！其实是说："你竟然没有礼貌！" **manners** 礼貌；具有抽象名词性质，虽是复数形式，作单数用，所以前面用 There's，而不用 There're。 **Tə-oo banches o voylets trod into the mad.** = Two bunches of violets (were) trod into the mud. 不用 were，是名词句。

60 **romantic figure** 楚楚动人者。

61 **hardly older** 不大会（比二十岁）年纪更大。

62 **sailor hat** （妇女戴的）低顶草帽。 **exposed to the dust and soot of London** 听任暴露于伦敦的尘土和煤灰中（势必沾满灰尘）。

soot of London and has seldom if ever been brushed. Her hair needs washing rather badly: its mousy color can hardly be natural. She wears a shoddy black coat that reaches nearly to her knees and is shaped to her waist. She has a brown skirt with a coarse apron. Her boots are much the worse for wear. She is no doubt as clean as she can afford to be; but compared to the ladies she is very dirty. Her features are no worse than theirs; but their condition leaves something to be desired; and she needs the services of a dentist.]

THE MOTHER How do you know that my son's name is Freddy, pray?

THE FLOWER GIRL Ow, eez yə-ooa san, is e? Wal, fewd dan y' də-ooty bawmz a mather should, eed now bettern to spawl a pore gel's flahrzn than ran awy athaht pyin. Will ye-oo py me f'them? [*Here, with apologies, this desperate attempt to represent her dialect without a phonetic alphabet must be abandoned as unintelligible outside London.*]

THE DAUGHTER Do nothing of the sort, mother. The idea!

---

63 **seldom if ever** 即便曾经有过也是极其难得地；实际意义 = seldom or never。**needs washing rather badly** 极需要洗。need 后面用主动形式的动名词，表示被动的意思。注意：不能说 need being washed。badly 口语中常作"非常"解。

64 **its mousy** [ˈmaʊsi] **color can hardly be natural** 她头发的灰褐颜色不大可能是天然如此。can 这里作"可能"解，不是"能够"的意思。 **shoddy** 质量差的，以次充好的（如充羊毛的）。

65 **reaches nearly to her knees** 几乎齐膝。 **reach to** 伸延到……。

66 **shaped** [ʃeɪpt] **to her waist** 裁制得适合她的腰身。

67 **the worse for wear** 穿得破旧了的；破旧不堪的。the 是副词。 **no doubt** 的确，固然；注意下面用 but ...。 **as she can afford to be** 尽她所能地干净；be 后省略 clean。

68 **the ladies** 上流社会妇人那一类人物。用 the 指“……那一类人物”。 **Her features** 她脸庞的各部，她的容貌。

69 **their condition leaves something to be desired** 它们（her features）的状况还需改善；她的容貌还需修饰。 leaves something (much, nothing) to be desired 都是习语，分别作“还需改善”（“还需大大改善”、“无需改善，完美无缺”）解。

70 **the services of a dentist** 牙医服务（指修补、矫正、洗洁等）。注意用复数形式 services。

71 **How do you know that my son's name is Freddy, pray?** 你怎么知道我儿子的名字叫 Freddy？卖花女对此没有回答。再次问她后，她才回答（见后）。 **pray** = please. 请问。

73 **Ow, eez yə-ooa san, is e?** = Oh, he is your son, is he? **Wal, fewd dan y' də-ooty bawmz a mather should, eed now bettern to spawl a pore gel's flahrzn than ran awy athaht pyin.** = Well, if you'd (= you had) done your duty by him as a mother should, he'd (= he would) know better than to spoil a poor girl's flowers and then run away without paying. 唉，假如你尽到了一个母亲应尽的（教育子女的）责任，他应该懂得道理，不至于弄坏了一个穷苦女孩的花，钱也不给就跑掉了。这是虚拟句：if you had done ... , he would know ... ，假如你过去做了……，他现在就懂……了；事实是你过去没有做，所以他现在不懂。 **done your duty by him** 尽了你对他的责任；注意用 by。 **know better than** （后接带 to 的不定式）懂得，明白，因而不至于……。

75 **Will ye-oo py me f'them?** = Will you pay me for them (= the flowers)?

76 **Here, with apologies** [əˈpɒədʒɪz], **this desperate** [ˈdespərət] **attempt to represent** [reprɪˈzent] **her dialect without a phonetic alphabet** [ˈælfəbet] **must be abandoned as unintelligible outside London.** 至此以后，将放弃这种不用音标，勉强描述她一口伦敦方言的做法，因为在伦敦以外（的人）无法理解，抱歉。注意 with apologies 中用复数。

79 **Do nothing of the sort.** 决不要干这样的事；一个钱也不要给她。 **The idea!** （亏她想得出这样的）好主意！岂有此理！

THE MOTHER Please allow me, Clara. Have you any pennies?

THE DAUGHTER No. Ive nothing smaller than sixpence.

THE FLOWER GIRL [*hopefully*] I can give you change for a tanner, kind lady.

THE MOTHER [*to Clara*] Give it to me. [*Clara parts reluctantly.*] Now [*to the girl*] this is for your flowers.

THE FLOWER GIRL Thank you kindly, lady.

THE DAUGHTER Make her give you the change. These things are only a penny a bunch.

THE MOTHER Do hold your tongue, Clara. [*to the girl*] You can keep the change.

THE FLOWER GIRL Oh, thank you, lady.

THE MOTHER Now tell me how you know that young gentleman's name.

THE FLOWER GIRL I didnt.

THE MOTHER I heard you call him by it. Dont try to deceive me.

THE FLOWER GIRL [*protesting*] Who's trying to deceive you? I called him Freddy or Charlie same as you might yourself if you was talking to a stranger and wished to be pleasant.

THE DAUGHTER Sixpence thrown away! Really, mamma, you might have spared Freddy that. [*She retreats in disgust behind the pillar.*]

An elderly gentleman of the amiable military type rushes into the shelter, and closes a dripping umbrella. He is in the same plight as Freddy, very wet about the ankles. He is in evening

80 **Please allow me** = Please allow me to do something of the sort. 让我给一点钱。**Clara** [ˈkleərə] 女子名。 **pennies** 便士。penny 有两个复数式：指一个一个便士的钱币时用 pennies；计值用 pence。

81 **sixpence** [ˈsɪkspens] 六便士，这里指英国当时六便士面值的银币。当时英国一镑 = 二十先令，一先令 = 十二便士；六便士即半先令。现已取消先令，一镑 = 一百便士。

82 **change** [tʃeɪndʒ] 找头。 **tanner** （俚语）英国旧时的六便士银币。

84 **parts** （口语）出钱，付款。

86 **Thank you kindly, lady.** 多谢你，女士。用 kindly 来修饰自己对对方的道谢，在意义上讲是不妥当的，但事实上用得很多。 **lady** 这里用来称对方，现在不是正规的用语。

89 **Do hold your tongue** 住嘴。 Do hold 加重 hold 的语气；Do 要重读。 **You can keep the change** 你不用找我钱了。keep the change 是惯用语；不说 Do not give me the change。

95 **call him by it** 用 Freddy 的名字叫他；注意用 by。

96 **protesting** 抗议；辩白。 **protest** 动词读 [prəˈtest]，名词读 [ˈprəʊtest]。

97 **Charlie** [ˈtʃɑːli] Charlie 和 Freddy 等都是很普通的男子名。 **same as** 正规英语用 the same as 或 just as。 **you might yourself** = you might yourself call him Freddy or Charlie. **if you was** 正规英语应作 if you were；这里是虚拟语气。

98 **be pleasant** [ˈplezənt] 使人喜悦；这里是"表示亲热"的意思。

99 **you might have spared Freddy that** 你大可把那个（白白扔掉的六便士）省下给 Freddy。spare 可以接双宾语，spare Freddy that 比 spare that to Freddy 普通，尤其如果这里不用 that 而用了 the sixpence。

102 **rushes into the shelter** 冲进躲避处。比较：前面有过 running for shelter，那 shelter 是抽象名词，作"掩蔽"解；这里的 shelter 是普通名词，是具体的掩蔽的地方，所以用冠词 the。

dress, with a light overcoat. He takes the place left vacant by the daughter.

THE GENTLEMAN Phew!

THE MOTHER [*to the gentleman*] Oh, sir, is there any sign of its stopping?

THE GENTLEMAN I'm afraid not. It started worse than ever about two minutes ago. [*He goes to the plinth beside the flower girl; puts up his foot on it; and stoops to turn down his trouser ends.*]

THE MOTHER Oh dear! [*She retires sadly and joins her daughter.*]

THE FLOWER GIRL [*taking advantage of the military gentleman's proximity to establish friendly relations with him*] If it's worse, it's a sign it's nearly over. So cheer up, Captain; and buy a flower off a poor girl.

THE GENTLEMAN I'm sorry. I havnt any change.

THE FLOWER GIRL I can give you change, Captain.

THE GENTLEMAN For a sovereign? Ive nothing less.

THE FLOWER GIRL Garn! Oh do buy a flower off me, Captain. I can change half-a-crown. Take this for tuppence.

THE GENTLEMAN Now dont be troublesome: theres a good girl. [*trying his pockets*] I really havnt any change – Stop: heres three hapence, if thats any use to you. [*He retreats to the other pillar.*]

THE FLOWER GIRL [*disappointed, but thinking three halfpence better*

---

105 **light overcoat** 薄大衣。厚大衣称 heavy overcoat。 **the place left vacant** 被

空出的地方。left 是过去分词，修饰 the place；vacant 是补语。

108 **any sign of its stopping** 它（雨）停的任何迹象。

110 **I'm afraid not** = I'm afraid there's not any sign of its stopping. **It started worse than ever** 情况比原来更糟了。这里指雨开始下得更大了。

114 **taking advantage** [əd'vɑːntɪdʒ] **of** 利用，趁……的机会；是习语。 **proximity** [prɒk'sɪməti] 靠近；接近。

115 **If it's worse, it's a sign it's nearly over.** sign 后面省略 that；第一和第三个 it 代替 rain，第二个 it 是虚词（expletive），和 that it's nearly over 同位。

116 **Captain** 是"队长"或"陆军上尉"、"海军上校"。这里是卖花女对军人的胡乱称呼。 **buy a flower off a poor girl** 从穷苦女孩子手里买一枝花。注意用 off，有"让我卖掉一枝花"的意思。

118 **change** 零钱；是不可数名词。

119 **change** 找头；是不可数名词。

120 **For a sovereign** ['sɒvrɪn]**?** = Can you give me change for a sovereign? Sovereign 是当时的一金镑硬币。 **Ive nothing less** = I've nothing less than a sovereign. 我没有比一金镑小的钱币。

121 **Garn** 英国俚语，表示不信、轻蔑等意，犹言"去你的!"、"得了吧! "，是从 go on 转讹而来。

122 **change half-a-crown** 兑开两先令六便士的硬币。当时英国有五先令的硬币，称 crown；也有两先令六便士的硬币，称 half-a-crown。 **Take this for tuppence** ['tʌpəns]. 出两便士买这个吧。

123 **Now dont be troublesome** ['trʌbəlsəm] 好啦，别纠缠不清了。Now 这里是语气词，引出命令、请求、劝慰等。 **troublesome** 使人感觉麻烦的；讨厌的；不是"感觉麻烦的"。 **theres a good girl** 这才是个好姑娘。

124 **trying his pockets** 在口袋里摸摸看。 **Stop** 等一等看。 **heres three hapence** ['heɪpəns] 这里有一个半（⅓ × 3）便士。 **hapence** 半便士；正规写作 halfpence（也读 ['heɪpəns]），是 halfpenny ['heɪpni] 的复数。halfpennies 计值用 halfpence。一个半便士是一个数额，所以动词用单数。

127 **better than nothing** 比没有好些；聊胜于无。

than nothing] Thank you, sir.

THE BYSTANDER [*to the girl*] You be careful: give him a flower for it. Theres a block here behind taking down every blessed word youre saying. [*All turn to the man who is taking notes.*]

THE FLOWER GIRL [*springing up terrified*] I aint done nothing wrong by speaking to the gentleman. Ive a right to sell flowers if I keep off the kerb. [*hysterically*] I'm a respectable girl: so help me, I never spoke to him except to ask him to buy a flower off me. [*General hubbub, mostly sympathetic to the flower girl, but deprecating her excessive sensibility. Cries of* Dont start hollerin. Who's hurting you? Nobody's going to touch you. Whats the good of fussing? Steady on. Easy, easy, *etc., come from the elderly staid spectators, who pat her comfortingly. Less patient ones bid her shut her head, or ask her roughly what is wrong with her. A remoter group, not knowing what the matter is, crowd in and increase the noise with question and answer:* Whats the row? What-she do? Where is he? A tec taking her down. What! him? Yes: him

---

129 **You be careful** 比 Be careful 语气重。

130 **it** 指 three hapence。 **block** （俚语）家伙（只指男人）。 **every blessed** [ˈblesɪd] **word** 每一个词。blessed 这里用以加强 every 的语气，带有俚俗的口气，但比说 every damned word 文雅些。

132 **I aint done nothing wrong** = I haven't done anything wrong / I've done nothing wrong.

134 **keep off the kerb** 对街沿石保持距离；不走到街沿石。 **kerb** = kerbstone. 人行道的镶边石，街沿石；是英国用语，在美国称 curb(stone)。 **respectable** 正派的；这里不作"可敬的"解。 **so help me** 也作 so help me God，是赌

咒用语；犹言“天晓得”，表示千真万确的。

136 **General hubbub** [ˈhʌbʌb] 众人的喧闹。

137 **deprecating** [ˈdeprəkeɪt] **her excessive sensibility** 责怪她过分的敏感（神经过敏）。 **Cries** 是后面 come from the elderly staid spectators 的主语。Cries of 后面的 Dont start hollerin 到 Easy easy, etc. 是你一声、我一声 Cries 的内容。 **hollerin** = hollering. 吵闹。土语中总将 -ing 读作 -in。

138 **Whats the good of fussing?** 大惊小怪有什么好处？ **good** 作名词，是“好处”、“用处”的意思。

139 **Steady on** [ˈstedi ɒn] 且慢；停下来。**Easy, easy** Easy 是 Be easy、Take it easy 之略，意思是“不要急”、“定心”。 **etc.** [ˌetˈsetərə] 是拉丁语 et cetera 的缩写，也写作 &c,= and so on,等等。这里 etc. 指上文众人所说的种种话以外还有其他的话，并不是说话中有这个词。 **the elderly staid** [steɪd] **spectators** 年老持重的旁观者们。

141 **shut her head** 住嘴，= shut her mouth. 比较：open one's head,（美国俚语）开口，说话。 **what is wrong with her** 她出了什么事。注意：用 with。

142 **not knowing what the matter is** 不知是什么事情。这里 the matter 是字面的意义：这事情。比较：not knowing what is the matter 是“不知出了什么事”的意思，这里的 the matter 是习语，作“麻烦”、“毛病”解，基本上 = wrong，具有形容词的性质。 **crowd in** 拥挤到人群中来。

143 **question and answer** 照理，question 和 answer 都是可数名词，应作 questions and answers，但两词用 and 连接，成了一对，故可用单数。后面许多话都是回答的内容。 **Whats the row** [raʊ]**?** 吵嚷什么？ **What-she** [ˈwɒtʃɪ] **do?** = What does she do? 这里 What-she 连写，表示说话的人把两个词念在一起。

144 **A tec taking her down.** = A tec is taking her down. 一个侦探在把她（说的话）记下来。 **tec** 俚语，= detective；指剧本开首的那个 one man，即 the note taker。 **take down** 记下，录下；是习语。 **What! him?** 什么！他吗？这是 What! Is it he? 的省略句。照理 him 应作 he，主格作表语，但口语中常用宾格。 **him over there** = It's him over there. **over there** 他正在那边。

over there: Took money off the gentleman, *etc.*]

THE FLOWER GIRL [*breaking through them to the gentleman, crying wildly*] Oh, sir, dont let him charge me. You dunno what it means to me. Theyll take away my character and drive me on the streets for speaking to gentlemen. They –

THE NOTE TAKER [*coming forward on her right, the rest crowding after him*] There! There! There! There! Who's hurting you, you silly girl? What do you take me for?

THE BYSTANDER It's aw rawt: e's a genleman: look at his bə-oots. [*explaining to the note taker*] She thought you was a copper's nark, sir.

THE NOTE TAKER [*with quick interest*] Whats a copper's nark?

THE BYSTANDER [*inapt at definition*] It's a – well, it's a copper's nark, as you might say. What else would you call it? A sort of informer.

THE FLOWER GIRL [*still hysterical*] I take my Bible oath I never said a word –

THE NOTE TAKER [*overbearing but good-humored*] Oh, shut up, shut up. Do I like a policeman?

THE FLOWER GIRL [*far from reassured*] Then what did you take down my words for? How do I know whether you took me down right? You just shew me what youve wrote about me. [*The note taker opens his book and holds it steadily under her nose,*

---

145 **Took money** = She took money.

146 **breaking through them** 从人群中挤出去（或冲出去）。

147 **charge** 控告。 **You dunno** [ˈdʌnəʊ] **what it means to me.** 你不知道这（控告我）意味着什么。 **dunno** 口语，= don't know.

148 **Theyll take away my character** [ˈkærəktə] 他们会拿掉我的品行证明书；毁我的名声。They 泛指警察局人员。 **drive me on the streets** 把我赶到街头去流浪。

151 **There!** 感叹词，用以引起注意、表示安慰或加强语气等。

152 **take me for...** 当我是……

153 **It's aw rawt: e's a genleman: look at his bə-oots** = It's all right: he's a gentleman: look at his boots. 没有问题，他是个上等人，看他的皮鞋。意思是从他的皮鞋可以看得出，他不是警察手下的密探（见下句）。

154 **She thought you was a copper's nark** 她原以为你是警察手下的密探。was 是 were 之讹。 **copper** 警察；是俚语。 **nark** （警察手下的）密探；也是俚语。

157 **inapt at definition** 不善于下定义。inapt 作"不熟练于某事的"解时，介词用 at；作"对某事不恰当的"解时，用 for。 **well** 语气词。It's a 后面应该说出个 copper's nark 的定义来，但是说不出，打了个顿，含糊地说了声 well，接下去还是个 copper's nark。

158 **as you might say** 有如你们（如果说到这种人时）会这样称呼的。 **What else would you call it?** 还能叫它什么呢？ it 指 copper's nark 这个名称。 **A sort of informer.** You would call it a sort of informer. **informer** 现在只作"告密者"解；"报告者"用 informant。

160 **I take my Bible oath** 我对《圣经》发誓。 **take an oath** = swear. 发誓这里后面省略引起同位从句的连词 that。 **never said a word** - 没有说过一句（不正经的或违法的）话。这句话没说完，被人喝住了（见下句）。

164 **far from reassured** 还是不放心的；极不放心。 **far from** 习语；极不。from 虽是介词，后面可接形容词；也可作 far from being reassured。

165 **took me down right** 正确地把我记下来。 **right** 这里是副词，= rightly；在动词后面通常用 right。

166 **shew** 是 show 的古老拼法，萧伯纳爱用此式。 **youve wrote** 是 you've written 之讹。

though the pressure of the mob trying to read it over his shoulders would upset a weaker man.] Whats that? That aint proper writing. I cant read that.

THE NOTE TAKER I can. [*reads, reproducing her pronunciation exactly*] 'Cheer ap, Keptin; n'baw ya flahr orf a pore gel.'

THE FLOWER GIRL [*much distressed*] It's because I called him Captain. I meant no harm. [*to the gentleman*] Oh, sir, dont let him lay a charge agen me for a word like that. You –

THE GENTLEMAN Charge! I make no charge. [*to the note taker*] Really, sir, if you are a detective, you need not begin protecting me against molestation by young women until I ask you. Anybody could see that the girl meant no harm.

THE BYSTANDERS GENERALLY [*demonstrating against police espionage*] Course they could. What business is it of yours? You mind your own affairs. He wants promotion, he does. Taking down people's words! Girl never said a word to him. What harm if she did? Nice thing a girl cant shelter from the rain without being insulted, etc., etc., etc. [*She is conducted by the more sympathetic demonstrators back to her plinth, where she resumes her seat and struggles with her emotion.*]

THE BYSTANDER He aint a tec. He's a blooming busybody: thats

---

168 **trying to read it over his shoulders** 想从他肩背后看他写的东西。这个分词短语修饰 the mob。

169 **would upset a weaker man** 是虚拟语气，= would upset him if he were a weaker man than he is。would upset 的主语是 the pressure。 **That aint**

proper writing. 那不是正规文字（因为那是些特殊的缩记符号）。

171 **reproducing** 重新念出；模仿。

172 **Keptin** = Captain. **n'baw ya flahr orf a pore gel** = and buy a flower off a poor girl.

173 **It's because I called him Captain.** 卖花女误会，以为因为她称人 Captain 被认为犯了错误。

174 **meant** [ment] **no harm** 没有恶意。

175 **lay a charge agen** (= against) **me** 告我一状；控告我；指责我。

176 **Charge! I make no charge.** Charge! 在这里是名词，承接上文 lay a charge。**make no charge** 没有控告；没有指责。

177 **you need not begin protecting me against molestation by young women until I ask you.** you need not begin protecting me ... until I ask you，在我请求你之前，你不必保护起我来。 **protecting me against molestation by young women** 保护我不受年轻女子的缠扰。protect 后表示不受重大损害用 against，表示不受一般损害用 from。

180 **the bystanders generally** 一般旁观者；generally 指作者"笼统地"说"旁观者"。**police espionage** [ˈespɪənɑːʒ] 警察局的密探行为。espionage 一般指"间谍活动"。

181 **Course they could** = Of course they could. **they could** 承接上文 Anybody could see ...。Anybody 是单数，但因概念上是许多人，所以英美人往往用复数 they 作 anybody 的代词。对于 everybody 也是这样。 **What business is it of yours?** of yours 修饰 business。全句 = What's your business? 这关你什么事？ **You mind your own affairs** 你管你自己的事就是了（可不用管别人的事）。

182 **He wants promotion, he does.** 加 he does 强调 He wants promotion。 **Taking down people's words!** 这是动名词短语构成的单部句。

183 **Girl** = The girl. **What harm if she did?** = What harm is there if she said a word to him?

184 **Nice thing** = It's a nice thing that ... . 这里 nice 是反语：糟糕的。

185 **etc., etc., etc.** 犹言"等等，等等"，相当于 and so on and so forth。

187 **struggles with her emotion** 跟她自己（激动）的情绪挣扎；竭力使自己镇静下来（一时还镇静不下来）。

188 **a blooming busybody** [ˈbɪzɪbɒdi] 太爱管闲事的人。 **blooming** 这里是俚语，与 blessed 一样是 bloody、damned 等诅咒语的委婉的说法，此处用以加重 busybody 的语气，没有具体意义。

what he is. I tell you, look at his bə-oots.

THE NOTE TAKER [*turning on him genially*] And how are all your people down at Selsey?

THE BYSTANDER [*suspiciously*] Who told you my people come from Selsey?

THE NOTE TAKER Never you mind. They did. [*to the girl*] How do you come to be up so far east? You were born in Lisson Grove.

THE FLOWER GIRL [*appalled*] Oh, what harm is there in my leaving Lisson Grove? It wasnt fit for a pig to live in; and I had to pay four-and-six a week. [*in tears*] Oh, boo-hoo-oo –

THE NOTE TAKER Live where you like: but stop that noise.

THE GENTLEMAN [*to the girl*] Come, come! He cant touch you: you have a right to live where you please.

A SARCASTIC BYSTANDER [*thrusting himself between the note taker and the gentleman*] Park Lane, for instance. Id like to go into the Housing Question with you, I would.

THE FLOWER GIRL [*subsiding into a brooding melancholy over her basket, and talking very low-spiritedly to herself*] I'm a good girl, I am.

THE SARCASTIC BYSTANDER [*not attending to her*] Do you know where *I* come from?

THE NOTE TAKER [*promptly*] Hoxton.

Titterings. Popular interest in the note taker's performance increases.

---

190 **turning on him genially** 和蔼地转向他（说）。 **your people** 你的家属。

191 **down at Selsey** [ˈselsi] Selsey，地名，所在不详；down，说“南方”、“乡村”、“内地”都用 down。

192 **come from** 出生于（某地）。

194 **Never you mind** = Never mind. 用 you 加重语气。 **mind** = mind who told me that your people come from Selsey. **They did.** = They（人们）told me that your people come from Selsey.

195 **come to be up so far east** 向东跑这么远到城里来。come 后接不定式，表示“终于”或“开始”。 **up** 从乡村到城市用 up。 **Lisson** [ˈlɪsn] **Grove** 地名，看上文当在伦敦以西郊区。

197 **It wasnt fit for a pig to live in** 那地方（很糟，）给猪待在里面都不行。

198 **four-and-six** 四先令六便士。（现行英国币制已废除先令，见前。） **in tears** 在流泪。 **boo-hoo-oo** – 哭闹声。因而 boohoo 作“哭闹”解，名词读作 [ˈbuːhuː]，动词读作 [ˌbuːˈhuː]。

199 **Live where you like** 你爱住在哪里就住在哪里。

200 **Come, come!** Come 作感叹词，这里表示不耐烦，也可用以引起注意或表示鼓励等。

201 **have a right to live** 有居住的权利。也可说 have the right to live；也可说 have a (或 the) right of living，但不如用不定式普遍。

203 **Park Lane** 伦敦一街，是高级住宅区。那里当然轮不到卖花女居住；这是讽刺 the note taker 和 the gentleman 对卖花女说的她有权利要住哪里就住哪里。 **go into the Housing** [ˈhaʊzɪŋ] **Question** 研究住房问题。 **go into** 探讨；深入研究；是习语。 **the Housing Question** 住房问题是当时英国正争议着的一大社会问题，用大写字母开头，表示专题。

204 **I would** 句末加 I would，重复句首的 Id (= I would)，是强调语气。

205 **subsiding** [səbˈsaɪdɪŋ] **into a brooding** [ˈbruːdɪŋ] **melancholy** [ˈmelənkəli] （从原来的哭闹）平静下来，转入闷闷不乐。melancholy 是不可数名词，这里用 a，是“一种……”的意思。 **over her basket** 低头对着她的篮子。

207 **attending to** 注意；理会。

208 ***I*** 斜体，要重读，强调“我”，表示“你认得出别人是哪里人，能说出我是哪里人吗”的口气。

209 **Hoxton** [ˈhɒkstən] 地名，所在不详。

210 **Titterings** （周围的人）嗤嗤的笑声。 **Popular interest** 大众的兴趣。

THE SARCASTIC ONE [*amazed*] Well, who said I didnt? Bly me! you know everything, you do.

THE FLOWER GIRL [*still nursing her sense of injury*] Aint no call to meddle with me, he aint.

THE BYSTANDER [*to her*] Of course he aint. Dont you stand it from him. [*to the note taker*] See here: what call have you to know about people what never offered to meddle with you?

THE FLOWER GIRL Let him say what he likes. I dont want to have no truck with him.

THE BYSTANDER You take us for dirt under your feet, dont you? Catch you taking liberties with a gentleman!

THE SARCASTIC BYSTANDER Yes: tell him where he come from if you want to go fortune-telling.

THE NOTE TAKER Cheltenham, Harrow, Cambridge, and India.

THE GENTLEMAN Quite right.

Great laughter. Reaction in the note taker's favor. Exclamations of He knows all about it. Told him proper. Hear him tell the

---

212 **Well, who said I didnt?** = Well, who said I didn't come from Hoxton? 这是反问(rhetoric question)，强调表示"唉，一点不错，我确是 Hoxton 人。" **Bly me!** 俚语；表示惊讶；也作 Blimey ['blaɪmi]；是由 (God) blind me 转讹而来。

214 **nursing her sense of injury** 感觉很受伤。 **Aint no call to meddle with me, he aint.** 句首的 Aint = He aint (= He hasn't); 口语中有时省略主语。 **call** 理由；必要。Aint no call 是双重否定，应作 Has no call。

216 **Dont you stand it from him** = Dont stand it from him. 中间用 you，加强语

气。 stand it from him 忍受他那一套。it 并无具体所指，有些语法家称为“it 的泛用（the vague use of 'it'）”。

217 **See here** 也说 Look here，是引起注意的口头语，意思是“听我说”，犹如说 I say。

218 **know about people** 知道关于人们的事情。 **what** 应作 who 或 that。 **offered to meddle with you** 要来干预你。 **offered** 表示“主动”、“起劲”的意思。

219 **I dont want to have no truck with him.** 双重否定；= I'll have no truck with him. **truck** 交往；交道；是口语。

221 **take us for dirt under your feet** 把我们当作你脚底下的垃圾；极度蔑视我们。 **dirt** 统指肮脏东西；是不可数名词。

222 **Catch you taking liberties with a gentleman!** 料你不敢跟（有身份的）绅士胡来！（言下之意你只敢欺侮卖花女等。）Catch somebody doing something 有“发现某人做某事（决不放过；料你不敢）”的意思，如 Catch me smoking again! 你瞧着吧，我决不再抽烟！ **take liberties** (也作 liberty) **with** 对……放肆；随意对待。

223 **come from** 应作 comes from。

224 **go fortune-telling** 进行算命。go doing 通常作“出去做某事”解，如 go shopping，出去买东西；也作“进行……”、“继续……”解，如 Don't go telling me lies，别继续对我撒谎。

225 **Cheltenham** [ˈtʃeltənəm], **Harrow** [ˈhærəʊ], **Cambridge** [ˈkeɪmbrɪdʒ], **and India** [ˈɪndɪə]. 出生于 Cheltenham，在哈罗公学、剑桥大学念的书，在印度工作过。Cheltenham，英格兰西南部 Gloucester [ˈglɒstə] 郡的一个城市，是旅游胜地和文化中心；Harrow，英国的著名公学，哈罗公学、伊顿（Eton）公学的学生大多是上层子弟；Cambridge，剑桥大学，它和牛津（Oxford）大学是英国历史最悠久的著名大学；India 指此人当时是英国在印度的殖民地官员。

227 **Reaction in the note taker's favor** 有利于 the note taker 的反应，群众佩服起他来了。这是省略谓语的名词句。 **Exclamations of** ……的惊叫（惊叹）声。后面不单是接 He knows all about it，而是接到 etc. 为止的一段话。

228 **He knows all about it.** 他对这些情况全都知道。it 泛指人们的种种情况。 **Told him proper.** = He told him proper. him 指 the gentleman. **proper** 这里作副词，= properly；是方言。 **Hear him tell the toff** him 指 the note taker。

toff where he come from? *etc.*

THE GENTLEMAN May I ask, sir, do you do this for your living at a music hall?

THE NOTE TAKER Ive thought of that. Perhaps I shall some day.

The rain has stopped; and the persons on the outside of the crowd begin to drop off.

THE FLOWER GIRL [*resenting the reaction*] He's no gentleman, he aint, to interfere with a poor girl.

THE DAUGHTER [*out of patience, pushing her way rudely to the front and displacing the gentleman, who politely retires to the other side of the pillar*] What on earth is Freddy doing? I shall get pneumownia if I stay in this draught any longer.

THE NOTE TAKER [*to himself, hastily making a note of her pronunciation of 'monia'*] Earlscourt.

THE DAUGHTER [*violently*] Will you please keep your impertinent remarks to yourself.

THE NOTE TAKER Did I say that out loud? I didnt mean to. I beg your pardon. Your mother's Epsom, unmistakeably.

THE MOTHER [*advancing between the daughter and the note taker*]

---

229 **toff** 上流人士；时髦人物；是英国口语；这里指 the gentleman。 **come from** 应作 comes from，已见前。根据上文，这里既指"出生于（何地）"，也指"受教育于（什么学校）"、"从（什么地方）来"。

230 **do this** 指讲出别人的出生地和在何处上学、何处工作等。 **for your living** 借以为生。 **living** 生计。

231 **music hall** 表演歌舞和杂耍的游艺场。在美国往往指“音乐厅”。

232 **Ive thought of that.** 我想到过那个。that 指上文讲的到游艺场去替人算命，借以为生。 **I shall some day.** = I shall do this for my living (或 for a living) at a music hall some day. **some day** 将来有一天。

234 **drop off** 一个个离去。

235 **He's no gentleman, he aint, to interfere with a poor girl.** 他要干涉一个贫苦的女孩子，（当然）不是个上等人，他（决）不是（上等人）。 **no** = not a. **interfere** 干涉，是不及物动词，后面用介词 with。

237 **out of patience** [ˈpeɪʃəns] 不耐烦的。这是习语，作定语，不能作状语。说“对……不耐烦”时，后面介词用 with。 **pushing her way rudely to the front** 粗鲁地挤到前面。

238 **displacing** 取代……的位置。

239 **What on earth** 究竟什么。 **on earth** 习语，加强 what 的语气。 **pneumownia** [njʊˈmaʊnɪə] = pneumonia [njuːˈməʊnɪə]. 肺炎。土音把 [əʊ] 念作 [aʊ]。

240 **any longer** 再……下去；是习语，用于否定、疑问或假定。

241 **making a note of her pronunciation of ‘monia’** 把她说 pneumonia 时 “monia” 的发音记录下来。 **Earlscourt** [ˈɜːlzkɔːt] 地名，所在不详；反正把 pneumonia 念成 pneumownia 是 Earlscourt 的土音。

243 **Will you please keep your impertinent** [ɪmˈpɜːtɪnənt] **remarks to yourself.** 请你不要对别人胡说八道！ Will you please... 原是客气的问句形式，但这里却是不客气的命令。 **keep your remarks to yourself** 不要说出口；不要对人说。 **impertinent** 不恰当的；无礼的。

245 **say that out loud** 大声说出（Earlscourt）那个地名。 **I didnt mean to** = I didnt mean to say that out loud. 我并不是有意大声说出那个来。 **I beg your pardon.** 我请你原谅；对不起。这句话是常用的口语，在听不清对方说什么，要求再说一遍时，也有此话，有时简略作 Beg pardon。

246 **Your mother's Epsom** [ˈepsəm] 你母亲是 Epsom 人。Epsom 在伦敦之南的城市，其西南郊外有大赛马场，著名的 Derby 赛马就在此举行。

How very curious! I was brought up in Largelady Park, near Epsom.

THE NOTE TAKER [*uproariously amused*] Ha! Ha! What a devil of a name! Excuse me. [*to the daughter*] You want a cab, do you?

THE DAUGHTER Dont dare speak to me.

THE MOTHER Oh please, please, Clara. [*Her daughter repudiates her with an angry shrug and retires haughtily.*] We should be so grateful to you, sir, if you found us a cab. [*The note taker produces a whistle.*] Oh, thank you. [*She joins her daughter.*]

The note taker blows a piercing blast.

THE SARCASTIC BYSTANDER There! I knowed he was a plain-clothes copper.

THE BYSTANDER That aint a police whistle: thats a sporting whistle.

THE FLOWER GIRL [*still preoccupied with her wounded feelings*] He's no right to take away my character. My character is the same to me as any lady's.

THE NOTE TAKER I dont know whether youve noticed it; but the rain stopped about two minutes ago.

THE BYSTANDER So it has. Why didnt you say so before? And us losing our time listening to your silliness! [*He walks off towards the Strand.*]

THE SARCASTIC BYSTANDER I can tell where you come from. You

---

248 **curious** 稀奇的；难以理解的。这里不作“好奇的”解。 **was brought up** 被抚养大；被教育。 **Largelady** [ˈlɑːdʒˌleɪdi] **Park** 所在地不详。

250 **uproariously** [ʌpˈrɔːrɪəsli] **amused** 感到有趣得大声嘻嘻哈哈起来；哄然失笑。 **What a devil** [ˈdevəl] **of a name** （Largelady Park）是多怪的一个名字呀！a devil of a ... 是习语，表示“讨厌”、“奇怪”、“有趣”，其中的 devil（原义“魔鬼”）没有具体意义。

251 **Excuse me** 原谅我。因为他脱口而出用了 devil 这个不文雅的词，有失礼貌，所以请人原谅。

252 **Dont dare speak to me** 别放肆对我说话。 **dare** 有“胆大妄为”的意思。

253 **please, please** 表示“劝阻”、“安慰”等意，犹如说：“好了，好了。” **repudiates** [rɪˈpjuːdɪeɪts] **her** 拒绝她；不听母亲的劝阻。

254 **We should be so grateful to you, sir, if you found us a cab.** 这是虚拟语气。found us a cab = would find us a cab. 注意 found 可接双宾语。

255 **produces** 拿出。

256 **thank you.** The mother 看见 the note taker 拿出哨子替她叫车子，所以谢谢他。

257 **blows a piercing blast** [blɑːst] 吹出尖锐刺耳的哨子声。 **blast** 喇叭、汽笛或哨子等的声音。

258 **knowed** 早知道，是 knew 之讹。 **plain-clothes** [ˈpleɪnkləʊðz] **copper** 便衣警察。

260 **police whistle** 警笛。 **sporting whistle** 裁判员或教练员用的哨子。

262 **preoccupied with** 被……缠住，被……迷住。 **wounded** [ˈwuːndɪd] **feelings** 被伤害的感情；认为被冤枉的感觉。

264 **as any lady's** = as any lady's character to her.

265 **I dont know whether youve noticed it; but...** = I dont know whether you have noticed it that ... 英美人常在这样的语气中用 but，如： I am sorry, but I cant accept it. 对不起，我不能接受。

267 **So it has.** = Yes, it (= the rain) has stopped. 雨是停了。这里也可承上文说 So it did = Yes, it stopped two minutes ago. 注意：这和倒装形式 So has it 等涵义不同，如：He has learnt it; so has she. 他学会了，她也学会了。 **And us losing our time listening to your silliness** 而我们却浪费时间（在这）听你胡说。us 不可改作 we。

come from Anwell. Go back there.

THE NOTE TAKER [*helpfully*] Hanwell.

THE SARCASTIC BYSTANDER [*affecting great distinction of speech*] Thenk you, teacher. Haw haw! So long. [*He touches his hat with mock respect and strolls off.*]

THE FLOWER GIRL Frightening people like that! How would he like it himself?

THE MOTHER It's quite fine now, Clara. We can walk to a motor bus. Come. [*She gathers her skirts above her ankles and hurries off towards the Strand.*]

THE DAUGHTER But the cab – [*Her mother is out of hearing.*] Oh, how tiresome! [*She follows angrily.*]

All the rest have gone except the note taker, the gentleman, and the flower girl, who sits arranging her basket, and still pitying herself in murmurs.

THE FLOWER GIRL Poor girl! Hard enough for her to live without being worrited and chivied.

THE GENTLEMAN [*returning to his former place on the note taker's left*] How do you do it, if I may ask?

THE NOTE TAKER Simply phonetics. The science of speech. Thats my profession: also my hobby. Happy is the man who can

---

271 **Anwell** 是 Hanwell [ˈhænwəl] 的讹读，土话中不但常脱落 [h] 音，且有时

会在没有 h 的元音前凭空加上 [h] 的音，如 Alex 讹读作 [ˈhælɪks]。

272 ***H*anwell** 在伦敦西郊，有疯人院。作者用此地名，可能有取笑 the note taker 是疯子之意。H 斜体，表示说话的人强调 [h] 音，纠正前面说话人的发音错误。

273 **affecting great distinction of speech** 做作地发音非常清晰。 **Thenk you** Thank you 之讹。

274 **teacher** 用 teacher 是因为 the note taker 纠正了 the sarcastic bystander 的发音之故，含有讽刺之意。 **Haw haw** [ˈhɔːˈhɔː] 伦敦某些上流人士的笑声。 **So long** 再见。正常用于极熟的亲友间。 **touches his hat** 举手到帽檐致敬。 **mock respect** 假装的敬意。 **mock** 假装的。常有揶揄之意。

277 **it** 承上文，指 being frightened。

281 **But the cab –** 可是出租车（就不叫了吗）?

284 **pitying herself in murmurs** 喃喃咕咕地自觉可怜。

286 **Hard enough for her to live without being worrited and chivied.** 她不受烦扰，不受折磨，生活已够苦恼（再要受到烦扰和困惑，更无法生活了）。Hard 是 It is hard 之略；it 是虚词，引起同位语 to live ...。worrited 是 worried 之讹。chivied，其原形动词是 chivy [ˈtʃɪvi]，也作 chivvy 或 chevy [ˈtʃevi]，作“折磨”解，是英国用语。

289 **How do you do it, if I may ask?** 假如我可以问的话，（我要请问）你如何做到（说出各人来自什么地方）的？这里的 if 是特殊用法。类似的例子如：We met once at a party, if you remember. 你如果记得的话，（你该记得）我们有一次在聚会上见过面。“见过面”是客观事实，并不是假如他记得才见过面，假如他不记得就没有见过面。if 的这种用法很普遍。

290 **Simply phonetics.** = It's simply phonetics. 或 I do it simply by phonetics. 名词句。 **The science of speech** 是 phonetics 的同位语，独立成为一个名词句。

291 **Happy is the man** 是 The man is happy 的倒装形式，一方面着重 Happy 的语气，一方面使 the man 紧跟后面的定语从句 who can make a living by his hobby。

make a living by his hobby! You can spot an Irishman or a Yorkshireman by his brogue. *I* can place any man within six miles. I can place him within two miles in London. Sometimes within two streets.

THE FLOWER GIRL Ought to be ashamed of himself, unmanly coward!

THE GENTLEMAN But is there a living in that?

THE NOTE TAKER Oh yes. Quite a fat one. This is an age of upstarts. Men begin in Kentish Town with £80 a year, and end in Park Lane with a hundred thousand. They want to drop Kentish Town; but they give themselves away every time they open their mouths. Now I can teach them –

THE FLOWER GIRL Let him mind his own business and leave a poor girl –

THE NOTE TAKER [*explosively*] Woman: cease this detestable boohooing instantly; or else seek the shelter of some other place of worship.

THE FLOWER GIRL [*with feeble defiance*] Ive a right to be here if I like, same as you.

THE NOTE TAKER A woman who utters such depressing and disgusting sounds has no right to be anywhere – no right to live.

---

292 **spot an Irishman** [ˈaɪərɪʃmən] **or a Yorkshireman** [ˈjɔːkʃəmən] **by his brogue** [brəʊg] 从土音中确定（说话的人）是爱尔兰人或约克郡人。约克郡（York 或 Yorkshire）位于英吉利东北部。 **brogue** 爱尔兰土音；（泛指）土音。

293 ***I* can place any man within six miles.** 我能说出任何人的出生地（或生活的

地方)，误差不出六英里。 **place** 这里是及物动词，作“说出……的位置”、“确定”解。

294 **Sometimes within two streets.** 这是省略句，承上句，= Sometimes I can place him within two streets in London.

296 **Ought to be ashamed of himself, unmanly** [ʌnˈmænli] **coward** [ˈkaʊəd]**!** Ought 前省去主语 He，= He ought；unmanly coward 是 He 的同位语，也可把全句理解为倒装句，= The unmanly coward ought to be ashamed of himself. **ashamed of himself** 为他自己害臊。注意 ashamed 后用 of。 **unmanly coward** 字面意义是“没有男子气的胆小鬼”，这里称“可鄙的人”。

298 **But is there a living in that?** 可是在那(说出各人来自什么地方)里面有生计(可寻)吗？能以此为生吗？

299 **Quite a fat one.** = There's quite a fat living in that. 在那个行当里有大好的生计。fat 修饰 living，犹如汉语中“肥差”、“肥缺”中的“肥”字。 **quite a** 也可说 a quite，口语中多说 quite a。 **an age of upstarts** [ˈʌpstɑːts] 暴发户时代。upstart 作动词时读 [ʌpˈstɑːt]，作“(使)突然跃起”，“使崛起”解。

300 **Kentish Town** 伦敦西北部的工业区。 **Park Lane** 已见前。

301 **drop Kentish Town** 改掉 Kentish Town 的口音。

302 **give themselves away** (说出土音)露出马脚。

304 **Let him mind his own business and leave a poor girl –** him 指 the note taker。leave a poor girl – 话未说完，后面该有 alone；leave ... alone 是习语，是“让……去”，“不管”，“不干预”的意思。

306 **explosively** 爆发似地；大发雷霆地。 **Woman** 用 woman 作称呼是极粗野无礼的。 **boohooing** [buːˈhuːɪŋ] 哭闹。boohoo 作名词时读 [ˈbuːhuː]，见前注。

307 **or else** 否则；要不然。与 or 同义，语气较重。 **seek the shelter of some other place of worship** 找个另外的教堂去躲避(不要在这儿 St. Paul 教堂前胡闹)。**place of worship** 做礼拜的地方；教堂。

309 **if I like** = if I like to be here.

310 **same as you** 正规英语是 the same as you。

312 **has no right to be anywhere** 任何地方都没有权利待。不作“无权到处去，而只能在某些地方”解。

Remember that you are a human being with a soul and the divine gift of articulate speech: that your native language is the language of Shakespear and Milton and The Bible; and dont sit there crooning like a bilious pigeon.

THE FLOWER GIRL [*quite overwhelmed, looking up at him in mingled wonder and deprecation without daring to raise her head*] Ah-ah-ah-ow-ow-ow-oo!

THE NOTE TAKER [*whipping out his book*] Heavens! What a sound! [*He writes; then holds out the book and reads, reproducing her vowels exactly.*] Ah-ah-ah-ow-ow-ow-oo!

THE FLOWER GIRL [*tickled by the performance, and laughing in spite of herself*] Garn!

THE NOTE TAKER You see this creature with her Kerbstone English: the English that will keep her in the gutter to the end of her days? Well, sir, in three months I could pass that girl off as a duchess at an ambassador's garden party. I could even get her a place as lady's maid or shop assistant, which requires better English.

THE FLOWER GIRL What's that you say?

---

313 **the divine** [dɪˈvaɪn] **gift of articulate** [ɑːˈtɪkjələt] **speech** 神圣天赋的声音，清楚的语言。这个词组和上面 a soul 同属介词 with 的宾语。

314 **native language** 本国语言。

315 **the language of Shakespear** [ˈʃeɪkspɪə] **and Milton** [ˈmɪltən] **and The Bible** 莎士比亚、弥尔顿和《圣经》的语言。这种语言被认为是英国语言的典范。

Shakespear，通常作 Shakespeare；William Shakespeare (1564–1616) 是英国戏剧家兼诗人。John Milton (1608–1674) 是英国诗人，《失乐园》(*Paradise Lost*) 的作者。The Bible，此处指 1611 年承英王 James 一世之旨英译出版的《圣经》。A and B and C 比普通说 A, B, and C 语气强。

316 **crooning like a bilious** [ˈbɪlɪəs] **pigeon** 像生气的鸽子那样叽里咕噜。crooning 原义是"低调哼（消沉的）调子"。

317 **overwhelmed** [ˌəʊvəˈwelmd] 被（the note taker 的一通训斥）压倒；弄得不知所措。 **in mingled wonder and deprecation** [ˌdeprɪˈkeɪʃən] 在惊愕和反抗相混杂的心情下。 **deprecation** 不以为然；反对。

318 **Ah-ah-ah-ow-ow-ow-oo!** 在无奈中发出的呼叫声，没有具体意义。

320 **whipping out his book** 倏地拿出他的笔记簿来。这里 book = notebook。 **Heavens!** 天哪！ 啊呀！ 也作 Good (或 Great, Gracious) Heavens，一般说，heavens 指"天空"，常用大写开首的 heaven 指"天堂"、"上帝"。但 Heavens 这个感叹语中用复数。 **What a sound!** = what a sound it is!

321 **reproducing her vowels** 重新读出她的元音。模仿她的 Ah-ah-ah-ow-ow-ow-oo 的声音。

323 **tickled** 原义是"被使觉得痒"，转义为"被逗得发笑"。 **laughing in spite of herself** 不由自主地大笑起来。

325 **creature** 人（含有怜爱或轻蔑之意）。 **Kerbstone English** 街头英语；俚俗的英语。 **kerbstone** 见前注。

326 **keep her in the gutter to the end of her days** 使她终身颠沛街头。 **gutter** 街沟，也作"贫民区"、"贫民窟"解。

327 **pass that girl off as a duchess** 让那个姑娘冒充公爵夫人。duchess 也指"女公爵"。 **pass ... off as ...** 使……冒充……，是习语。这里的 as 也可用 for。

328 **garden party** 游园会。 **get her a place as lady's maid** 给她找一个伺候贵妇人的女仆的差事。 **lady's maid** 在贵妇人身边主要侍候梳妆的女侍；这里作为一种职位，放在 as（作为……身份；担任）后面，所以省略冠词。

329 **shop assistant** 店员。这是英国说法，在美国称 (store) clerk，或 salesman、saleswoman。

331 **What's that you say?** = what's that that you say? 第一个 that 指上面 the note taker 说的话；第二个 that 是关系代词，是从句中 say 的宾语；作宾语的关系代词可以省略。

THE NOTE TAKER Yes, you squashed cabbage leaf, you disgrace to the noble architecture of these columns, you incarnate insult to the English language: I could pass you off as the Queen of Sheba. [*to the gentleman*] Can you believe that?

THE GENTLEMAN Of course I can. I am myself a student of Indian dialects; and –

THE NOTE TAKER [*eagerly*] Are you? Do you know Colonel Pickering, the author of Spoken Sanscrit?

THE GENTLEMAN I am Colonel Pickering. Who are you?

THE NOTE TAKER Henry Higgins, author of Higgins's Universal Alphabet.

PICKERING [*with enthusiasm*] I came from India to meet you.

HIGGINS I was going to India to meet you.

PICKERING Where do you live?

HIGGINS 27A Wimpole Street. Come and see me tomorrow.

PICKERING I'm at the Carlton. Come with me now and lets have a jaw over some supper.

HIGGINS Right you are.

THE FLOWER GIRL [*to Pickering, as he passes her*] Buy a flower, kind gentleman. I'm short for my lodging.

PICKERING I really havnt any change. I'm sorry. [*He goes away.*]

---

332 **Yes, you squashed** [skwɒʃt] **cabbage leaf, you disgrace to the noble architecture** [ˈɑːkɪtektʃə] **of these columns, you incarnate** [ɪnˈkɑːnət] **insult to the English language: I could pass you off as the Queen of Sheba** [ˈʃiːbə]. 前面

三个 you 是呼唤语（vocative），cabbage leaf、disgrace 和 insult 分别为它们的同位语，体现了说话人激动和咄咄逼人的气势。全句直译为：“是啊，你这压烂了的菜瓣皮，你这使高贵的廊柱建筑丢脸的东西，你这对英国语言而言活生生的污辱——我可以让你冒充示巴的女王。**disgrace** 丢脸；丢脸的人。**these columns** 指 St. Paul 教堂的廊柱，剧中人在这些廊柱间躲雨。**incarnate** 化身的；人体化的；这里如作动作“赋予形体”、“体现”语法上也可通，但与全句语气不符；注意如作动词，重音在前，读 [ˈɪnkɑːneɪt]，也有读 [ɪnˈkɑːneɪt] 的。**the Queen of Sheba** 《旧约圣经·列王纪上》所载亚拉伯西南部示巴的女王，曾朝觐以色列王所罗门（Solomon）。

336 **a student of Indian dialects** [ˈdaɪəlekts] 研究印度方言的人。**student** 一般指大、中学生（不指小学生，小学生称 pupil），但也指研究某项学问的人，甚至可能是专家、学者，像这里的 gentleman 就是后者。**and –** and 后面话没有说完，就被打断了。

338 **Colonel** [ˈkəːnəl] **Pickering** [ˈpɪkərɪŋ] Pickering 上校。

339 **the author of Spoken Sanscrit** [ˈsænskrɪt] 《梵语口语》的作者。照例书名应作斜体或加引号，但萧伯纳常用正体，也不加引号。**Sanscrit** = Sanskirt.（印度的）梵语；梵文。

341 **Henry Higgins** [ˈhɪgɪnz] 本剧主人公之一，对卖花女进行语言训练，使其成为“贵妇人”，犹如希腊神话中雕刻出一个活美人的 Pygmalion，所以剧名为 *Pygmalion*（见前言）。**Higgins's** [ˈhɪgɪnzɪz] **Universal Alphabet** [ˈælfəbet] 《希氏通用字母表》，书名。

346 **27A Wimpole** [ˈwɪnpəʊl] **Street** 英美习惯，门牌号码写在前，街名在后。

347 **the Carlton** [ˈkɑːltən] 指 Carlton Club。是英国保守党的俱乐部，1832 年由威灵顿（Wellington）公爵创立。**have a jaw over some supper** 一面吃点晚饭，一面谈谈。**jaw** 喋喋不休地说话；是口语。**some supper** 用 some，有“随便吃点什么”的意思；注意前面用 over，同样的用例如“over a cup of tea”。

349 **Right you are** = You are right. 是口语，= Right! 或 Right oh!，都是表示同意、赞成。

351 **short for my lodging** [ˈlɒdʒɪŋ] 没有足够的钱付房钱；注意用 for。

HIGGINS [*shocked at the girl's mendacity*] Liar. You said you could change half-a-crown.

THE FLOWER GRIL [*rising in desperation*] You ought to be stuffed with nails, you ought. [*flinging the basket at his feet*] Take the whole blooming basket for sixpence.

The church clock strikes the second quarter.

HIGGINS [*hearing in it the voice of God, rebuking him for his Pharisaic want of charity to the poor girl*] A reminder. [*He raises his hat solemnly; then throws a handful of money into the basket and follows Pickering.*]

THE FLOWER GIRL [*picking up a half-crown*] Ahow-ooh! [*picking up a couple of florins*] Aaahow-ooh! [*picking up several coins*] Aaaaaah-ow-ooh! [*picking up a half-sovereign*] Aaaaaaaaaaahow-ooh!!!

FREDDY [*springing out of a taxicab*] Got one at last. Hallo! [*to the girl*] Where are the two ladies that were here?

THE FLOWER GIRL They walked to the bus when the rain stopped.

FREDDY And left me with a cab on my hands! Damnation!

THE FLOWER GIRL [*with grandeur*] Never mind, young man. *I'm* going home in a taxi. [*She sails off to the cab. The driver puts his hand behind him and holds the door firmly shut against her. Quite

---

353 **mendacity** [men'dæsəti] 虚假；说谎。卖花女刚才说能兑开 half-a-crown（两先令六便士的硬币，见前注），怎么现在又说付不出房钱，分明在说谎。**Liar**

['laɪə] 说谎的人。这里可以当作是呼唤语，也可当是 You are a liar 之略。

355 **You ought to be stuffed with nails, you ought.** 你该被塞满一肚子的钉子。肚子里塞满钉子，当然是活不成了，所以也就是“该死”的意思。句末重复 you ought，是加强语气。

356 **Take the whole blooming basket for sixpence.** （你）出六便士把整篮（花）拿去（买去）。**blooming** 见前注。

359 **it** 指教堂的时钟敲起的钟声。 **Pharisaic** [ˌfærɪ'seɪik] **want of charity** 法利塞人般没有慈悲心的。法利塞人（Pharisee ['færɪsi:]）是犹太教的一派，《圣经》中称他们是言行不一的伪善的人。

360 **A reminder** = It is a reminder. 教堂的时钟是提醒我（应该慈善）的信号。 **raises his hat** 举帽（脱帽）致敬。

363 **a couple** ['kʌpl] 一对，即“两个”，但口语中常泛指“两三个”，甚至“几个”。

364 **florins** ['flɒrɪnz] 两先令的银币。

365 **half-sovereign** ['hɑ:f'sɒvrɪn] 半英镑的金币。这使卖花女大为惊奇，所以“哇哇”地大叫起来。

366 **Got one** = I've got one 或 I got one. one 指 a taxicab。

369 **And left me with a cab on my hands!** 而把一辆出租车留在我手上了。And 紧接上面卖花女说她们去乘公共汽车而言，所以后面 left 前的主语也省去了。leave somebody with something 是“把某物留下给某人”的意思。 **on my hands** 由我照管（或处理），有“棘手”之意，这是习语；比较另一习语 on hand：即待处理的，手头现有的；在美国还作“即将发生”、“在场”等解。注意两个习语中 hand 的单复数。 **Damnation** [dæm'neɪʃn]**!** 动词 damn 的名词形式，这里作感叹词，是“该死！”的意思。

370 **grandeur** ['grændʒə] 庄严；伟大；富丽堂皇。 **young man** 用以称呼人，犹言“小伙子”。

371 **sails off** 昂然走去。 **sail** 作“傲慢（或潇洒）地行走”解，常用于女人。 **puts his hand behind him and holds the door firmly shut against her** 手伸到背后，紧紧按住关着的门，不让她上车（因为看她是穷苦的卖花女，料她乘不起出租车）。shut 这里是过去分词，作宾语 the door 的补足语。

understanding his mistrust, she shews him her handful of money.] A taxi fare aint no object to me, Charlie. [*He grins and opens the door.*] Here. What about the basket?

THE TAXIMAN Give it here. Tuppence extra.

LIZA No: I dont want nobody to see it. [*She crushes it into the cab and gets in, continuing the conversation through the window.*] Goodbye, Freddy.

FREDDY [*dazedly raising his hat*] Goodbye.

TAXIMAN Where to?

LIZA Bucknam Pellis [Buckingham Palace].

TAXIMAN What d'ye mean – Bucknam Pellis?

LIZA Dont you know where it is? In the Green Park, where the King lives. Goodbye, Freddy. Dont let me keep standing there. Goodbye.

FREDDY Goodbye. [*He goes.*]

TAXIMAN Here? Whats this about Bucknam Pellis? What business have you at Bucknam Pellis?

LIZA Of course I havnt none. But I wasnt going to let him know that. You drive me home.

TAXIMAN And wheres home?

LIZA Angel Court, Drury Lane, next Meiklejohn's oil shop.

---

374 **aint no object** 是"双重否定", = is no object. **no object** 不成问题；是习语，尤其用于广告文字中，如 Money no object：报酬不计。 **Charlie** [ˈtʃɑːli] 这是一个极普通的男子名，卖花女并不认识 the driver，是随口乱叫的，同她

前面叫别人 Freddy 一样。

376 **Give it here.** 把它（这一篮花）交给我，放在这里。 **Tuppence extra.** 另加两便士（车钱）。 **Tuppence** = Twopence. 都读 [ˈtʌpəns]。

377 **Liza** [ˈlaɪzə] 卖花女的名；她的姓是 Doolittle。Liza 是 Elizabeth [ɪˈlɪzəbəθ] 的昵称。这里突然不用 the flower girl 而用 Liza，是表示她摆起架子，丢掉了卖花女的“低贱”身份。 **dont want nobody to see it** = don’t want anybody to see it 或 want nobody to see it. it 指一篮花。

380 **dazedly** [ˈdeɪzɪdli] 被弄得头昏眼花地；茫然。

381 **Where to?** = Where are you going (to)? 或 Where am I to take you to?

382 **Bucknam Pellis** [ˈbʌknəmˈpelɪs] 是括号中 Buckingham Palace [ˈbʌkɪŋəmˈpælɪs] 的误读。白金汉宫，是现今英国王宫。

383 **What d’ye** (= do you) **mean – Bucknam Pellies?** 你说白金汉宫是什么意思？一个卖花女说要到王宫去，自然使人大惑不解。

384 **Green Park** 英国王家花园，是个小丘，树林特别青翠茂盛。 **the King** 指英王乔治六世，1936–1952 年在位；萧伯纳改写出版电影版是在 1941 年，这一段文字是在 1941 年改写本中插入的。

385 **Dont let me keep standing there.** 别让我使你老站在那里。我把你叫来的却难以处置的车子乘走了，你可以去了。

388 **Whats this about Bucknam Pellis?** 你要去白金汉宫，这是怎么回事？下面 Liza 的回答很清楚：她说要去白金汉宫是吹牛，是说给 Freddy 听的。

390 **I havnt none.** = I have none. = I have no business at all at Bucknam Pellis (Buckingham Palace).

391 **that** 指 I have no business at all at Buckingham Palace。

392 **wheres home** 承上文 drive me home 开车送我回家而问，= where is “home” = where is your home。

393 **Angel**[ˈeɪndʒl] **Court, Drury** [ˈdrʊəri] **Lane, next Meiklejohn’s** [ˈmɪkldʒɒnz] **oil shop** （家在）Drury Lane 路上的 Angel Court，就在 Meiklejohn 油店隔壁。英美地址的说法，一般是“门牌，街道，城镇，国家”，先小后大。 **Angel Court** 不可考，可能是虚构的。 **Drury Lane** 伦敦街名，旧时贵族住宅区，著名的大剧场 Drury Lane Theatre 所在地。 **Meiklejohn’s oil shop** 英美企业常用企业主的姓氏为名。 **next** 也可说 next to；单用 next，是介词；next to 中的 next 是形容词，有时也作副词，如：He sits next to me.

TAXIMAN That sounds more like it, Judy. [*He drives off.*]

Let us follow the taxi to the entrance to Angel Court, a narrow little archway between two shops, one of them Meiklejohn's oil shop. When it stops there, Eliza gets out, dragging her basket with her.

LIZA How much?

TAXIMAN [*indicating the taximeter*] Cant you read? A shilling.

LIZA A shilling for two minutes!!

TAXIMAN Two minutes or ten: it's all the same.

LIZA Well, I dont call it right.

TAXIMAN Ever been in a taxi before?

LIZA [*with dignity*] Hundreds and thousands of times, young man.

TAXIMAN [*laughing at her*] Good for you, Judy. Keep the shilling, darling, with best love from all at home. Good luck! [*He drives off.*]

LIZA [*humiliated*] Impidence!

She picks up the basket and trudges up the alley with it to her lodging: a small room with very old wall paper hanging loose in the damp places. A broken pane in the window is mended

---

394 **That sounds more like it** 那（指上文 Liza 所说的地址）听起来（比起先

说的白金汉王宫）像话多了；那个地方才比较像是你这种人住的了。 **Judy** [ˈdʒuːdi] 普通的女子名，是 Taximan 随便乱叫的，正像 Liza 对 Taximan 乱叫 Charlie 一样。

396 **one of them** (the two shops) **Meiklejohn's oil shop** them 后省略 being，是独立结构（absolute construction），是伴随说明的短语。

397 **Eliza** [ɪˈlaɪzə] 即 Liza，同是 Elizabeth 的昵称。

400 **taximeter** [ˈtæksɪˌmiːtə] （出租车凭以计算车费的）计程器。 **Cant you read?** 你看不懂计程器吗？ **read** 读数。

402 **Two minutes or ten: it's all the same.** ten = ten minutes. it 指 two minutes or ten。**all the same** 习语，作"（虽然……）还是、依然"解。这里是不管时间是两分钟或十分钟，车费都一样。注意：不能因为这里是说两者相同而用 both the same。

403 **I dont call it right** 我并不认为这（两分钟和十分钟车费相同）是合理的 = 我认为不合理。但是不说 I call it not right。

404 **Ever been in a taxi before?** = Have you ever been in a taxi before? 你以前乘过出租汽车吗?

405 **Hundreds and thousands of times** 几百几千次；许许多多次。省略主语和谓语动词，= I have been in a taxi hundreds and thousands of times. 注意：这里 hundreds 和 thousands 用复数，但 several hundred（或 thousand) times 中的 hundred 和 thousand 直接修饰中心词 times，用单数。

407 **Good for you** 你干得好；你运气好。是口语，这里有讥讽的意思。 **Keep the shilling** （看你苦恼）还是留着这一先令（别付车钱了）吧。（有轻视的意味。）

408 **with best love from all at home** 带着我全家至诚的爱。这类的话也常用作书信结尾的问候语。 **Good luck!** = I wish you good luck! 常用在告别时，表示祝愿。其实 Good-bye 也表示祝愿，它是从 God be with you（愿上帝与你同在，即保佑你）衍变过来的。

410 **Impidence** 是 Impudence [ˈɪmpjədəns] 的误读；意为"大胆妄为；无礼"，指 Taximan 对穷人的轻视态度。

411 **trudges** [ˈtrʌdʒɪz] **up the alley** [ˈæli] 沿着巷子吃力地走进去。up 这里是介词。

412 **hanging**[ˈhæŋɪŋ] **loose in the damp places** 在这几个潮湿处快要脱落下来。不及物动词 hang 的现在分词修饰 wall paper（糊墙纸）。

with paper. A portrait of a popular actor and a fashion plate of ladies' dresses, all wildly beyond poor Eliza's means, both torn from newspapers, are pinned up on the wall. A birdcage hangs in the window; but its tenant died long ago: it remains as a memorial only.

These are the only visible luxuries: the rest is the irreducible minimum of poverty's needs: a wretched bed heaped with all sorts of coverings that have any warmth in them, a draped packing case with a basin and jug on it and a little looking glass over it, a chair and table, the refuse of some suburban kitchen, and an American alarum clock on the shelf above the

---

414 **fashion plate of ladies' dresses** 一件件女服的时式样板。 **fashion plate** 有时也借喻作“服装时髦的人”解。

415 **all wildly beyond poor Eliza's means** 都远远超过贫穷的 Eliza 的资力（根本买不起）。从语法上讲，all 是代词，指 dresses，整个词组是省略了分词 being 的一个独立结构,即 = all being wildly beyond poor Eliza's means。也可说 all 修饰 beyond，即“(不是某一件衣裳超过，而是)全部都超过(她的资力)”。**beyond ... means** 修饰 dresses。 **wildly** 相差极远，犹如上海话说“野豁豁”。**both torn from newspapers** 两者（portrait 和 fashion plate）都是从报纸上扯下来的。结构同上条注。可以认为 both 后省略 being；也可认为 both 修饰分词 torn，torn 修饰 portrait 和 fashion plate。

416 **are pinned up** 被用大头针钉起来。主语是 portrait 和 fashion plate。

417 **hangs** 悬挂；这里是不及物动词；它也可作及物动词，如 hang a birdcage in the window；它的过去式和过去分词都是 hung。hang 作“绞死”、“吊死”解时，过去式和过去分词都是 hanged，间或也用 hung。 **its tenant** [ˈtenənt] 鸟笼的居住者（指原来关在笼中的那只鸟）。

418 **memorial** [məˈmɔːrɪəl] 纪念物。鸟死笼空，只好把空笼子挂着作纪念。注意：亲友间赠送的纪念品不能说是 memorial，应该说 keepsake。

419 **visible** [ˈvɪzəbl] **luxuries** [ˈlʌkʃəriz] （眼前）看得见的（非生活必需的）奢侈品。把报上扯下的画像和空鸟笼称为“奢侈品”是幽默地说明卖花女的贫穷。看得见的“奢侈品”是这些，另外不在眼前、看不见的“奢侈品”，也可想而知。**the rest** 其他不属“奢侈品”的东西；生活必需品。the rest 可作单数，也可作复数，视其所指是单数或复数而定。这里后面的表语是 minimum（单数），故作单数。如拿后面具体列举的许多家具作表语，the rest 就作复数，如：The rest are a bed, a packing case, a chair and table, etc. **irreducible minimum** [ˈmɪnɪməm] **of poverty's needs** 贫苦（生活）必须的无可减少的最小极限；即使生活贫苦也缺一不可的必需品。注意：这里 needs 用复数。

420 **wretched** [ˈretʃɪd] **bed** 破旧不堪的床。它后面的 packing case、chair and table 等都是进一步说明上面 the rest 所指的具体内容，也可说是 the rest 的同位语。**all sorts of coverings that have any warmth in them** 各式各样只要能保暖的覆盖物（如被头）。**all sorts of** 也可说 all sort of，= all kind(s) of。**have any warmth** 照字面讲，不通，因覆盖物本身里面没有温度，故应理解为“（对人体）有保暖（御寒）作用”。

421 **draped packing case** 遮着布的装货（粗板）箱。

422 **a basin and jug** 面盆和水壶。这两样东西作为一套用具，故合用一个冠词。**a little looking glass over it** 箱子上面（放着）一面小镜子。looking glass 和 basin and jug 并列，是 with 的介词宾语。**over it** 在箱子的上方（墙上）。

423 **a chair and table** 一对桌椅。作为一组，故合用一个冠词。和 bed 及 packing case 并列。**the refuse of some suburban** [səˈbɜːbən] **kitchen** 不知哪家郊区（人家）厨房（不要而丢掉）的垃圾。这个名词词组是 a chair and table 的同位语。注意 refuse 在这里是名词，读 [ˈrefjuːs]；作“拒绝”解的动词读 [rɪˈfjuːz]。

424 **an American alarum** [əˈleərəm] **clock** 美国货闹钟。“闹钟”在美国称 alarm clock，现在在英国也多称 alarm clock。

unused fireplace: the whole lighted with a gas lamp with a penny in the slot meter. Rent: four shillings a week.

Here Eliza, chronically weary, but too excited to go to bed, sits, counting her new riches and dreaming and planning what to do with them, until the gas goes out, when she enjoys for the first time the sensation of being able to put in another penny without grudging it. This prodigal mood does not extinguish her gnawing sense of the need for economy sufficiently to prevent her from calculating that she can dream and plan in bed more cheaply and warmly than sitting up without a fire. So she takes off her shawl and skirt and adds them to the miscellaneous bedclothes. Then she kicks off her shoes and gets into bed without any further change.

---

425 **unused** [ˌʌnˈjuːzd] 不用的。这个词也作“没有用过的”，即“新的”解，这里不是此义。另外，它又与 to 连用作“不习惯于……的”解，读 [ʌnˈjuːst]，如：He is unused to society. 他不善于交际。 **the whole** 整个房间。前面讲了许多零星家具用品，现在讲整个房间，故用 the whole。 **lighted** 被照亮着；是过去分词，可理解为因在说明词中，所以前面省略了 was，也可理解为前面省略了 being，the whole being lighted ... slot meter 是个独立结构。 **a gas lamp with a penny in the slot meter** 在自动收费计（的投钱口）里投入了一枚一便士硬币（因而点燃着）的煤气灯。

426 **Rent: four shillings a week.** = The rent is four shillings a week. 在说明词中可以用公式的写法，省略动词；Rent 前冠词也省略。

427 **chronically weary** [ˈwɪəri] 极度疲劳。 **chronically** 作“剧烈地”、“顽固地”解，是英国用法。 **sits** 主语是 Eliza。

428 **her new riches** 她新得来的财富，即 Higgins 扔给她的一把钱币。 **planning what to do with them** 计划着怎样处置它们（这些钱币）。 **what to do with** 是习语，除“怎样处置”、“怎样对付”外，还可作“怎样与……相处”、“怎样忍受”解。

429 **the gas goes out** 煤气灯熄灭。投入一便士，使用时间已结束。

430 **sensation** 激动的感觉。 **put in another penny without grudging** [ˈgrʌdʒɪŋ] **it** 毫不吝惜地再投入一枚一便士钱币（使煤气灯继续点下去）。 **it** 指 another penny。

431 **This prodigal** [ˈprɒdɪgəl] **mood does not extinguish her gnawing** [ˈnɔːɪŋ] **sense of the need for economy sufficiently to prevent her from calculating** 这种（不在乎一便士的）挥霍心情不足以完全消除她想到需要节俭的痛苦意识，（不足以）使她不盘算着……。 **sufficiently** 修饰 extinguish；does not extinguish sufficiently，消除得还不够。 **gnawing** 原义“咬的”，转义“令人痛苦的”。

434 **sitting up** 坐着不就寝。 **without a fire** 不生火；没有生火炉。

435 **adds them to the miscellaneous** [ˌmɪsəˈleinjəs] **bedclothes** 把它们(shawl 和 skirt)加盖在杂七杂八的被褥上面。比较：add to 和 add ... to 的不同用法，例如：This adds to the expense. 这要增加费用。

436 **gets into bed** 上床。注意：和 go to bed 以及前三行的 in bed 一样，bed 前都不用冠词。

437 **without any further change** 没有任何其他的变化；只踢掉一双鞋子，不另换什么睡衣之类。

第二幕
剧情提要

卖花女 Liza 昨天得到 Higgins 扔给她的一把钱，以为出得起给语音学专家 Higgins 教授的学费，今天一早就登门来请他授课。Higgins 问她打算付多少钱。她说："人家请真正的法国先生教法语，一个小时给一先令半；你教我本国语言，我至多给一先令。"Higgins 替她计算，她出一先令抵得上百万富翁出六、七十镑！当然，他不要她的钱，但是他要用她作试验。他说能在三至六个月里使她冒充公爵夫人参加大使馆的招待会。Pickering 和他打赌：如果试验成功，他愿承担这次试验的一切费用。

Liza 的父亲 Doolittle 得知 Liza 在这里，找上门来。他是个倒垃圾的工人，愤世嫉俗，玩世不恭。他说："两位先生看上了我的女儿，可不能白占我便宜。"他要 Higgins 给他五个英镑。Higgins 给他十镑，他只要五镑。他说："五镑正够和老伴去吃喝玩乐一番，钱一多，就舍不得乱花，乐不起来了。"所谓"老伴"，算是 Liza 的后娘，却一直没肯和他正式结婚。Doolittle 发表了一大套言论，Higgins 认为他大可当个牧师或议员。

Higgins 开始了对 Liza 非常严格的语音训练。Liza 既是他的学生，又成了任他呼来唤去的女管家。

ACT II

Next day at 11 a.m. Higgins's laboratory in Wimpole Street. It is a room on the first floor, looking on the street, and was meant for the drawing room. The double doors are in the middle of the back wall; and persons entering find in the corner to their right two tall file cabinets at right angles to one another against the walls. In this corner stands a flat writing-table, on which are a phonograph, a laryngoscope, a row of tiny organ pipes with a bellows, a set of lamp chimneys for singing flames with burners attached to a gas plug in the wall by an india-rubber tube, several tuning-forks of different sizes, a life-size image of half a human head, shewing in section the vocal organs, and a box containing a supply of wax cylinders for the phonograph.

Further down the room, on the same side, is a fireplace, with a comfortable leather-covered easy-chair at the side of the hearth

---

1 **laboratory** 实验室；研究室。英国多读 [lə'bɒrətri]，美国读 ['læbrətɔːri]。**in Wimpole Street** 英国说"在……街"、"在街上"用 in，美国用 on。

2 **first floor** 在英国，"底层"称 ground floor；first floor 是我国所说的"二楼"。在美国 first floor 指"底层"，"二楼"称 second floor，和我国说法相同。**looking on the street** 看出去是街景；（楼面）临街。**was meant** [ment] **for** 原是准备作……之用的。上下文用现在时，这里用过去时，表示原先的情况。

3 **double doors** 《新英和大辞典》用复数，指“双扇双关的门”或“双重门”；《韦氏国际词典》用单数，指“双扇门”，则复数当指两个或两个以上双扇门了。

4 **persons entering** = persons who enter / persons when they enter. **corner to their right** 他们右边的角落。这里的 to 也可用 at。

5 **file cabinets** [ˈkæbɪnəts] 文件柜。**at right angles to one another** 彼此形成直角。**one another** 过去一般语法书上说限用于三个或三个以上事物之间，each other 才用于两者之间，实际上两语通用。

6 **stands a flat writing-table** = a flat writing-table stands. 因句首有状语短语 In this corner，所以主谓倒装。 **writing-table** 写字台（似乎着重在供写字用，未必如 desk 有许多抽屉）。

7 **phonograph** [ˈfəʊnəgrɑːf]（老式的）录音机。 **laryngoscope** [ləˈrɪŋgəskəʊp]（医学上或语音学、声学上用的）喉镜。 **a row** [rəʊ] **of tiny** [ˈtaɪni] **organ pipes with a bellows** 装有风箱的一排小小的风琴管。风箱用以吹响琴管。注意：作“划船”解和口语中作“吵架”解的 row 均读 [raʊ]，词源各不相同。 **bellows** 只有复数式，常用作单数。

8 **a set of lamp chimneys for singing flames with burners attached to a gas plug in the wall by an indiarubber tube** 一组罩住试音火的灯罩，配有（烧煤气的）灯头，灯头用橡皮管接在墙上的煤气插头上。 **singing flames** 随声音颤动而起落的煤气火焰（装置）。 **with burners** 修饰 lamp chimneys。 **indiarubber** 一般分写成 india rubber。

10 **tuning-forks** 音叉。 **a life-size image** [ˈɪmɪdʒ] **of half a human head, shewing** (= showing) **in section the vocal organs** 一具同比例的半人头模型，以断面显示各种发音器官。shewing in section，这里 = shewing in longitudinal (或 vertical) section：以纵截面。“横截面”为 cross section。

12 **wax cylinders** [ˈsɪlɪndəz] （老式录音机录音用的）蜡管。

14 **Further down the room** 在房间里更前面些的地方。在舞台上，down 指靠台前的一面，up 指靠台后的一面。

15 **at the side of the hearth** [ˈhɑːθ] **nearest the door** 在壁炉旁边最近房门处。at the side of 中的 at 也可用 on，如下文有 On the other side of ... 。hearth 原指“壁炉（fireplace）的炉床”，转义为“炉边”；这里借指“壁炉”。

nearest the door, and a coal-scuttle. There is a clock on the mantelpiece. Between the fireplace and the phonograph table is a stand for newspapers.

On the other side of the central door, to the left of the visitor, is a cabinet of shallow drawers. On it is a telephone and the telephone directory. The corner beyond, and most of the side wall, is occupied by a grand piano, with the keyboard at the end furthest from the door, and a bench for the player extending the full length of the keyboard. On the piano is a dessert dish heaped with fruit and sweets, mostly chocolates.

The middle of the room is clear. Besides the easy-chair, the piano bench, and two chairs at the phonograph table, there is one stray chair. It stands near the fireplace. On the walls, engravings: mostly Piranesis and mezzotint portraits. No paintings.

---

16 **nearest the door** 最靠近门处（可能靠近门处除 easy-chair 外还有其他东西，而 easy-chair 靠门最近）。nearest the door 并非修饰 hearth，而是和 at the side of the hearth 一起修饰 easy-chair。door 当是指上文的 double doors，虽是双扇的门，但仍是"门"的概念，故此处可用单数 door。 **coal-scuttle** 煤斗；和 easy-chair 并列，是 with 的介词宾语。

17 **mantelpiece** [ˈmæntlpiːs] （壁炉顶上的）壁炉架。

18 **stand for newspapers** 放报纸的架子。

20 **On it is a telephone and the telephone directory** [dəˈrektəri] 柜（cabinet）上是电话和电话簿。状语短语 On it 放句首，故主谓倒装。这里的 is 按语

法应用 are，因为主语是两样东西，但英语中常有这种情况，可以理解为说了 is a telephone，又想到 the telephone directory，所谓 after-thought；也可理解为 = a telephone with the telephone directory，两者作为一组东西。

21 **The corner beyond, and most of the side wall, is occupied by a grand piano** ([pɪˈænəʊ]，也可读作 [pɪˈɑːnəʊ]) 这里 beyond = beyond the cabinet；The corner beyond the cabinet 是在舞台口的角落。and 连接的前后两个位置，作为一个空间，故后面用 is occupied。 **grand piano** 大钢琴（乐器名，不照字面作"大的钢琴"解）。

22 **keyboard at the end furthest from the door** 大钢琴背朝 side wall，键盘朝外，所以说"键盘在离门（the double doors in the middle of the back wall）最远的一端"。 **furthest** further 比 farther 常用；后者限用于"距离"；这里是指距离，所以改用 farthest 也可。

23 **a bench for the player** 弹琴的人坐的长凳子。bench 与 keyboard 并列，是 with 的介词宾语。 **extending the full length of the keyboard** （凳子）同键盘一样长。注意：extending 在这里是不及物动词。the full length of the keyboard 作状语。比较及物动词 extend 的例子：extend the length（延长长度）。

24 **a dessert** [dɪˈzɜːt] **dish heaped with fruit and sweets, mostly chocolates** [ˈtʃɒkləts] 堆满水果和糖果——大半是巧克力糖的果盘。heaped 是过去分词，修饰 dessert dish。 **fruit** 统称"水果"，是不可数名词用单数；强调多种水果时，用复数，如 the fruits in season now（现在当季的几种水果）。 **sweets** 统称"糖果"用复数；指一块、两块糖时，说 a sweet、two sweets；美国称 candy，可统指"糖果"，也可指一块糖，因而单复数都可用，如 give the boy some candy（或 candies)。 **chocolates** 这里指一块块巧克力糖，是可数名词，作 sweets 的同位语，chocolate 作为巧克力这种物质时，是不可数名词。

26 **clear** （房间）没放东西的。

27 **one stray chair** 一把散置的（或不成套的）椅子。用 one 而不用 a，是强调"一把"（不是"两把，三把"）。

28 **engravings** 版画；雕版印刷品。它前面用逗号，省略 are。

29 **Piranesis** [pɪrəˈneɪzɪz] Piranesi 的一些作品。Giambattista Piranesi (1720–1778)，是意大利雕刻家兼画家；这里以人名用作可数名词，是指其作品。 **mezzotint** [ˈmetsəʊtɪnt] **portraits** 金属版印刷的肖像画。 **No paintings.** = There are no paintings. **paintings** 油画水彩画，别于上面的印刷品。

Pickering is seated at the table, putting down some cards and a tuning-fork which he has been using. Higgins is standing up near him, closing two or three file drawers which are hanging out. He appears in the morning light as a robust, vital, appetizing sort of man of forty or thereabouts, dressed in a professional-looking black frock-coat with a white linen collar and black silk tie. He is of the energetic, scientific type, heartily, even violently interested in everything that can be studied as a scientific subject, and careless about himself and other people, including their feelings. He is, in fact, but for his years and size, rather like a very impetuous baby 'taking notice' eagerly and loudly, and requiring almost as much watching to keep him out of unintended mischief. His manner varies from genial bullying when he is in a good humor to stormy petulance when anything goes wrong; but he is so entirely frank and void of malice that he remains likeable even in his least reasonable moments.

---

30 **cards** 卡片；资料卡。

31 **standing up near him** 在他身旁稍后些处。up 指靠后台一面，见前注。

32 **hanging** [ˈhæŋɪŋ] **out** （抽屉）开着，口子下倾；拖出在外面。

33 **a robust** [rəʊˈbʌst], **vital, appetizing** [ˈæpɪtaɪzɪŋ] **sort of man** 一种强壮、活力充沛、令人喜爱的人。注意：sort of 和 kind of 一样，后面的名词用单数，无冠词，很少用复数；即使 sorts of 和 kinds of 后面有时也用单数。**appetizing** 原义是“开胃的”。

34 **forty or thereabouts** 四十岁左右。thereabouts 一般读 [ˈðeərəˌbaʊts]；在 there or thereabouts（附近；左右）这一习语中读 [ˌðeərəˈbaʊts]；thereabouts 有时也作 thereabout。 **dressed** 这里是过去分词。 **professional-looking** 看

上去很专业的样子。 **professional** 职业的。这里指“从事专门职业（常指医生、律师、牧师）的”。“-looking”是构词成分，常接在形容词后面，表示“看上去像什么样子”的意思，如 angry-looking（像在发火）。

35 **frock-coat** （男子的）礼服大衣，简称 frock。

36 **scientific type** 从事科学研究的那种人的类型；不作“科学的类型”解。**heartily, even violently interested** 强烈地、甚至狂热地感兴趣。

38 **careless about himself and other people, including their feelings** 不顾自己，不顾别人，包括（不顾会不会伤）别人的感情。

39 **but for his years and size** 除了他（已经是四十左右的）年纪和（高大的）个子的缘故；若不考虑他的年龄和个子；这是插入的状语短语，修饰 is，is 接后面表语 rather like ... **but for** = except for。

40 **impetuous** [ɪmˈpetjʊəs] 激动的；是名词 impetus [ˈɪmpɪtəs]（动力）衍生的形容词。 **'taking notice' eagerly and loudly** 开始懂事，因而样样都哗啦哗啦要管；分词词组修饰 baby。 taking notice 这里不作“注意”解，而指婴孩的“开始懂事”，因为是一种特殊的用法，故加引号。

41 **requiring almost as much watching** 需要几乎同样程度的看管。require watching 中的 watching 形式是主动语态，意义是被动的，可改用不定式 to be watched，却不可改用 being watched。requiring almost as much watching 后面省略 as a very impetuous baby 'taking notice' eagerly and loudly requires to keep him out of unintended mischief。 **keep him out of unintended mischief** [ˈmɪstʃɪf] 不让他无意中闯乱子。 keep him out of 作“使他保持在……之外”、“使免于……”，“使……不”解；这里和 keep him from 同义。

42 **varies** [ˈveərɪz] 变化不同。 **varies from ... to ...** 变化于……与……之间；一会儿……，一会儿……。这里是 varies from genial [ˈdʒiːnɪəl] bullying [ˈbʊlɪɪŋ] to stormy petulance [ˈpetjʊləns]，时而和和气气地欺辱人，时而大发雷霆。

43 **when he is in a good humor** 当他高兴的时候，修饰 bullying。 **when anything goes wrong** 当有什么事情出了毛病（不顺他心）的时候，修饰 petulance。goes wrong 原义“走入歧路”，转义“出岔”；是习语。

44 **void of malice** [ˈmælɪs] 绝无恶意的。这里 void 是形容词；void of malice 和 frank 并列。

45 **remains likeable even in his least reasonable moments** 即使在他最不讲理的时候也还是可爱的。likeable = likable。

HIGGINS [*as he shuts the last drawer*] Well, I think thats the whole show.

PICKERING It's really amazing. I havnt taken half of it in, you know.

HIGGINS Would you like to go over any of it again?

PICKERING [*rising and coming to the fireplace, where he plants himself with his back to the fire*] No, thank you: not now. I'm quite done up for this morning.

HIGGINS [*following him, and standing beside him on his left*] Tired of listening to sounds?

PICKERING Yes, It's a fearful strain. I rather fancied myself because I can pronounce twenty-four distinct vowel sounds; but your hundred and thirty beat me. I cant hear a bit of difference between most of them.

HIGGINS [*chuckling, and going over to the piano to eat sweets*] Oh, that comes with practice. You hear no difference at first; but you keep on listening, and presently you find theyre all as different as A from B. [*Mrs Pearce looks in: she is Higgins's housekeeper.*] Whats the matter?

MRS PEARCE [*hesitating, evidently perplexed*] A young woman asks to see you, sir.

HIGGINS A young woman! What does she want?

---

46 **thats the whole show** 要给你看的全给你看了。犹言"全本《西厢记》尽在于此"。比较：美国口语中 be the whole show 是"当主角"、"一手包办"

的意思。

48 **havnt taken half of it in** 懂得不到一半。**take in** 懂得；是习语；另外还可作“接受”、“轻信”等解。

50 **go over** 这个习语有许多意义。这里作“把……来一遍”解。

51 **plants** [plɑːnts] **himself** 使他自己站立着；站立不动。

52 **not now** = I shouldn't（也可说 wouldn't) like to go over any of it now. **done up** 精疲力竭。也作 done in，都是习语；这里的 done 是形容词。 **I'm quite done up for this morning** 这一个早晨（听下来）我累极了。

54 **Tired of ...** = Are you tired of ...（你因为……而厌倦了吗？）

56 **fearful strain** （听发音录音听得）非常吃力。fearful 作“非常”、“极度”解，是口语。 **fancied myself** （妄）自以为（能力强）。

58 **your hundred and thirty beat me** 你的一百三十个（元音）弄得我稀里糊涂。 beat 使迷惑；使为难；是口语。 **hundred and thirty** hundred 和十位或个位数之间通常用 and（在美国通常不用 and）；这里 hundred 前加 one 也可。一百三十个元音见于英国语言学家 Henry Sweet（1845–1912）所著语音学著作中；萧伯纳原是以 Henry Sweet 作为剧中人 Henry Higgins 的原型，见前言。 **cant hear a bit of** 在……中一点也听不出。 **difference between most of them** 它们（这一百三十个元音）中的大多数之间（所存在）的区别。 **between** 旧语法书中常说限用于两个之间，实际也可像 among 一样用于三个或三个以上之间。这里也可理解为许多元音的每两个之间，如 [ɛ] 和 [e]，[ʌ] 和 [ə]。

60 **that comes with practice** 那（分辨一百三十个元音）是随着练习而来的；多听听就听得出来了。

62 **presently you find theyre all as different as A from B** 不久之后你就会觉得全像 A 和 B 那样（明显地）不同。 **different** 后一般接 from，英国用法也有接 to，也有（主要在美国）接 than 的。

63 **Pearce** [ˈpɪəs] 姓氏。 **housekeeper** 女管家。这词也作“女主人”解；犹如 hostess，是“（宴会上的）女主人”，又可作“（车、船和飞机上的）女服务员”等解。

64 **Whats the matter?** 出了什么事？是惯用语。 **the matter** 是 wrong 的意思。

65 **young woman** 因为来访的是卖花女，所以不客气地称 woman；倘是来 Higgins 家的“上等”女客，就称 lady 了。

MRS PEARCE Well, sir, she says youll be glad to see her when you know what she's come about. She's quite a common girl, sir. Very common indeed. I should have sent her away, only I thought perhaps you wanted her to talk into your machines. I hope Ive not done wrong; but really you see such queer people sometimes – youll excuse me, I'm sure, sir –

HIGGINS Oh, thats all right, Mrs Pearce. Has she an interesting accent?

MRS PEARCE Oh, something dreadful, sir, really. I dont know how you can take an interest in it.

HIGGINS [*to Pickering*] Lets have her up. Shew her up, Mrs Pearce. [*He rushes across to his working table and picks out a cylinder to use on the phonograph.*]

MRS PEARCE [*only half resigned to it*] Very well, sir. It's for you to say. [*She goes downstairs.*]

HIGGINS This is rather a bit of luck. I'll shew you how I make records. We'll set her talking; and I'll take it down first in Bell's Visible Speech; then in broad Romic; and then we'll

---

69 **what she's** (= she has) **come about** 她为了什么事而来的。 **common girl** 粗俗的姑娘。

70 **I should have sent her away, only I thought ...** 我本想打发她走的，可是我想…… should have sent her away 是表示过去与事实相反的虚拟语气，实际上是没有 sent her away。 **only** 这里是连词，= but。连在一起，可以理解为 I should have sent her away if I had not thought ...，即 I did not send her away, for I thought ...。

71 **wanted her to talk into your machines** [mə'ʃiːnz] 要她对着你的录音机器说

话（给你录音）。 **wanted** 是“将要”而并非“过去要”，所以用过去时，是因为它用在过去时 thought 引起的从句中，语法上叫做“时态的呼应”。如以为 Higgins 原先曾约好她来录音的，那么 wanted 应改为 had wanted。

72 **done wrong** 做错；犯错误；这是习语。比较：另一习语 do wrong to somebody，常作 do somebody wrong：委屈（或冤枉）某人；说（某人）坏话。

73 **I'm sure** 我相信。语气很轻，实际上只是“大概”的意思；I'm certain 才是“我确实相信”、“我肯定”的意思。

75 **accent** 口音。这里不作“重音”解。作“口音”解的例子还有如 The French guest speaks German with a French accent. 那位法国客人说德语带法国口音。

76 **something dreadful** 难听的东西（口音）。something 在口语中也作副词用，有“相当”、“非常”的意思。 **dreadful** 原义“可怕的”，转义“糟透的”，犹如上海方言说“吓(坏)人的”。 **really** 真的。不是修饰前面的 dreadful，而是修饰全句，表示“我说这话是千真万确的”，另举两例：Really, that's a flat lie. 真的，那是彻头彻尾的谎言。Really?（你说的）是真的吗？ **I dont know how you can take an interest in it** 我不知道你怎么会对它（那种糟透的口音）感兴趣；在我看来是毫无意义的。

78 **have her up** 让她上来。up 是宾语补足语，her up（她上来）有逻辑上的主谓关系，因此构成 have 的复合宾语。 **Shew her up** 带领她上来。这个 up 是副词，修饰 shew，表示“方向”、“去处”；和 have her up 的 up 不同，须仔细辨别。 **shew** show 的旧式拼法。

79 **rushes across to his working table** 匆匆跑到房间另一端他的工作台那里。 **across** 也可说 across the room，即 across the middle part of the room。working table，就是指前面讲的 writing-table。 **to use** = to be used.

81 **only half resigned to it** 只是一半屈从于；相当勉强地听从主人的命令；听从是出于无可奈何。only 修饰 half。 **It's for you to say** 由你说了算。It 是不及物动词不定式 to say 的先行词。

84 **records** 纪录，唱片。这里是录好音的录音筒（cylinders）。record，名词读 [ˈrekɔːd]，动词读 [rɪˈkɔːd]。现在录音机按钮上的 record 字样，应读 [rɪˈkɔːd]。 **set her talking** 使她说话。talking 是 her 的宾语补足语，her 与 talking 在逻辑上有主谓关系，her talking 这个主谓结构也称为是 set 的复合宾语。 **take it down first in Bell's Visible** [ˈvɪzəbl] **Speech** 先用倍耳“视语音标”把它（她说的话）记录下来。 **Bell's Visible Speech** Alexander Melville Bell（1819–1905）是生于

get her on the phonograph so that you can turn her on as often as you like with the written transcript before you.

MRS PEARCE [*returning*] This is the young woman, sir.

The flower girl enters in state. She has a hat with three ostrich feathers, orange, sky-blue, and red. She has a nearly clean apron, and the shoddy coat has been tidied a little. The pathos of this deplorable figure, with its innocent vanity and consequential air, touches Pickering, who has already straightened himself in the presence of Mrs Pearce. But as to Higgins, the only distinction he makes between men and women is that when he is neither bullying nor exclaiming to the heavens against some feather-weight cross, he coaxes women as a child coaxes its nurse when it wants to get anything out of her.

HIGGINS [*brusquely, recognizing her with unconcealed disappointment, and at once, babylike, making an intolerable grievance of it*] Why, this is the girl I jotted down last night. She's no use: I've got all the records I want of the Lisson Grove lingo; and I'm not

---

苏格兰的美国语音学家兼教育家，1867 年著《视语》，设计了一套音标表示发音器官的实际位置，后改称“器官音标”（Organic Alphabet）。

85 **broad Romic** [ˈrəʊmɪk] 宽式罗马字音标。这是英国语言学家 Henry Sweet 创制的一种用罗马字母标识的音标，分“宽”、“狭”（narrow）两式，“狭式”比“宽式”更精密。

86 **get her on the phonograph** 用录音器把她（说的话）录下来。on the phonograph 是 her 的宾语补足语。 **can turn her on as often as you like** 可以随时打开她的（录音）。 as often as you like 你想（打开）多少次就多少次。

87 **written transcript** ['trænskrɪpt] 书写的音标。

89 **in state** 庄严地；是习语。 **ostrich** ['ɒstrɪtʃ] **feathers** ['feðəz] 鸵鸟毛。

91 **The pathos** ['peɪθɒs] **of this deplorable figure** 凄惨动人的寒酸形象，后接 touches (感动) Pickering。

92 **with its innocent** ['ɪnəsnt] **vanity** ['vænəti] **and consequential** [ˌkɒnsɪ'kwenʃl] **air** 带着天真的虚荣自满和自以为了不起的神气。its 指这形象（figure's）。

93 **has already straightened himself in the presence of Mrs Pearce** 在 Mrs Pearce 出现的时候已经站立起来。Pickering 的彬彬有礼和 Higgins 的任性放肆始终形成鲜明对比。

94 **the only distinction he makes between men and women** 他对（待）男女的唯一区别。西俗对妇女应更有礼貌，而 Higgins 不但不分男女，而且不分尊卑，都不重礼貌。

96 **when he is neither bullying nor exclaiming to the heavens against some featherweight cross** 当他既不盛气凌人，又不为了些鸡毛蒜皮的糟心事发誓赌咒时。 **cross** 从"十字架"转义为"折磨"、"苦难"。

97 **coaxes women as a child coaxes its nurse when it wants to get anything out of her** 像小孩子为了得到某种东西时哄保姆那样去哄女人。 **coaxes** 用甜言蜜语劝诱。its 和 it 代 child('s)；英语中常用 it 代 baby 或幼小的 child，相反常用 she 代国家、船舶等。

99 **brusquely**['bruːskli] 粗暴地（说）。 **recognizing** ['rekəgnaɪzɪŋ] **her** 见面而认出她（就是曾经在一起避雨的卖花女）。 **unconcealed disappointment** 毫不掩饰的失望；明显表现出来的失望。

100 **making an intolerable grievance of it** 把这（识出就是卖花女）当作是无法忍受的倒霉事，叫苦连天。 **Why** 这里是感叹词，表示发现什么或不耐烦等意思。

101 **the girl I jotted down** 我（把她的口音）记录下来的那个姑娘，girl 后省略 whom。 **jotted** 简略地摘记；草草写下。 **no use** = of no use. 无用的。是习语，与 (of) no good 同义。

102 **lingo** 方言；难懂的语言。犹如说某人讲的像"外国话"，带有开玩笑的贬义。

going to waste another cylinder on it. [*to the girl*] Be off with you: I dont want you.

THE FLOWER GIRL Dont you be so saucy. You aint heard what I come for yet. [*to Mrs Pearce, who is waiting at the door for further instructions*] Did you tell him I come in a taxi?

MRS PEARCE Nonsense, girl! What do you think a gentleman like Mr Higgins cares what you came in?

THE FLOWER GIRL Oh, we *are* proud! He aint above giving lessons, not him: I heard him say so. Well, I aint come here to ask for any compliment; and if my money's not good enough I can go elsewhere.

HIGGINS Good enough for what?

THE FLOWER GIRL Good enough for yə-oo. Now you know, dont you? I'm come to have lessons, I am. And to pay for em tə-oo: make no mistake.

HIGGINS [*stupent*] Well!!! [*recovering his breath with a gasp*] What do you expect me to say to you?

THE FLOWER GIRL Well, if you was a gentleman, you might ask me to sit down, I think. Dont I tell you I'm bringing you business?

HIGGINS Pickering: shall we ask this baggage to sit down, or shall

---

103 **Be off with you** 去！滚开！这里的 with 没有具体意义，只是与副词连用构成祈使句。

105 **Dont you be so saucy.** 你不要这样无礼；Dont you 是加强 Dont 的语气。 **saucy** （对尊长）无礼的。 **aint** (= haven't) **heard what I come for yet**

你还没有听我说我是为什么来的。这里 come 也可用 came。yet 修饰 heard。

107 **instructions** 作“命令”、“指示”解是可数名词，且常作复数；作“教育”、“训练”解是不可数名词。 **Did you tell him I come in a taxi?** 在过去时 Did tell 后面的间接引语中的这个 come 按严格的语法应用 had come，实际上通常用 came。

108 **Nonsense** 胡说！这里作感叹词。 **girl** 单独 girl 一词作呼唤语很不客气，与亲热地称 my girl 截然不同。 **What do you think a gentleman like Mr Higgins cares what you came in?** 你认为像 Higgins 先生这样的绅士会在意你是乘什么来的吗？ cares 的宾语是 what you came in 这个宾语从句；句首的 what 是状语宾语（adverbial objective），修饰 cares。 **cares** 把……放在心上；关心。

110 **Oh, we *are* proud!** 噢，我们这种人是光明正大的；别把我们看作不自珍重的人。**aint** (= isn't) **above giving lessons** 并非不肯授课。 above 不屑……的。

111 **not him** = He is not above giving lessons. 重复以强调。him 用宾格代替主格，常见于这种上下文的口语中。 **I aint** (= haven't) **come here to ask for any compliment** [ˈkɒmplɪmənt] 我不是来讨你恭维的；不因为我出钱请你教课，就要你把我当个好主顾那样来奉承我。

112 **if my money's not good enough I can go elsewhere** 假如我（出）的钱（你嫌）不够的话，我可以到别处去（请教）。

115 **yə-oo** = you. 为要强调 you，读成了 [jəuː]。

116 **have lessons** 听课；上课。**And to pay for em tə-oo** = And I'm to pay for them (the lessons), too. 而且我听课是要付钱的。

117 **make no mistake** 别弄错；我说的话是千真万确的。

118 **stupent** 感到惊慌失措。 **Well!!!** 这个感叹词可以表示许多意思，这里表示惊讶，后面用三个惊叹号，表示非常非常惊讶。 **recovering his breath with a gasp** （被卖花女气得）喘着粗气才能恢复呼吸。 **What do you expect me to say to you?** 你道我会对你说什么？What 是 say 的宾语。**expect** 忖度；不是“希望”的意思，如：You're not expected. 没想到你会来；不是“不希望你来”。

120 **Well** 这个 Well 和上面的“Well!!!”不同，仅是个语气词，有“那么”的意思。**if you was a gentleman, you might ask me to sit down** 这是虚拟语气，you was 应作 you were；you might ask 是 ask 的委婉说法，言外有责怪 Higgins 的意思。

121 **bringing you business** [ˈbɪznəs] 给你带生意来。

123 **baggage** 原是“行李”的意思，这里是对女人的蔑称，犹言“贱货”、“婊子”。Higgins 身为专家、教授，举止言语极其粗鲁。 **or** = otherwise. 否则。

we throw her out of the window?

THE FLOWER GIRL [*running away in terror to the piano, where she turns at bay*] Ah-ah-oh-ow-ow-ow-oo! [*wounded and whimpering*] I wont be called a baggage when Ive offered to pay like any lady.

Motionless, the two men stare at her from the other side of the room, amazed.

PICKERING [*gently*] But what is it you want?

THE FLOWER GIRL I want to be a lady in a flower shop stead of sellin at the corner of Tottenham Court Road. But they wont take me unless I can talk more genteel. He said he could teach me. Well, here I am ready to pay him – not asking any favor – and he treats me zif I was dirt.

MRS PEARCE How can you be such a foolish ignorant girl as to think you could afford to pay Mr Higgins?

THE FLOWER GIRL Why shouldnt I? I know what lessons cost as well as you do; and I'm ready to pay.

HIGGINS How much?

THE FLOWER GIRL [*coming back to him, triumphant*] Now youre talking! I thought youd come off it when you saw a chance of

---

125 **running away in terror** 因恐惧而逃跑。 **turns at bay** 处于困兽斗的状态。这是习语，常作 turn to bay、stand at bay、be at bay。

126 **wounded** [ˈwuːndɪd] 这是由 wound 的过去分词变成的形容词，原义“受伤的”，转义“受了委屈的”。注意：wound（伤），不要和 wind [waɪnd]（绕、绞）的过去时和过去分词 wound 混淆。

127 **offered** 提供；主动提出。

130 **But what is it you want?** it 后面省略关系代词 that；过去的修辞学上常说句首不能用 And 或 But，事实上这很普遍。

131 **stead of sellin** = instead of selling. stead 是误用；又，没受过教育的人常把 -ing 读作 -in，即把 [ŋ] 读作 [n]。

132 **Tottenham** [ˈtɒtnəm] **Court Road** 伦敦街名。

133 **take** 雇用；录用。 **genteel** [dʒenˈtiːl] 这里该用 genteelly，意思为"斯文地"，此词常讽刺地含有"假斯文"的意思。

134 **asking any favor** 要求任何恩惠。ask 作"请求"解时，通常限于请求无形的东西，而 ask for 则请求有形、无形的东西一般都可以用，如 ask for a ticket、ask for help。

135 **zif I was dirt** = as if I was dirt. 仿佛我是垃圾；当我垃圾（不当我人）。 **as if** 仿佛；后面用虚拟语气，was 也可用 were。 **dirt** 垃圾。是不可数名词，不能说 a dirt 或 dirts。

137 **could afford to pay** 付得起。afford 作"负担得起"解时，常与 can 连用，后面接不定式，但有时也可直接接名词或代词，如 can't afford a new car = can't afford to buy a new car。当然文中 afford to pay Mr Higgins 不能说 afford Mr Higgins。

138 **Why shouldnt I?** = Why shouldnt I think I can afford to pay Mr Higgins? 为什么我不能认为我是付得起 Higgins 先生的（学费）呢？ **I know what lessons cost as well as you do** 我同你（们）一样清楚地知道学费要多少。what 是疑问代词，作 cost 的宾语。 **as well as you do** = as well as you know what lessons cost 这里 as well as ... 是"像……一样清楚（well）"；不要和习语 as well as 混淆，如：He gives me clothes as well as food. 他不但给我吃的，还给我穿的。

141 **coming back to him, triumphant** [traɪˈʌmfənt] （从钢琴处）回到他面前，得意洋洋。这里 triumphant 是形容词，作表语，也称主语补足语，说卖花女回到 Higgins 面前后的神态，倘改用副词 triumphantly，那就修饰 coming，是"得意洋洋地回到他面前"的意思，说的是回过来时一路上的神态。 **Now youre talking!** 现在你（才像是）说人话了；你现在这样说才对（我们可以谈下去了）。言下之意，Higgins 刚才蛮横无理，简直是胡闹。这是口语中的惯用语。

142 **youd come off it** = you would come off it. 你会不再胡闹的。come off it 是口语中的习语，是"不再胡说八道"、"不再胡闹"的意思。

getting back a bit of what you chucked at me last night. [*confidentially*] Youd had a drop in, hadnt you ?

HIGGINS [*peremptorily*] Sit down.

THE FLOWER GIRL Oh, if youre going to make a compliment of it –

HIGGINS [*thundering at her*] Sit down.

MRS PEARCE [*severely*] Sit down, girl. Do as youre told.

THE FLOWER GIRL Ah-ah-ah-ow-ow-oo! [*She stands, half rebellious, half bewildered.*]

PICKERING [*very courteous*] Wont you sit down? [*He places the stray chair near the hearthrug between himself and Higgins.*]

LIZA [*coyly*] Dont mind if I do. [*She sits down. Pickering returns to the hearthrug.*]

HIGGINS Whats your name?

THE FLOWER GIRL Liza Doolittle.

HIGGINS [*declaiming gravely*]

Eliza, Elizabeth, Betsy and Bess,
They went to the woods to get a bird's nes':

PICKERING They found a nest with four eggs in it:

HIGGINS They took one apiece, and left three in it.

They laugh heartily at their own fun.

LIZA Oh, dont be silly.

MRS PEARCE [*placing herself behind Eliza's chair*] You mustnt speak to the gentleman like that.

LIZA Well, why wont he speak sensible to me?

143 **what you chucked at me last night** 昨夜你扔给我的东西（即一大把金银钱币）。what 是 chucked 的宾语。**confidentially** [ˌkɒnfɪˈdenʃəli] 私下地；不足与外人道。书信、文件上写个 confidential，表示“秘密”。

144 **had a drop in** 喝了点酒（喝醉了，所以会给那么多钱）。

145 **peremptorily** [pəˈremptrəli] 命令式地；专横地。

146 **if youre going to make a compliment of it** – 如果你把这（叫我坐）作为一种歉意；如果你客气点叫我坐（那么我就坐）。破折号表示话未说完就被打断了。

147 **thundering** 怒喝（犹如雷鸣）。

148 **Do as youre told.** = Do as youre told to do.

149 **half rebellious** [rɪˈbeljəs], **half bewildered** 一半对抗，一半惶惑；既要反抗，又不知所措。

151 **courteous** [ˈkɜːtɪəs] 彬彬有礼的；殷勤的。

153 **Liza** [ˈlaɪzə] 这里应作 The Flower Girl，因为接下去又用 The Flower Girl，且方始报出 Liza 的名字。 **Dont mind if I do.** = I dont mind if I sit down. Dont 不要误解为祈使语气而认为 = You dont。mind 这里作“反对”解，全句字面意思是：“假如我坐，我也不反对”，实际是“我并不反对坐下”，即“我坐下好了”。

156 **Doolittle** [ˈduːlɪtl] 姓氏。

158 **Eliza** [ɪˈlaɪzə], **Elizabeth** [ɪˈlɪzəbəθ], **Betsy** [ˈbetsi] **and Bess** [bes] 这一行起的四行是 Higgins 和 Pickering 一唱一和拿 Liza 的名字开玩笑的一首打油诗。Eliza、Betsy、Bess，跟 Liza 一样，都是 Elizabeth 的昵称，诗中作为四个人。

159 **bird's nes'** = bird's nest. 鸟巢。也作 bird-nest。这里 nest 省去 t，为和上行末的 Bess 押韵。

161 **apiece** 各；每人。

162 **laugh heartily at** 因……而开怀大笑。注意：这里 laugh 和 at 不构成习语；习语 laugh at 作“嘲笑”、“对……付之一笑”解。

163 **silly** 傻的；无聊的。

166 **speak sensible** = speak sensibly. 合情合理地说话。

HIGGINS Come back to business. How much do you propose to pay me for the lessons?

LIZA Oh, I know whats right. A lady friend of mine gets French lessons for eighteenpence an hour from a real French gentleman. Well, you wouldnt have the face to ask me the same for teaching me my own language as you would for French; so I wont give more than a shilling. Take it or leave it.

HIGGINS [*walking up and down the room, rattling his keys and his cash in his pockets*] You know, Pickering, if you consider a shilling, not as a simple shilling, but as a percentage of this girl's income, it works out as fully equivalent to sixty or seventy guineas from a millionaire.

PICKERING How so?

HIGGINS Figure it out. A millionaire has about £150 a day. She earns about half-a-crown.

LIZA [*haughtily*] Who told you I only –

HIGGINS [*continuing*] She offers me two-fifths of her day's income for a lesson. Two-fifths of a millionaire's income for a day

---

167 **Come back to business** 言归正传。

169 **A lady friend of mine** 我的一个上等女性朋友。卖花女在当时的社会中自不算“上等”。

170 **eighteenpence** 十八便士。当时英国币制，一先令 = 十二便士。这里不说 a shilling and sixpence 或 a shilling and a half，而说 eighteenpence，犹如英语中往往不说 a year and a half 等，而说 eighteen months。

171 **wouldnt have the face to ask me the same for teaching me my own language**

as you would for French 总没有这脸皮（总不好意思）要求我付同你教法语一样的学费来教我学母语；要你教母语总该比要你教外国语的学费低些。as you would for French = as you would ask (me) for teaching (me) French. 这里的 as 是代词，和上面 the same 呼应，在它引起的从句中作 ask 的直接宾语（间接宾语是 me）。ask 接双宾语，如此处作“请求”、“要求”解外，也可作“问”解，如：ask him a question（问他个问题）。 **the same** 同样的学费。

173 **Take it or leave it.** 要么接受，要么放弃；（你肯收一先令）就收它，否则就不收它（我不请你教就是）。

174 **walking up and down the room** 在房间里走来走去。up and down 是习语，虽有“上上下下”、“前前后后”等多种意义，但此处未必是说“向舞台的后部(up) 和向舞台的前部（down）”来回走。 **rattling** 使发出叮叮当当（或格格）的声音。

175 **consider a shilling, not as a simple shilling, but as a percentage of this girl's income** 把一个先令不单纯看作是一个先令，而看作是这个姑娘（全部）收入的百分之几。 **consider** 接复合宾语，中间通常不用 as，如 consider him a true scholar（认为他是真正的学者）；这里用 as 是“作为……（来考虑）”。 **not ... but ...** 不是……，而是……；是习语。注意：not 和 but 后面的语法成分必须对等，如：He is not an actor, but a singer. 他不是演员，而是歌手。不能说 He is not an actor, but is a singer.

177 **it works out as fully equivalent** [ɪˈkwɪvələnt] **to** 这（一先令）算起来足足抵得上……

178 **guineas** [ˈɡɪnɪz] 基尼；旧时英国金币，值二十一先令，也作为二十一先令的计值单位。现在作为计值单位，是一又百分之五镑，即一镑五便士（新币制一镑 = 一百便士）。 **from a millionaire** [mɪljəˈneə] 百万富翁拿出来的。

179 **How so?** 怎么会是这样的？这是口语中的惯用语。

180 **Figure** [ˈfɪɡə] **it out.** 你把它算出来看。这里的 it 指 Higgins 刚才所说卖花女的一先令相当于百万富翁的六、七十基尼的说法。 **has** 有（多少）收入；= has an income of。 **£150** 一百五十英镑，读作 one hundred and fifty pounds 或 pound one hundred fifty。

183 **two-fifths** 五分之二。 **fifth** 除作“第五”解外，还可作“五分之一”解，并可用复数（其他序数词也是这样）；二个五分之一就是五分之二。但二分之一是 half，不是 second。

would be somewhere about £60. It's handsome. By George, it's enormous! it's the biggest offer I ever had.

LIZA [*rising, terrified*] Sixty pounds! What are you talking about? I never offered you sixty pounds. Where would I get –

HIGGINS Hold your tongue.

LIZA [*weeping*] But I aint got sixty pounds. Oh –

MRS PEARCE Dont cry, you silly girl. Sit down. Nobody is going to touch your money.

HIGGINS Somebody is going to touch you, with a broomstick, if you dont stop snivelling. Sit down.

LIZA [*obeying slowly*] Ah-ah-ah-ow-oo-o! One would think you was my father.

HIGGINS If I decide to teach you, I'll be worse than two fathers to you. Here! [*He offers her his silk handkerchief.*]

LIZA Whats this for?

HIGGINS To wipe your eyes. To wipe any part of your face that feels moist. Remember: thats your handkerchief; and thats your sleeve. Dont mistake the one for the other if you wish to become a lady in a shop.

Liza, utterly bewildered, stares helplessly at him.

MRS PEARCE It's no use talking to her like that, Mr Higgins: she

---

185 **It's handsome.** 这（一课的学费六十英镑）是可观的（数目）。 **By George**

发誓用语，表示“真的”；有时只是激动地感叹。这用语现在似乎已经过时了。

186 **offer** 出价。这里指愿付的学费金额。

188 **get –** 破折号表示话未说完被打断了；后面该有类似 such a big sum，或至少有 it 等词。

189 **Hold your tongue** 住嘴；是习语；= Shut up。

192 **touch your money** 要你的钱。 **touch** 有“动脑筋取得”等意思。

193 **touch you, with a broomstick** 用扫帚柄打你。这里承上文所用 touch，也用 touch 一词，而意义不同，是幽默的说法。

195 **One would think you was my father.** 人们会当你是我老子的（我老子对我才这样凶）。 **was** 正规英语中用 were。这里用 was (were) 而不用 are，是因为主句中用 would 而不是用 will 的缘故。

197 **worse than two fathers to you** 比两个老子更叫你难受。上文 Liza 说 Higgins 凶得好比是她老子，所以他这样说。

198 **Here** 这儿；喏；是拿东西给人时常用语。 **offers her his silk handkerchief** 主动把他的丝手帕给她。handkerchief 读 [ˈhæŋkətʃɪf]，复数式是 handkerchiefs [-tʃɪfs]，现在也读作 [ˈhæŋkətʃi:f]，复数式作 handkerchieves [-tʃi:vz]。

199 **Whats this for?** 这（手帕）作什么用？ for 的介词宾语是 what。

200 **To wipe your eyes.** = It's for you to wipe your eyes. **that feels moist** 摸上去觉得湿的。 **feels** 作“接触着感觉（如何）”解，类似用例如：The air feels cold. 觉得空气冷。

202 **Dont mistake the one for the other** 不要把两者相互弄错；不要把手帕当袖子用、把袖子当手帕用。 **mistake A for B** 把 A 误作为 B。

204 **utterly** 全然；一般修饰贬义词，如 utterly ruined（彻底垮掉），utterly exhausted（精疲力竭）。 **helplessly** 不知所措地；无可奈何地。

205 **It's no use talking to her like that** 那样对她讲没有用。It 是虚词（expletive），除可以引起同位的不定式和名词性从句外，也可像这里这样引起同位的动名词，甚至名词，如：It's of vital importance education. 教育是头等重要的。用动名词一般指当前的事实，用不定式一般指泛说的行为。

doesnt understand you. Besides, youre quite wrong: she doesnt do it that way at all. [*She takes the handkerchief.*]

LIZA [*snatching it*] Here! You give me that handkerchief. He gev it to me, not to you.

PICKERING [*laughing*] He did. I think it must be regarded as her property, Mrs Pearce.

MRS PEARCE [*resigning herself*] Serve you right, Mr Higgins.

PICKERING Higgins: I'm interested. What about the ambassador's garden party? I'll say youre the greatest teacher alive if you make that good. I'll bet you all the expenses of the experiment you cant do it. And I'll pay for the lessons.

LIZA Oh, you are real good. Thank you, Captain.

HIGGINS [*tempted, looking at her*] It's almost irresistible. She's so deliciously low – so horribly dirty –

LIZA [*protesting extremely*] Ah-ah-ah-ah-ow-ow-oo-oo!!! I aint dirty: I washed my face and hands afore I come, I did.

PICKERING Youre certainly not going to turn her head with flattery, Higgins.

MRS PEARCE [*uneasy*] Oh, dont say that, sir: theres more ways than one of turning a girl's head; and nobody can do it better than Mr Higgins, though he may not always mean it. I do

---

206 **she doesnt do it that way at all** 她根本不那样做的（不用手帕擦眼泪鼻涕的）。does not do 用现在时表示经常的、习惯的动作。it 指擦眼泪鼻涕。

that way = in that way.

208 **Here! You give me that handkerchief.** 不行！你把那块手帕给我！ **Here!** 那可不行！（你抢去手帕这件事）太不应该啊！ **You give me ...** = Give me ... 祈使句中用 You 比不用 You 语气重。 **gev** (= gave) **it to me, not to you.** 它（手帕）是给我的，不是给你的。注意：give the handkerchief to me 也可用双宾语，说 give me the handkerchief，但在用 it 的情况下，在英国比较少说 give me it（往往说 give it me）。这里 to me 和 to you 对照，更不能用双宾语了。

210 **He did.** = He gave it to Liza.

212 **resigning** [rɪˈzaɪnɪŋ] **herself** 使自己勉强服从；无可奈何。 **Serve you right** 是习语，= It serves you right. 它（这里是指 Liza 抓去手帕当自产）给了你应有的报应。也就是"活该"的意思。

213 **What about the ambassador's garden party?** 在第一幕中 Higgins 曾说要训练卖花女，使她在大使馆的游园会上冒充公爵夫人，这里问他这事怎么样。

215 **make that good** 实现那个话(使卖花女得以冒充公爵夫人)。make good 是习语，作"实现（计划、诺言）"解。 **bet you all the expenses of the experiment you cant do it** 跟你打赌——倘我输，由我负担（训练卖花女使之能冒充公爵夫人的）全部试验费用——你不可能办到这件事。在句法上，bet you 的 you 是 bet 的间接宾语，you cant do it（you 前省去连词 that）这个从句是 bet 的直接宾语，expenses 是状语宾语（adverbial objective）。

217 **real good** = really good. 口语中有将 real 作副词的。

218 **tempted** 受了诱惑，因而产生了兴趣。

219 **deliciously low** 美妙地低贱；低贱得可爱。这是萧伯纳的幽默之笔。修饰词和被修饰词词义褒贬相反，在修辞学上原有此一格，叫做"矛盾修饰法"（oxymoron）；英国大诗人弥尔顿（Milton）常用这种修辞手法，极端的例子可举丁尼生（Tennyson）的"and faith unfaithful kept him falsely true"（不忠的忠心使他一直虚假地真诚）。 **horribly dirty** 脏得吓人；极脏。horribly 在口语中可作"非常"解。

221 **afore I come** = before I came. afore 在古文和方言中 = before，在航海用语中作"在（……）前面"解，= in front (of)。come 此处应用 came。

225 **turning a girl's head** = turning her head with flattery. 用恭维使她妄自尊大；捧得她忘乎所以。Higgins 称她 deliciously low 和 horribly dirty，当然不是恭维话。Pickering 把这说成是恭维，是句俏皮话。

hope, sir, you wont encourage him to do anything foolish.

HIGGINS [*becoming excited as the idea grows on him*] What is life but a series of inspired follies? The difficulty is to find them to do. Never lose a chance: it doesnt come every day. I shall make a duchess of this draggletailed guttersnipe.

LIZA [*strongly deprecating this view of her*] Ah-ah-ah-ow-ow-oo!

HIGGINS [*carried away*] Yes: in six months – in three if she has a good ear and a quick tongue – I'll take her anywhere and pass her off as anything. We'll start today: now! this moment! Take her away and clean her, Mrs Pearce. Monkey Brand, if it wont come off any other way. Is there a good fire in the kitchen?

MRS PEARCE [*protesting*] Yes; but –

HIGGINS [*storming on*] Take all her cloths off and burn them. Ring up Whiteley or somebody for new ones. Wrap her up in brown paper til they come.

LIZA Youre no gentleman, youre not, to talk of such things. I'm a good girl, I am; and I know what the like of you are, I do.

---

227 **wont encourage** [ɪnˈkʌrɪdʒ] **him to do anything foolish** 不要鼓励他干出任何蠢事来。“蠢事”指训练卖花女冒充公爵夫人。

228 **the idea grows on him** 这想法（指训练卖花女冒充公爵夫人）在他头脑里滋长（越想越感兴趣）。 **What is life but a series of inspired follies?** 除了一系列心血来潮的蠢事之外，人生是什么呢？人生只是一系列心血来潮的蠢事而已。 **but** = except. **inspired** 受灵感启示的；心血来潮的；兴之所致的。

229 **The difficulty is to find them to do. Never lose a chance: it doesnt come every day.** 困难在于找到这种心血来潮的蠢事去干。（找到也不容易）不要失掉（这种干蠢事的）机会，这种机会不是每天都有的。

230 **make a duchess of this draggletailed guttersnipe** （通过语音训练）使这个破破烂烂的穷女孩变成公爵夫人。draggletailed 是由 draggle（拖得又脏又湿）+ tail（尾巴）+ ed 构成的，作“懒散邋遢的”解，用于女人，与 slattern 同义。guttersnipe 是 gutter（沟）和 snipe（鹬，也作“可鄙的人”解）构成的，是对流浪儿或拾荒者的蔑称。

232 **this view of her** 对她的这个看法，即把她看作是破烂的穷女孩。比较：this view of hers（她的这种看法）。

233 **carried away** 由于激动而失去自制；得意忘形。 **in six months** = I shall make a duchess of this draggletailed guttersnipe in six months. **has a good ear and a quick tongue** 有能辨别各种发音的耳朵和能很快学会发各种音的舌头。

234 **take her anywhere and pass her off as anything** 带她到任何地方去，使她冒充任何（高贵的）人物。

235 **now! this moment!** = We'll start now! We'll start this moment. Higgins 的激动和急躁，活现纸上，如闻其声。

236 **Monkey Brand** = Use (或 Clean her with) Monkey Brand. Monkey Brand 猴牌洗涤剂。当是去污粉之类，不是一般盥洗用的香皂。

237 **it wont come off** 污垢洗不掉。 **it** 这里没有先行词；泛指污垢。 **a good fire** 烧得很旺的炉火。

239 **Yes; but –** = Yes, there is a good fire in the kitchen, but – 旺的炉火是有，可是——（话未说完。）

240 **storming on** 继续大发雷霆；不待 Mrs Pearce 话说完，他自管自大叫大嚷。**Ring up Whiteley** [ˈwaɪtli] **or somebody for new ones.** 打电话给 Whiteley 或（别的）什么人，叫他送新衣服来。Whiteley 当是个成衣商。 **ones** = clothes.

242 **brown paper** 牛皮纸。 **til** = till.

243 **Youre no gentleman** 你不是正派的上等人。这里 no = not a，但又与 not a 有不同意义，例如：He is not a scholar. 他不是学者（可能是干部、画家等）。而 He is no scholar 却有“此人不学无术，根本不是什么学者”的意思。 **youre not** 按语法 = youre not a gentleman，而承上文，只是重复强调 Youre no gentleman。

244 **what the like of you are** 像你这样的一类人是什么样的人。

HIGGINS We want none of your Lisson Grove prudery here, young woman. Youve got to learn to behave like a duchess. Take her away, Mrs Pearce. If she gives you any trouble, wallop her.

LIZA [*springing up and running between Pickering and Mrs Pearce for protection*] No! I'll call the police, I will.

MRS PEARCE But Ive no place to put her.

HIGGINS Put her in the dustbin.

LIZA Ah-ah-ah-ow-ow-oo!

PICKERING Oh come, Higgins! be reasonable.

MRS PEARCE [*resolutely*] You must be reasonable, Mr Higgins: really you must. You cant walk over everybody like this.

Higgins, thus scolded, subsides. The hurricane is succeeded by a zephyr of amiable surprise.

HIGGINS [*with professional exquisiteness of modulation*] *I* walk over everybody! My dear Mrs Pearce, my dear Pickering, I never had the slightest intention of walking over anyone. All I propose is that we should be kind to this poor girl. We must help her to prepare and fit herself for her new station in life. If I did not express myself clearly it was because I did not wish to hurt her delicacy, or yours.

---

245 **Lisson Grove prudery** [ˈpruːdəri] 贫民区的假正经。 **Lisson Grove** 卖花女

居住的贫民区，见第一幕。**prudery** 规矩特多、忌讳特多；过分拘谨；假正经。

246 **Youve got to** 你必须；你得。**have got to** 口语，= have to；口语中还有说成 got to 的。

247 **wallop** [ˈwɒləp] 痛打；是口语，犹如我们说“揍”。

251 **Ive no place to put her** 不必说 Ive no place to put her in。

252 **dustbin** [ˈdʌstbɪn] 垃圾箱。这是英国语；美国称 ash can。

254 **come** 得了。这里有感叹词的意味，叫人注意。

256 **walk over everybody** 对每个人都强凶霸道，不顾人家怎样想。**walk over** 是习语；它还有一个意义是“轻易胜过”。

257 **subsides** [səbˈsaɪdz] 平息下来。subside 作“平息”解时，可用于 The debators subsided，也可用于 His anger（或 excitement 等）subsided。**The hurricane** [ˈhʌrɪkən] **is succeeded by a zephyr** [ˈzefə] **of amiable** [ˈeɪmɪəbl] **surprise** [səˈpraɪz] 照字面译为“飓风被和蔼的惊讶的微风所替代。”实际是说：Higgins 原在大发雷霆，Mrs Pearce 说他强凶霸道，他还不自知，所以觉得惊讶，但是他对这指责并不暴跳如雷，而是转而和蔼地作了辩解。hurricane 和 zephyr 都是比喻。

259 **professional exquisiteness** ([ˈekskwɪzɪtnɪs]，现在也读作 [ɪkˈskwɪzɪtnɪs]) **of modulation** 专家的优美音调。**modulation** 这里是指音调的抑扬顿挫。收音机上的 FM 就是 frequency modulation（频率调制，即“调频”）的简写。***I* walk over everybody!** 我对任何人都强凶霸道吗！（别人可能强凶霸道）我才不强凶霸道呐！

262 **help her to prepare and fit herself for her new station in life** 帮助她准备和适应（她作为公爵夫人等的）新的社会地位。help her 后面接不定式时，英国用法往往有不定式记号 to，美国不用 to，prepare 和 fit 合用反身代词 herself 和介词 for。prepare oneself for 和 prepare for 意义基本相同，常可互用，但应指出：（1）prepare for 比 prepare oneself for 普遍，更口语化；（2）prepare himself for bad news（对坏消息作好思想准备）之类的用例中，不能用 prepare for；（3）prepare for the examination 单纯是“准备考试”的意思，而 prepare oneself for the examination 是指“为某种重要考试（如留学考试）作好各方面的准备”。

263 **If** 是“如果说”的意思。

264 **express myself clearly** 把自己（的意思）表达得清楚，即“表达清楚”。**it** 指 I did not express myself clearly 这件事。

265 **hurt her delicacy** [ˈdelɪkəsi], **or yours** 伤害她的或者你们的脆弱的情感。

Liza, reassured, steals back to her chair.

MRS PEARCE [*to Pickering*] Well, did you ever hear anything like that, sir?

PICKERING [*laughing heartily*] Never, Mrs Pearce: never.

HIGGINS [*patiently*] Whats the matter?

MRS PEARCE Well, the matter is, sir, that you cant take a girl up like that as if you were picking up a pebble on the beach.

HIGGINS Why not?

MRS PEARCE Why not! But you dont know anything about her. What about her parents? She may be married.

LIZA Garn!

HIGGINS There! As the girl very properly says, Garn! Married indeed! Dont you know that a woman of that class looks a worn out drudge of fifty a year after she's married?

LIZA Whood marry me?

HIGGINS [*suddenly resorting to the most thrillingly beautiful low tones in his best elocutionary style*] By George, Eliza, the streets will be strewn with the bodies of men shooting themselves for your sake before Ive done with you.

MRS PEARCE Nonsense, sir. You mustnt talk like that to her.

LIZA [*rising and squaring herself determinedly*] I'm going away. He's off his chump, he is. I dont want no balmies teaching me.

HIGGINS [*wounded in his tenderest point by her insensibility to his*

---

266 **steals back to** 偷偷地回到……；不声不响地回到……。

271 **take a girl up like that** 那样（随便）捡个姑娘（收留下来）。

273 **Why not?** = Why can I not (或 can't I) take up a girl like that.

274 **Why not!** 这里承接上文而用惊叹号，表示"还问得出为什么不！"

276 **Garn!** 去你的！得了吧！见第一章注。

277 **There!** 这里是感叹词，引起注意，等于说 Look (here)! **Married indeed!** 真结婚了！真有结婚了的事！这是反话。

278 **looks a worn out drudge** [drʌdʒ] **of fifty a year after she's married** 结婚一年之后看上去就像个五十来岁油尽灯枯的苦工。worn out 通常写作 worn-out，是从 wear out（使）疲惫、（使）耗尽衍生的形容词。a year 修饰 after。she's = she is。

280 **Whood marry me?** = Who would marry me? 是虚拟语气，省略诸如 even if I should like to get married 的条件从句。

281 **resorting** [rɪˈzɔːtɪŋ] **to** 诉诸；求助于；采取（手段）。 **thrillingly beautiful** 惊人地漂亮的；悦耳之极的。

282 **elocutionary** [ˌeləˈkjuːʃənəri] **style** 朗诵的语调。 **the streets will be strewn with the bodies of men shooting themselves for your sake** 街上会铺满为你而开枪自杀的男人们的尸体。意思是："多少男人会因得不到你而自杀呢"。shooting 是现在分词，修饰 men。

284 **before Ive done with you** 在我结束对你的训练之前；不消等到我把你完全训练成贵妇人（就有许许多多人争着要娶你为妻）。 **have done with** 停止，结束；是习语。在美国也作 be done with。注意：不要和另一习语 do with（对付；容忍）相混。

286 **squaring herself** 摆架势；是口语。

287 **off his chump** 头脑失常；发疯；是俚语；= off his head。 **chump** 原义"厚木块"、"厚肉块"，俚语中作"头"解。 **I dont want no balmies** [ˈbɑːmɪz] **teaching me.** 我不要疯子来教我。这里 dont 和 no 是"双重否定"。balmies teaching me 是动名词词组构成的复合宾语。 **balmies** 原义"香的"等，俚语中 = barmy，愚蠢的；疯的。原是形容词，这里用作名词。

288 **wounded in his tenderest point by her insensibility to his elocution** 她对他（音调优美）的朗诵无动于衷刺痛了他（感情）的最敏感处。 **tender point** （身体上）最易感到酸痛之处，也称 tender spot。

elocution] Oh, indeed! I'm mad, am I? Very well, Mrs Pearce: you neednt order the new clothes for her. Throw her out.

LIZA [*whimpering*] Nah-ow. You got no right to touch me.

MRS PEARCE You see now what comes of being saucy. [*indicating the door*] This way, please.

LIZA [*almost in tears*] I didnt want no clothes. I wouldnt have taken them. [*She throws away the handkerchief.*] I can buy my own clothes.

HIGGINS [*deftly retrieving the handkerchief and intercepting her on her reluctant way to the door*] Youre an ungrateful wicked girl. This is my return for offering to take you out of the gutter and dress you beautifully and make a lady of you.

MRS PEARCE Stop, Mr Higgins. I wont allow it. It's you that are wicked. Go home to your parents, girl; and tell them to take better care of you.

LIZA I aint got no parents. They told me I was big enough to earn my own living and turned me out.

MRS PEARCE Wheres your mother?

LIZA I aint got no mother. Her that turned me out was my sixth stepmother. But I done without them. And I'm a good girl, I am.

HIGGINS Very well, then, what on earth is all this fuss about? The girl doesnt belong to anybody – is no use to anybody but me.

---

289 **Oh, indeed!** 哦，当真！（表示惊讶、讽刺等。） **I'm mad, am I?** 这是一种比较少见的句型。一个陈述句后面加上一个"附加疑问句"（tag

question），一般是前后两句，一正一反或一反一正；这里前句与后句都是肯定句，带有愤怒的反问口气；“我疯了，我疯吗？”其实自己不承认疯。

291 **Nah-ow.** = Now. 这里有感叹词的作用，可以表示各种意思，这里有“瞧你”的意思。

292 **comes of** 因……而得到的结果。 **what comes of** = the result of.

293 **This way, please.** = Come this way, please. 这是口语中引路的常用语。

294 **in tears** 流着泪。注意：tear，一滴眼泪；是可数名词，读 [tɪə]；作“撕”解的动词 tear 读 [teə]。 **I wouldnt have taken them.** 这是虚拟语气；（即使买了衣服来给我）我也不会拿的。

297 **on her reluctant way to the door** 在她并不情愿地向门口走去的途中。注意 reluctant way 之类不同于中国说法的“外国话”。

298 **wicked** [ˈwɪkɪd] 邪恶的。口语中作“讨厌的”、“令人不愉快的”解，这里就是这意思。下文 Mrs Pearce 称 Higgins 才是 wicked，当然不可能说她主人“邪恶”。

299 **my return** 我所得到的报答。 **take you out of the gutter** 把你从泥沟里拉出来。 **gutter** 原义“沟”，转义“民居住处”；the gutter 再转作“贫困”、“卑贱”解。

301 **It's you that are wicked** 不好的是你；是你不好。这种句型的说法是强调 you are wicked 中的 you。照语法，that 是关系代词，它的先行词是 It，这样，that 后面的动词应用 is，但习惯上常把 you 做 that 的先行词，因而 that 后用 are；而且也有把这里的 that 改用 who 的，但不很普遍。

304 **aint got no parents** 没有父母。aint = haven't. haven't got（口语）= haven't. 这里又是“双重否定”。 **big** 大。原指体积而言，这里 = grown-up / old。 **earn my own living** 我自己谋生。

305 **turned me out** 把我赶出来。turned 和前面 told 并列。

307 **Her that** 照语法该作 She that 或 She who；但口语中一般用 her 而不用 she。

308 **stepmother** 后母。前一句说没有 mother 是说亲生母亲已经不在。从后面剧情中知道，这个“后母”实际上当时并没有同 Liza 的父亲正式结婚；结婚是在他突然继承了一笔财产，成了暴发户之后的事。 **I done without them** 应作 I have done without them（我已经不需要他们了）。 **do without** 没有……也行；是习语。

310 **what on earth is all this fuss about** 这一切的大惊小怪都是干吗呀？完全无需小题大做。on earth 强调 what。about 是介词，what 是它的宾语。

311 **anybody but me** 除我之外的任何人。but = except.

[*He goes to Mrs Pearce and begins coaxing.*] You can adopt her, Mrs Pearce: I'm sure a daughter would be a great amusement to you. Now dont make any more fuss. Take her downstairs; and –

MRS PEARCE But whats to become of her? Is she to be paid anything? Do be sensible, sir.

HIGGINS Oh, pay her whatever is necessary: put it down in the housekeeping book. [*impatiently*] What on earth will she want with money? She'll have her food and her clothes. She'll only drink if you give her money.

LIZA [*turning on him*] Oh you are a brute. It's a lie: nobody ever saw the sign of liquor on me. [*to Pickering*] Oh, sir: youre a gentleman: dont let him speak to me like that.

PICKERING [*in good-humored remonstrance*] Does it occur to you, Higgins, that the girl has some feelings?

HIGGINS [*looking critically at her*] Oh no, I dont think so. Not any feelings that we need bother about. [*cheerily*] Have you, Eliza?

LIZA I got my feelings same as anyone else.

HIGGINS [*to Pickering, reflectively*] You see the difficulty?

PICKERING Eh? What difficulty?

HIGGINS To get her to talk grammar. The mere pronunciation is easy enough.

LIZA I dont want to talk grammar. I want to talk like a lady in a flower-shop.

---

312 **adopt her** 收养她；收她为养女。

316 **whats to become of her** 她将变成什么呢；她今后怎么样。口语中常说 What has become of him（或 it 等）? 他（这件事等）现在情况怎么样了？ **Is she to be paid anything?** 要付她点钱吗？动词 be（这里是 Is）后接不定式表示"计划"、"规定"等。

317 **Do be** Be 的强调式，Do 要重读。

318 **whatever is necessary** 需要的一切；比 what (= that which) is necessary 语气强。 **put it down in the housekeeping book** 把它（付出的钱）记在家用账上。 **book** 账簿。簿记学叫 bookkeeping。

320 **She'll only drink** 这里有"徒然让她去喝酒"的意思。

322 **turning on him** 突然（怀着恶意地）转身向他。 **brute** [bru:t] 原义"畜生"；这里指"蛮不讲理的人"。 **lie** 原义"谎话"，这里只是"胡说"的意思。

323 **sign of liquor** [ˈlɪkə] 喝酒的痕迹。

325 **Does it occur to you, Higgins, that ...** Higgins，你想到过……吗。 **occur to you** 在你头脑中出现；被你想到。it 是虚词，引起后面与它同位的 that 从句。

326 **has some feelings** 有情感（上的反应）。注意：这里的 feelings 即使前面没有 some，也用复数，同 hurt somebody's feelings（伤某人感情）等语中的 feelings 一样。

327 **Not any feelings that we need bother about.** = She has not any feelings that we need bother about. 她没有需要我们去烦心的情感；她的情感不关我们的事。need 在否定句和疑问句中作助动词，所以 bother 前没有 to。

328 **Have you** = Have you any feelings that we need bother about?

329 **I got my feelings same as anyone else** = Ive (got) my feelings just as anyone else (has his feelings). got 这里不是过去时，而是在不正规的口语中作 have got 用，= have。same 是副词，same as 应用 just as（这里 as 是连词）。

330 **the difficulty** 难处。指 Liza 不但语音是土腔，而且语法也不对，还要教她语法，这就困难了。

332 **To get her to talk grammar** = The difficulty is to get her to talk grammar. **talk grammar** = talk grammatically. 符合语法地说话。

334 **I want to talk like a lady in a flower-shop.** 我要讲话讲得像花店里的上等女子；像花店里的女店员一样说话，而不再用街头的卖花女的语言。

MRS PEARCE Will you please keep to the point, Mr Higgins. I want to know on what terms the girl is to be here. Is she to have any wages? And what is to become of her when youve finished your teaching? You must look ahead a little.

HIGGINS [*impatiently*] Whats to become of her if I leave her in the gutter? Tell me that, Mrs Pearce.

MRS PEARCE Thats her own business, not yours, Mr Higgins.

HIGGINS Well, when Ive done with her, we can throw her back into the gutter; and then it will be her own business again; so thats all right.

LIZA Oh, youve no feeling heart in you: you dont care for nothing but yourself. [*She rises and takes the floor resolutely.*] Here! Ive had enough of this. I'm going [*making for the door*]. You ought to be ashamed of yourself, you ought.

HIGGINS [*snatching a chocolate cream from the piano, his eyes suddenly beginning to twinkle with mischief*] Have some chocolates, Eliza.

LIZA [*halting, tempted*] How do I know what might be in them? Ive heard of girls being drugged by the like of you.

Higgins whips out his penknife; cuts a chocolate in two; puts one half into his mouth and bolts it; and offers her the other half.

---

336 **Will you please keep to the point, Mr Higgins.** 请你不要岔开话，Higgins 先

生。 **Will you please ...** = Please. 所以虽是主谓倒装的疑问句形式，句末不用问号而用句号。 **keep to the point** 扣住论点；不离主题。

337 **on what terms** 以什么条件。注意：terms 作“条件”解时用复数，前面介词用 on。

338 **wages** 工钱；常用复数。比较：wages 指支付体力劳动的“工钱”；salary 指支付脑力劳动的“薪金”，pay 统指“工资”，军饷称 soldier's pay。

339 **look ahead a little** 稍微向前看看；考虑得远一些。

342 **her own business, not yours** 她自己的事，不是你的事（与你无关）。

346 **feeling heart** 同情的心；恻隐之心。 **dont care for nothing but yourself** 不顾别人，只顾自己。这是“双重否定”，dont care 应作 care。 **nothing but** 除……之外没有其他；只有。这是习语。比较：另一习语 anything but：除……之外的任何一切；根本不……。这两个习语中的 but 都是介词，= except。

347 **takes the floor** 站起来（准备走开）。take the floor 有时作“发言”解，这里不是。

348 **Ive had enough of this.** 我对这（蛮横无理）已经受够了。 **making for the door** 走向门口。 **make for** 向……前进；是习语。

350 **chocolate cream** 奶油夹心巧克力糖。cream（奶油）原是不可数名词，和 chocolate 构成复合词，是一块一块的糖，所以是可数名词。 **his eyes suddenly beginning to twinkle with mischief** [ˈmɪstʃɪf] 他的眼睛忽然开始闪闪发出恶作剧的光芒。这是个“独立结构”，表示 snatching 时的状态。

352 **halting, tempted** 受到引诱（想吃）而停止（往门口跑）。tempted 是过去分词，修饰 halting。 **what might be in them** 它们（指巧克力糖）里面可能会有什么。might 比 may 表示更大的嫌疑。

353 **Ive heard of girls being drugged by the like of you** 我听到过姑娘们被像你这样的人用药物麻醉。girls being drugged ... 是 heard of 的复合宾语。 **drug** 名词作“药”解，也指“麻醉药”、“毒品”。作动词用时只指“（使）服麻醉药”、“（使）受到麻醉药的毒而失去知觉”解。

354 **whips out his penknife** 一下掏出小摺刀（旧称“小洋刀”）。whips out 已见第一幕 whipping out his book 一语中。

355 **bolts** 原义“射”、“窜”，这里作“囫囵吞下”解。

HIGGINS Pledge of good faith, Eliza. I eat one half: you eat the other. [*Liza opens her mouth to retort: he pops the half chocolate into it.*] You shall have boxes of them, barrels of them, every day. You shall live on them. Eh?

LIZA [*who has disposed of the chocolate after being nearly choked by it*] I wouldnt have ate it, only I'm too ladylike to take it out of my mouth.

HIGGINS Listen, Eliza. I think you said you came in a taxi.

LIZA Well, what if I did? Ive as good a right to take a taxi as anyone else.

HIGGINS You have, Eliza; and in future you shall have as many taxis as you want. You shall go up and down and round the town in a taxi every day. Think of that, Eliza.

MRS PEARCE Mr Higgins: youre tempting the girl. It's not right. She should think of the future.

HIGGINS At her age! Nonsense! Time enough to think of the future when you havnt any future to think of. No, Eliza: do as this lady does: think of other people's futures; but never think of your own. Think of chocolates, and taxis, and gold, and diamonds.

---

357 **Pledge** [pledʒ] **of good faith** 真诚的保证；自己吃给她看，保证不是给她吃什么毒品。Pledge 是 It（指我吃一半）is a（或 my) ledge 的省略。 **the other** = the other half.

358 **pops** pop 原是个拟声词，表示“砰”或“啪”的一声。用作动词，表示突然发生的动作；这里是“突然投掷”、“突然塞进”的意思。

359 **shall** shall 用于第二、第三人称表示说话人的意向，读 [ʃæl]，不读 [ʃəl]，这里和后面好几处 you shall 中的 shall 都表示说话人“允诺”，有时也表示“命令”、“威吓”。

360 **live on them** 靠(吃)巧克力糖生活。 **Eh?** 用以征求对方同意；好不好？是不是？

361 **disposed of** 处理掉；这里是“吃掉”。

362 **wouldnt have ate it** 本来不要吃的。这是虚拟语气，表示与过去的事实相反，实际上她已经吃了。ate 是 eaten 之误。 **only** 这里是连词，= but。 **ladylike** 像贵妇人的；有大家闺秀风度的。

364 **Listen** 听(我讲)；实际上只是叫对方注意。

365 **as good a right to take a taxi as anyone else** 有同任何其他人一样充分的乘出租车的权利。 **as anyone else** = as anyone else has a good right to take a taxi.

367 **You have** = You have as good a right to take a taxi as anyone else.

368 **go up and down and round the town** 在城里来来去去兜圈子。 **up and down** 来来去去；到处；是习语。 round 原义“围绕着”，实际上也是“在……的各处”的意思；美国多用 around。 go round 常是“（在……）到处兜一兜”的意思。

372 **At her age!** = She should think of the future at her age!（你竟然说）她这年纪（该想想未来）！意思是“她（这年纪）才无需考虑未来呐！” **Time enough to think of the future when you havnt any future to think of** = There is time enough ... / You have time enough ... 到你没有任何未来可以考虑的时候再去考虑未来，也有足够的时间（也不迟）。“未来”就是“前途”，即：到无路可走的时候，再找出路也不迟。这是萧伯纳典型的俏皮话。you 泛指“任何人”，也可理解为是对 Liza 说的。 **future** 未来；也就是“（自己的）前途”。

373 **do as this lady does** 照这位太太（指 Mrs Pearce）那样做。冒号后面是 Mrs Pearce 的做法。

374 **think of other people's futures; but never think of your own** 考虑别人的未来，而决不考虑你自己的未来。Higgins 说 Mrs Pearce 的做法是这样的，且把它说得像条处世格言，这分明是讽刺 Mrs Pearce 专管闲事而不想想自己的未来，可能她自己的未来还没有着落呢。 **futures** 别人各有各的未来或前途，故用复数。 **your own** = your own future.

375 **chocolates, and taxis, and gold, and diamonds** [ˈdaɪəməndz] 叠用一连串 and，比单用末一个 and 语气强。全不用 and 也比用一个 and 语气强。

LIZA No: I dont want no gold and no diamonds. I'm a good girl, I am. [*She sits down again, with an attempt at dignity.*]

HIGGINS You shall remain so, Eliza, under the care of Mrs Pearce. And you shall marry an officer in the Guards, with a beautiful moustache: the son of a marquis, who will disinherit him for marrying you, but will relent when he sees your beauty and goodness –

PICKERING Excuse me, Higgins; but I really must interfere. Mrs Pearce is quite right. If this girl is to put herself in your hands for six months for an experiment in teaching, she must understand thoroughly what she's doing.

HIGGINS How can she? She's incapable of understanding anything. Besides, do any of us understand what we are doing? If we did, would we ever do it?

PICKERING Very clever, Higgins; but not to the present point. [*to Eliza*] Miss Doolittle –

LIZA [*overwhelmed*] Ah-ah-ow-oo!

HIGGINS There! Thats all youll get out of Eliza. Ah-ah-ow-oo! No use explaining. As a military man you ought to know that. Give her her orders: thats enough for her. Eliza: you are to live here for the next six months, learning how to speak

---

378 **with an attempt at dignity** 要作出庄严的样子。

379 **remain so** = remain a good girl. 依旧是个正经姑娘。 **under the care of** 在……照管下。

380 **an officer in the Guards** 禁卫军军官。 **the Guards** 王家禁卫军。

381 **moustache** [məˈstɑːʃ] 小胡子。“大胡子”是 beard [bɪəd]。 **the son of a marquis** [ˈmɑːkwɪs], **who will disinherit** [ˌdɪsɪnˈherɪt] **him for marrying you** 侯爵的儿子，侯爵会因为他儿子娶了你而剥夺他儿子的继承权。who 前后有逗号，= and he (marquis)，它引起的从句叫做“非限制性定语从句”，别于“限制性定语从句”，如：He is the first (man) who got the news. 他是第一个得到消息的人。（who 前没有逗号。） **for** 表示原因。

382 **will relent** 会变得仁慈；宽恕他儿子娶 Liza 为妻。

384 **but** 在 Excuse me、sorry 等语后常用 but 接所要请人原谅的事。

385 **If this girl is to put herself in your hands** 要是想使这个姑娘自愿把自己交托给你（由你支配）。

386 **she must understand thoroughly what she's doing** 必须使她彻底了解她正在做的是怎么回事。

388 **How can she?** = How can she understand thoroughly what she's doing? **incapable of** 不能；不会。它同 capable 一样，后面接介词 of。比较：able 和 unable 后面接不定式。

390 **If we did, would we ever do it?** 如果我们明白（我们所做的事）的话，我们还会去做它吗？这是虚拟语气，意思是“正因为我们不明白，所以我们才会去做”。 **did** = understood what we were (或 are) doing. **ever** 用在疑问句中加强语气。 **do it** = do what we are doing.

391 **Very clever** = That (你说的话) is very clever. **not to the present point** 无关现在的主题；说到题外去了。

392 **Miss Doolittle** – Liza 从没有被人称过 Doolittle 小姐，所以 Pickering 这样称呼她，她受宠若惊，Pickering 话还没说下去，她听见这称呼就大叫起来。

394 **Thats all youll get out of Eliza.** 那（Ah-ah-ow-oo 的大叫声）就是你会从 Eliza 那里得到的一切；你只可能得到这样的反应。

395 **No use explaining.** = It's no use explaining. It 是可以引起同位的动名词，已见前注。 **As a military man** 作为一个军人。

396 **that** 指“只可能得到这样的反应”。 **Give her her orders** 对她下她（该执行）的命令。这句和 Give her your orders（给她下你的命令）是一样意思。 **thats enough for her** 那（指“给她下命令”）对她已经足够（不必跟她解释，反正解释她也不懂）。

beautifully, like a lady in a florist's shop. If youre good and do whatever youre told, you shall sleep in a proper bedroom, and have lots to eat, and money to buy chocolates and take rides in taxis. If youre naughty and idle you will sleep in the back kitchen among the black beetles, and be walloped by Mrs Pearce with a broomstick. At the end of six months you shall go to Buckingham Palace in a carriage, beautifully dressed. If the King finds out youre not a lady, you will be taken by the police to the Tower of London, where your head will be cut off as a warning to other presumptuous flower girls. If you are not found out, you shall have a present of seven-and-sixpence to start life with as a lady in a shop. If you refuse this offer you will be a most ungrateful wicked girl; and the angels will weep for you. [*to Pickering*] Now are you satisfied, Pickering? [*to Mrs Pearce*] Can I put it more plainly and fairly, Mrs Pearce?

MRS PEARCE [*patiently*] I think youd better let me speak to the girl properly in private. I dont know that I can take charge of her or consent to the arrangement at all. Of course I know you dont mean her any harm; but when you get what you call interested in people's accents, you never think or care what may happen to them or you. Come with me, Eliza.

HIGGINS Thats all right. Thank you, Mrs Pearce. Bundle her off to the bathroom.

---

398 **good** 好好的；与下文 naughty and idle 对照。

400 **money** 和 lots to eat 并列，是 have 的宾语；money 后面接 to buy chocolates 和 (to) take rides（乘车）in taxis 两个并列的不定式词组修饰它。

401 **sleep in the back kitchen among the black beetles** 睡在后厨房蟑螂堆里。 **black beetles** = cockroaches [ˈkɒkrəʊtʃɪz]. 蟑螂。among the black beetles 与 in the back kitchen 并列，修饰 sleep。

403 **you shall go to Buckingham Palace in a carriage** [ˈkærɪdʒ], **beautifully dressed** 给你坐着四轮马车到白金汉王宫去，穿得漂漂亮亮的。beautifully dressed 修饰 you。

405 **be taken by the police to the Tower** [ˈtaʊə] **of London** 被警察抓（去关）到伦敦塔里去。 **the police** 警察局；警务人员们。 **the Tower of London** 简称 the Tower，在伦敦泰晤士河北岸，是十一世纪建造的王宫，后改为监狱，现又改作博物馆，收藏历代兵器尤多。

407 **presumptuous** [prɪˈzʌmptjʊəs] 自以为是的；放肆的。

408 **you shall have a present of seven-and-sixpence to start life with as a lady in a shop** 要使你得到的赠礼是：你将以七先令六便士的收入开始，从此做一个花店里的店员小姐。

410 **a most ungrateful wicked girl** 一个很不领情的坏姑娘。 **a most** 很；非常；和用以表示形容词最高级的 the most（最）不同。 **ungrateful** 不领情的；忘恩负义的；也作“讨厌的”解。

411 **the angels** [ˈeɪndʒlz] **will weep for you** 天使们要为你哭泣（婉惜她拒绝接受这条件）。

412 **Can I put it more plainly and fairly** 我还能把话说得更清楚、更公平吗？这是反问，意思是“我说得再明白、公平不过了”。

415 **in private** 私下。

416 **consent to** 同意。consent 是不及物动词，介词用 to，不能直接接宾语。

417 **mean her any harm** 对她怀恶意。mean 这里接双宾语。 **get what you call interested in people's accents** 对人们的口音感到所谓兴趣。 **what you call** 插在 get interested（感到兴趣）两个词中间，= what is called = so-called。

418 **what may happen to them or you** 对他们或者对你（自己）会产生什么（后果）。

420 **Bundle her off** 把她撵走。

LIZA [*rising reluctantly and suspiciously*] Youre a great bully, you are. I wont stay here if I dont like. I wont let nobody wallop me. I never asked to go to Bucknam Palace, I didnt. I was never in trouble with the police, not me. I'm a good girl –

MRS PEARCE Dont answer back, girl. You dont understand the gentleman. Come with me. [*She leads the way to the door, and holds it open for Eliza.*]

LIZA [*as she goes out*] Well, what I say is right. I wont go near the King, not if I'm going to have my head cut off. If I'd known what I was letting myself in for, I wouldnt have come here. I always been a good girl; and I never offered to say a word to him; and I dont owe him nothing; and I dont care; and I wont be put upon; and I have my feelings the same as anyone else –

Mrs Pearce shuts the door; and Eliza's plaints are no longer audible.

Eliza is taken upstairs to the third floor greatly to her surprise; for she expected to be taken down to the scullery. There Mrs Pearce opens a door and takes her into a spare bedroom.

MRS PEARCE I will have to put you here. This will be your bedroom.

LIZA O-h, I couldnt sleep here, missus. It's too good for the likes of me. I should be afraid to touch anything. I aint a duchess

---

422 **bully** [ˈbʊli] 恃强欺弱的人。

424 **I never asked to go to Bucknam Palace** 我从没有要求过到 Buckingham Palace。事实她是说过的，但并没有真要去白金汉宫。Liza 这样辩解，无非说明自己并没有做过越轨的事，是个 good girl。 **I was never in trouble with the police, not me.** 我从来没有和警察（局）有过纠葛，我没有过。 **not me** 口语中习惯用 not me，不用 not I。

426 **answer back** 回嘴；顶嘴。

430 **not if I'm going to have my head cut off** = I wont go near the King even if I'm going to have my head cut off. 即使（要是不去就要）杀我的头，我也不要到国王跟前去。 **have my head cut off** 让我的头被砍掉；cut 是过去分词，cut off 作宾语补足语，my head 和 cut off 之间有逻辑上的主谓关系，my head cut off 构成复合宾语。 **If I'd known what I was letting myself in for, I wouldnt have come here.** 假如我早知道我会遭遇到什么，我才不会来这里呢。这里表示与过去事实相反的虚拟语气，事实是早先不知道是这么回事，所以她来了。

432 **say a word** 说（几）句话；a word 并不真限于"一个词"，犹如 Drop me a line（简单写封信给我）中的 a line 不真限于"一行"。

433 **dont owe him nothing** 是"双重否定"，= dont owe him anything 或 owe him nothing，一点不欠他什么。 **dont care** 不放在心上；不以为意。

434 **be put upon** 被欺骗；上当。 **the same as anyone else** = just as anyone else has his feelings.

436 **plaints are no longer audible** [ˈɔːdəbl] 抱怨声不再听得见。

438 **greatly to her surprise** 使她大为惊异。

439 **scullery** [ˈskʌləri] 厨房的洗涤间；碗碟贮藏室，即前面曾见的 back kitchen。 **There** 指 the third floor（ground floor 以上的第三层楼，即我国所说的"四楼"）。spare bedroom 空余没有人住的卧室。

443 **It's too good for the likes of me.** 这（卧室）对我这样的人是太好了。 **the likes of me** 像我这样（贫穷或不行）的人；是口语。

444 **I aint** (= am not) **a duchess yet** 我还不是公爵夫人。做了公爵夫人，才配住这卧室，碰这里的东西。

yet, you know.

MRS PEARCE You have got to make yourself as clean as the room: then you wont be afraid of it. And you must call me Mrs Pearce, not missus. [*She throws open the door of the dressingroom, now modernized as a bathroom.*]

LIZA Gawd! Whats this? Is this where you wash clothes? Funny sort of copper I call it.

MRS PEARCE It is not a copper. This is where we wash ourselves, Eliza, and where I am going to wash you.

LIZA You expect me to get into that and wet myself all over! Not me. I should catch my death. I knew a woman did it every Saturday night; and she died of it.

MRS PEARCE Mr Higgins has the gentlemen's bathroom downstairs; and he has a bath every morning, in cold water.

LIZA Ugh! He's made of iron, that man.

MRS PEARCE If you are to sit with him and the Colonel and be taught you will have to do the same. They wont like the smell of you if you dont. But you can have the water as hot as you like. There are two taps: hot and cold.

LIZA [*weeping*] I couldnt. I dursnt. It's not natural: it would kill me. Ive never had a bath in my life: not what youd call a proper one.

MRS PEARCE Well, dont you want to be clean and sweet and decent, like a lady? You know you cant be a nice girl inside if youre a dirty slut outside.

LIZA Boohoo!!!

---

448 **not missus** [ˈmɪsəz] 不要称我 missus（因为我不是这里的主妇）。 **missus** 口语；= missis [ˈmɪsɪz]，太太。 **throws open the door** 猛推开门。 **dressingroom, now modernized as a bathroom** （原来的）梳妆室，现在已被加以现代化（加上现代设备），改作浴室。

450 **Gawd** = God. 是土音。 **Whats this?** 是指着浴盆问的。 **Funny sort of copper I call it.** = I call it a funny sort of copper. 我认为这是一种奇异的洗涤槽。 **Funny** 口语，作"奇怪的"解。 **copper** 金属洗涤槽，洗涤炊具或洗衣用；是可数名词，这里因用在 sort of 后面，所以不加冠词。

452 **wash ourselves** 洗澡。

454 **Not me.** = I won't get into that (= the copper) and wet myself all over. 在这种句型中，常用 me 代替 I，已见前。

455 **catch my death** = catch my death of cold. 得可能致死的感冒；是习语。 **did it** 指洗澡。

458 **in cold water** 前面加逗号，有"而且是用冷水"的意思。

459 **Ugh!** 惊叫声，可读作 [ɜː]，表示"厌恶"、"惊吓"。 **He's made of iron, that man.** 他那个人是铁打的。that man 是 He 的同位语。

460 **sit with him and the Colonel and be taught** 和他（Higgins）和 Pickering 上校坐在一起，跟他们学习（语音）。

461 **do the same** = has a bath every morning.

462 **if you dont** = if you dont have a bath every morning.

464 **I couldnt** 是虚拟语气，= I couldn't do it if I had to do it，有"叫我洗我也不洗"的意思。 **I dursnt** [ˈdɜːsnt] = I dursn't do it if I had to do it. durst = dared; dursnt = dare not.

465 **not what youd call a proper one** = Ive never had what you'd call a proper bath in my life. 我一生没有洗过你们称为正规的澡。从下文看，Liza 过去洗澡时衣服都不脱干净，更谈不上使用正式的浴缸。

468 **cant be a nice girl inside if youre a dirty slut outside** 如果你外表是个邋遢婆，就不能内心是个好姑娘。slut 是"懒妇"、"荡妇"的意思，是个很不好听的字眼，所以 Liza 听了，"Boohoo!!!"地大哭起来。

MRS PEARCE Now stop crying and go back into your room and take off all your clothes. Then wrap yourself in this [*taking down a gown from its peg and handing it to her*] and come back to me. I will get the bath ready.

LIZA [*all tears*] I cant. I wont. I'm not used to it. Ive never took off all my clothes before. It's not right: it's not decent.

MRS PEARCE Nonsense, child. Dont you take off all your clothes every night when you go to bed?

LIZA [*amazed*] No. Why should I? I should catch my death. Of course I take off my skirt.

MRS PEARCE Do you mean that you sleep in the underclothes you wear in the daytime?

LIZA What else have I to sleep in?

MRS PEARCE You will never do that again as long as you live here. I will get you a proper nightdress.

LIZA Do you mean change into cold things and lie awake shivering half the night? You want to kill me, you do.

MRS PEARCE I want to change you from a frowzy slut to a clean respectable girl fit to sit with the gentlemen in the study. Are you going to trust me and do what I tell you or be thrown out and sent back to your flower basket?

LIZA But you dont know what the cold is to me. You dont know how I dread it.

MRS PEARCE Your bed wont be cold here: I will put a hot water bottle in it. [*pushing her into the bedroom*] Off with you and undress.

474 **get the bath ready** 把洗澡水准备好。ready 是宾语补足语，the bath ready 构成复合宾语。

475 **all tears** 满面是泪的；是形容词短语。 **I cant.** = I can't take off all my clothes. **I wont.** = I won't take off all my clothes. **I'm not used to it.** = I'm not used to taking off all my clothes. 我不习惯于把所有衣裳脱得精光。

477 **Dont you take off all your clothes every night when you go to bed?** Mrs Pearce 这样反问 Liza，是因为她认为晚上睡觉总得脱光身上的衣服，换上睡衣的。

479 **Why should I?** = Why should I take off all my clothes every night when I go to bed? **I should catch my death.** 这是虚拟语气，省略 if I took off all my clothes when I go to bed。

483 **What else have I to sleep in?** （除了白天随身穿的内衣外）我另外有什么衣裳可穿上睡觉的呢？ Liza 贫困，哪里另有睡衣之类？ What 是 have 的宾语。

484 **will never do that again as long as you live here** 你住在这里的期间，再不用那样做（再不用穿随身的内衣睡觉）。**as long as** 在整个……的期间；只要是……

485 **nightdress** 妇女或儿童穿的直统的睡衣；也称 nightgown。分衣裤的睡衣称 pyjama(s)，美国称 pajama(s)。

486 **Do you mean change into cold things and lie awake shivering half the night?** 你的意思是要我换上冰冷的衣裳，半个夜里躺在床上醒着发抖吗？ change 和 lie 都是不及物动词，在语法上是把动词 change 和 lie 用作省去了 to 的不定式。

490 **or be thrown out and sent back to your flower basket** 还是被撵出去，送回到你卖花的篮子那儿去（仍旧到街头去卖花）呢？

492 **what the cold is to me** 冷对我是怎么回事；我多怕冷。

494 **hot water bottle** 取暖的热水瓶或热水袋；不是保暖用的热水瓶，后者称 vaccum flask、vaccum bottle 或 thermos bottle、thermos flask，或单称 thermos。

495 **Off with you and undress.** 去，把衣服脱掉。**Off with you** 走开；滚开；是习语；这里的 Off 可理解为前面省略动词 Be，= Be off。也可当作不及物动词，作“离开”解。

LIZA Oh, if only I'd a known what a dreadful thing it is to be clean I'd never have come. I didnt know when I was well off. I – [*Mrs Pearce pushes her through the door, but leaves it partly open lest her prisoner should take to flight.*]

Mrs Pearce puts on a pair of white rubber sleeves, and fills the bath, mixing hot and cold, and testing the result with the bath thermometer. She perfumes it with a handful of bath salts and adds a palmful of mustard. She then takes a formidable looking long handled scrubbing brush and soaps it profusely with a ball of scented soap.

Eliza comes back with nothing on but the bath gown huddled tightly round her, a piteous spectacle of abject terror.

MRS PEARCE Now come along. Take that thing off.

LIZA Oh I couldnt, Mrs Pearce: I reely couldnt. I never done such a thing.

MRS PEARCE Nonsense. Here: step in and tell me whether it's hot enough for you.

LIZA Ah-oo! Ah-oo! It's too hot.

MRS PEARCE [*deftly snatching the gown away and throwing Eliza down*

---

497 **if only I'd a known what a dreadful thing it is to be clean I'd never have come** 要是我早知道要弄干净是这么可怕，我决不会来（受这罪呢）。这是表示与过去事实相反的虚拟语气，事实是事先不知，所以来了。 **if only** 要

是……就好；是习语。 **I'd a known** = I should have known. 土音把 have 的轻音 [əv] 读成 [ə]，所以写成 a。what 是 it is 的表语；it 是虚词，引起同位语 to be clean。

498 **I didnt know when I was well off.** 过去我过好日子的时候，还不知道（要弄干净有这样可怕）。 **well off** 富裕；光景好；是习语。萧伯纳幽默地让 Liza 认为过去不脱衣服洗澡，不换睡衣睡觉是“过好日子”，发人深思。

499 **leaves it partly open lest her prisoner should take to flight** （Mrs Pearce）让门半开着，（可以看守 Liza），怕她的俘虏逃跑。 **lest** 恐怕；以防；是连词，它所引起的状语从句中一般用 should。 **take to flight** 逃走；take to 有“趋于”、“采取”的意思。

502 **mixing hot and cold** 调匀热水和冷水。 **testing the result with the bath thermometer** [θə'mɒmɪtə] 用浴缸温度计测量（冷热水调匀后的）结果（温度）。

503 **perfumes it with a handful of bath salts** 加把浴盐使洗澡水香。 **perfume** 香水，香（名词），读 ['pɜːfjuːm]。这里是及物动词（洒香水于……；使香），读 [pɜː'fjuːm]。 **bath salts** 浴盐（使水软而香）。

504 **a palmful** ['pɑːmfʊl] **of mustard**['mʌstəd] 一手心的芥末。浴水中放芥末，当是为使皮肤发热祛寒。 **formidable** ['fɔːmɪdəbl] **looking** 看起来模样可怕的；也写作 formidable-looking。

505 **long handled** 长柄的；也写作 long-handled，是由形容词 + 名词 + ed 构成的。 **soaps it profusely** [prə'fjuːsli] 把它（刷子）擦足了肥皂。soap 作动词，既可作“上肥皂于……”解，如这里的 soap a brush，又可作“用肥皂擦洗”解。 **a ball of scented soap** 一块（圆形的）香皂。soap 是物质名词，“一块肥皂”说 a cake (或 piece) of soap；a soap 是“一种肥皂”。

507 **with nothing on but the bath gown huddled tightly round her** 除了胡乱地紧裹在她身上的浴衣之外，一点不穿什么；裤子也不穿，只包着一件浴衣。 **on** 被穿在身上。 **nothing but** 只有；是口语；but = except。

508 **a piteous** ['pɪtɪəs] **spectacle of abject** ['æbdʒekt] **terror** ['terə] 一副可怜相，显出无可奈何的惊恐。

500 **Take that thing off.** 把那东西脱掉。that thing 指 bath gown。

510 **reely** really 的土音。 **I never done** 应作 Ive never done。 **such a thing** 指脱掉光身包着的浴衣；脱得精光。

515 **throwing Eliza down on her back** 把 Eliza 仰面朝天推下（浴缸）。

on her back] It wont hurt you. [*She sets to work with the scrubbing brush.*]

Eliza's screams are heartrending.

Meanwhile the Colonel has been having it out with Higgins about Eliza. Pickering has come from the hearth to the chair and seated himself astride of it with his arms on the back to cross-examine him.

PICKERING Excuse the straight question, Higgins. Are you a man of good character where women are concerned?

HIGGINS [*moodily*] Have you ever met a man of good character where women are concerned?

PICKERING Yes: very frequently.

HIGGINS [*dogmatically, lifting himself on his hands to the level of the piano, and sitting on it with a bounce*] Well, I havnt. I find that the moment I let a woman make friends with me, she becomes jealous, exacting, suspicious, and a damned nuisance. I find that the moment I let myself make friends with a woman, I become selfish and tyrannical. Women upset everything. When you let them into your life, you find that the woman is driving at one thing and youre driving at another.

PICKERING At what, for example?

HIGGINS [*coming off the piano restlessly*] Oh, Lord knows! I suppose

516 **sets to work** 开始工作；开始替 Eliza 擦洗。 **set to** 开始；是习语；set 可作不及物动词，如这里的 set to work；也可作及物动词，如 set her to work。to 是介词，work 是名词，不是动词。在 set to scrubbing 这样的结构中，可以认为 to 是介词，以动名词为介词宾语，也可认为 to 是副词，scrubbing 是现在分词，是 set to 的补语。

519 **having it out with** 与……争辩明白；是习语；也作"与……决一雌雄"解。

521 **seated himself astride of it with his arms on the back** （面朝椅背）跨坐在椅子上，手臂搭在椅背上。

523 **Excuse the straight question** 恕我直问。excuse 的宾语可以是被请求原谅的人，也可以是被请求原谅的事情。

524 **good character** 性格好。 **where women are concerned** 在涉及女人之处；关于女人方面。

527 **very frequently** = I have very frequently met men of good character where women are concerned.

528 **lifting himself on his hands to the level of the piano** 用手撑着（钢琴），使自己升高到和钢琴一样高。

529 **I havnt.** = I havn't met a man of good character where women are concerned.

530 **becomes jealous, exacting, suspicious, and a damned nuisance** [ˈnjuːsns] 变得妒忌，苛求，猜疑，（变成）讨厌之极的人。and 所连接的应该是词类相同的词语，但这里 and 前面是三个形容词，and 后面是一个名词词组，并列作 becomes 的表语，口语中常有这种情况。如在 and 后加 becomes 则 and 前后词语的词类相同，但读起来反不自然。

532 **the moment** 相当于连词 as soon as 或 when。

533 **tyrannical** [tɪˈrænɪkl] 专横的。这是从 tyrant [ˈtaɪrənt]（暴君；专横的人）派生的形容词。

534 **let them into your life** 让她们进入你的生活；你生活中有了女人。

535 **driving at** 意向；意指。

536 **At what, for example?** = What, for example, are the woman and you driving at (respectively)?

537 **Lord knows!** 天知道！谁知道！ = God knows! / Heaven knows!

the woman wants to live her own life; and the man wants to live his; and each tries to drag the other on to the wrong track. One wants to go north and the other south; and the result is that both have to go east, though they both hate the east wind. [*He sits down on the bench at the keyboard.*] So here I am, a confirmed old bachelor, and likely to remain so.

PICKERING [*rising and standing over him gravely*] Come, Higgins! You know what I mean. If I'm to be in this business I shall feel responsible for that girl. I hope it's understood that no advantage is to be taken of her position.

HIGGINS What! That thing! Sacred, I assure you. [*rising to explain*] You see, she'll be a pupil; and teaching would be impossible unless pupils were sacred. Ive taught scores of American millionairesses how to speak English: the best looking women in the world. I'm seasoned. They might as well be blocks of wood. *I* might as well be a block of wood. It's –

Mrs Pearce opens the door. She has Eliza's hat in her hand. Pickering retires to the easy-chair at the hearth and sits down.

HIGGINS [*eagerly*] Well, Mrs Pearce: is it all right?

---

538 **live her own life** 过她自己的生活。动词 live 和名词 life 是同源的，因此这里的 life 叫做“同源宾语”（cognate object）。

539 **live his** = live his own life. **the wrong track** 错路；指一个不是要去的方向。“错路”虽不是专指，也未必只有一条，但习惯在 wrong 前面用 the，而不

用 a，如买错了一本书，说 Sorry to have bought the wrong book。

540 **the other south** = the other wants to go south. 这里的 south 和前面的 north 一样，是副词，= southward / to the south。

541 **hate the east wind** 讨厌东风。可能因为在英国，春天的东风比较阴冷，所以有人不喜欢东风。hate 原义“恨”，口语中常作“不喜欢”、“讨厌”解。

542 **sits down on the bench at the keyboard** 在琴键跟前凳子上坐下。 **So here I am** 所以我在这里（Higgins 的 laboratory 里）。 **a confirmed old bachelor** [ˈbætʃələ] 一个坚定的老独身汉。可以说前面省去 being。

543 **and likely to remain so** 而且大概将一直如此（即保持独身）。

544 **standing over him** 居高临下似地站在他面前。stand over 带有“监督”的意思。

545 **be in this business** 参加这事情（指训练 Liza）。business 这里不作“生意”解。

546 **it's understood that ...** 这是被默认（或不言而明）的；大家同意。 **no advantage is to be taken of her position** 不占她（贫苦无依）的处境的便宜。 **take advantage of** 趁机利用。

548 **That thing!** 指 Pickering 所说希望大家同意的 no advantage is to be taken of her position。 **Sacred, I assure you.** = I assure that she is sacred. 神圣不可侵犯的。

549 **teaching would be impossible unless pupils were sacred** 除非学生是神圣不可侵犯的，否则教学无法进行。这是虚拟语气，意思是“必须尊重学生，才能施教”。**unless** = if ... not.

550 **scores of** 几十个；许多。score 原义“二十”，单复数同形；用 scores 时，作“许多”解；和 dozen(s) 的用法相同。

551 **the best looking women in the world** 天下最漂亮的女人；是 millionairesses [ˌmɪljəˈneərəsɪz]（有百万家财的女人）的同位语。Higgins 的意思是说，他对“财貌双全”的女人尚且无动于衷，决不会对一个贫穷的“邋遢婆”动什么坏脑筋。 **best looking** 最好看的，也写作 best-looking，是 good-looking 的最高级。**in the world** 习语；强调语气，未必实有“在这世界上”的意思。

552 **seasoned** 由及物动词 season（给予锻炼；使适应）的过去分词演变成的形容词，作“经过风雨的”、“老练的”解，这里指“不会为女色所动的”。 **They might as well be blocks of wood** 她们不妨是（等于是）一块块木头。 **might as well** 不妨；……为宜；后面还可接第二个 as，如：You might as well do it by yourself as ask for his help. 你求他帮助，还不如自己做。

556 **is it all right** 事情（指帮 Liza 洗澡和对她的安排）顺利吗？没有问题吧？

MRS PEARCE [*at the door*] I just wish to trouble you with a word, if I may, Mr Higgins.

HIGGINS Yes, certainly. Come in. [*She comes forward.*] Dont burn that, Mrs Pearce. I'll keep it as a curiosity. [*He takes the hat.*]

MRS PEARCE Handle it carefully, sir, please. I had to promise her not to burn it; but I had better put it in the oven for a while.

HIGGINS [*putting it down hastily on the piano*] Oh! thank you. Well, what have you to say to me?

PICKERING Am I in the way?

MRS PEARCE Not in the least, sir. Mr Higgins: will you please be very particular what you say before the girl?

HIGGINS [*sternly*] Of course. I'm always particular about what I say. Why do you say this to me?

MRS PEARCE [*unmoved*] No, sir: youre not at all particular when youve mislaid anything or when you get a little impatient. Now it doesnt matter before me. I'm used to it. But you really must not swear before the girl.

HIGGINS [*indignantly*] *I* swear! [*most emphatically*] I never swear. I detest the habit. What the devil do you mean?

MRS PEARCE [*stolidly*] Thats what I mean, sir. You swear a great deal too much. I dont mind your damning and blasting, and what the devil and where the devil and who the devil –

HIGGINS Mrs Pearce: this language from your lips! Really!

MRS PEARCE [*not to be put off*] – but there is a certain word I must ask you not to use. The girl used it herself when she began to

557 **if I may** = if I may trouble you with a word. 这是客气话。

559 **Dont burn that** 别烧掉那个（指 Liza 的草帽，见下面舞台指示）。

560 **curiosity** [ˌkjʊərɪˈɒsɪti] 珍奇的东西；古玩。

561 **had to promise her not to burn it** 已经不得不答应她不烧掉这帽子。

562 **had better put it in the oven** [ˈʌvn] **for a while** 最好在烘箱里烘一会儿（以消毒）。 **had better** 还是……好；后接没有 to 的不定式。

565 **in the way** 有妨碍的；碍事的；是习语。

566 **Not in the least** = You are not in the least in the way. **Not in the least** 毫不；是习语。 **be very particular what you say before the girl** 在姑娘面前说话要非常注意。 **particular** 讲究的；这里指说话要文雅，忌粗俗、诅咒。注意：这里 particular 后直接接 what you say，不及下面 Higgins 回答的 particular about what I say 的说法正规。

570 **unmoved** 不为所动；无视她主人的严肃（sternly）责问。

572 **Now it doesnt matter before me** 这（指说话不注意）在我面前是无所谓的。 **Now** 语气词，引起一个话头，没有具体意义。 **matter** 有关紧要。 **I'm used to it** 我对这（说话不注意）已经（听）惯了。

573 **swear before the girl** 在这姑娘面前诅咒（指下文所说的用 the devil 等诅咒语）。

574 ***I* swear!** 我诅咒！意思是"我才不诅咒呢！"

575 **the habit** = the habit of swearing. **the devil** [ˈdevl] 原义"魔鬼"，用作诅咒语，加强 what、where 等疑问词的语气，如这里的 What the devil。

576 **Thats what I mean** 我就是指那个；指你刚才脱口而出的 What the devil（之类的诅咒）。 **swear a great deal too much** 诅咒得实在太多。too much 修饰 swear；a great deal 又修饰 too。 **a great deal** = much，这里作为状语短语。

577 **I dont mind your damning and blasting, and what the devil** 我不介意你用 damn 和 blast（诅咒），和用 what the devil（之类的诅咒语）。要是这里在 What the devil 和 Where the devil 等加上引号，更易理解。

579 **this language from your lips** 从你嘴里说出这样的话。这是个名词词组，构成单部句，可称为"名词句"。this language 指 Mrs Pearce 说了的一连串诅咒语。顺便一提，有时 language 一词也单独有"诅咒语"之意，= bad language。

580 **not to be put off** 不让被打断说话。 **put off** 是习语，有"推迟"、"搪塞"、"去掉"等多种意义。**a certain word** 某一个词；从下文看，当指 bloody，原义"出血的"、

enjoy the bath. It begins with the same letter as bath. She knows no better: she learnt it at her mother's knee. But she must not hear it from your lips.

HIGGINS [*loftily*] I cannot charge myself with having ever uttered it, Mrs Pearce. [*She looks at him steadfastly. He adds, hiding an uneasy conscience with a judicial air.*] Except perhaps in a moment of extreme and justifiable excitement.

MRS PEARCE Only this morning, sir, you applied it to your boots, to the butter, and to the brown bread.

HIGGINS Oh, that! Mere alliteration, Mrs Pearce, natural to a poet.

MRS PEARCE Well, sir, whatever you choose to call it, I beg you not to let the girl hear you repeat it.

HIGGINS Oh, very well, very well. Is that all?

MRS PEARCE No, sir. We shall have to be very particular with this girl as to personal cleanliness.

HIGGINS Certainly. Quite right. Most important.

MRS PEARCE I mean not to be slovenly about her dress or untidy

---

"血污的"，作为诅咒语，极为恶俗，尤为妇女所忌讳（taboo）。bloody 作形容词，犹如"他妈的"，又可用作副词，有"非常"的意思，当然同样是非常恶俗的字眼。

582 **It begins with the same letter as bath.** 这个词的首字母和 bath（的首字母）相同；指 bloody 这个词。 **as bath** = as 'bath' begins with. as 是关系代词。

583 **knows no better** 不懂得更多（而只能如此）；只懂这一点。它的反义词组是 know better：懂得更多（而不至于如此）；后面还能跟 than，如：He

knows better than to quarrel. 他知道不能吵嘴。这里的 better 是副词。 **at her mother's knee** （抱）在她母亲膝盖上（的时候），即“从小”的意思。注意：这里 knee 用单数；而 on one's knees（跪着）中 knees 是复数；这是习惯用法。

585 **charge myself with** 指责自己犯……的过错；认（罪）。

586 **adds** （说了其他的话之后）加上一句；补充说。 **hiding an uneasy conscience** [ˈkɒnʃəns] **with a judicial** [dʒʊˈdiʃəl] **air** 做出慎重的样子，掩盖内心不安（因为他自己知道确实常要诅咒）。

587 **Except** Except 引起的这个介词短语在语法上是紧接上面一句的。

588 **extreme and justifiable** [ˈdʒʌstɪfaɪəbl] **excitement** 极度的、有道理的激动；尽管是大发雷霆，却有道理。

589 **Only this morning** 就在今天早晨。不是“只有今天早晨”的意思。 **applied it to your boots** 对你的鞋子使用诅咒；说到鞋子就用了诅咒语。英国人所说的 boot，美国人往往称 shoe；而美国人说的 boot，英国人往往称 high boot。

590 **the butter** 专指家里买着的或 Higgins 吃的 butter，所以前面用定冠词，下面 the brown bread 同。 **brown bread** 用糙面粉做的面包；麸皮面包。

591 **Oh, that!** 噢，（我道是什么，原来是）那个（指诅咒 boots、butter 和 brown bread）。 **Mere alliteration** [əˌlɪtəˈreɪʃən] （我说 bloody boots、bloody butter、bloody brown bread）只是双声而已。前后诸词的首字母相同（这里是 b），在作诗法中称为 alliteration（头韵法；犹如我国所称“双声叠韵”的“双声”）。 **natural to a poet** 对诗人是自然的。修饰 alliteration。萧伯纳在本剧序言中谈到语音学家 Henry Sweet，私淑大诗人 John Milton，而 Higgins 是以 Sweet 为原型的。所以这里 Higgins 以诗人自命，是萧伯纳幽默之笔。

593 **whatever you choose to call it** 不管你爱叫它什么。whatever 在这里 = no matter what，引起表示让步的状语从句；choose to = like to；it 指说 bloody boots 等。

594 **repeat** 重复说；再说。

595 **Is that all?** 话说完了吗？要对人说的话说完后，常说 That's all.

599 **I mean not to be slovenly** [ˈslʌvnli] **about her dress** 我的意思是（她）不要衣衫不整洁。注意：这里 I mean 后面接不定式和 I mean to go（我要去）的意义不同，前者 not to be slovenly 的主体不是 mean 的主语 I，而是 Liza；而后者 to go 的主体就是 mean 的主语 I。 **slovenly** 是名词 sloven（衣衫不整的人；懒散的人）+ ly 构成的形容词。 **dress** 这里是不可数名词；统称“服装”。

in leaving things about.

HIGGINS [*going to her solemnly*] Just so. I intended to call your attention to that. [*He passes on to Pickering, who is enjoying the conversation immensely.*] It is these little things that matter, Pickering. Take care of the pence and the pounds will take care of themselves is as true of personal habits as of money. [*He comes to anchor on the hearthrug, with the air of a man in an unassailable position.*]

MRS PEARCE Yes, sir. Then might I ask you not to come down to breakfast in your dressing-gown, or at any rate not to use it as a napkin to the extent you do, sir. And if you would be so good as not to eat everything off the same plate, and to remember not to put the porridge saucepan out of your hand on the clean tablecloth, it would be a better example to the girl. You know you nearly choked yourself with a fishbone in the jam only last week.

HIGGINS [*routed from the hearthrug and drifting back to the piano*] I may do these things sometimes in absence of mind; but

---

600 **leaving things about** 把（用过的）东西到处乱放（不收拾）。

601 **Just so.** 正是如此；是口头常用习语。 **call your attention to** 叫你注意。

603 **It is these little things that matter** 要紧的就是这些小事情。It 是虚词，以 that 从句作它的同位从句。

604 **Take care of the pence and the pounds will take care of themselves** 这是谚语，直译"如果你当心便士，英镑自会当心自己（无需你当心）"。意思是"小钱省了，大钱自省"，推而广之，"小事谨慎，大事自成"。祈使句 + and

+ 陈述句，表示“如果……，那么……”，这是一个习惯句型。 **pence** penny 有两个复数形式，指多个便士的硬币用 pennies，计值用 pence。

605 **is as true of personal habits as of money** （谚语）对金钱是正确的，对个人习惯也同样正确。is 的主语是一句谚语。 **as of money** = as it is true of money.

606 **comes to anchor** [ˈæŋkə]（坐）定下来；是习语，也作 come to anchor，原义“抛锚”。 **the air of a man in an unassailable position** 处于无懈可击的地位的人的神气。

608 **might I ask you** 比 may I ask you 婉转，是客气的说法。Might you = Please，也是客气说法。 **come down to breakfast**（从楼上）下来吃早饭。breakfast 是名词。

609 **not to use it as a napkin to the extent you do** 不要像你那样经常把它（dressing-gown，梳妆时穿的晨衣）当作餐巾用。 **to the extent**（程度）**you do** = to the extent to which you use it as a napkin.

610 **be so good as not to** 请你不要……。be so good as to ... = please; 是惯用客套语。

611 **eat everything off the same plate** 用同一只盆子吃各种东西。按正式用餐规矩，一道菜用一只盆。注意这里用介词 off。 **to remember** 接 would be so good as，和前面的 not to eat 并列。 **remember not to put the porridge saucepan out of your hand on the clean tablecloth** 记住不要放手把粥锅放在干净桌布上。 **remember** 后接简单不定式，是“记住，不要忘记去做（某事）”的意思；后接动名词时，意思是“记得（过去所做的事）”，如 remember meeting him some time ago（记得过去什么时候见到过他）；但用了完成不定式，又是“记得（过去所做的事）”的意思，如 remember to have met him some time ago。

613 **it** 指 if 从句中所讲的内容。

614 **nearly choked yourself with a fishbone in the jam** 差一点被果酱里的鱼骨头梗死。可见 Higgins 吃饭时不按规矩，乱七八糟。

616 **routed from the hearthrug** 从炉前地毯上败退下来。上文刚说 Higgins 站定在炉前地毯上一副无懈可击的神气，现在被 Mrs Pearce 历数他粗野的举止，只得认输，败下阵来。

617 **in absence of mind** 在心不在焉的时候。

surely I dont do them habitually. [*angrily*] By the way: my dressing-gown smells most damnably of benzine.

MRS PEARCE No doubt it does, Mr Higgins. But if you will wipe your fingers –

HIGGINS [*yelling*] Oh very well, very well: I'll wipe them in my hair in future.

MRS PEARCE I hope youre not offended, Mr Higgins.

HIGGINS [*shocked at finding himself thought capable of an unamiable sentiment*] Not at all, not at all. Youre quite right, Mrs Pearce: I shall be particularly careful before the girl. Is that all?

MRS PEARCE No, sir. Might she use some of those Japanese dresses you brought from abroad? I really cant put her back into her old things.

HIGGINS Certainly. Anything you like. Is that all?

MRS PEARCE Thank you, sir. Thats all. [*She goes out.*]

HIGGINS You know, Pickering, that woman has the most extraordinary ideas about me. Here I am, a shy, diffident sort of man. Ive never been able to feel really grown-up and tremendous, like other chaps. And yet she's firmly persuaded that I'm an arbitrary overbearing bossing kind of person. I cant account for it.

Mrs Pearce returns.

MRS PEARCE If you please, sir, the trouble's beginning already.

618 **By the way** 顺便提起。Higgins 认输，总不甘心，寻找话题，又图反扑。

619 **smells most damnably** [ˈdæmnəbli] **of benzine** [ˈbenziːn, benˈziːn] 糟透地尽是汽油味道。 **smells** 发出……的气味，介词用 of。 **benzine** 和 benzene（苯）读音完全相同。 **most** 非常。 **damnably** 该死地；口语中又作“非常”解。

620 **But if you will wipe your fingers –** 话未说完，意思是：然而要是你肯（用抹布之类而不用晨衣）擦手指（晨衣不会肮脏到非用汽油清洗不可了）。

622 **wipe them in my hair in future** 今后在我头发上擦手指。Higgins 使气说蛮话了。

625 **finding himself thought capable of an unamiable** [ʌnˈeɪmɪəbl] **sentiment** 发觉自己被人认为会有不和蔼的情绪（发脾气）。 **thought** 过去分词，是 finding 的宾语补足语；himself 和 thought 有逻辑上的主谓关系，构成复合宾语。

628 **Might she use** 比 May she use 婉转，更客气。

629 **from abroad** 从国外。 **abroad** 到国外；在国外；说“从国外”，要用 from abroad。 **put her back into her old things** 给她重新穿她的旧衣服。things 用复数，指“个人用品”。

631 **Anything you like.** = You may do anything (that) you like.

634 **Here I am** （在我看来，）我就是这样一个人。 **a shy, diffident sort of man** 一种羞怯、犹豫的人；这是 I 的同位语。注意 : sort of、kind of 后面的可数名词不用冠词。

635 **grown-up and tremendous** 成熟和了不起的。 **tremendous** 原义“可怕的”，口语中作“巨大的”、“非凡的”解。

636 **chaps** 家伙；人；与 fellow 和美国人说的 guy 一样，有熟不拘礼的用语，有时有鄙意。 **And yet she's firmly persuaded** [pəˈsweɪdɪd] 然而她被使得深信；但她深信。 **an arbitrary** [ˈɑːbɪtrəri] **overbearing bossing kind of person** 一种武断的傲慢的发号施令的人。这里三个形容词之间既无逗号，又无 and，那就该理解为 bossing 修饰 kind，over-bearing 修饰 bossing kind，arbitrary 又修饰 overbearing bossing kind；如有逗号或 and，则三个形容词就并列修饰 kind。 **bossing** 由名词 boss（头目；老板）演化为动词，再由动词的分词用作形容词。

637 **account for it** 说明它的道理。can't account for it 便是“莫名其妙”。

640 **If you please** 一般用于请求或命令，= please，又作“信不信由你”解；这里有“你瞧，出事了”的意思。

Theres a dustman downstairs, Alfred Doolittle, wants to see you. He says you have his daughter here.

PICKERING [*rising*] Phew! I say!

HIGGINS [*promptly*] Send the blackguard up.

MRS PEARCE Oh, very well, sir. [*She goes out.*]

PICKERING He may not be a blackguard, Higgins.

HIGGINS Nonsense. Of course he's a blackguard.

PICKERING Whether he is or not, I'm afraid we shall have some trouble with him.

HIGGINS [*confidently*] Oh no: I think not. If theres any trouble he shall have it with me, not I with him. And we are sure to get something interesting out of him.

PICKERING About the girl?

HIGGINS No. I mean his dialect.

PICKERING Oh!

MRS PEARCE [*at the door*] Doolittle, sir. [*She admits Doolittle and retires.*]

Alfred Doolittle is an elderly but vigorous dustman, clad in the costume of his profession, including a hat with a back brim covering his neck and shoulders. He has well marked and rather interesting features, and seems equally free from fear and conscience. He has a remarkably expressive voice, the result of a habit of giving vent to his feelings without reserve. His

641 **Alfred** [ˈælfrɪd] **Doolittle** 卖花女 Liza Doolittle 的父亲；是 dustman [ˈdʌstmən] 的同位语。 **wants** = who wants. 口语中，在 There's a dustman who wants to see you 的句型中 who 常省略。

643 **Phew** [fjuː]**!** 唷！哼！表示惊讶，反感等。 **I say!** 常用引起话头，也用以表示惊讶、反感。按照美国用法，说 Say!

644 **Send the blackguard up** 带那流氓（指 the dustman）上来。Higgins 惯于出言不逊。

646 **may not be** 可能不是；不作"不可能是"解。

648 **Whether he is or not** = Whether he is a blackguard or he is not a blackguard. 不管他是不是流氓。这是个状语从句。 **we shall have some trouble with him** 我们将在他那里有些麻烦。注意：有麻烦（have trouble）的是我们，不是他。

650 **I think not** = I think (that) we shall not have any trouble with him. = I don't think we shall have any trouble with him. **If theres any trouble he shall have it with me, not I with him.** 如果要有什么麻烦的话，（我要叫）他在我这里得到麻烦，而不是我在他那里得到麻烦。 he shall 第二、三人称后用 shall 表示说话人的意志。 **not I with him** = I shall not have trouble with him.

653 **About the girl?** = Shall we get something interesting about the girl out of him?

656 **Doolittle, sir.** Doolittle 是 Mrs Pearce 向主人通报来客的名字（用姓氏而不冠以 Mr，显然不客气），sir 是称呼主人。

658 **clad in the costume** [ˈkɒstjuːm] **of his profession** 穿着他（倒垃圾）行业的服装；倒垃圾的打扮。 **clad** 是 clothe 的不规则变化的过去分词，等于规则变化的 clothed。 **costume** （各行业、时代、地区特殊的）服装。

659 **a back brim covering his neck and shoulders** （帽子的）后沿（垂在脑后）遮盖着他的头颅和肩膀（为倒垃圾遮尘）。

660 **well marked** [mɑːkt] **and rather interesting features** 轮廓非常清楚而且相当有趣的面貌。 **features** 面貌，即眉、目、口、鼻等各个 feature 的综合；用复数。

661 **equally free from fear and conscience** 同等地没有恐惧和良心不安（的样子）；用 equally，表示既无恐惧又无不安。 **free from** 没有……的。

662 **remarkably expressive voice** 非常能表达感情的嗓子。

663 **the result of a habit of giving vent to his feelings without reserve** 无保留地发泄感情的习惯的结果。the result ... 这个名词词组是 voice 的同位语，也可理解为

present pose is that of wounded honor and stern resolution.

DOOLITTLE [*at the door, uncertain which of the two gentlemen is his man*] Professor Iggins?

HIGGINS Here. Good morning. Sit down.

DOOLITTLE Morning, Governor. [*He sits down magisterially.*] I come about a very serious matter, Governor.

HIGGINS [*to Pickering*] Brought up in Hounslow. Mother Welsh, I should think. [*Doolittle opens his mouth, amazed. Higgins continues.*] What do you want, Doolittle?

DOOLITTLE [*menacingly*] I want my daughter: thats what I want. See?

HIGGINS Of course you do. Youre her father, arnt you? You dont suppose anyone else wants her, do you? I'm glad to see you have some spark of family feeling left. She's upstairs. Take her away at once.

DOOLITTLE [*rising, fearfully taken aback*] What!

HIGGINS Take her away. Do you suppose I'm going to keep your daughter for you?

DOOLITTLE [*remonstrating*] Now, now, look here, Governor. Is this reasonable? Is it fairity to take advantage of a man like this? The girl belongs to me. You got her. Where do I come in? [*He sits down again.*]

HIGGINS Your daughter had the audacity to come to my house and ask me to teach her how to speak properly so that she

the result 的前面省略 which (voice) is；倘不省略，便是一个非限制性定语从句。 **give vent to** 发泄；吐露。 **His present pose is that of wounded** [ˈwuːndɪd] **honor and stern resolution** [ˌrezəˈluːʃən]. 他目前是表示(感到)有损了体面和(抱着)坚定决心的姿态。 **that** = the pose；如用 one，则 = a pose。

665 **uncertain which of the two gentlemen is his man** 吃不准两位先生中哪一位是他（要找）的人。his man 指 Higgins。uncertain 后可用 about，也可直接接疑问词。

666 **Iggins** 是 Higgins 的误读。伦敦土音常脱落 [h] 音。

668 **Morning** 把 Good morning 说成 Morning，是很随便的说法；初次见面这样说，显然不合适，但 Doolittle 无视礼仪，而且他也实在没有教养。 **Governor** 原义"统治者"、"行政长官"、"总督"；在英国俚语中用以称呼主人、老板等，犹言"老爷"。 **magisterially** [ˌmædʒɪˈstɪərɪəli] 以主人（或长官）的神气；威严地。

670 **Brought up** = He (Doolittle) was brought up. **Hounslow** [ˈhaʊnzləʊ] 在伦敦之西，Middlesex 郡一城市。 **Mother Welsh** = His mother is Welsh: 他母亲是威尔士（Wales）人。

671 **opens his mouth, amazed** （Doolittle 听了）惊奇得张开了嘴巴。

675 **you do** = you want your daughter.

676 **suppose** = think.

677 **have some spark of family feeling left** 有点对家属的感情被遗留着(没有消失)；还有父女之情。 **spark** 原义"火星"，转义"一点"。 left 是过去分词，作 have 的宾语补足语，some spark of family feeling left 称作复合宾语。

679 **taken aback** 吃了一惊。

680 **keep your daughter for you** 替你养活你女儿。

682 **look here** 叫人注意的用语，并不一定有"瞧这儿"的意思。

683 **fairity** 是 fair（公平的）之误。

684 **Where do I come in?** 我的份儿呢？这是句惯用语。

686 **had the audacity** [ɔːˈdæsəti] **to ...** 胆敢。 **audacity** 大胆；放肆。卖花女来请专家教课，被视为"胆大妄为"。

could get a place in a flower-shop. This gentleman and my housekeeper have been here all the time. [*bullying him*] How dare you come here and attempt to blackmail me? You sent her here on purpose.

DOOLITTLE [*protesting*] No, Governor.

HIGGINS You must have. How else could you possibly know that she is here?

DOOLITTLE Dont take a man up like that, Governor.

HIGGINS The police shall take you up. This is a plant – a plot to extort money by threats. I shall telephone for the police. [*He goes resolutely to the telephone and opens the directory.*]

DOOLITTLE Have I asked you for a brass farthing? I leave it to the gentleman here: have I said a word about money?

HIGGINS [*throwing the book aside and marching down on Doolittle with a poser*] What else did you come for?

DOOLITTLE [*sweetly*] Well, what *would* a man come for? Be human, Governor.

HIGGINS [*disarmed*] Alfred: did you put her up to it?

DOOLITTLE So help me. Governor. I never did. I take my Bible oath I aint seen the girl these two months past.

HIGGINS Then how did you know she was here?

DOOLITTLE [*'most musical, most melancholy'*] I'll tell you, Governor, if youll only let me get a word in. I'm willing to tell you. I'm

---

688 **This gentleman and my housekeeper** 指 Pickering 上校和 Mrs Pearce。

690 **You sent her here on purpose.** 是你有意派了她来(设计讹诈)。 **on purpose**

故意地；是习语。

693 **You must have.** = You must have sent her here on purpose. **How else could you** = Or else (= Otherwise) how could you.

695 **take a man up like that** 那样对待人；那样看人。

696 **take you up** 把你逮捕。上文说 take up，这里接着也说 take up，但意思不同，是个双关语（pun）。 **plant** 欺诈；骗局；是俚语。 **plot** 阴谋。

697 **telephone for** 打电话叫……来。

698 **directory** = telephone directory. 电话号码簿。

699 **a brass** [brɑːs] **farthing** [ˈfɑːðɪŋ] 一文钱；极小数的金额。 **farthing** 英国过去四分之一便士的铜币。 **leave it to the gentleman here** 这事情让这里这位先生讲一句（公道话）。

701 **marching down on Doolittle with a poser** 大步朝前走到 Doolittle 面前责问他。 **down** 朝台前方向。 **poser** 难题。这里不作“装腔作势（pose）的人”解。

702 **What else** （要不是钱，又是）别的什么。

703 **Well, what *would* a man come for?** 是呀，一个人到这里为啥？（总有目的的嘛；用 Doolittle 下面自己的话说：“总不会把女儿白白送人。”）这是虚拟语气，省略诸如 if I might ask you 之类的条件从句。 **Be human** 要讲人情（别不讲道理而胡说）。

705 **disarmed** 原义“被解除了武装”，转义“火气被消了”，“平了气”。 **put her up to it** 指使她做这件事；（故意）派她来的。 **put up to** 是口语；既有“唆使”之意，也有“告诉”、“指导”之意。

706 **So help me** 天晓得；我说的是千真万确的。已见前注。 **I take my Bible oath** 我可以对《圣经》发誓；我发誓。

707 **these two months past** = for the past two months.

709 **‘most musical, most melancholy’** “（声调）非常悦耳，非常凄婉”。这个舞台指示放在引号里，因为这里引用英国诗人弥尔顿（John Milton, 1680–1674）的抒情长诗《沉思的人》（*Il Penseroso* [ɪl ˌpensəˈrəʊzəʊ]）中的第六十二行诗句；这里四个词都用 m 开首，这叫做头韵法（alliteration）。

710 **get a word in** 插入一句话；插话。 **I'm willing to tell you. I'm wanting to tell you. I'm waiting to tell you.** 三句话同一句型，又连用三个以 w 开头的动词，似乎铿锵有力，俨然雄辩家的口吻，实际上只是前面说了的 I'll tell you 的重复，无怪 Higgins 接着大加讽刺和挖苦。

wanting to tell you. I'm waiting to tell you.

HIGGINS Pickering: this chap has a certain natural gift of rhetoric. Observe the rhythm of his native woodnotes wild. 'I'm willing to tell you: I'm wanting to tell you: I'm waiting to tell you.' Sentimental rhetoric! Thats the Welsh strain in him. It also accounts for his mendacity and dishonesty.

PICKERING Oh, please, Higgins: I'm west country myself. [*to Doolittle*] How did you know the girl was here if you didnt send her?

DOOLITTLE It was like this, Governor. The girl took a boy in the taxi to give him a jaunt. Son of her landlady, he is. He hung about on the chance of her giving him another ride home. Well, she sent him back of her luggage when she heard you was willing for her to stop here. I met the boy at the corner of Long Acre and Endell Street.

HIGGINS Public house. Yes?

---

712 **natural gift of rhetoric** ['retərɪk] 演说的天赋。 **rhetoric** 英国指"演说术"，美国指"修辞学"。

713 **the rhythm** ['rɪðəm] **of his native woodnotes wild** 纯朴而奔放的诗歌的节奏。his native woodnotes wild 一语出于弥尔顿《欢乐的人》（*L' Allegro* [læ'leɪgrəʊ]）一诗第一百三十四行。萧伯纳以语言学家 Henry Sweet 作为 Higgins 的原型，而 Sweet 热衷于弥尔顿（前注中已提及），所以这里 Higgins 随口引用了弥尔顿。 **woodnotes** 原指"林中的鸟叫"，转义为"朴素的诗（或歌）"。 **wild** 修饰 woodnotes；弥尔顿常把定语放在被修饰的中心词后面。

715 **Sentimental rhetoric!** 感伤的浮夸的语言！这是个名词句。 **Welsh strain**

in him 他的威尔士的本色。前面 Higgins 曾听 Doolittle 话音，说他母亲是威尔士人。 **It also accounts for his mendacity** [men'dæsəti] **and dishonesty.** 这也说明他虚伪和不老实的原因。It 指 Welsh strain。Higgins 说威尔士人虚伪，当然是他的偏见，犹如大文豪约翰生（Samuel Johnson, 1709–1784）对苏格兰人有偏见。also 指 Welsh strain 既是浮夸的根源，又是虚伪的根源。

717 **please** 这里有"请别这么说"的意思。 **I'm west country myself.** 我自己就是（英国）西部地方人。Wales 在英国西部；Pickering 出生于 Cheltenham，在英格兰西南部，英格兰西部（尤其西南部）和苏格兰西部称 west country。注意：这里用 I'm west country = I come from the west country.

719 **send her** 派她（到这里来）。

720 **It was like this** 事实情况是这样的。 **took** 给……搭车。

721 **give him a jaunt** 给他兜个圈子。 **jaunt** 短途游览。 **Son of her landlady, he is.** = He is the (或 a) son of her landlady. 口语中常有这种句型。在正常叙述中，如那房东太太只有一个儿子，son 前用 the；如有几个儿子，而说的是其中某一个，则用 a，全不用冠词也可，因为在 father、mother、son、daughter 等词前常省略冠词。 **hung about** 徘徊；在 Liza 身边打转。 **hung** hang 的过去时。hang about 是习语；也作 hang around。

722 **on the chance of** 期待；怀着……的希望。 **giving him another ride home** 让他再乘一次车回家。 **home** 修饰名词 ride；可说是副词作定语用。

723 **sent him back of her luggage** 叫他回去拿她的行李。 **luggage** 统称"行李"，是不可数名词。 **you was** you were 之误。

724 **stop here** 逗留在这里，住在 Higgins 家。 **at the corner of Long Acre and Endell Street** 在 Long Acre 和 Endell Street 的转角处；虽四叉路口有四个转角处，但习惯不用 a corner of ...，而用 the corner of ...。

726 **Public house.** = You met the boy at the corner of Long Acre and Endell Street in a (或 the) public house. 这里如果专指某家酒店，用 the public house，不专指哪一家，则用 a。 **public house** 小客栈；在英国也指"小酒店"。

DOOLITTLE The poor man's club, Governor: why shouldnt I?

PICKERING Do let him tell his story, Higgins.

DOOLITTLE He told me what was up. And I ask you, what was my feelings and my duty as a father? I says to the boy, 'You bring me the luggage,' I says –

PICKERING Why didnt you go for it yourself?

DOOLITTLE Landlady wouldnt have trusted me with it, Governor. She's that kind of woman: you know. I had to give the boy a penny afore he trusted me with it, the little swine. I brought it to her just to oblige you like, and make myself agreeable. That's all.

HIGGINS How much luaggage?

DOOLITTLE Musical instrument, Governor. A few pictures, a trifle of jewelry, and a bird-cage. She said she didnt want no clothes. What was I to think from that, Governor? I ask you as a parent what was I to think?

HIGGINS So you came to rescue her from worse than death, eh?

DOOLITTLE [*appreciatively: relieved at being so well understood*] Just so, Governor. Thats right.

PICKERING But why did you bring her luggage if you intended to take her away?

DOOLITTLE Have I said a word about taking her away? Have I now?

HIGGINS [*determinedly*] Youre going to take her away, double quick. [*He crosses to the hearth and rings the bell.*]

DOOLITTLE [*rising*] No, Governor. Dont say that. I'm not the

---

727 **The poor man's club** = The public house is the poor man's club. 这里的 the 都不是专指，而是泛指某一类型的人或物。The poor man's club 中的 the 是属于 poor man 的冠词。 **why shouldnt I?** = why shouldnt I meet him in the public house? 为什么我不能（在小酒店里遇见他）呢？也就是“为什么我不能去小酒店喝两杯呢”的意思。

729 **what was up** 发生什么事。 **what was my feelings and my duty** 这里表语虽是复数，但主语 what 是单数，所以动词用 was，而不用 were。

730 **I says** 是 I say 之误。

732 **go for it yourself** 你自去拿取行李。

733 **trusted me with it** 放心把行李交给我。

735 **afore** 方言，= before。 **the little swine** 那小猪崽；是 the boy 的同位语。

736 **just to oblige you like** 可以算是为你效劳。 **like** 在这里是口语中的一种用法，有“仿佛”、“可以说”的意思。 **make myself agreeable** 使我讨（你的）欢喜些；讨好（你）。

737 **That's all** 我要说的就是这些（全在这里了）。

739 **Musical instrument** [ˈɪnstrəmənt] 乐器。它和下面的 pictures、jewelry、bird-cage 是她所谓的“行李”。 **a trifle of** 一些些。

741 **What was I to think from that** 从（她说她不用拿衣服）那句话，我当时会怎么想。

743 **rescue her from worse than death** 把她从比死更坏的处境中救出去（以免女儿受污辱）。worse 在这里作名词。

744 **relieved at being so well understood** 因（他的意思）那么充分地被了解而宽慰。

746 **bring her luggage** 把她的行李带来。这里的 her 是定语，不是间接宾语。

750 **Youre going to take her away** = You shall take her away = Take her away. **double quick** 加倍地快；速即。这两个词是副词，double 修饰副词 quick，quick 又修饰 take；也可以看作是个复合动词，作“快走”、“跑步”解，它还可作复合名词用。

751 **crosses to the hearth** 穿过（房间的中央部分）到壁炉跟前。 **rings the bell** 按铃（唤 Mrs Pearce 来让 Doolittle 把女儿带走）。

man to stand in my girl's light. Heres a career opening for her, as you might say; and –

Mrs Pearce opens the door and awaits orders.

HIGGINS Mrs Pearce: this is Eliza's father. He has come to take her away. Give her to him. [*He goes back to the piano, with an air of washing his hands of the whole affair.*]

DOOLITTLE No. This is a misunderstanding. Listen here –

MRS PEARCE He cant take her away, Mr Higgins: how can he? You told me to burn her clothes.

DOOLITTLE Thats right. I cant carry the girl through the streets like a blooming monkey, can I? I put it to you.

HIGGINS You have put it to me that you want your daughter. Take your daughter. If she has no clothes go out and buy her some.

DOOLITTLE [*desperate*] Wheres the clothes she come in? Did I burn them or did you missus here?

MRS PEARCE I am the housekeeper, if you please. I have sent for some clothes for your girl. When they come you can take her away. You can wait in the kitchen. This way, please.

Doolittle, much troubled, accompanies her to the door; then hesitates; finally turns confidentially to Higgins.

DOOLITTLE Listen here, Governor. You and me is men of the world, aint we?

753 **stand in my girl's light** 妨碍我女儿的前程。stand in somebody's light 原义是“挡住某人的光”，转义为“妨碍某人的前程”；是习语。 **a career opening for her** 放在她面前的事业；前程。Doolittle 并不知道他女儿要受语音训练，所以他所谓 career，并不是说她受教育可有光明前程，而是他误会 Higgins 看上了她，她可以交运了。

754 **as you might say** 有如（假如你们要说起来）你们会这么说的。

757 **with an air of washing his hands of the whole affair** 带着对整件事情撒手不管（今后不干他事）的神气。

760 **You told me to burn her clothes.** 你叫我把她的衣服都烧了。（叫她怎么出去呢？）

762 **carry the girl through the streets like a blooming monkey** 把女儿像只该死的（光身的）猴子一样背着穿过大街小巷。 **carry** 带；有“运载”的意思，包括“挑”、“掮”、“抱”、“背”等；与本身没有这些含义的 bring（拿来）、take（拿去）不同。 **blooming** 诅咒语，已屡见前。

763 **I put it to you.** 我把问题向你提出；我问你怎么办。 **it** 上面一句提出的问题。

764 **You have put it to me that you want your daughter.** 你向我提出了要女儿嘛。这里的 it 引起 that 从句构成的同位语。

765 **buy her some** = buy her some clothes = buy some clothes for her.

766 **Wheres the clothes she come in?** 应作 Where are the clothes she came in? 她来的时候穿的衣服哪去了呢？

767 **or did you missus here** 还是你的这位太太呢。后面省略 burn them。

768 **sent for some clothes** 叫人去买些衣服来。在 send for ... 的结构中，拿东西来的可能就是派去的人，也可能派去的人只是通知，而拿东西来的是另外的人；也可以指“打电话去买或借”。

770 **This way, please.** 请这边走；指引去厨房的路。

771 **accompanies her to the door** 照字面解释，应是“陪她（或送她）到门口”，但这里 accompanies 实在是 follows（跟随）的意思。

772 **turns confidentially to Higgins** 引为知己地转向 Higgins。turns to 除“转向……”外，还有“求助于……”的意思。

773 **You and me is** 是 You and I are 之误。 **men of the world** 老于世故的人。

HIGGINS Oh! Men of the world, are we? Youd better go, Mrs Pearce.

MRS PEARCE I think so, indeed, sir. [*She goes, with dignity.*]

PICKERING The floor is yours, Mr Doolittle.

DOOLITTLE [*to Pickering*] I thank you, Governor. [*to Higgins, who takes refuge on the piano bench, a little overwhelmed by the proximity of his visitor; for Doolittle has a professional flavor of dust about him*] Well, the truth is, Ive taken a sort of fancy to you, Governor; and if you want the girl, I'm not so set on having her back home again but what I might be open to an arrangement. Regarded in the light of a young woman, she's a fine handsome girl. As a daughter she's not worth her keep; and so I tell you straight. All I ask is my rights as a father; and youre the last man alive to expect me to let her go for nothing; for I can see youre one of the straight sort, Governor. Well, whats a five-pound note to you? And whats Eliza to me? [*He turns to his chair and sits down judicially.*]

---

775 **Men of the world, are we?** 意即 We are men of the world. 这种把表语移前的说法，在口语中很普遍，尤其像这一句，Men of the world 是重复对方的话，说在前面，语气紧凑而自然。 **Youd better go** 你最好走开；你去吧。Higgins 叫她去，一是他不准备叫 Doolittle 带他女儿走，因而没有 Mrs Pearce 的事了，另一方面可能他要跟 Doolittle 谈谈，恐怕 Mrs Pearce 在场不方便。

778 **The floor is yours** 现在由你发言，这是会议上的用语，Pickering 在这场合说的话，带有幽默之意。

780 **takes refuge** [ˈrefju:dʒ] 躲避；避难。 **a little overwhelmed by the proximity** [prɒkˈsɪməti] **of his visitor** 因为对他的来客（Doolittle）的靠近有点受不了，这个以过去分词 overwhelmed 为中心的分词短语，表示 take refuge 的原因。

781 **has a professional flavour of dust about him** 他身边有一股（倒垃圾工人的）职业性的垃圾气味。Dust 统指“尘土”，在英国也作“垃圾”解，都是不可数名词；a dust 不是“一颗灰尘”，而是“一阵灰尘”。

782 **the truth is, ...** = the truth is that ... 实际情况是；实在是。 **taken a sort of fancy to you** 对你产生了某种喜爱；有些喜欢你。**take a fancy to** 对……中意；喜欢；是习语；注意介词用 to。

783 **I'm not so set on** 我并不是那么坚决要……

784 **but what** 而不……，= that not，是习语，用于否定或疑问语后面。另举一例：Nobody saw the play but what it impressed him deeply. 没有人看了这戏而不深为感动的。but what 也作 but that，也可单用 but；but what 多用于口语中。 **I'm not so set on having her back home again but what I might be open to an arrangement.** 全句的意思是：“我并不是那么坚决要她重新回家去而不能商量解决的”，要她留在这里，也好商量。

785 **Regarded in the light of a young woman** 被作为一个年轻女人来看。 **in the light of** 作为……；是习语；也作“按照”解。

786 **she's not worth her keep** 她不值得被扶养。注意：her keep 是“她的被扶养”；keep 是名词。

787 **tell you straight** 直率对你讲；这里 straight 是副词。 **rights as a father** 作为一个父亲（应有）的各种权利。 **youre the last man alive to expect** 你是活在世上的最后会指望的人……；实际就是“你决不会指望”之意。 **be the last man to** 决不……；是习语；加上一个 alive，犹如 on earth，只是加强语气，并无具体意义。

788 **let her go for nothing** 白白让她走掉；女儿给人要去，而老子一无所得。

789 **the straight sort** 直爽的一类（人）。 **Well, whats a five-pound note to you? And whats Eliza to me?** 唉，一张五镑的钞票对你算得了什么？ Eliza 对我又算得了什么？（而你要 Eliza，我拿五镑好花用，岂不两便？） **note** = banknote.

791 **judicially** 慎重地。

PICKERING I think you ought to know, Doolittle, that Mr Higgins's intentions are entirely honorable.

DOOLITTLE Course they are, Governor. If I thought they wasnt, I'd ask fifty.

HIGGINS [*revolted*] Do you mean to say that you would sell your daughter for £50?

DOOLITTLE Not in a general way I wouldnt; but to oblige a gentleman like you I'd do a good deal, I do assure you.

PICKERING Have you no morals, man?

DOOLITTLE [*unabashed*] Cant afford them, Governor. Neither could you if you was as poor as me. Not that I mean any harm, you know. But if Liza is going to have a bit out of this, why not me too?

HIGGINS [*troubled*] I dont know what to do, Pickering. There can be no question that as a matter of morals it's a positive crime to give this chap a farthing. And yet I feel a sort of rough justice in his claim.

DOOLITTLE Thats it, Governor. Thats all I say. A father's heart, as it were.

PICKERING Well, I know the feeling; but really it seems hardly right –

DOOLITTLE Dont say that, Governor. Dont look at it that way. What am I, Governors both? I ask you, what am I? I'm one of the undeserving poor: thats what I am. Think of what that

---

792 **Higgins's** [ˈhɪɡɪnzɪz] **intentions are entirely honorable** Higgins 的用意是

全然光明正大的；只是对 Eliza 进行语言训练，决无任何坏心意。说某人的 intentions are honorable，一般说某人“是诚意求婚而不是想勾引”；但这里并无求婚的意思。

794 **Course they are** = Of course, they (= his intentions) are entirely honorable. **If I thought they wasnt** = If I thought (that) they weren't entirely honorable. 这是虚拟语气；thought 不是指过去时；wasnt 是 werent 之误。

795 **I'd ask fifty** = I would ask fifty pounds 那我就将要求五十镑了。虚拟语气。这里 ask 也可用 ask for。

798 **Not in a general way I wouldnt** 在一般情况下我不会（拿五十镑卖掉女儿）。这是“双重否定”。wouldnt = wouldn't sell my daughter for £50. **to oblige a gentleman like you** 为了报效像你这样的一位先生。这个不定式词组作目的状语，修饰 'd (= would) do。

799 **do a good deal** 做一笔克己的交易。 **deal** 交易；如 fair deal（公平交易）。**good** 这里是“对对方有利”的意思。

800 **morals** 道德，用复数。

803 **have a bit out of this** 从这件事中得到一点（好处）。

805 **There can be no question that ...** ……是不可能有问题的；毫无问题。

806 **positive crime** 绝对的罪过；错尽，错绝。

807 **feel a sort of rough justice in his claim** 觉得他提出的要求中有一种大致上的公平（也有一点道理）。

809 **Thats it** 那就是了；对啦；口语中常用的习语。 **Thats all I say.** 我所说的就是那个意思；all 后面省略 that。 **as it were** 仿佛；可以说是；是习语。注意：不要和 as it was 混淆；as it is (过去时用 was) 是“现在（或过去）实际情况如此”、“事实上”、“既然如此”的意思。

811 **really it seems hardly right** – 似乎总不大对——话未说完。“不对”指为 Liza 之事而给他钱。

813 **Dont say that, Governor.** that 指 Pickering 说的 it seems hardly right。 **Governor** 这里是称呼 Pickering。

815 **the undeserving poor** 不配救济的穷人们。 **what that means** 那（指 to be one of the undeserving poor）意味着什么。

means to a man. It means that he's up agen middle class morality all the time. If theres anything going, and I put in for a bit of it, it's always the same story: 'Youre undeserving; so you cant have it.' But my needs is as great as the most deserving widow's that ever got money out of six different charities in one week for the death of the same husband. I dont need less than a deserving man: I need more. I dont eat less hearty than him; and I drink a lot more. I want a bit of amusement, cause I'm a thinking man. I want cheerfulness and a song and a band when I feel low. Well, they charge me just the same for everything as they charge the deserving. What is middle class morality? Just an excuse for never giving me anything. Therefore, I ask you, as two gentleman, not to play that game on me. I'm playing straight with you. I aint pretending to be deserving. I'm undeserving; and I mean to go on being undeserving. I like it; and thats the truth. Will you take advantage of a man's nature to do him out of the price of his own daughter what he's brought up and fed and clothed

---

816 **up agen** (= against) **middle class morality all the time** 老是与中产阶级伦理道德相抵触。 **up against** 面临；与……冲突；是习语。 **middle class** 在英国指贵族和雇佣劳动者之间的阶级，即资产阶级和自由职业者。萧伯纳经常抨击中产阶级伦理道德。 **all the time** 老是，= always; 在英国通常指“在某一段时间内老是……”。

817 **theres anything going** 有什么事在进行；这里指“有什么救济或慈善活动”。 **going** 可视为形容词，作“进行中的”、“现行的”解。 **put in for a bit of it** 申请一些救济。 **put in for** 申请；是习语。It 指上文 anything，即“救济”。

818 **the same story** 老一套。

819 **needs** 生活必需的种种；用复数。 **the most deserving widow's** 最配受救济的寡妇的需要。widow's 后省略 needs。严格地说，这里 widow's 不妥，因为下面的关系代词 that 指 widow's needs 不妥（needs 不大可能 got money out of ...）；the most deserving widow's 改作 those (= needs) of the most deserving widow 才对，这样下面的 that 指 the most deserving widow，完全符合语法。

820 **ever got money out of six different charities in one week for the death of the same husband** 曾经因为同一个丈夫的死亡而在一个星期里从六个慈善团体得到救济金。 **charity** 作"慈善"解是不可数名词；作"慈善团体"解是可数名词。 **in one week** 同 in a week，强调一。注意用 ever 和过去时 got（不用现在时 gets）。

822 **I dont eat less hearty than him** 我吃得并不比他少；我的胃口并不比他（的胃口）小。 **hearty** 应作 heartily，痛快，胃口好。 **than him** = than he eats. 在文学中多作 than he，口语中多说 than him。

823 **I drink a lot more** 我喝酒比他多得多；more 后省略 than he drinks。**a lot** 许多；这里是副词短语；修饰 more。

824 **cause** = because. **a thinking man** 有思想的人。

825 **band** 乐队。 **want a band** 有个乐队（听听音乐）。 **feel low** 觉得情绪低落；不起劲。 **they charge me just the same for everything as they charge the deserving** 他们对什么都要我支付和受救济的人们同样的费用；衣食住行样样需要同样的开支。 **charge** 使支付；可接双宾语。

827 **Just an excuse** = It's (middle class morality is) just an excuse 只是一个借口而已。

828 **play that game on me** 对我耍那个（middle class morality 的）花招。

829 **playing straight with you** 和你们坦率地打交道。 straight 这里是副词；比较：play fair（公平地比赛）和 play foul（比赛犯规；作弊）中的 fair 和 foul 都是副词。 **pretending to be deserving** 假装是配受救济的。deserving 是形容词作表语，并不和 be 构成进行式。

831 **like it** 喜欢这样；it 指 to go on being undeserving 或 being undeserving。

832 **take advantage of a man's nature** 利用一个人的本性（宁肯不配救济）而占他便宜。 **do him out of the price of his own daughter** 剥夺他应得的他自己女儿的代价；要他把他的女儿给你们而你们不给他钱。

833 **what** 应作 that 或 whom。 **clothed** [kləʊðd] 给……衣穿。

by the sweat of his brow until she's growed big enough to be interesting to you two gentlemen? Is five pounds unreasonable? I put it to you; and I leave it to you.

HIGGINS [*rising, and going over to Pickering*] Pickering: if we were to take this man in hand for three months, he could choose between a seat in the Cabinet and a popular pulpit in Wales.

PICKERING What do you say to that, Doolittle?

DOOLITTLE Not me, Governor, thank you kindly. Ive heard all the preachers and all the prime ministers – for I'm a thinking man and game for politics or religion or social reform same as all the other amusements – and I tell you it's a dog's life any way you look at it. Undeserving poverty is my line. Taking one station in society with another, it's – it's – well, it's the only one that has any ginger in it, to my taste.

HIGGINS I suppose we must give him a fiver.

PICKERING He'll make a bad use of it, I'm afraid.

DOOLITTLE Not me, Governor, so help me I wont. Dont you be afraid that I'll save it and spare it and live idle on it. There wont be a penny of it left by Monday: I'll have to go to work same as if I'd never had it. It wont pauperize me, you bet. Just one good spree for myself and the missus, giving

---

834 **by the sweat** [swet] **of his brow** 靠（满头大汗地）辛勤劳动；是习语。**growed** grown 之误。

835 **Is five pounds unreasonable?** 五镑不合理（意即太贵）吗？ five pounds 作为一个金额，用单数。

836 **I put it to you; and I leave it to you.** 我把问题向你提出，让你回答。这口吻和前面连用 I'm waiting to tell you 等三句的口吻相仿，都是描摹出他“演说的天赋”。

838 **take this man in hand for three months** 训练他三个月。**take in hand** 拿在手上；有“承担”、“处理”等意思，这里指“进行语言训练”。 **could choose between a seat in the Cabinet and a popular pulpit in Wales** 能在内阁阁员和威尔士群众布道师两者中间选择（担任）一个。

840 **that** 指 Doolittle 受三个月训练可成为阁员或布道师的设想。

841 **thank you kindly** 这句话很普通；有些咬文嚼字的人认为不妥，因为自称对人“谢”得 kindly，有自誉为有礼貌的意味。

843 **game for** 对……极有兴致的；有劲。game 是形容词，后面介词用 for。 **same as** = the same as = in the same way as.

844 **amusements** 娱乐。在 Doolittle 看来，politics、religion、social reform 等也不过都是开开玩笑的事。 **it's a dog's life any way you look at it** 无论你怎么看，它总是极苦的生活。 **it** 泛指社会上一切形形式式的事物。 **any way** = however，有连词的作用。 **a dog's life** 苦难的生活。

845 **Undeserving poverty is my line.** 不配救济的穷困是我的行业。 **Taking one station in society with another** 拿社会上各个行当相比。 **another** = another station in society. society 作“社会”解时前面不用冠词。

846 **it's the only one that has any ginger** ['dʒɪndʒə] **in it, to my taste** 只有这个行当才有劲，才配我胃口。it 指 undeserving poverty。ginger 原义“生姜”，口语中转作“劲头”解。 **to taste** 配胃口的；合适的；是习语。

848 **fiver** = a five-pound note.

849 **make a bad use of** 不好好利用；滥花（钱）。

850 **so help me** 天晓得；我可以保证；见前注。 **I wont** = I wont make a bad use of it (指 the fiver).

851 **live idle on it** 靠这五镑闲混过日子。 **There wont be a penny of it left** = Not a penny of it will be left.

852 **by Monday** 至迟到星期一。

853 **same as if** = (just 或 all) the same as if. 土语中 same 这样的用法，已屡见前注。as if 后用虚拟语气。 **you bet** 你可以打赌，你可以确信。

854 **good spree** 狂欢一场（例如痛饮一顿）。 **the missus** 口语中称“妻子”，其实当时 Doolittle 和他所谓的 missus 尚未正式结婚，只是“情妇”；见前。

pleasure to ourselves and employment to others, and satisfaction to you to think it's not been throwed away. You couldnt spend it better.

HIGGINS [*taking out his pocket book and coming between Doolittle and the piano*] This is irresistible. Lets give him ten. [*He offers two notes to the dustman.*]

DOOLITTLE No, Governor. She wouldnt have the heart to spend ten; and perhaps I shouldnt neither. Ten pounds is a lot of money: it makes a man feel prudent like; and then goodbye to happiness. You give me what I ask you, Governor: not a penny more, and not a penny less.

PICKERING Why dont you marry that missus of yours? I rather draw the line at encouraging that sort of immorality.

DOOLITTLE Tell her so, Governor: tell her so. I'm willing. It's me that suffers by it. Ive no hold on her. I got to be agreeable to her. I got to give her presents. I got to buy her clothes something sinful. I'm a slave to that woman, Governor, just because I'm not her lawful husband. And she knows it too. Catch her marrying me! Take my advice, Governor: marry Eliza while she's young and dont know no better. If you dont

---

855 **employment to others** 与前面的 pleasure 和后面的 satisfaction 并列，是 giving 的宾语。 **Giving employment to others** 使别人有生意做。

856 **throwed away** 被丢掉；自费。throwed 是 thrown 之误。

857 **couldnt spend it better** 后面省略 than give it to me。

859 **This is irresistible** 这话极有说服力（无法不听从）。 **give him ten** 给他十

镑。Doolittle 原来只要五镑，Higgins 听了他那番话，心悦诚服，愿意加倍奉敬。**two notes** 两张（五镑）钞票。

861 **wouldnt have the heart to spend ten** 舍不得花十镑。这是虚拟语气，省略 if I were given ten 或 I got ten。 **have the heart to** （接不定式）忍心（常用于否定句中）。

862 **I shouldnt neither** = I shouldnt have the heart to spend ten either. 用了 neither，变成"双重否定"。

863 **feel prudent like** 觉得有些拘谨（不肯随意花用了）。口语中 like 这样的用法已见前注。 **and then goodbye to happiness** 那就向快乐告别了；那就没有愉快了。

864 **not a penny more** = don't give me a penny more than I ask you to give.

866 **rather draw the line at encouraging that sort of immorality** 我总觉该有个界限，不能（超越这界限而）鼓励那样的不道德；如鼓励不道德，那就过分了。 **draw the line at** 也作 draw a line at，是习语，后面所接的是不该做的事。这里的 that sort of immorality 指 Doolittle 和一个女人不结婚而姘居。

868 **It's me that suffers by it.** 由于这个情况（不结婚）而受害的是我。It's me 在口语中比 It's I 普遍。that 是关系代词，它的先行词是 It，不是 me，所以从句中用 suffers 而不用 suffer。但习惯上也有不用 that 而用 who 的；既用 who，先行词变成是 me，从句中自不能用 suffers 而要用 suffer 了。英国语法家 Quirk 曾举 It's me who's to blame 的例子，说是 informal English。

869 **Ive no hold on her.** 我控制不住她；我管不住她。 **got to** = have got to = have to. 这是口语用法。 **agreeable to her** 合她的意的；讨她喜欢的。

870 **buy her clothes something sinful** = buy her rather sinful clothes. 买相当邪气的衣服给她。something 这里是副词，是口语用法，既可作"多少有点"解，也可作"非常"解。

872 **lawful husband** 合法的（正式结了婚的）丈夫。

873 **Catch her marrying me!** 要是她会跟我结婚，你抓住问我！即"你瞧着，她决不会跟我结婚"的意思。 **marry Eliza while she's young and dont know no better** 趁 Eliza 年轻还不懂事的时候娶她。(待她懂得了不正式结婚的便宜，就不肯跟你结婚了。) dont know no better 是双重否定；dont 是 doesn't 之误。所以整个词组应作 doesn't know better。know better 是习语，作"懂得更多（因而不做某事）"，后面有时接 than；这里是 know better than to marry you 的意思。

youll be sorry for it after. If you do, she'll be sorry for it after; but better her than you, because youre a man, and she's only a woman and dont know how to be happy anyhow.

HIGGINS Pickering: if we listen to this man another minute, we shall have no convictions left. [*to Doolittle*] Five pounds I think you said.

DOOLITTLE Thank you kindly, Governor.

HIGGINS Youre sure you wont take ten?

DOOLITTLE Not now. Another time, Governor.

HIGGINS [*handing him a five-pound note*] Here you are.

DOOLITTLE Thank you, Governor. Good morning. [*He hurries to the door, anxious to get away with his booty. When he opens it he is confronted with a dainty and exquisitely clean young Japanese lady in a simple blue cotton kimono printed cunningly with small white jasmine blossoms. Mrs Pearce is with her. He gets out of her way deferentially and apologizes.*] Beg pardon, miss.

THE JAPANESE LADY Garn! Dont you know your own daughter?

DOOLITTLE } *exclaiming simultaneously* { Bly me! it's Eliza!
HIGGINS } Whats that? This!
PICKERING } By Jove!

LIZA Dont I look silly?

HIGGINS Silly?

---

875 **for it** 因为不娶她。 **after** 应说 afterwards。

876 **better her than you** = It's better for her to be sorry than for you to be sorry. / It's better that she (should) be sorry than you (should) be sorry.

877 **dont know** 是 doesn't know 之误。

879 **shall have no convictions left** 将没有信念被留存（而不被打破）。Higgins 怕自己彻底怀疑起 middle class morality 的信念。 **left** 过去分词，作宾语补足语。 **Five pounds I think you said.** = I think you said 'five pounds.'

883 **Not now.** = I wont take ten (pounds) now. **Another time** = I will take ten (pounds) another time. 我下次拿十镑。

885 **Good morning** 可用作上午的告别语，一般两词都重读；见面时用，一般重音放在 morning 上。

886 **get away with his booty** 拿了他要得的五镑钞票离去。 **booty** 战利品；掠夺所得。

887 **exquisitely** [ɪkˈskwɪzɪtli] **clean young Japanese lady** 高雅清洁的年轻日本贵妇人；即 Eliza，她穿着和服。

888 **kimono** [kɪˈməʊnəʊ] 和服；和服式晨衣；是日本语"着物"的音读。 **printed cunningly** 精巧地印着花样；cunning 有"狡猾"、"精巧"和"熟练"几个解释。

889 **gets out of her way** 给她让路。out of somebody's way 是 in somebody's way（妨碍；阻挡）的反义习语。

890 **deferentially** [ˌdefəˈrenʃəli] 恭敬地。Doolittle 认不出自己女儿，还当是日本贵妇人，所以恭而敬之。 **Beg pardon** 对不起；是 (I) beg your pardon 之略。 **miss** 小姐；不带姓名地作为称呼，常用于仆人对主人等的场合；正规的称呼是 madam。

891 **Garn!** 去你的！见前注。

892 **exlaiming simultaneously** [ˌsɪməlˈteɪnɪəsli] 也有人（尤其美国人）读作 [ˌsaɪməlˈteɪnɪəsli] 同时叫喊。Doolittle 叫喊 Bly me! it's Eliza! Higgins 叫喊 Whats that? This! Pickering 叫喊 By Jove! 三人的叫喊混成一片。 **Bly me!** = Blimey! 感叹词，表示惊讶。

894 **By Jove!** 指神名的发誓、诅咒语；天哪！ **Jove** 即罗马神话中的诸神之王 Jupiter [ˈdʒuːpɪtə]。

895 **Dont I look silly?** 我看上去不傻里傻气吗？因众人看见她都惊叫，所以她这样问。

MRS PEARCE [*at the door*] Now, Mr Higgins, please dont say anything to make the girl conceited about herself.

HIGGINS [*conscientiously*] Oh! Quite right, Mrs Pearce. [*to Eliza*] Yes: damned silly.

MRS PEARCE Please, sir.

HIGGINS [*correcting himself*] I mean extremely silly.

LIZA I should look all right with my hat on. [*She takes up her hat; puts it on; and walks across the room to the fireplace with a fashionable air.*]

HIGGINS A new fashion, by George! And it ought to look horrible!

DOOLITTLE [*with fatherly pride*] Well, I never thought she'd clean up as good looking as that, Governor. She's a credit to me, aint she?

LIZA I tell you, it's easy to clean up here. Hot and cold water on tap, just as much as you like, there is. Woolly towels, there is; and a towel horse so hot, it burns your fingers. Soft brushes to scrub yourself, and a wooden bowl of soap smelling like primroses. Now I know why ladies is so clean. Washing's a treat for them. Wish they could see what it is for the like of me!

HIGGINS I'm glad the bathroom met with your approval.

LIZA It didnt: not all of it; and I dont care who hears me say it. Mrs Pearce knows.

HIGGINS What was wrong, Mrs Pearce?

MRS PEARCE [*blandly*] Oh, nothing, sir. It doesnt matter.

897 **dont say anything to make the girl conceited about herself.** 别说什么会使得姑娘自负的话。Mrs Pearce 怕 Higgins 夸耀她好看。

901 **Please** 这是要 Higgins 注意，因为她又在 Eliza 面前说 damned 了。

904 **a fashionable air** 时髦的气派。

906 **by George** 指神名的发誓，诅咒语，表示千真万确。 George 指英国的守护神（patron）St. George。 **And it ought to look horrible!** 而且它（指 new fashion）应该看上去吓人！要时髦得吓人；那当然是讽刺。

908 **fatherly pride** 父亲的骄傲。 **clean up** 弄得干干净净，面目一新。

909 **a credit to me** 为我增光的人。 **a credit** 增光的事物。

911 **Hot and cold water on tap, just as much as you like, there is.** = There is hot and cold water on tap, just as much as you like. **on tap** 在龙头里，随手可以放出的。

912 **Woolly towels** [ˈtaʊəlz], **there is; and a towel horse so hot, it burns your fingers.** = There are woolly towels and so hot a towel horse that it burns your fingers. **Woolly** 羊毛般柔软的。 **towel horse** 手巾架，也称 towel rack。 **burns** 烫。这里不作“烧”解。 **your** 泛指“人们的”。

914 **soap smelling like primroses** 闻上去像樱草花香的肥皂。soap 是不可数名词。

915 **ladies is** ladies are 之误。 **Washing's a treat for them.** 洗澡对她们是一种享乐（因为她们有那么舒适的设备）。

916 **Wish** = I wish. 口语中常把 I wish, I hope 等语中的 I 略去。

918 **met with your approval** [əˈpruːvəl] 得到你的赞赏。

919 **It didnt** = It didn't meet with my approval. **not all of it** = not all of it meet with my approval. 并不是浴室的一切我都赞赏。她对浴室挂着照见她身体的镜子，大不以为然。 **dont care who hears me say it** 不怕谁听见我说这话(话在下面)。

921 **What was wrong** 出了什么问题；有什么不对头。

922 **blandly** 若无其事地。 **nothing** = nothing was wrong. **doesnt matter** 无关紧要。

LIZA I had a good mind to break it. I didnt know which way to look. But I hung a towel over it, I did.

HIGGINS Over what?

MRS PEARCE Over the looking-glass, sir.

HIGGINS Doolittle: you have brought your daughter up too strictly.

DOOLITTLE Me! I never brought her up at all, except to give her a lick of a strap now and again. Dont put it on me, Governor. She aint accustomed to it, you see: that's all. But she'll soon pick up your free-and-easy ways.

LIZA I'm a good girl, I am; and I wont pick up no free-and-easy ways.

HIGGINS Eliza: if you say again that youre a good girl, your father shall take you home.

LIZA Not him. You dont know my father. All he come here for was to touch you for some money to get drunk on.

DOOLITTLE Well, what else would I want money for? To put into the plate in church, I suppose. [*She puts out her tongue at him. He is so incensed by this that Pickering presently finds it necessary to step between them.*] Dont you give me none of your lip; and dont let me hear you giving this gentleman any of it neither, or youll hear from me about it. See?

---

923 **had a good mind to break it** 真想砸了它（镜子）。 **I didnt know which way to look.** 我不知该朝哪边看（才能不看见镜子里自己赤裸的身子）。

924 **hung a towel over it** 在这（镜子）上面挂条毛巾（把它遮住）。

927 **brought your daughter up too strictly** 把女儿管教得太严了。

929 **except to give her a lick of a strap now and again** 除了时而给她吃一顿皮鞭子。 **lick** 原义“舔”，俚语作“用鞭子抽打”、“猛击”解。

931 **aint** (= is not) **accustomed to it** 不习惯于此（对着镜子洗澡）。

932 **pick up** 学会。 **free-and-easy ways** 各种随随便便的习惯；随便的生活方式。

935 **your father shall take you home** 我就要你父亲把你带回家去。shall 用于第二、第三人称，表示说话人的意向。

937 **Not him** = He shall not take me home. 我才不让他带我回家呢。在 Not him 这样的结构中，常用宾语而不用主语。 **All he come here for was to touch you for some money to get drunk on.** 他来到这里，所为的就是向你要几个钱去喝个醉。All 后面省略 that。come 是 came 之误。 **All he came here for** 他来到这里的全部目的，即仅有的目的。**touch** 俚语中作“向……商借（或求事）”、“偷窃”、“敲诈勒索”等解。句末的 on 可有可无；to get drunk on 是不定式短语作定语，修饰 money；如不用 on，则 to get drunk 是不定式短语作状语，修饰 touch，说明要钱的目的。

939 **To put into the plate in church, I suppose.** 我想（要么）在教堂里捐献掉。教堂里做礼拜时，用盘子（plate）收集献金。church 作“教堂里做礼拜”解时，前面不用冠词，如 go to church、church begins at eight o'clock。

940 **puts out her tongue at him** 对他伸出舌头（嗤笑他说到教堂里捐钱）。

941 **incensed by this** 被这（伸舌头的）动作所惹怒。 **presently finds it necessary to step between them** 立即觉得有必要走到他们（父女）中间（以防 Doolittle 打女儿）。 **it** 虚词，引起不定式短语。

942 **Dont you give me none of you lip** 别说无礼的话。这一句里用了“双重否定”；Dont you 加强 Dont 的语气。 **lip** 无礼的话；多嘴嚼舌；是俚语，常用于 none of your lip 一语中。

943 **dont let me hear you giving this gentleman any of it neither** 应作 dont let me hear you give this gentleman any of it either，it 指 lip（失礼的话）。

944 **or youll hear from me about it** 否则你会从我这里受到（关于你多嘴无礼的）训责。 **hear** 有“受到批评（或训责）”的意思。 **it** 指说无礼的话这件事。 **See?** = You see? 你知道了吗?

HIGGINS Have you any further advise to give her before you go, Doolittle? Your blessing, for instance.

DOOLITTLE No, Governor: I aint such a mug as to put up my children to all I know myself. Hard enough to hold them in without that. If you want Eliza's mind improved, Governor, you do it yourself with a strap. So long, gentlemen. [*He turns to go.*]

HIGGINS [*impressively*] Stop. Youll come regularly to see your daughter. It's your duty, you know. My brother is a clergyman; and he could help you in your talks with her.

DOOLITTLE [*evasively*] Certainly, I'll come, Governor. Not just this week, because I have a job at a distance. But later on you may depend on me. Afternoon, gentlemen. Afternoon, maam. [*He touches his hat to Mrs Pearce, who disdains the salutation and goes out. He winks at Higgins, thinking him probably a fellow-sufferer from Mrs Pearce's difficult disposition, and follows her.*]

LIZA Dont you believe the old liar. He'd as soon you set a bulldog on him as a clergyman. You wont see him again in a hurry.

HIGGINS I dont want to, Eliza. Do you?

LIZA Not me. I dont want never to see him again, I dont. He's a disgrace to me, he is, collecting dust, instead of working at his trade.

PICKERING What is his trade, Eliza?

---

946 **Your blessing** 你（对女儿）的祝福。

947 **mug** 笨蛋；是俚语；原指“嘴”、“脸”、“丑脸”。 **put up my children to**

all I know myself 把我自己所懂得的全都教给我的子女。 **put up to** 教……做（某事）；是习语。

948 **Hard enough to hold them in without that** 不那样（把我自己所懂得的全教给他们），已经够难管束他们了。Hard 是 It is hard 之略。 **hold in** 约束；是习语。**without that** = without putting up my children to all I know myself.

950 **do it** = improve Eliza's mind. 教育她。

954 **help you in your talks with her** 在你对她说服教育方面帮助你。注意：help 后面介词用 in。**talks with** 参照动词短语 talk with，除"与……谈话"外，还作"说服"解。

955 **Not just this week** = I wont come just this week.

956 **have a job at a distance** 在远处有工作要做。job 这里指"短活"、"任务"。 **at a distance** 在附近的远处，如父亲在上海，儿子在东北工作，不能说 My son is working at a distance. **later on you may depend on me** 以后你可以相信我；你放心，我会来的。

957 **Afternoon** = Good afternoon. **maam** [mæm, məm] 常写作 ma'am，是口语；= madam。

958 **touches his hat to** 向……用手碰帽檐（致敬礼）。 **disdains the salutation** 不理 Doolittle 的致意。salutation 这里指既称 Mrs Pearce 为 maam，又向她致敬礼。

959 **fellow-sufferer from Mrs Pearce's difficult disposition** 同是 Mrs Pearce 的难弄的脾气的受害者。

961 **He'd as soon you set a bulldog on him as a clergyman.** 他宁可你叫条恶狗去咬他，也不愿你叫个牧师去缠他；他对牧师比恶狗还怕。He'd = He would. **would as soon ... as ...** 宁可……而不要……。句中的 would 有谓语动词的作用，后面省去连词 that。 **set ... on** 指使；是习语，这里的 set 是动词过去时。 **bulldog** 斗牛犬（一种猛犬）。 **as a clergyman** = as you set a clergyman on him.

962 **You wont see him again in a hurry.** 你短期内不会再见他。

965 **collecting dust, instead of working at his trade** 收集（拾）垃圾而不务正业。他的正业是挖土工（navvy），见下文。

LIZA Talking money out of other people's pockets into his own. His proper trade's a navvy; and he works at it sometimes too – for exercise – and earns good money at it. Aint you going to call me Miss Doolittle any more?

PICKERING I beg your pardon, Miss Doolittle. It was a slip of the tongue.

LIZA Oh, I dont mind; only it sounded so genteel. I should just like to take a taxi to the corner of Tottenham Court Road and get out there and tell it to wait for me, just to put the girls in their place a bit. I wouldnt speak to them, you know.

PICKERING Better wait til we get you something really fashionable.

HIGGINS Besides, you shouldnt cut your old friends now that you have risen in the world. Thats what we call snobbery.

LIZA You dont call the like of them my friends now, I should hope. Theyve took it out of me often enough with their ridicule when they had the chance; and now I mean to get a bit of my own back. But if I'm to have fashionable clothes, I'll wait. I should like to have some. Mrs Pearce says youre going to give me some to wear in bed at night different to what I wear in the daytime; but it do seem a waste of money when you could get something to shew. Besides, I never could fancy

---

968 **Talking money out of other people's pockets into his own. His proper trade's a navvy** 上文问 What is his trade? Eliza 接着回答：（他的行当变成是专门）把别人腰包里的钱弄到自己腰包里（骗人家的钱）了。他的正业是挖土工

（倒不认真干）。 **navvy** 开沟筑路的挖土工；是英国用语。

969 **works at it** 做（挖土）工。it = the job as a navvy.

970 **for exercise** （工作只是）为了运动运动。 **earns good money** 挣大钱。 **Aint you going to call me Miss Doolittle any more?** 你（听了我爹的这行径）不会再（尊敬我）称我 Doolittle 小姐了吧。按前文 Pickering 曾随口称她 Miss Doolittle，使她哇哇叫起来，她实在不喜欢人家这样叫她。

972 **Miss Doolittle** 又叫她 Miss Doolittle 了。Pickering 客气已成习惯。 **It was a slip of the tongue.** 这（上次称她 Miss Doolittle）是口误。a slip of the pen 是"笔误"。

974 **I dont mind** 我并不介意；没关系。 **only it sounded so genteel** [dʒen'tiːl] 可是（Miss Doolittle）这称呼听起来太文雅了些。 **genteel** 高雅的；常含讽刺意，作"装斯文的"解。

976 **get out there and tell it to wait for me** 在那里下车，叫车子（停着）等我。 **put the girls in their place a bit** 叫（那边街道的）那些姑娘安分些（不要再像过去那样来耻笑我）。 **put somebody in his place** 使某人安分，不得越规；是习语。

978 **Better wait** = You had better wait. 还是等……好。 **get you something really fashionable** 给你买真正时髦的衣服。

980 **cut your old friends** 不理睬你的老朋友。 **now that you have risen in the world** 因为你在社会上地位升高了的缘故。

983 **Theyve took it out of me often enough with their ridicule** ['rɪdɪkjuːl] **when they had the chance** 她们一有机会就耻笑我，耻笑得我够多的了。 **take it out of** 以（某人）出气；使（某人）受气；里面的 it 无所指，是习语。Theyve took 是 Theyve taken 之误。

984 **mean to get a bit of my own back** 要稍微报复报复。 **get one's own back** 报复，犹言"翻本"，是习语。

987 **different** = which（指前面的 some，即 some clothes) are different. different 后面一般介词用 from，有时（尤其英国人）也用 to；美国人有时用 than。

988 **it do seem a waste of money** 这（另外给我睡衣）确实好像是浪费金钱。do 是 does 之误。seem 这里也可说 seem to be。waste 前面的 a 不用也可。

989 **shew** = show. 显示；炫耀；出风头。 **never could fancy changing into cold things** 决不会喜欢（脱下身上温暖的衣服）换上冷的衣服（睡衣）。

changing into cold things on a winter night.

MRS PEARCE [*coming back*] Now, Eliza. The new things have come for you to try on.

LIZA Ah-ow-oo-ooh! [*She rushes out.*]

MRS PEARCE [*following her*] Oh, dont rush about like that, girl. [*She shuts the door behind her.*]

HIGGINS Pickering: we have taken on a stiff job.

PICKERING [*with conviction*] Higgins: we have.

There seems to be some curiosity as to what Higgins's lessons to Eliza were like. Well, here is a sample: the first one.

Picture Eliza, in her new clothes, and feeling her inside put out of step by a lunch, dinner, and breakfast of a kind to which it is unaccustomed, seated with Higgins and the Colonel in the study, feeling like a hospital out-patient at a first encounter with the doctors.

Higgins, constitutionally unable to sit still, discomposes her still more by striding restlessly about. But for the reassuring presence and quietude of her friend the Colonel she would run for her life, even back to Drury Lane.

HIGGINS Say your alphabet.

LIZA I know my alphabet. Do you think I know nothing? I dont need to be taught like a child.

992 **try on** 试穿。

994 **She shuts the door behind her.** 她（出房间）随手关门。her 指 Mrs Pearce，而不是 Eliza。

996 **have taken on a stiff job** 承担了一项棘手的工作。

998 **There seems to be some curiosity as to ...** 看来（有些读者）会好奇地想到……

999 **the first one** 第一课。one 指 lesson。

1000 **Picture** （请读者们）想一想。 **feeling her inside put out of step** 觉得她的肠胃被搞乱了。 **inside** 口语，作“肚子”解。 **put** 是过去分词，作宾语补足语。 **out of step** 原义脚步不齐；转义“失调”、“混乱”。

1001 **to which it is unaccustomed** 它（她的肠胃）所不习惯那种的。

1002 **seated** 是过去分词。如“请坐”，常说 Please be seated.

1003 **a hospital out-patient** 医院的门诊病人。 **a first encounter** 一个初次的相会。比较：the first encounter，初次相会。

1005 **constitutionally unable to sit still** 生性坐不定。 **discomposes her still more by striding restlessly about** 由于他不停地大步走来走去，弄得她更加心神不宁。Eliza 原已像第一次见到医生的门诊病人那样局促不安，现在更加不安了，所以用 still more。

1006 **But for the reassuring presence and quietude** [ˈkwaɪətjuːd] **of her friend the Colonel** 要不是她的朋友 Pickering 上校的在场使她心安且平静。 **But for** 要不是；是习语；含有虚拟语气，这里 = If it were not for，所以下面用 would run，而不用 will run。

1007 **run for her life** 拼命地跑；逃命。

1008 **even back to Drury Lane** Drury Lane 是 Liza 家的所在地，见第一幕末尾(p.38)。说“即使回到老家去”，可见她把她的家看作是最可怕的去处。

1009 **Say your alphabet** [ˈælfəbet]. 背出你的字母表。an alphabet 是一种语言的全套字母，不是一个字母；“一个字母”称 a letter。

1010 **dont need to be taught** 也可以说 need not be taught。

HIGGINS [*thundering*] Say your alphabet.

PICKERING Say it, Miss Doolittle. You will understand presently. Do what he tells you; and let him teach you in his own way.

LIZA Oh well, if you put it like that – Ahyee, bəyee, cəyee, dəyee –

HIGGINS [*with a roar of a wounded lion*] Stop. Listen to this, Pickering. This is what we pay for as elementary education. This unfortunate animal has been locked up for nine years in school at our expense to teach her to speak and read the language of Shakespear and Milton. And the result in Ahyee, Bə-yee, Cə-yee, Də-yee. [*to Eliza*] Say A, B, C, D.

LIZA [*almost in tears*] But I'm sayin it. Ahyee, Bəyee, Cə-yee –

HIGGINS Stop. Say a cup of tea.

LIZA A cappətə-ee.

HIGGINS Put your tongue forward until it squeezes against the top of your lower teeth. Now say cup.

LIZA C-c-c – I cant. C-Cup.

PICKERING Good. Splendid, Miss Doolittle.

HIGGINS By Jupiter, she's done it at the first shot. Pickering: we shall make a duchess of her. [*to Eliza*] Now do you think you could possibly say tea? Not tə-yee, mind: if you ever say bə-yee, cə-yee, də-yee again you shall be dragged round the room three times by the hair of your head. [*fortissimo*] T, T, T, T.

1012 **thundering** （像打雷般）怒喝。

1013 **presently** 马上；不久。

1015 **if you put it like that –** 如果你那样说；如果你要我念；话未说完，没说出的意思是“我就念吧”。 **Ahyee, bəyee, cəyee, dəyee** Liza 用伦敦土音把 [eɪ]、[biː]、[siː]、[diː] 念成 [ˈɑːjiː]、[ˈbəjiː]、[ˈsəjiː]、[ˈdəjiː]。

1016 **with a roar of a wounded lion** 用受伤的狮子（一般）的吼声；比喻“怒吼”。 **Listen to this** 听这个（指 Liza 念 ABCD 的发音）。

1017 **This is what we pay for as elementary education.** 这就是我们出钱（纳税）办的小学教育。 **This unfortunate animal** 这个畜生般的可怜人；指 Liza。

1018 **locked up for nine years in school** 在学校里关了九年；受了九年教育（当指英国的义务教育）。

1019 **at our expense** 由我们负担费用。 **to teach her to speak and read the language of Shakespear and Milton** 教她说和读莎士比亚及弥尔顿（所用）的语言（规范英语）。 **to teach her ...** 这个格式在这里似乎不合理，该改作 to be taught。

1022 **But I'm sayin it.** 可我是在念你所教我念的东西嘛。其实她接下来念出来的还是 Ahyee、Bəyee、Cə-yee。

1024 **cappətə-ee** Liza 把 cup of tea 念成 [kæpəˈtəjiː]。

1025 **Put your tongue forward until it squeezes against the top of your lower teeth.** 把你的舌头向前伸到顶住你下面牙齿的上端。

1027 **C-c-c –** Liza 一下念不出 [kʌp]，因此尽是 [k-k-k-] 的。 **C-Cup** 终于念出了 [k-kʌp]。

1029 **By Jupiter** 发誓，诅咒用语，见前 By Jove 条注。 **done it at the first shot** 一炮就打响；一试就试成（正确念出 cup 的音）。

1031 **could possibly** 有可能会。用了 possibly，有“是否可能竟然不会”的意思。 **Not tə-yee** = Do not say tə-yee. 不要念成 [təjiː]。 **mind** 注意；也作 mind you。 **if you ever say bə-yee, cə-yee, də-yee again** 如果再念一声 [ˈbəjiː][ˈsəjiː][ˈdəjiː]。 **ever** 有“只要有一次”的意思。

1032 **you shall be dragged round the room three times by the hair of your head** 我要你被揪着头发在房间里拖着转三圈。注意：drag somebody by the hair 之类的结构中习惯用 the，不用 his；又如 catch him by the arm 这说法与 catch his arm 略有不同；前者侧重抓住其人，后者仅是抓住其臂。

1033 **fortissimo** [fɔːˈtɪsɪməʊ] 极响；极强；音乐用语；是意大利语。 **T, T, T, T.** Higgins 连续发 [tiː] 音，教 Liza 学着念。

LIZA [*weeping*] I cant hear no difference cep that it sounds more genteel-like when you say it.

HIGGINS Well, if you can hear that difference, what the devil are you crying for? Pickering: give her a chocolate.

PICKERING No, no. Never mind crying a little, Miss Doolittle: you are doing very well; and the lessons wont hurt. I promise you I wont let him drag you round the room by your hair.

HIGGINS Be off with you to Mrs Pearce and tell her about it. Think about it. Try to do it by yourself: and keep your tongue well forward in your mouth instead of trying to roll it up and swallow it. Another lesson at half-past four this afternoon. Away with you.

Eliza, still sobbing, rushes from the room.

And that is the sort of ordeal poor Eliza has to go through for months before we meet her again on her first appearance in London society of the professional class.

1035 **I cant hear no difference** 我听不出（你念的和我念的 T 的音）有什么区别。Liza 用了“双重否定”。 **cep that it sounds more genteel-like when you say it** 只是你念的 T 听起来比较文雅。这就说明她能够听出区别来。cep = except.

1037 **what the devil are you crying for?** 你还哭什么呢？ the devil 加强 what 的语气，但那是诅咒语，Higgins 却经常会脱口而出，使用这种语词。

1039 **Never mind crying a little** 稍许哭哭不要紧。mind 作“介意”解，后面接动名词。

1041 **drag you round the room by your hair** 前面注中刚说过，在这样的句型中，习惯用 by the hair，这里用 by your hair，可能为了突出“你的”的意思。

1042 **Be off with you to Mrs Pearce** 到 Mrs Pearce 那里去。 **Be off with** 也作 Off with；用于祈使句；去！去掉……！ **tell her about it.** 把它（指 this lesson，这一课所教的）告诉她。

1043 **Think about it** 想想它（指 this lesson，这一课所教的）。 **Try to do it by yourself** 独自试着做它（指这一课所教的），自己练习。 **keep your tongue well forward in your mouth** 把舌头在嘴里好好（充分地）向前伸着。

1044 **instead of trying to roll it up and swallow it** 而不是拼命把舌头卷起来吞下去。“吞下去”当然是挖苦的话。

1045 **half-past** 一般分写，不用连字号。

1046 **Away with you.** 去！ Away with 是习语。

1048 **ordeal** [ɔːˈdiːl] 苦难；折磨。 **go through** 经历；通过。

1049 **we meet her again** 我们再次在戏中看到她出现。

1050 **London society of the professional class** 伦敦专门职业者阶级的社交界。

第三幕
剧情提要

在 Higgins 教授的母亲家里。这天是她的会客日。她一向不要儿子在会客日到她家里来，因为他不拘礼仪，谈吐粗野。这回他说还将有个卖花女 Liza 来访，更使 Higgins 太太不安。Higgins 把他和 Pickering 打赌的事情告诉她，说明 Liza 是先来这里做个试验的。

正在这时，Freddy 和他的母亲及妹妹——Eynsford Hill 太太和 Clara 小姐——来了。他们虽然家道中落，可母女俩始终装得一派大家风范。

接着 Liza 来了。她服饰华丽，举止优雅，开始时说话也确实斯文得体。可是她渐渐越说越不像话，最终街头卖花女的原形毕露。Higgins 太太啼笑皆非；Eynsford Hill 太太表示惊愕万分；Freddy 却说这正是最时髦的语言；Clara 竟当场学起“时髦”来。

训练工作自得继续进行。六个月的期限未满，而 Liza 竟已成功地在大使馆招待会上冒充公爵夫人。一位青年语言学家肯定她是匈牙利王族，不可能是英国人，因为英国女人没有一个能说这样正确的英语，只有外国人才能说得那么好。又有位太太则说 Liza 的言谈与维多利亚女王一般无二。

试验成功。Higgins 教授打赌赢了。可是 Liza 精疲力竭，再也受不了了。

ACT III

It is Mrs Higgins's at-home day. Nobody has yet arrived. Her drawing room, in a flat on Chelsea Embankment, has three windows looking on the river; and the ceiling is not so lofty as it would be in an older house of the same pretension. The windows are open, giving access to a balcony with flowers in pots. If you stand with your face to the windows, you have the fireplace on your left and the door in the right-hand wall close to the corner nearest the windows.

Mrs Higgins was brought up on Morris and Burne Jones; and her room, which is very unlike her son's room in Wimpole Street, is not crowded with furniture and little tables and nicknacks. In the middle of the room there is a big ottoman; and this, with the carpet, the Morris wallpapers, and the Morris chintz window curtains and brocade covers of the ottoman and its cushions, supply all the ornament, and are much too handsome to be hidden by odds and ends of useless things. A few

---

1 **at-home day** 接待客人的日子；会客日。at home 除“在家”、“在国内”等解释外，还可作“在家接待客人”解，如：I am not at home today. 我今天不会客。 **at-home** 对客人的接待；家庭招待会。

2 **a flat on Chelsea Embankment** Chelsea 堤岸上的（一幢房子中的）一套公寓。 **flat** 一套公寓；这是英国说法，美国人叫 apartment。 **Chelsea** 伦敦西南部、泰晤士河北岸的一个区，过去画家、作家多居此。Chelsea 堤岸实是 Chelsea 区里的泰晤士河岸。注意：Chelsea Embankment 前面没有 the；介词用 on。

3 **windows looking on the river** 临河的窗；河指泰晤士河。

4 **an older house of the same pretension** 同样气派的较老的房子。过去房子的天花板较高，现在的低。

5 **giving access** [ˈækses] **to** 通往。

7 **close to the corner nearest the windows** 贴近靠窗的角落。close 是形容词，修饰 door。

9 **was brought up on Morris** [ˈmɒrɪs] **and Burne Jones** [bɜːnˈdʒəʊnz] 是受着 Morris 和 Burne Jones 的影响而形成她的艺术修养的。 **bring up** 使成长；教育；培养。 **Morris** William Morris（1834–1896），英国诗人兼工艺美术家，信奉社会主义，主张社会主义改革，曾开设工厂，所制工艺美术品，风行一时。 **Burne Jones** 是复姓，其全名为 Edward Burne Jones（1833–1898），英国画家，美术设计家，拉斐尔前派（Pre-Raphaelite）的巨匠，Morris 的终身好友。

10 **very unlike her son's room in Wimpole Street** 跟她儿子（Henry Higgins）在 Wimpole Street 的房间（见第二幕）大不相同。儿子是语言学家，房间里放满了家具和实验仪器等，而他母亲的房间布置得很雅致，处处显现出她崇尚时新的拉斐尔前派的艺术情趣。母子性格迥然不同。

11 **crowded with furniture** 放满家具。 **furniture** 家具的集称，是不可数名词。"一件家具"应作 a piece (或 an article 或 a bit) of furniture。 **nicknacks** [ˈnɪknæks] 零星的装饰物（家具或服装等）；小摆设。nicknack 也作 knicknack。

12 **ottoman** [ˈɒtəmən] 没有靠背和扶手的厚垫长榻或长凳，也指厚垫脚凳；这里指前者。

13 **this** 指 ottoman。 **Morris wallpapers** Morris 和他的几个同伴们设计的那种糊墙纸。下面 Morris chintz 中的 Morris 也是这个意思。

14 **brocade** [brəˈkeɪd] **covers** 织锦缎套子。

15 **its cushions** [ˈkʊʃnz] ottoman 上放的垫子。 **supply all the ornament** 构成全部的装饰。这里 supply 的主语是 this (= ottoman)，按语法应改用 supplies；但 this 后面用介词 with 引起一连串其他东西，所以在概念上 supply 的主体是多样东西，而不是一个 ottoman；也可以说这里的介词 with 实际上起了连词 and 的作用。 **are much too handsome to be hidden by odds and ends of useless things** = are so handsome that they should not be hidden ...（这些家具和装饰）太漂亮了，

good oil-paintings from the exhibitions in the Grosvenor Gallery thirty years ago (the Burne Jones, not the Whistler side of them) are on the walls. The only landscape is a Cecil Lawson on the scale of a Rubens. There is a portrait of Mrs Higgins as she was when she defied the fashion in her youth in one of the beautiful Rossettian costumes which, when caricatured by people who did not understand, led to the absurdities of popular estheticism in the eighteen-seventies.

In the corner diagonally opposite the door Mrs Higgins, now over sixty and long past taking the trouble to dress out of the fashion, sits writing at an elegantly simple writing-table with a bell button within reach of her hand. There is a Chippendale chair further back in the room between her and the window

---

不能让没用的零星东西来遮盖掉；加上零星东西反而要遮盖原已非常漂亮的布置。这里 are 和 supply 并列，主语同样是 this，按语法应改用 is，如上条所注。 **odds and ends** 零零碎碎的东西（或事情）；是习语。

17 **exhibitions**[ˌeksɪˈbɪʃnz] **in the Grosvenor** [ˈgrəʊvnə] **Gallery thirty years ago** 三十年前在 Grosvenor 画廊展出的展品。 **the Grosvenor Gallery** 在伦敦 Bond Street，创立于 1876 年，是著名的美术展览馆，也称 the Grosvenor；注意前面有 the，Grosvenor 中的 s 不发音。

18 **the Burne Jones, not the Whistler** [ˈwɪslə] **side of them** 它们（这些油画展品）属于 Burne Jones（拉斐尔前派）的，而不属于 Whistler（印象派）的。Burne Jones 后面省略 side of them；或按照严格的标点法，在 Whistler 后面应加逗号，表示 Burne Jones 和 Whistler 并列地修饰 side。 **Whistler** James Abbott McNeill Whistler（1834–1903），居住在英国的美国旧派油画家兼蚀刻画家。

19 **The only landscape** [ˈlændskeɪp] **is a Cecil** ([ˈsesl] 或 [ˈsɪsl]) **Lawson** [ˈlɔːsn] 唯一的一幅风景画是 Cecil Lawson 的作品。 **landscape** 风景画；一片风景；是可数名词。 **Cecil Lawson** 英国风景画家，善作巨幅风景画；前面用 a，表示他的作品；下面 a Rubens 也指作品。

20 **on the scale of a Rubens** [ˈruːbɪnz] 像 Rubens 的画那种画幅的。 **Rubens** Peter Paul Rubens（1577–1640），欧洲中世纪佛兰德（Flanders）画家，所作多为巨幅画。 **a portrait** [ˈpɔːtreɪt] **of Mrs Higgins as she was** 一张 Mrs Higgins 当时模样的肖像。比较：a portrait of Mrs Higgins's: Mrs Higgins 所有（或所画、所拍摄）的肖像画（或照片）。

21 **when she defied the fashion in her youth** 在她年轻时与当时流行的服装式样相对抗；敢于打扮得新奇；修饰 as she was 的 was。

22 **Rossettian** [rɒˈsetɪən] **costumes** [ˈkɒstjuːmz] Rossetti 画派风格的服装。 **Rossetti** Dante Gabriel Rossetti（1828–1882），英国诗人兼画家，和他妹妹 Christina Georgina Rossetti 及上述 Burne Jones 等，都是拉斐尔前派的中心人物。 **costumes** （某一时代、地区、或某一类人等特殊的）服装。 **when caricatured** [ˈkærɪkətʃʊəd] **by people who did not understand** 一经被不懂的人们歪曲地模仿；修饰 led；这个插入的状语从句把 which 和 led（主语和谓语）隔开了。 **when caricatured** = when the Rossettian costumes were caricatured.

23 **led to the absurdities of popular estheticism** [iːsˈθetɪsɪzəm] **in the eighteen-seventies** 导致 19 世纪 70 年代（1870–1879）流行的唯美主义的种种荒唐行为。 **led to** 通往；导致。 **estheticism** = aestheticism.

25 **diagonally** [daɪˈægənəli] **opposite the door** 斜对着门的。 **diagonally** 成对角线地；斜对面地。

26 **long past taking the trouble to dress out of the fashion** 早过了费心定要穿得不同于流行服装的年纪；不再别出心裁，务求穿得不同流俗。past 是介词；这个介词短语和上面的 now over sixty 并列，都修饰 Mrs Higgins。

27 **elegantly** [ˈelɪgəntli] **simple** 典雅朴素的；朴素雅致的。 **with a bell button within reach of her hand** 有个伸手可以按到的电铃按钮。

28 **Chippendale** [ˈtʃɪpəndeɪl] **chair** Chippendale 风格的椅子。**Chippendale** Thomas Chippendale（1718–1779），英国著名的家具设计家。

29 **further back in the room** 在房间的再往后处；在舞台上更靠近后台处。下面 further forward 正与此相反。

nearest her side. At the other side of the room, further forward, is an Elizabethan chair roughly carved in the taste of Inigo Jones. On the same side a piano in a decorated case. The corner between the fireplace and the window is occupied by a divan cushioned in Morris chintz.

It is between four and five in the afternoon.

The door is opened violently; and Higgins enters with his hat on.

MRS HIGGINS [*dismayed*] Henry! [*scolding him*] What are you doing here today? It is my at-home day: you promised not to come. [*As he bends to kiss her, she takes his hat off, and presents it to him.*]

HIGGINS Oh bother! [*He throws the hat down the table.*]

MRS HIGGINS Go home at once.

HIGGINS [*kissing her*] I know, mother. I came on purpose.

MRS HIGGINS But you mustnt. I'm serious, Henry. You offend all my friends: they stop coming whenever they meet you.

HIGGINS Nonsense! I know I have no small talk; but people dont mind. [*He sits on the settee.*]

MRS HIGGINS Oh! Dont they? Small talk indeed! What about your large talk? Really, dear, you mustnt stay.

HIGGINS I must. Ive a job for you. A phonetic job.

MRS HIGGINS No use, dear. I'm sorry; but I cant get round your

31 **Elizabethan** [ɪˌlɪzəˈbi:θn] **chair roughly carved in the taste of Inigo** [ˈɪnɪgəʊ] **Jones** 照 Inigo Jones 的风格、雕刻线条豪放的伊丽莎白式椅子。 **Elizabethan chair** 英国女王伊丽莎白一世（Elizabeth [ɪˈlɪzəbəθ] I, 1533–1603）时代的式样的椅子。 **Inigo Jones** 英国建筑家兼舞台设计师（1573–1652）。

32 **On the same side a piano in a decorated** [ˈdekəreɪtɪd] **case**. 同一边上，有一台琴箱上有花纹装饰的钢琴。这是句省略句，a piano 前面省略 stands 或 (there) is 等谓语动词。

33 **divan** [dɪˈvæn] **cushioned in Morris chintz** 用 Morris 擦光印花布做面子的软垫的靠壁长榻。

36 **with his hat on** 戴着帽子。 **on** 被戴着。按礼仪，进房间应脱去帽子；Higgins 既不经通报，也不轻叩房门，猛然开门直闯进来，到室内又不脱帽，都说明他不拘礼节。

41 **Oh bother!** 啊，讨厌！ 也作 Oh bother it! 英国人常用以表示轻蔑或不耐烦，这里是表示对脱帽不耐烦而发出的感叹。

43 **came on purpose** 故意来的（特意凑在 Mrs Higgins 的会客日带 Liza 来试试他训练的成果）。

44 **mustnt** = mustn't come. 不该来。 **I'm serious** 我是当真的（不是跟你开玩笑）。

45 **stop coming** 从此不来（怕碰到专门要得罪客人的 Higgins）。

46 **I have no small talk** 我不会敷衍聊天。 **small talk** 交际场中的闲谈；是习语；是不可数名词。 **people dont mind** 人们不在乎我不会敷衍聊天。

47 **settee** [seˈti:] 有靠背和扶手的长椅；有如一般的“长沙发”。

48 **Dont they?** = don't they mind? 他们不在乎吗？是反问句。 **Small talk indeed!** (“敷衍客套”, 你倒说得好！你把我们的谈话）全算是敷衍客套吗？ **What about your large talk?** 你的高谈阔论又算什么呢？ **large talk** 大话；是名词习语；动词习语作 talk large（说大话）；这里是针对上文 Higgins 说 small talk 而讽刺他的。

50 **Ive a job for you.** 我要你做件事。

51 **No use** （在做这件事上我是）没有用的；（我）不能。 **I'm sorry; but ...** 口语中常在 I'm sorry 后面接 but ... 表示所遗憾的事，实际上 = I'm sorry that ... **get round** 克服……困难；弄通；学会；说服。round 是介词。

vowels; and though I like to get pretty postcards in your patent shorthand, I always have to read the copies in ordinary writing you so thoughtfully send me.

HIGGINS Well, this isnt a phonetic job.

MRS HIGGINS You said it was.

HIGGINS Not your part of it. Ive picked up a girl.

MRS HIGGINS Does that mean that some girl has picked you up?

HIGGINS Not at all. I dont mean a love affair.

MRS HIGGINS What a pity!

HIGGINS Why?

MRS HIGGINS Well, you never fall in love with anyone under forty-five. When will you discover that there are some rather nice-looking young women about?

HIGGINS Oh, I cant be bothered with young women. My idea of a lovable woman is somebody as like you as possible. I shall never get into the way of seriously liking young women: some habits lie too deep to be changed. [*rising abruptly and walking about, jingling his money and his keys in his trouser pockets*] Besides, theyre all idiots.

MRS HIGGINS Do you know what you would do if you really loved me, Henry?

HIGGINS Oh bother! What? Marry, I suppose.

MRS HIGGINS No. Stop fidgeting and take your hands out of your pockets. [*With a gesture of despair, he obeys and sits down again.*] Thats a good boy. Now tell me about the girl.

HIGGINS She's coming to see you.

52 **in your patent shorthand** 用你独创的速记法书写的。patent 原义“专利的”，口语中作“别出心裁的”解。

53 **copies in ordinary writing** 用通常的书写法写的副本（用以对照阅读速记法写的稿本）。

54 **you so thoughtfully send me** 你考虑那么周到（怕我看不懂你的速记）而特意寄给我的。you 前面省略代替 copies 的关系代词 that 或 which。

57 **Not your part of it.** （这）不是要你做的那一部分；这不是你的事。 **picked up** 无意中拣得；弄到；是习语。Higgins 说 picked up a girl，语义含糊，引起下文他母亲的误会。

59 **love affair** 恋爱事；常指风流韵事。

60 **What a pity!** 多可惜！真遗憾！这是个常用语。

62 **you never fall in love with anyone under forty-five** 你从没有爱上过任何一个四十五岁以下的女人。（实际上是说她儿子总不好好找个年轻的对象，并非说他爱上过的都是四十五岁以上的女人。）

64 **about** 在周围存在着。

65 **I cant be bothered with young women** 我不可能为年轻女人烦心；我受不了她们的麻烦。

66 **somebody as like you as possible** 尽可能像你（越像你越好）的那么一个人。

67 **get into the way of** 变成习惯于……

68 **some habits lie too deep to be changed** 有些习惯根深蒂固,无法改变;积重难返。

69 **walking about** 来回走着。about 是副词，是“在附近、周围”的意思。 **jingling his money and his keys in his trouser pockets** 把两只裤袋里的钱币和钥匙搅得叮当作响。

73 **Marry, I suppose.** = I should marry, I suppose. = I suppose (that) I should marry if I really loved you. 我想我要是真正爱你（母亲），我该娶媳妇吧。Higgins 知道他母亲心里盼他结婚成家。

74 **fidgeting** [ˈfɪdʒɪtɪŋ] 烦躁；坐立不安。

76 **Thats a good boy.** 那才是个好孩子。Mrs Higgins 把他当个小孩子，事实上他也确实像个任性的小孩子，见第二幕场景说明末尾对 Higgins 的描绘。

MRS HIGGINS I dont remember asking her.

HIGGINS You didnt. *I* asked her. If youd known her you wouldnt have asked her.

MRS HIGGINS Indeed! Why?

HIGGINS Well, it's like this. She's a common flower girl. I picked her off the kerbstone.

MRS HIGGINS And invited her to my at-home!

HIGGINS [*rising and coming to her to coax her*] Oh, thatll be all right. Ive taught her to speak properly; and she has strict orders as to her behavior. She's to keep to two subjects: the weather and everybody's health – Fine day and How do you do, you know – and not to let herself go on things in general. That will be safe.

MRS HIGGINS Safe! To talk about our health! about our insides! perhaps about our outsides! How could you be so silly, Henry?

HIGGINS [*impatiently*] Well, she must talk about something. [*He controls himself and sits down again.*] Oh, she'll be alright: dont you fuss. Pickering is in it with me. Ive a sort of bet on that I'll pass her off as a duchess in six months. I started on her some months ago; and she's getting on like a house on fire. I shall

---

78 **I dont remember asking her.** 我不记得曾经请过她；实际就是说"我并没有请过她"。asking her 后面省略 to come to see me。比较：Remember to ask her to come. 记住（别忘了）请她来。remember 后面接动名词表示曾经发生的事，后面接不定式表示应该要做的事。

79 **You didnt.** = You didnt ask her. **If youd known her you wouldnt have asked her.** 要是你曾经认识她，你就不会请她来了；这是表示与过去事实相反的虚拟语气，事实上正因为你不认识她（不知道她是个“下等女人”），你才要她来。

82 **it's like this** 事情是这样的。这是个常用语。 **off the kerbstone** 在人行道的镶边石外边；即“在马路上”；参看第一幕 keep off the kerb 注。

84 **invited her to my at-home** 邀请她来参加我接待客人的招待会。

86 **she has strict orders as to her behavior** 关于她的举止行为我都给了严格的指示。she has orders 不是“她有指示”，而是“她受到了指示”。orders 作“指示”、“命令”解，常用复数。

87 **She's** (= she is) **to keep to two subjects** （规定）她（说话）只许限于两个话题。be + 不定式表示“安排”、“意图”、“可能性”等。 **keep to** 保持；是习语。

88 **Fine day and How do you do** Fine day 和 How do you do 是说话限于 the weather 和 everybody's health 的两个例子。

89 **not to let herself go on things in general** 不让她谈到一般话题。这个不定式短语承接 She's，和上面 to keep to two subjects 并列。

91 **To talk about our health!** = Is she to talk about our health! **about our insides!** 谈我们身体的内部吗？身体内部如 stomach，bowels，womb 等在中产阶级的“高雅”谈话中是忌讳的。

92 **about our outsides!** 谈我们身体的外部吗！前面说了 insides，接下说与它相对的 outsides：leg，belly，buttocks 也是忌讳的，身体的里里外外全在忌讳之列，这是萧伯纳对中产阶级道德礼仪的讽刺。

94 **she must talk about something** 必须让她说些什么；她总该说些什么。

95 **dont you fuss** 别大惊小怪的；比 dont fuss 语气重。

96 **Pickering is in it with me.** Pickering 和我一起参与了这件事。it 指和 Pickering 打赌对 Liza 作语音训练的试验这件事。 **Ive a sort of bet on** 我对……（认为必胜而）可以说是打了赌。 **a sort of bet** 有点像是打赌。 **sort of** 有点儿；几乎；这是习语，不但可放在名词前面，还可以放在形容词、动词等前面，如：He's sort of tired. I sort of hope so. **have a bet on** 后面接 that - 从句，表示打赌认为必胜的内容。

97 **started on her** 开始训练她。

98 **getting on** 进展。 **like a house on fire** （像着火的房子猛烈而迅速地燃烧那样）迅猛地。这是习语。

win my bet. She has a quick ear; and she's been easier to teach than my middle-class pupils because she's had to learn a complete new language. She talks English almost you talk French.

MRS HIGGINS Thats satisfactory, at all events.

HIGGINS Well, it is and it isnt.

MRS HIGGINS What does that mean?

HIGGINS You see, Ive got her pronunciation all right; but you have to consider not only how a girl pronounces, but what she pronounces; and that's where –

They are interrupted by the parlormaid, announcing guests.

THE PARLORMAID Mrs and Miss Eynsford Hill. [*She withdraws.*]

HIGGINS Oh Lord! [*He rises; snatches his hat from the table; and makes for the door; but before he reaches it his mother introduces him.*]

Mrs and Miss Eynsford Hill are the mother and daughter who sheltered from the rain in Covent Garden. The mother is well bred, quiet, and has the habitual anxiety of straitened means. The daughter has acquired a gay air of being very much at home in society: the bravado of genteel poverty.

MRS EYNSFORD HILL [*to Mrs Higgins*] How do you do? [*They shake hands.*]

MISS EYNSFORD HILL How d'you do? [*She shakes.*]

MRS HIGGINS [*introducing*] My son Henry.

100 **because she's had to learn a complete new language** 因为她得学习一种全新的语言。卖花女学公爵夫人的语言，等于从头学一种外语。但正因从头学起，教学倒反而容易。

101 **She talks English almost you talk French.** 她现在讲英语几乎和你讲法语一样（好）。

102 **Thats satisfactory, at all events.** 不管怎样，至少那也不错了。（我法语虽说得不太好，她说英语能像我说法语那样好，也够了。）

103 **it is and it isnt** = it is satisfactory and it isnt satisfactory. 英语讲得好，但（同时）还不够；见下文说明。

105 **got her pronunciation all right** 把她的发音弄得很好了。all right 是宾语补足语，与 her pronunciation 有逻辑上的主谓关系，因而这个逻辑上的主谓结构也称作是 got 的复合宾语。

106 **what she pronounces** 她发音的内容是什么；她说的是什么话。

107 **and that's where –** 话未说完，被打断了。后面应有 it isn't satisfactory 之类的话，意思是“而不够之处就在于此”。

108 **parlormaid** 客厅女仆（负责餐桌侍候和开门、通报来客等）。 **announcing guests** 通报客人来到。

109 **Mrs and Miss Eynsford** [ˈeɪnsfəd] **Hill** 就是第一幕开始时剧院散了场在教堂的廊下躲雨和叫车子的母女俩，当时和她们一起的还有这老太太的儿子 Freddy。他们就是在那里和 Higgins，Pickering 及 Eliza 相遇的。Eynsford Hill 是复姓。

110 **Oh Lord!** 天哪！表示惊奇的感叹语，也作 Good Lord! 或 Lord God! 等。 **makes for** 走向，向……走去。

113 **well bred** 教养良好的。也写作 well-bred。bred 是 breed 的过去分词。

114 **the habitual** [həˈbɪtʃʊəl] **anxiety** [æŋˈzaɪəti] **of straitened means** （长年因）经济拮据（而养成）的习惯性的忧心忡忡。Enysford Hill 是个破落户。

115 **acquired a gay air** 学会了作出一副明朗快乐的神气。 **at home in society** 善于交际。 **at home** 自在；熟练。society 作“社会”、“社交”解，都是不可数名词。

116 **the bravado** [brəˈvɑːdəʊ] **of genteel** [dʒenˈtiːl] **poverty** 大户人家破落后（强装出来的）浮夸的大胆无畏；穷酸的强作放浪。

119 **She shakes.** = She shakes hands with Mrs Higgins.

120 **My son Henry.** = This is my son Henry.

MRS EYNSFORD HILL Your celebrated son! I have so longed to meet you, Professor Higgins.

HIGGINS [*gumly, making no movement in her direction*] Delighted. [*He backs against the piano and bows brusquely.*]

MISS EYNSFORD HILL [*going to him with confident familiarity*] How do you do?

HIGGINS [*staring at her*] Ive seen you before somewhere. I havnt the ghost of a notion where; but Ive heard your voice. [*drearily*] It doesnt matter. Youd better sit down.

MRS HIGGINS I'm sorry to say that my celebrated son has no manners. You mustnt mind him.

MISS EYSNFORD HILL [*gaily*] I dont. [*She sits in the Elizabethan chair.*]

MRS EYSNFORD HILL [*a little bewildered*] Not at all. [*She sits on the ottoman between her daughter and Mrs Higgins, who has turned her chair away from the writing-table.*]

HIGGINS Oh, have I been rude? I didnt mean to be.

He goes to the central window, through which, with his back to the company, he contemplates the river and the flowers in Battersea Park on the opposite bank as if they were a frozen desert.

The parlormaid returns, ushering in Pickering.

THE PARLORMAID Colonel Pickering. [*She withdraws.*]

PICKERING How do you do, Mrs Higgins?

121 **longed to meet you** 一直盼望见到你；久仰。

123 **making no movement in her direction** 不向她（Mrs Enysford Hill）的方向移动；没有迎上前去。 **Delighted.** = I'm delighted to meet you. Higgins 对刚介绍给他认识的客人这样简单草率（curt）地打招呼，显然不礼貌。

124 **backs against the piano** 背靠钢琴。 **bows** [baʊz] **brusquely**[ˈbru:skli] 粗鲁地点点头。注意：作“鞠躬”和“船头”解的 bow 都读 [baʊ]，作“弓”解的 bow 读 [bəʊ]，词源各不相同。

125 **with confident familiarity** 以大胆亲昵的态度（表示惯于交际）。

127 **Ive seen you before** 我以前见过你；也可作 I saw you before。 **I havnt the ghost of a notion** 毫无概念；一点印象都没有。 **the ghost of** 一点儿，只用于否定意义，如不能说 I have the ghost of a notion.

128 **where** = where Ive seen you before. **Ive heard your voice** 我听过你说话的声音。当然此处不是“我听见了你的声音”的意思。

130 **has no manners** 没有礼貌。 **manners** 礼貌；用复数。

132 **I dont.** = I dont mind him. 我不怪他；我不介意他（没有礼貌）。 **sits in the Elizabethan chair** 注意 chair 前介词用 in，不用 on。比较：下文 on the ottoman。

133 **Not at all.** 重复并强调她女儿已经说的 I dont (mind him)。

134 **turned her chair away from the writing-table** 把原来对着写字台的椅子转过来。

136 **I didnt mean to be.** 我不是有意无礼。后面省略了 rude。

137 **with his back to the company** 背向着在一起的人们。 **company** 同伴们。

138 **contemplates the river** 凝视着（泰晤士）河。 **Battersea** [ˈbætəsɪ] **Park on the opposite bank** 对岸的 Battersea 公园。Battersea Park 是在伦敦 Battersea 区靠泰晤士河的大花园，对岸就是 Mrs Higgins 家所在的 Chelsea Embankment。

139 **as if they were a frozen desert** （Higgins 心不在焉，因而泰晤士河对岸公园中的花木，在他看来）仿佛是一片沉寂的沙漠。 **as if** 仿佛，它所引起的从句用虚拟语气。注意：作“沙漠（的）”解的 desert 读 [ˈdezət]，作“功过”和“舍弃”解的 desert 读 [dɪˈzɜ:t]，词源各不相同。

140 **ushering** [ˈʌʃərɪŋ] **in Pickering** 引进 Pickering。

141 **Colonel Pickering** 这里通报 Pickering 上校来到，不是在称呼客人。

MRS HIGGINS So glad youve come. Do you know Mrs Eysnford Hill – Miss Eysnford Hill? [*Exchange of bows. The Colonel brings the Chipendale chair a little forward between Mrs Hill and Mrs Higgins, and sits down.*]

PICKERING Has Henry told you what weve come for?

HIGGINS [*over his shoulder*] We were interrupted: damn it!

MRS HIGGINS Oh Henry, Henry, really!

MRS EYNSFORD HILL [*half rising*] Are we in the way?

MRS HIGGINS [*rising and making her sit down again*] No, no. You couldnt have come more fortunately: we want you to meet a friend of ours.

HIGGINS [*turning hopefully*] Yes, by George! We want two or three people. Youll do as well as anybody else.

The parlormaid returns, ushering Freddy.

THE PARLORMAID Mr Eynsford Hill.

HIGGINS [*almost audibly, past endurance*] God of Heaven! another of them.

FREDDY [*shaking hands with Mrs Higgins*] Ahdedo?

MRS HIGGINS Very good of you to come. [*introducing*] Colonel Pickering.

FREDDY [*bowing*] Ahdedo?

MRS HIGGINS I dont think you know my son, Professor Higgins.

FREDDY [*going to Higgins*] Ahdedo?

143 **So glad** = I'm so glad.

144 **Exchange of bows.** 相互鞠躬。这是单部（one-element）的名词句。

147 **what weve come for** 我们为什么而来的；我们来的目的。

148 **over his shoulder** （回头）隔着自己的肩膀（对 Pickering 说）。over one's (或 somebody's) shoulder 可另举一谚语为例：Think of the devil and he is looking over your shoulder (也作 and he will appear). 犹言"说曹操，曹操就到"。

149 **really!** 你真的是！你竟然说出 damn it 这样粗俗的诅咒话来！

150 **half rising** 欠身要站起（准备告辞的样子）而尚未完全站起。 **Are we in the way?** 我们在这里有妨碍吗？（因为听见 Higgins 说 We were interrupted。）

151 **making her sit down again** 拉她（Mrs Eynsford Hill）重新坐下。 **You couldnt have come more fortunately** 你来得不能再巧了（来得正巧）。这里的 fortunately 犹如"Fortunately you have come."中的 Fortunately，是修饰全句，而不是修饰 have come，因此 fortunate 指的不是 You，而是 You have come 这件事。

155 **Youll do as well as anybody else.** 你们（Eynsford Hill 母女俩）像任何人一样顶用。 **do** 这里是"行"、"应付得了"的意思。 **as well as** 像……一样好；这里不是作"也"、"又"解的习语。

156 **ushering Freddy** 引进 Freddy。ushering 和上面看到的 ushering in 意思相同。 **Freddy** Mrs Eynsford Hill 的儿子，见前。

158 **past endurance** = being past endurance. **God of Heaven!** 老天爷！感叹语。 **another of them** = there's (或 there comes) another of them. 又来了一个 Eynsford Hill 家的人！

160 **Ahdedo?** = How d'ye do? (How do you do?)

161 **Very good of you to come.** = It's very good of you to come. 多蒙光临。

164 **I dont think you know my son, Professor Higgins.** 你不认识我的儿子 Higgins 教授吧。这里 know 不是"知道"的意思；know my son, Professor Higgins 不是"知道我儿子 Higgins 教授的名字"，而是"认识我儿子 Higgins 教授"。说"知道某人（的名字）"、"知道有某人"该用 know of。例如：I know of him, but I dont know him (personally). 我知道他（知道有这么个人），但并不认识他（和他有过交往）。

HIGGINS [*looking at him much as if he were a pickpocket*] I'll take my oath Ive met you before somewhere. Where was it?

FREDDY I dont think so.

HIGGINS [*resignedly*] It dont matter, anyhow. Sit down.

He shakes Freddy's hand, and almost slings him on to the ottoman with his face to the window; then comes round to the other side of it.

HIGGINS Well, here we are, anyhow! [*He sits down on the ottoman next Mrs Eynsford Hill, on her left.*] And now, what the devil are we going to talk about until Eliza comes?

MRS HIGGINS Henry: you are the life and soul of the Royal Society's soirée; but really youre rather trying on more commonplace occasions.

HIGGINS Am I? Very sorry. [*beaming suddenly*] I suppose I am, you know. [*uproariously*] Ha, ha!

MISS EYNSFORD HILL [*who considers Higgins quite eligible matrimonially*] I sympathize. *I* havnt any small talk. If people would only be frank and say what they really think!

HIGGINS [*relapsing into gloom*] Lord forbid!

MRS EYNSFORD HILL [*taking up her daughter's cue*] But why?

---

166 **much as if he were a pickpocket** 在很大程度上仿佛他是个扒手；完全当他是扒手似的。 **much** 修饰 as if；as if 引起的从句用虚拟语气，所以用 he were，在现代口语中也用 he was。 **I'll take my oath** 我发誓。oath 后面省

略连词 that。说“发誓”，take an oath，make an oath，swear an oath 都可以。

169 **resignedly** [rɪˈzaɪnɪdli] 无可奈何地。注意 -edly 的发音。 **It dont matter** 是 It doesnt matter 之讹。英美人说话常有这种错误；Higgins 身为语言专家，偶尔也不守语言规则。 **anyhow** 无论如何。这里是说“无论以前有没有见过面，反正（不成问题）”。

170 **almost slings him on to the ottoman with his face to the window** （Higgins）脸朝着窗户（看也不朝 Freddy 看），（和 Freddy 握了手）几乎把他推到了厚垫长凳上去。

171 **comes round to the other side of it** 绕到它（厚垫长凳）的另一边。

173 **here we are** 我们都在这里了；人都到了。

174 **next Mrs Eynsford Hill, on her left** 在 Mrs Eynsford Hill 的左侧旁边。这两个介词短语，都修饰 sits。 **what the devil** 诅咒语。the devil 加强 what 的语气，没有具体意思；见前注。

176 **the life and soul of the Royal Society's soirées** [ˈswɑːreɪz] 皇家学会晚会上的台柱。 **life and soul** 生命和灵魂，比喻众望所归的中坚分子。 **the Royal Society** 英国皇家学会，创立于 1645 年，是英国科学家的组织，犹如我国的“科学院”，它的正式名称为 The Royal of London for Improving Natural Knowledge。

177 **trying** 使人难受的；是形容词。 **on more commonplace occasions** [əˈkeɪʒnz] 在（与皇家学会晚会相比而言）较为平常的场合中。

179 **Am I?** = Am I rather trying on more commonplace occasions? 后面 I suppose I am 的 am 后面省略同样的表语。 **beaming** beam 原义“发光”，转义“微笑”。

181 **considers Higgins quite eligible** [ˈelɪdʒəbl] **matrimonially** [ˌmætrɪˈməʊnɪəli] 认为 Higgins 在婚姻上是十分合格的；认为 Higgins 是个可取的结婚对象。consider + 宾语 + 宾语补足语，在宾语补足语前面不用 as；但如将 consider 换用同义的 regard，则宾语补足语前须用 as，如 She regards him as eligible.

182 **If people would only be frank and say what they really think!** 但愿人们坦率说出他们所真正想的！ If only（或 If ... only ...）这个句型——虚拟语气的条件从句没有主句而独立存在，从“只要……（省略表示“就好了”意思的主句）”转而表示“但愿……！”

184 **relapsing into gloom** 又阴郁起来。 **Lord forbid!** 或作 God forbid! 这是表示祈愿的虚拟语气，= May Lord (或 God) forbid! 愿上帝禁止！ 上帝保佑，不要如此！

185 **taking up her daughter's cue** 接着她女儿的话往下说；为女儿帮腔。

HIGGINS What they think they ought to think is bad enough, Lord knows; but what they really think would break up the whole show. Do you suppose it would be really agreeable if I were to come out now with what *I* really think?

MISS EYNSFORD HILL [*gaily*] Is it so very cynical?

HIGGINS Cynical! Who the dickens said it was cynical? I mean it wouldnt be decent.

MRS EYNSFORD HILL [*seriously*] Oh! I'm sure you dont mean that, Mr Higgins.

HIGGINS You see, we're all savages, more or less. We're supposed to be civilized and cultured – to know all about poetry and philosophy and art and science, and so on; but how many of us know even the meanings of these names?[*to Miss Hill*] What do you know of poetry? [*to Mrs Hill*] What do you know of science? [*indicating Freddy*] What does he know of art or science or anything else? What the devil do you imagine I know of philosophy?

MRS HIGGINS [*warningly*] Or of manners, Henry?

THE PARLORMAID [*opening the door*] Miss Doolittle. [*She withdraws.*]

HIGGINS [*rising hastily and running to Mrs Higgins*] Here she is, mother. [*He stands on tiptoe and makes signs over his mother's head to Eliza to indicate to her which lady is her hostess.*]

186 **What they think they ought to think is bad enough** 他们认为他们应该想的已经够糟（实际想的更糟了）。What = That which；they ought to think 前面省略（但不可加入）连词 that；第一个 think 的宾语是 which。which they ought to think 是修饰 that 的定语从句。兹用方括弧表示定语从句，表解如下，更为清楚：That [which they think they ought to think] is bad enough.

187 **Lord knows** = God knows.（只有）上帝知道；天晓得。 **what they really think would break up the whole show** 他们实际上所想的（倘说出来）势必拆穿表面一套的全部西洋镜，大煞风景。 **what** (=that which) **they really think** 他们实际上所想的；与上面"他们认为应该想的"对比。这里用 would 是虚拟语气，省略一个 if they were to come out with it 或 if it were spoken out 之类的条件从句。 **break up the whole show** 也作 give the (whole) show away；拆穿西洋镜；泄露内幕。

188 **it would be really agreeable** 那会是真正令人愉快的，it 指 if – 从句中所讲的事。 **if I were to come out now with what *I* really think** 假如现在我把实际所想的说出来。 **come out with** 发表；说出；是习语。

190 **Is it so very cynical** [ˈsɪnɪkl]**?** 那是非常尖酸刻薄的吗？ it 指 what you really think；cynical 含有"玩世不恭"、"愤世嫉俗"的意思。

191 **the dickens** 是 the devil 的委婉说法，和 the devil 一样加在 who，what 等后面作加强语气，没有具体意思。 **it wouldnt be decent** [ˈdiːsnt] 那将是不登大雅之堂的。decent 是"合乎礼仪的"之意。

193 **mean that** 指不登大雅之堂那个意思。that 是代词，指 that it wouldnt be decent。

195 **more or less** 或多或少地；不同程度地；修饰 ’re (= are)。 **We’re supposed to be** 我们被认为是……；我们算是……

203 **warningly** 用警告、告诫地口气（说）。 **Or of manners** 承接上文，与 of philosophy 并列。Higgins 自己说"看我懂什么哲学"，Mrs Higgins 接上去问他"又懂什么礼貌"，是用挖苦的口吻训斥儿子。

205 **Here she is, mother.** 妈妈，她（Miss Doolittle，即 Liza）来了。

206 **on tiptoe** 踮着脚尖。 **makes signs over his mother’s head** 从他母亲头顶后面打暗号。

207 **to indicate to her which lady is her hostess** [ˈhəʊstəs] 指给她（Eliza）看哪一位是她的女主人。 **hostess** 聚会或宴会的女主人。

Eliza, who is exquisitely dressed, produces an impression of such remarkable distinction and beauty as she enters that they all rise, quite fluttered. Guided by Higgins's signals, she comes to Mrs Higgins with studied grace.

LIZA [*speaking with pedantic correctness of pronunciation and great beauty of tone*] How do you do, Mrs Higgins? [*She gasps slightly in making sure of the H in Higgins, but is quite successful.*] Mr Higgins told me I might come.

MRS HIGGINS [*cordially*] Quite right: I'm very glad indeed to see you.

PICKERING How do you do, Miss Doolittle?

LIZA [*shaking hands with him*] Colonel Pickering, is it not?

MRS EYNSFORD HILL I feel sure we have met before, Miss Doolittle. I remember your eyes.

LIZA How do you do? [*She sits down on the ottoman gracefully in the place just left vacant by Higgins.*]

MRS EYNSFORD HILL [*introducing*] My daughter Clara.

LIZA How do you do?

CLARA [*impulsively*] How do you do? [*She sits down on the ottoman beside Eliza, devouring her with her eyes.*]

FREDDY [*coming to their side of the ottoman*] Ive certainly had the pleasure.

MRS EYNSFORD HILL [*introducing*] My son Freddy.

LIZA How do you do?

208 **is exquisitely** [ɪkˈskwɪzɪtli] **dressed** 穿得美丽大方。注意：dress exquisitely 是指经常穿得美丽大方；而 is exquisitely dressed 是指在某一时如此，这个 dressed 可看作已由过去分词衍化为形容词。 **produces an impression of such remarkable distinction and beauty** 给人以一种异常高贵和美丽的印象。

209 **as she enters** 她进来的时候。修饰 produces。 **that they all rise, quite fluttered** 以致他们全部都站了起来，大为震动。that 与前面 such 相呼应。quite fluttered = being quite fluttered.

210 **Guided by Higgins's signals** = Being Guided by Higgins's signals. 受着 Higgins（指点哪个是女主人）的信号的引导；依他的指点。

211 **studied grace** 用心做出来的优美风姿。studied 是形容词。

212 **pedantic correctness of pronunciation** 学究式的正确发音；发音正确到过分拘泥的程度。

213 **gasps** [gɑːsps] **slightly in making sure of the H in Higgins** 为了一定要把 Higgins 中的 [h] 音发好，（吃力得）微微喘气。Liza 原来的伦敦土音基本不发 [h] 音，现在硬要发清楚，十分吃力。 **make sure** 弄确实；是习语；后面可接 of 引起的介词短语，也可接 that – 从句；接 that – 从句时，还可作"确信"解。

216 **Quite right** 对！好！也作 Right 或 Right you are，都是英国口语中表示同意的常用语。

219 **Colonel Pickering, is it not?** = Is it not Colonel Pickering? 这位（你）不是 Pickering 上校吗?

223 **just left vacant** = which has just been left vacant. 刚被让空的。

227 **beside Eliza** 在 Eliza 旁边。 **beside** 在现代英语中只作介词，意思是"在……旁边"；besides 的意思是"（除……之外）还有"，可作介词，也可作副词，这两个词不要混淆。 **devouring** [dɪˈvaʊərɪŋ] **her with her eyes** 用她（Clara）的眼睛吞噬她（Liza）；Clara 拼命看着 Liza。

228 **Ive certainly had the pleasure.** = Ive certainly had the pleasure of seeing (= meeting) you before. 我肯定曾经有幸见过你。

Freddy bows and sits down in the Elizabethan chair, infatuated.

HIGGINS [*suddenly*] By George, yes: it all comes back to me! [*They stare at him.*] Covent Garden! [*lamentably*] What a damned thing!

MRS HIGGINS Henry, please! [*He is about to sit on the edge of the table.*] Dont sit on my writing-table: youll break it.

HIGGINS [*sulkily*] Sorry.

He goes to the divan, stumbling into the fender and over the fire-irons on his way, extricating himself with muttered imprecations; and finishing his disastrous journey by throwing himself so impatiently on the divan that he almost breaks it. Mrs Higgins looks at him, but controls herself and says nothing.

A long and painful pause ensues.

MRS HIGGINS [*at last, conversationally*] Will it rain, do you think?

LIZA The shallow depression in the west of these islands is likely to move slowly in an easterly direction. There are no indications of any great change in the barometrical situation.

FREDDY Ha, ha! How awfully funny!

---

232 **infatuated** [ɪnˈfætʃʊeɪtɪd] = being infatuated. 着了迷；迷醉。

233 **By George, yes: it all come back to me!** 真是的，对了，这件事全部回到我

头脑里来了；一切我都记起来了。 By George 的确，表示感叹和发誓。

234 **Covent Garden!** 原来是在 Covent Garden（一起避雨时相见过的）；见第一幕。 **What a damned thing!**（又碰到 Eynsford Hill 家这些人）多倒霉的事！

236 **please!** 这里表示劝阻，叫 Higgins 不要说无礼的话。 **is about to sit** 正要坐（而还未坐）。

239 **stumbling into the fender and over the fire-irons on his way** 在他（走向靠壁长榻）去的途中绊着壁炉的围栏和火钳。stumble into（绊着）和 run into（撞着）的 into 并不完全是"进去"的意思。

240 **extricating** [ˈekstrɪkeɪtɪŋ] **himself with muttered imprecations** 低声诅咒着（从跌跌绊绊中）把自己摆脱出来。

241 **finishing his disastrous journey by throwing himself so impatiently on the divan** 那么不耐烦地往长榻上猛地一倒，以结束他（跌跌撞撞地走向长榻的）灾难的一段路。这里用 journey，多少有滑稽的意味。so 和后面 that he almost breaks it（以致他几乎把长榻压坏了）呼应。

243 **controls herself** 控制她自己；控制自己不以为然的感情。

244 **painful pause** 使人难堪的沉默（大家谈话中止）。

245 **conversationally** 作为攀谈地。 **Will it rain, do you think?** = Do you think it will rain?

246 **The shallow depression in the west of these islands is likely to move slowly in an easterly direction.** 这些岛（指 the British Isles）上西部轻微的低气压似乎将缓慢东移。Liza 不会谈天，而偏要学斯文，结果说出来的乃是气象预报的口吻，下一句也是如此，无怪惹人笑话。 easterly 除用于风指"来自东方的"外，都作"向东的"解。注意：in an easterly direction 一语中用 an，不用 the。

247 **There are no indications of any great change in the barometrical** [ˌbærəˈmetrɪkəl] **situation.** 气压情况没有任何巨大变化的迹象，完全是天气预报的口吻。 **barometrical** 气压表上的；气压上的。注意这一类词的名词和形容词的重音移位。

249 **How awfully funny!** = How awfully funny it is! 这（她说的话）多好笑！ **awfully** = very；是口语，读作 [ˈɔːfli]；比较：作"可怕地"解时读 [ˈɔːfəli]。

LIZA What is wrong with that, young man? I bet I got it right.

FREDDY Killing!

MRS EYNSFORD HILL I'm sure I hope it wont turn cold. Theres so much influenza about. It runs right through our whole family regularly every spring.

LIZA [*darkly*] My aunt died of influenza: so they said.

MRS EYNSFORD HILL [*clicks her tongue sympathetically*] !!!

LIZA [*in the same tragic tone*] But it's my belief they done the old woman in.

MRS HIGGINS [*puzzled*] Done her in?

LIZA Y-e-e-e-es, Lord love you! Why should she die of influenza? She come through diphtheria right enough the year before. I saw her with my own eyes. Fairly blue with it, she was. They all thought she was dead; but my father he kept ladling gin down her throat til she came to so sudden that she bit the bowl off the spoon.

MRS EYNSFORD HILL [*startled*] Dear me!

LIZA [*piling up the indictment*] What call would a woman with that strength in her have to die of influenza? What become

---

250 **What is wrong with that** 那个话有什么不对；说错了什么。注意：wrong 和 the matter 同义，后面也都用 with。 **young man** 小伙子；作为称呼，不客气。 **I bet I got it right.** 我敢打赌，我说得对。

251 **Killing!** 绝妙的！妙极！这是口语，作形容词。

252 **I'm sure I hope it wont turn cold.** 我希望天气不要转冷。 I'm sure 口头常用语，只表示“猜测”，有“我看”之意，并不作“我肯定”解；说“我肯定”，用 I'm certain。it 泛指天气。

253 **influenza** [ˌɪnflʊˈenzə] 流行性感冒；口语中常简称 flu。 **about** 在周围；这里作“流行”解；是副词。**It runs right through our whole family** 它(流行性感冒)把我全家整个儿染上。 **runs through** 贯穿。 **right** 完全地；彻底地。

255 **darkly** 语气深沉。 **died of** 因……（病）而死。 so they said 他们这么说。

256 **clicks her tongue** 咂嘴（发出啧啧声）。

257 **done the old woman in** 弄死了这个老太婆（她姑母）。done 是 did 之讹；do in 是俚语，是“谋害”、“搞垮”的意思。从这里开始，Liza 说话越来越不“文雅”，满口伦敦土话，完全显露本来面目。

260 **Lord love you!** 一般说 Lord (或 God) bless you! 感叹语；上帝保佑！天呐！ **Why should she die of influenza?** 她怎么会死于感冒呢？照语法该说 Why should she have died of influenza? 因为讲的是过去的事。

261 **come through diphtheria** [dɪfˈθɪərɪə] **right enough** 患了白喉也很好活过来了。**come through** 经历……而仍活着；渡过。这里 come 是 had come 之讹。**right** 好好地；顺利地。 **enough** 修饰 right。 **the year before** 在（她死的）前一年，注意：以过去为基点讲以前用 before；以现在为基点讲以前用 ago。

262 **I saw her with my own eyes** 我亲眼看见她（当时的样子）。 **Fairly blue with it, she was.** = She was fairly blue with it. 她病得已经不大有希望了。**Fairly** 相当；简直。 **blue** 脸色发青的。it 指 diphtheria。

263 **my father he** 这个 he 是多余的，比较：汉语口语中有时也说“我父亲他才真是个学者。”这个“他”同样是多余的。 **kept ladling** [ˈleɪdlɪŋ] **gin** [dʒɪn] **down her throat til she came to** 不断把白酒往她喉咙里舀，直到她苏醒过来(才不舀)。 **ladling** 舀；名词 ladle 是个“勺子”。 **gin** 杜松子酒，一种烈性白酒。**down** 这里是介词。 **til** 是 till 的古体，犹如 shew 是 show 的古体，但萧伯纳喜欢这些拼法，这是作家的癖好（mannerism）。 **came to** 恢复生机；苏醒；是习语；与 come to oneself 和 come to senses 同义。

264 **bit the bowl off the spoon** 把勺子盛汤的部分咬断了下来。

266 **Dear me!** （惊叹语）啊呀！喔唷！

267 **piling up the indictment** [ɪnˈdaɪtmənt] 添加控诉；继续控诉。 **What call would a woman with that strength in her have to die of influenza?** 一个力气那么大的女人怎么会因流感而死呢？ **call** 理由；必要；用于否定或疑问句中；这里是 have 的宾语，全句的意思是 She would have no call to die of influenza. 她不可能因流感而死。

of her new straw hat that should have come to me? Somebody pinched it; and what I say is, them as pinched it done her in.

MRS EYNSFORD HILL What does doing her in mean?

HIGGINS [*hastily*] Oh, thats the new small talk. To do a person in means to kill them.

MRS EYNSFORD HILL [*to Eliza, horrified*] You surely dont believe that your aunt was killed?

LIZA Do I not? Them she lived with would have killed her for a hat-pin, let alone a hat.

MRS EYNSFORD HILL But it cant have been right for your father to pour spirits down her throat like that. It might have killed her.

LIZA Not her. Gin was mother's milk to her. Besides, he'd poured so much down his own throat that he knew the good of it.

MRS EYNSFORD HILL Do you mean that he drank?

LIZA Drank! My word! Something chronic.

MRS EYNSFORD HILL How dreadful for you!

---

268 **What become of her new straw hat** 她的新草帽怎么了（弄到哪里去了）。become应作 became。**that should have come to me** 那(草帽)应该归我所有。这是虚拟语气，表示过去的与事实相反，即“应该归我而实际没有归我”。

270 **pinched** 原义作“拧”、“挤轧”等解；这里是俚语，是“盗窃”、“不告而取”的意思。 **them as pinched it done her in** 应作 they (或 those) who pinched it did her in 偷草帽的人（们）杀了她。前面说 Somebody 而这里又说 them，其实 Liza 心中只想到一个人（没想到可能有一个以上的人）。

272 **What does doing her in mean?** 清楚些，应写作 What does 'doing her in' mean? 下文 To do a person in means to kill them 同。

273 **new small talk** 新式的敷衍聊天。Higgins 讽刺敷衍聊天。 **To do a person in means to kill them.** them 是 him 之讹。

275 **to Eliza, horrified** 对 Eliza，惊讶地（说）。horrified 是指说话人 Mrs Eynsford Hill，并不是修饰 Eliza 的。horrify 原义“使惊恐”；口语中作“使震惊”、“使非常厌恶”解。

277 **Do I not?** = Do I not believe that my aunt was killed! 我不相信吗！（哪有不相信之理？）**Them she lived with** = They (或 Those) (whom) she lived with = They (或 Those) with whom she lived. **would have killed her for a hat-pin** 会为了（要她）帽子上的一枚别针而杀害她。这是虚拟语气，表示可能发生那样的事而未必真的曾经发生过。

278 **let alone a hat** 不要说是一顶帽子了；为了一顶帽子，更会杀害她了。 let alone 更不用说；何况；是习语；它后面还可跟名词以外的词，如 He cant read, let alone write. 他读也读不来，更谈不上写了。

279 **it cant have been right for your father to pour spirits down her throat like that** 你父亲那样把烈酒往她喉咙里灌不可能是对的（总也不对）。can 接完成不定式表示过去的可能。 **spirits** 烈性酒；常用复数。

280 **It might have killed her.** 这（指那样灌烈酒）会把她弄死的。这是虚拟语气；实际未必弄死。

281 **Not her.** （即使可能弄死别人，但）不可能弄死她。 **Gin was mother's milk to her** 杜松子酒对她（好比）是母乳。

282 **the good of it** 它（杜松子酒）的好处。

283 **drank** 喝酒。

284 **My word!** 哎呀！感叹语；也作 Upon my word。但 Upon my word 另有一个说法，= My word upon it，是“我保证这是真的”的意思。 **Something chronic** [ˈkrɒnɪk] 可理解为 (He drank) something chronically，（他喝得）相当厉害。 **Something** 俚语中作副词，= rather，见前注。 **chronic** 原义“长期的”、“慢性的”；这里作“剧烈的”解，是英国用法。这里的主语和谓语动词都省略，成了单部句。

285 **How dreadful for you!** = How dreadful it was for you! **dreadful** 原义“可怕的”，转义“糟透的”。

LIZA Not a bit. It never did him no harm what I could see. But then he did not keep it up regular. [*cheerfully*] On the burst, as you might say, from time to time. And always more agreeable when he had a drop in. When he was out of work, my mother used to give him fourpence and tell him to go out and not come back until he'd drunk himself cheerful and loving-like. Theres lots of women has to make their husbands drunk to make them fit to live with. [*now quite at her ease*] You see, it's like this. If a man has a bit of a conscience, it always takes him when he's sober; and then it makes him low-spirited. A drop of booze just takes that off and makes him happy. [*to Freddy, who is in convulsions of suppressed laughter*] Here! What are you sniggering at?

FREDDY The new small talk. You do it so awfully well.

LIZA If I was doing it proper, what was you laughing at? [*to Higgins*] Have I said anything I oughtnt?

MRS HIGGINS [*interposing*] Not at all, Miss Doolittle.

LIZA Well, thats a mercy, anyhow. [*expansively*] What I always say is –

HIGGINS [*rising and looking at his watch*] Ahem!

---

286 **Not a bit.** = Not at all. 一点不（糟）。 **It never did him no harm what I could see.** 我看不出这（喝酒）对他有什么害处。 **never did him no harm** 是"双重否定"，应作 never did him any harm。 **what** 是 that 之讹；这是关系代词 that 的一种习惯用法，如 He has never done it, that I know. 据我所知，他

从没有做过这件事。

287 **keep it up regular** 经常保持这个（喝酒的）习惯；经常喝酒。 **On the burst** = On the bust. 痛饮；闹饮。前面省略主语和谓语动词 He went。 **as you might say** 如你们所说的；用你们的话来说；指 On the burst 这句话。

288 **from time to time** 有时；时常；是习语。 **And always more agreeable** = And he was always more agreeable.

289 **had a drop in** 喝了一点酒；喝过酒；也是“喝醉”的一种轻飘的说法。

290 **not come back** 接 tell him 后，与 to go out 并列，因此应作 not to come back.

291 **drunk himself cheerful** 使自己喝得开心了。cheerful 是宾语补足语，himself cheerful 构成复合宾语。 **loving-like** 对人亲爱（的样子）的；与 cheerful 并列。 **-like** 构词成分；见前注。

292 **Theres lots of women has to make their husbands drunk.** 应作 There're lots of women who have to make their husbands drunk. drunk 是宾语补足语，their husbands drunk 构成复合宾语。

293 **to make them fit to live with** 以使他们可以好好地相处。 **at her ease** 舒畅；自在；也作 at ease。

294 **has a bit of a conscience** [ˈkɒnʃəns] 有点内疚。 **conscience** 良心。a good conscience 问心无愧；a bad conscience 心中有鬼。 **it always takes him** 它（内疚）总缠住他；使他终日不安。

295 **it makes him low-spirited** 它（指内疚缠住他一事）使他沮丧。 **A drop of booze just takes that off** （喝）一点酒正好驱散那（沮丧）。 **booze** 痛饮；也指“酒”。

297 **in convulsions of suppressed laughter** 在忍住的阵阵大笑中。 **convulsion** 捧腹大笑；用复数。

298 **sniggering** = snickering. 窃笑。

300 **proper** 规范英语应说 properly。 **what was you laughing at?** 你在笑什么? **laugh at** 可指单纯的笑，也可指“讥笑”；这里指前者。was 是 were 之讹。

301 **anything I oughtnt** = anything that I oughtnt to have said.

303 **thats a mercy** 那真是幸运；幸亏如此；这是口头常用语。 **expansively** 兴奋地；兴高采烈地。

305 **Ahem** （基本上发 [m] 音，也可发 [hm] 或 [əˈhem] 音）嗯；哼；引人注意或表示疑问，或在清嗓子时发出的声音。

LIZA [*looking round at him; taking the hint; and rising*] Well: I must go. [*They all rise. Freddy goes to the door.*] So pleased to have met you. Goodbye. [*She shakes hands with Mrs Higgins.*]

MRS HIGGINS Goodbye.

LIZA Goodbye, Colonel Pickering.

PICKERING Goodbye, Miss Doolittle. [*They shake hands.*]

LIZA [*nodding to the others*] Goodbye, all.

FREDDY [*opening the door for her*] Are you walking across the Park, Miss Doolittle? If so –

LIZA [*with perfectly elegant diction*] Walk! Not bloody likely. [*sensation*] I am going in a taxi. [*She goes out.*]

Pickering gasps and sits down. Freddy goes out on the balcony to catch another glimpse of Eliza.

MRS EYNSFORD HILL [*suffering from shock*] Well, I really cant get used to the new ways.

CLARA [*throwing herself discontentedly in to the Elizabethan chair*] Oh, it's all right, mamma, quite right. People will think we never go anywhere or see anybody if you are so old-fashioned.

MRS EYNSFORD HILL I daresay I am very old-fashioned; but I do hope you wont begin using that expression, Clara. I have got accustomed to hear you talking about men as rotters, and calling everything filthy and beastly; though I do think it horrible and unladylike. But this last is really too much. Dont you think so, Colonel Pickering?

306 **taking the hint** 懂得（Higgins 看表说“嗯”的）暗示。

307 **So pleased to have met you.** 遇到了你们很高兴；前面省略 I'm。这话用于分手时，见面时则用 (I'm) (so) pleased to meet you。

312 **Goodbye, all.** 大家再见；各位再见。

313 **the Park** 特指某一公园；这里可能就是对面的 Battersea Park（见 p.162）。

315 **with perfectly elegant diction** 用十分文静的声调。diction 一般指“措词”、“风格”；也指唱歌的“音调”，这里借用后一义。音调文雅，下文说出的却是粗话，妙极。 **Walk!** 走?（我才不走呢!）是 Walk? 的强调语气。 **Not bloody likely.** = It's not bloody likely that I should walk. 不见得我会走。bloody 是最犯忌讳的诅咒语，用以加强语气，没有具体意思。 **sensation** （bloody 一词使全场）震动。

318 **to catch another glimpse of Eliza** 去再看 Eliza 一眼。Freddy 已属意于她。

319 **suffering from shock** 受到震动而不安。 **get used to the new ways** 对新风尚习惯起来（听惯）。“新风尚”指说 bloody 那样的粗话等。

322 **it's all right, mamma, quite right** 这很好嘛，妈妈。it 泛指流行新风尚。quite right 与 all right 并列，重复强调说好。 **never go anywhere or see anybody** 从不到任何地方去，不会见任何人；没有社交活动；不见世面。这里的 or 也可用 nor，但在现代英语中不及用 or 普遍；如 anywhere 后加逗号，则 or 必须改用 nor。

324 **I daresay** 也作 I dare say。字面的意思是“我敢说”，实际只是“我想”、“大概”的意思。

325 **that expression** 指 bloody 这个词。

326 **hear you talking about men as rotters** 听你把 men 说作 rotters。 **rotters** （可恶或讨厌的）家伙；是英国俚语。 **hear you talking** 这里有“听你经常讲”的意思，而如用 hear you talk，便是“听见你在讲”的意思。

327 **calling everything filthy and beastly** 把什么都称为是 filthy 和 beastly。 **filthy** 不干净的，转义为“下流的”。 **beastly** 原义“野的”、“兽的”；口语中作“非常可恶的”、“糟透的”解。这些字眼都被认为是在文雅的语言中应该避免的，而偏流行于某些时髦人中间。 **I do think it horrible and unladylike.** 我确实认为那很讨厌且不像上等女孩该说的。it 并指上文 talking about men as rotters 和 calling everything filthy and beastly，把两者合起来视为一回事，所以不用 them。 **horrible** 其实这个词也不大“文雅”，却自己也溜出了口。

328 **this last** Liza 刚才最后说的这个词，指 bloody。

PICKERING Dont ask me. Ive been away in India for several years; and manners have changed so much that I sometimes dont know whether I'm at a respectable dinner-table or in a ship's forecastle.

CLARA It's all a matter of habit. Theres no right or wrong in it. Nobody means anything by it. And it's so quaint, and gives such a smart emphasis to things that are not in themselves very witty. I find the new small talk delightful and quite innocent.

MRS EYNSFORD HILL [*rising*] Well, after that, I think it's time for us to go.

Pickering and Higgins rise.

CLARA [*rising*] Oh yes: we have three at-homes to go to still. Goodbye, Mrs Higgins. Goodbye, Colonel Pickering. Goodbye, Professor Higgins.

HIGGINS [*coming grimly at her from the divan, and accompanying her to the door*] Goodbye. Be sure you try on that small talk at the three at-homes. Dont be nervous about it. Pitch it in strong.

CLARA [*all smiles*] I will. Goodbye. Such nonsense, all this early Victorian prudery!

HIGGINS [*tempting her*] Such damned nonsense!

CLARA Such bloody nonsense!

MRS EYNSFORD HILL [*convulsively*] Clara!

330 **away in India** 不在此地而在印度；和 absent in India 同义。

331 **dont know whether I'm at a respectable dinner-table or in a ship's forecastle** 不知我是在体面的宴席上，还是在船上的水手舱里；不知身在绅士淑女之间、还是在水手之间；分不清“高雅”和“粗俗”。 **forecastle** 读作 ['fəʊksl]，这个词可简作 fo'c'sle；艏楼水手舱；因而也用 the forecastle 作为水手们的集称，= crew。

334 **It's all a matter of habit.** 这全是习惯问题。这里连用三个 it，都是从指语言的雅俗转而指粗俗的语言。

335 **Nobody means anything by it.** 没有人说粗话有什么用意；说话粗俗并无恶意。 **quaint** 离奇的；妙。 **gives such a smart emphasis to things that are not in themselves very witty** 使本身原来并不怎么巧妙的话听来漂亮有劲。 **things** 可以泛指各种事物，这里指“话儿”。

339 **after that** 在说了那话之后；说完这话后。

342 **have three at-homes to go to still** 还要去赴三个社交会；还有三家人家今天是会客日，邀我们去作客。（她说这话表示她们交游广阔。）

345 **coming grimly at her** 一本正经地冲到她眼前。 **accompanying her to the door** 送她到门口。 **accompany somebody to** 陪送某人到（某处）去，已含有“去”的意思，所以不能说 accompany somebody to go to the airport 等。

346 **Be sure you try on** 你一定要试用。 **Be sure** 你一定要。后面省略连词 that。 **try on** 试用；试验；是习语；更常用于作“试穿”解；这里 try 是及物动词，on 是副词。

347 **Pitch it in strong.** 大干起来。 **Pitch in!** 努力（开始）干；是习语。strong = strongly.

348 **all smiles** 满面笑容的。 **Such nonsense, all this early Victorian prudery!** = All this Victorian prudery is such nonsense! 维多利亚王朝（1837-1901）早期的一本正经全是胡闹。 **early Victorian** 常写作 early-Victorian，维多利亚王朝早期的，指十九世纪上半叶；当时特别拘泥礼仪（prudery），举止言语多忌讳，迂腐不堪；所以后来 early-Victorian 也作“老式的”解。

350 **tempting** ['temptɪŋ] **her** 唆诱她（反对旧礼教）。

352 **convulsively** （听了）震惊得发抖地（说）。

CLARA Ha! Ha! [*She goes out radiant, conscious of being thoroughly up to date, and is heard descending the stairs in a stream of silvery laughter.*]

FREDDY [*to the heavens at large*] Well, I ask you – [*He gives it up, and comes to Mrs Higgins.*] Goodbye.

MRS HIGGINS [*shaking hands*] Goodbye. Would you like to meet Miss Doolittle again?

FREDDY [*eagerly*] Yes, I should, most awfully.

MRS HIGGINS Well, you know my days.

FREDDY Yes. Thanks awfully. Goodbye. [*He goes out.*]

MRS EYNSFORD HILL [*to Pickering*] It's no use. I shall never be able to bring myself to use that word.

PICKERING Don't. It's not compulsory, you know. Youll get on quite well without it.

MRS EYNSFORD HILL Only, Clara is so down on me if I am not positively reeking with the latest slang. Goodbye .

PICKERING Goodbye. [*They shake hands.*]

MRS EYNSFORD HILL [*to Mrs Higgins*] You mustnt mind Clara. [*Pickering, catching from her lowered tone that this is not meant for him to hear, discreetly joins Higgins at the window.*] We are so poor! And she gets so few parties, poor child! She doesnt quite know.

---

353 **She goes out radiant** 她走出去，神采焕发。radiant 是主语补足语。 **conscious of being thoroughly** ['θʌrəli] **up to date** 自己觉得十足地时髦了。conscious = being conscious，介词用 of。

354 **is heard descending the stairs in a stream of silvery laughter** 被听见在一连

串像银铃般清脆的笑声中走下楼梯。descending ... 这个分词短语是主语补足语，也算表语。

356 **to the heavens at large** 茫然对着天（说）；仰天长叹。 **the heavens** 复数，前面有 the，指“天”、“天空”。 **at large** 是习语，有“逍遥自在”、“详尽”、“笼统”等多种意义；这里指“广阔的（天）”。 **Well, I ask you –** 唉，我问你（指天）呵——没有说下去，下面当是“这是怎么回事？”之类的话。 **gives it up** 把这（问句）放弃了，话不说下去了。

360 **I should, most awfully.** = I should like to meet her again, most awfully. **awfully** 口语，原已有“十分”、“非常”的意思，再加 most（也是“十分”、“非常”的意思）修饰，热切之极。

361 **my days** = my at-home days. 我接待客人的日子（是哪几天）。

362 **Thanks awfully.** = Thanks very much. 十分感谢。Thanks = I thank you.

363 **It's no use.** （你们无论怎样对我，总是）没用；没办法。

364 **bring myself to uses that word** 使自己用那个词（指 bloody）； bloody 那个词说不出口。

365 **It's not compulsory** 这（使用 bloody 那个词）不是强迫的；不是非说 bloody 不可的。 **get on quite well without it** 不用那个词也可以很好地过下去；尽可不用它。

367 **Only** 只是；不过；是连词，多用于口语中。 **is so down on me** 那么怨恨我；对我有恶感；be down on 是习语。

368 **positively reeking with the latest slang** 确实散发着最新俚语的气味；满口难听的时髦俚语。 **reeking** 发出臭气；转义为“充满强烈的气息”。 **slang** “俚语”的总称，是不可数名词，如 This word is slang（不说 a slang）；a slang 是指“一种俚语”，如：Miners have a slang of their own. 矿工有矿工的俚语。

370 **You mustnt mind Clara.** 你千万别见怪我女儿 Clara（没规矩，学着说 bloody 等）。

371 **catching from her lowered tone that this is not meant for him to hear** 从她（说话）压低着的声音，知道这话不想让他听见。 **catching** 领会；理解。

372 **joins Higgins** 去和 Higgins 在一起。

373 **gets so few parties** 难得有机会参加聚会（或宴会）。Mrs Eynsford Hill 这话正戳穿她女儿 Clara 刚才说“还要去赴三个茶会”之类撑门面的谎言。**know** 懂。这里指“懂社交礼仪”。

[*Mrs Higgins, seeing that her eyes are moist, takes her hand sympathetically and goes with her to the door.*] But the boy is nice. Dont you think so?

MRS HIGGINS Oh, quite nice. I shall always be delighted to see him.

MRS EYNSFORD HILL Thank you, dear. Goodbye. [*She goes out.*]

HIGGINS [*eagerly*] Well? Is Eliza presentable? [*He swoops on his mother and drags her to the ottoman, where she sits down in Eliza's place with her son on her left.*]

Pickering returns to his chair on her right.

MRS HIGGINS You silly boy, of course she's not presentable. She's a triumph of your art and of her dressmaker's; but if you suppose for a moment that she doesnt give herself away in every sentence she utters, you must be perfectly cracked about her.

PICKERING But dont you think something might be done? I mean something to eliminate the sanguinary element from her conversation.

MRS HIGGINS Not as long as she is in Henry's hands.

HIGGINS [*aggrieved*] Do you mean that my language is improper?

MRS HIGGINS No, dearest: it would be quite proper – say on a canal barge; but it would not be proper for her at a garden party.

HIGGINS [*deeply injured*] Well I must say –

PICKERING [*interrupting him*] Come, Higgins: you must learn to

374 **her eyes are moist** 她（Mrs Eynsford Hill）的眼睛湿润（哭出来）了。

375 **the boy** 那男孩子，指 Freddy。

377 **quite nice** = the boy is quite nice.

380 **Is Eliza presentable** [prɪˈzentəbl]**?** Eliza 拿得出手吗？上得了场面吗？ **swoops on** 向……（像老鹰扑小鸡那样）猛扑上来；直冲到……上来。

385 **a triumph of your art and of her dressmaker's** 你的（语音训练）技术和她的裁缝的技术的成就。 **dressmaker** 做衣服（或童装）的裁缝。her dressmaker's = her dressmaker's art. **if you suppose for a moment** 要是你（即使）瞬间地想一想；你只要稍一想。

386 **doesnt give herself away in every sentence she utters** 她所说出来的每一句句子并不都露马脚。 **give herself away** 泄露秘密；露出卖花女本来的面目。Every sentence 后面省略关系代词 that（在 every ... 后面一般不用 which）。

387 **perfectly cracked about her** 完全对她发疯了。 **cracked** 原义"破碎了的"，转义为"神魂颠倒的"、"发疯的"。

388 **something might be done** 可以做些什么；可以采取补救办法，这是虚拟语气，省略 if we wanted to make sure that she would not give herself away 之类的条件从句。

389 **eliminate** [ɪˈlɪmɪneɪt] **the sanguinary** [ˈsæŋgwɪnəri] **element from her conversation** 把她谈话中恶俗的成分去掉。在英国有将 sanguinary（原义"血的"）来代替 bloody（原义也是"血的"）委婉说法，似乎的确"文雅"了，但何其怪也。

391 **Not as long as she is in Henry's hands.** 只要她在 Henry 手里，（bloody 这个词）总去不掉。（Henry Higgins 自己就经常说粗话。） **Not** = The sanguinary element cannot be eliminated from her conversation. **in Henry's hands** 在 Henry 的管教下。

393 **it would be quite proper – say on a canal** [kəˈnæl] **barge** 它（你的语言）只有在诸如运河的驳船上（使用）才算是很正当的。Mrs Higgins 认为她儿子的语言粗俗。 **say** 譬如说；例如；这是个插入语，= for instance。

396 **injured** 情感受伤的；受委屈的；过去分词作形容词。

know yourself. I havent heard such language as yours since we used to review the volunteers in Hyde Park twenty years ago.

HIGGINS [*sulkily*] Oh, well, if you say so, I suppose I dont always talk like a bishop.

MRS HIGGINS [*quieting Henry with a touch*] Colonel Pickering: will you tell me what is the exact state of things in Wimpole Street?

PICKERING [*cheerfully: as if this completely changed the subject*] Well, I have come to live there with Henry. We work together at my Indian Dialects; and we think it more convenient –

MRS HIGGINS Quite so. I know all about that: it's an excellent arrangement. But where does this girl live?

HIGGINS With us, of course. Where *should* she live?

MRS HIGGINS But on what terms? Is she a servant? If not, what is she?

PICKERING [*slowly*] I think I know what you mean, Mrs Higgins.

HIGGINS Well, dash me if I do! Ive had to work at the girl every day for months to get her to her present pitch. Besides, she's useful. She knows where my things are, and remembers my appointments and so forth.

MRS HIGGINS How does your housekeeper get on with her?

HIGGINS Mrs Pearce. Oh, she's jolly glad to get so much taken off her hands; for before Eliza came, she used to have to find things and remind me of my appointments. But she's got some silly bee in her bonnet about Eliza. She keeps saying

---

398 **know yourself** 知道你自己；有自知之明。

399 **used to review the volunteers** [ˌvɒlənˈtɪəz] **in Hyde** [haɪd] **Park** 过去常在海德公园检阅志愿兵。 **Hyde Park** 伦敦的大公园，因常在此举行政治性集会和发表政治性演说而著名。

402 **talk like a bishop** [ˈbɪʃəp] 像主教说话那样文雅。

403 **quieting Henry with a touch** 碰碰 Henry，叫他别说了。

404 **the exact state of things in Wimpole Street** 在 Wimpole Street 的确实情况。**things** 泛指事物、情况。Wimpole Street 是 Henry Higgins 的住所，Higgins 和 Pickering 在那里训练 Liza。

406 **work together at my Indian Dialects** 一起从事我所研究的印度方言的工作。也可能是一起从事我正在编写的《印度方言》一书的工作。萧伯纳对书名常既不斜写也不用引号。 **Indian** 印度的；印第安人的；此处指"印度的"；Pickering 是研究印度语言的，见第一幕。

408 **Quite so.** 正是这样；对；口语中常用语，有时单说一个 Quite!

410 **With us** = She lives with us.

411 **But on what terms?** 后面省略 does she live with you，她以什么关系和你们住在一起？ **terms** 条件；关系；用复数，前面介词用 on。 **If not, what is she?** 要不是佣人的话，她是什么呢？ If not = If she is not a servant. **What is she?** 她是什么身份（或职业）？

414 **Well, dash me if I do!** 唉，我可实在不懂！ dash 是 damn 的委婉说法。所以这句话的字面意思是"假如我懂，天打死我。" **work at the girl** 对这姑娘进行（训练）工作。

415 **get her to her present pitch** 使她达到她现在的程度。to her present pitch 是宾语补足语；her 和 to her present pitch 有逻辑上的主谓关系，构成 get 的复合宾语。

417 **and so forth** = and so on. 等等；诸如此类。

418 **get on with her** 同她相处。

419 **jolly** = very. 英国口语。 **get so much taken off her hands** 把许多（工作）从她手上摆脱掉。

421 **remind me of my appointments** 提醒我（什么时候有什么）约会。注意 remind 后面介词用 of。 **she's got some silly bee in her bonnet** 她胡思乱想。 **'s (= has) got** 口语，= has。 **have a bee in one's bonnet/head** 痴想；想痴；是习语。

'You dont *think*, sir': doesnt she, Pick ?

PICKERING Yes: thats the formula. 'You dont *think*, sir.' Thats the end of every conversation about Eliza.

HIGGINS As if I ever stop thinking the girl and her confounded vowels and consonants. I'm worn out, thinking about her, and watching her lips and her teeth and her tongue, not to mention her soul, which is the quaintest of the lot.

MRS HIGGINS You certainly are a pretty pair of babies, playing with your live doll.

HIGGINS Playing! The hardest job I ever tackled: make no mistake about that, mother. But you have no idea how frightfully interesting it is to take a human being and change her into a quite different human being by creating a new speech for her. It's filling up the deepest gulf that separates class from class and soul from soul.

PICKERING [*drawing his chair close to Mrs Higgins and bending over to her eagerly*] Yes, it's enormously interesting. I assure you, Mrs Higgins, we take Eliza very seriously. Every week – every day almost – there is some new change. [*closer again*] We keep

---

423 **You dont *think*** 你不想想；你不懂。Pick 是 Pickering 的昵称。欧美人名多昵称，例如称 Elizabeth 为 Eliza，Liza 等；但姓氏的昵称，除在极熟的亲友之外，一般不用，光用姓氏称呼人，不冠以 Mr 等，也只限极熟的亲友之间。

424 **thats the formula** 那（You dont *think*, sir）是（Mrs Pearce 的）公式般的惯用语。

426 **As if I ever stop thinking the girl and her confounded vowels and consonants.**

好像我不是一天到晚在为这姑娘和她那该死的元音和辅音（的发音）而操心似的（事实上我没有一刻不在操心）。As if I ever stop ...ing 直译是“好像我有停止……的任何时刻”，即“我不停地……着”。as if 引起的从句一般用虚拟语气，但现在口语中也用陈述语气，尤其是说 It looks (或 seems) as if ... 时，常用陈述语气。这里用 I stop，可以说是虚拟语气，也可以说是陈述语气，因为这里两者在形式上是相同的。

427 **worn out** 疲乏极了。

428 **not to mention** 更不用说；何况；这是习语，和前面已见的 let alone 用法相同。

429 **the quaintest of the lot** 所有（lips，teeth，tongue 和 soul）中最奇怪的。 **the lot** 全部。

430 **a pretty pair of babies** 可爱的一对婴儿；实际上 = a pair of pretty babies，一对可爱的婴儿。 **pretty** 常含反义，所以 pretty pair 犹如汉语说“这对活宝”。 **playing with your live** [laɪv] **doll** 玩着你们的活玩偶。玩某种游戏，用 play，有时用 play at，如 play (at) football (或 chess)；玩某种东西，用 play with，如 play with a ball，和这里的例子。注意：live 作形容词和副词时的发音。

432 **make no mistake** 别弄错；是习语。

433 **have no idea** 想不到。 **frightfully** 原义“可怕的”，口语作“非常的”解。

434 **take a human being** 拿来（指收留下来）一个人。类似的例子如 take pupils（收学生）。 **a human being** 一个作为生物的人；人类的一员。

435 **creating a new speech for her** 给她创造一种新的语言；使她学会高雅的语言。

436 **It's filling up the deepest gulf** 这（使她学会一种新语言这件事）填没了最深的鸿沟。 **filling** 这里是动名词；fill up the deepest gulf 是表语（或称主语补足语）；不该把 's (= is) filling 看作是进行式。 **separates class from class** 把（一个）阶级同（另一个）阶级分隔出来。 **class** 是可数名词，照理前面应有限定词（determinative），但这两个可数名词对偶地放在一起时，可不用限定词。

438 **bending over to her** 俯身过去对她（说）。

439 **enormously** enormous 是“巨大的”，enormously 作“非常地”解。 **I assure you** 我向你保证；请你放心；是常用语。

440 **take Eliza very seriously** 非常认真地对待 Eliza。

441 **new change** 新的变化；指 Eliza 不断地进步。 **keep records of every stage** 把每个（学习）阶段都做好（唱片、照片等）记录保存下来。

records of every stage – dozens of gramophone disks and photographs –

HIGGINS [*assailing her at the other ear*] Yes, by George: it's the most absorbing experiment I ever tackled. She regularly fills our lives up; doesnt she, Pick?

PICKERING We're always talking Eliza.

HIGGINS Teaching Eliza.

PICKERING Dressing Eliza.

MRS HIGGINS What!

HIGGINS Inventing new Elizas.

[*speaking together*]

HIGGINS You know, she has the most extraordinary quickness of ear:

PICKERING I assure you, my dear Mrs Higgins, that girl

HIGGINS just like a parrot. Ive tried her with every

PICKERING is a genius. She can play the piano quite beautifully.

HIGGINS possible sort of sound that a human being can make –

PICKERING We have taken her to classical concerts and to music

HIGGINS Continental dialects, African dialects, Hottentot

PICKERING halls; and it's all the same to her: she plays everything

---

442 **dozens of** 几十；许多。

444 **assailing her at the other ear** 对着她另一只耳朵开火（大喊大叫）。 **the most absorbing experiment I ever tackled** 我所进行过的最吸引人的试验。I ever tacked 也作 I have ever tacked；前面的关系代词 that 可用可不用。

445 **regularly fills our lives up** 每天把我们的生活占满了；她使我们老为她忙活。

447 **talking Eliza** 谈论 Eliza。这里把 Eliza 作为一个题材，所以用 talk，一般说谈论 Eliza 该用 talk about (或 of) Eliza。

449 **Dressing Eliza** 买衣服给 Eliza 穿，给她打扮，也可作"给 Eliza 穿衣服"解，如 she is dressing her baby；无怪 Mrs Higgins 听了要惊叫 What!（什么！你们还帮她穿衣服?）

451 **Inventing new Elizas** 创造新的 Eliza 来；使面貌日新。

452 **speaking together** 同时一起说话。这里用大括弧括在一起的上下两部分的说话，好比两部重唱的乐谱。括弧内的上半部和上半部连读，下半部同下半部连读。如 HIGGINS You know, she has the most extraordinary quickness of ear 连下去接读 just like a parrot ...；PICKERING I assure you, my dear Mrs Higgins, that girl 连下去接读 is a genius ...。

453 **quickness of ear** 耳朵灵；听觉灵敏；这里的 ear 指分辨各种发音的能力，是抽象名词。

462 **classical concerts** [ˈkɒnsəts] 演奏古典音乐的音乐会。

464 **Continental** [ˌkɒntɪˈnentl] 欧洲大陆的；首字母用大写。

465 **Hottentot** [ˈhɒtntɒt] （西南非洲的）霍屯督（人，也指其语言）。霍屯督语言多有如啧舌的倒吸气音，所以称 Hottentot clicks。

466 **halls** 指 music halls；表演歌舞和杂耍的游艺场；在美国往往指"音乐厅"。 **it's all the same to her** 这对她都一样。it 指无论带她到古典音乐会还是游艺场去。

466 **she plays everything she hears right off** 马上弹出她听到的一切（乐曲）。she hears 前面省略关系代词（that），she hear 修饰 everything。 **right off** = right away. 马上；立刻；是习语；这里修饰 plays，不是修饰 hears。

HIGGINS clicks, things it took me years to get hold of; and
PICKERING she hears right off when she comes home, whether it's

HIGGINS she picks them up like a shot, right away, as if she had
PICKERING Beethoven and Brahms or Lehar and Lionel Monckton;

HIGGINS been at it all her life.
PICKERING though six months ago, she'd never as much as touched a piano –

MRS HIGGINS [*putting her fingers in her ears, as they are by this time shouting one another down with an intolerable noise*] Sh–sh–sh–sh! [*They stop.*]

PICKERING I beg your pardon. [*He draws his chair back apologetically.*]

HIGGINS Sorry. When Pickering starts shouting nobody can get a word in edgeways.

MRS HIGGINS Be quiet, Henry. Colonel Pickering: dont you realize that when Eliza walked into Wimpole Street, something walked in with her?

PICKERING Her father did. But Henry soon got rid of him.

MRS HIGGINS It would have been more to the point if her mother had. But as her mother didnt something else did.

PICKERING But what?

468 **things it took me years to get hold of** 我费了几年功夫才掌握的东西（指各种语言）。things 后面省略关系代词，作 get hold of 的宾语。 **it** 虚词，引出和它同位的不定式短语 to get hold of (that)。

472 **picks them up like a shot** 一下就学会它们（指各种语言）。 **like a shot** 一下子；口语中也作"欣然"解；是习语。

473 **as if she had been at it all her life** 仿佛她一生都学这一行。 **at it** 从事于此；是习语。it 无所专指，是所谓 it 的泛用（the vague use of "it"）。

474 **Beethoven** [ˈbeɪtəʊvn] **and Brahms** [brɑːmz] 贝多芬和布拉姆斯（都是古典音乐家）。 **Beethoven** Ludwig van Beethoven（1770–1827），德国作曲家。 **Brahms** Johannes Brahms（1833–1897），德国作曲家。 **Lehar** [ˈleɪhɑː] **and Lionel** [ˈlaɪənl] **Monckton** [ˈmʌŋktən] 两个当时著名的音乐家。 **Lehar** Franz Lehar（1870–1948），匈牙利歌剧作曲家。 **Lionel Monckton** （1861–1924）英国作家，歌剧作曲家。

477 **she'd never as much as touched a piano** 她连碰也没碰过钢琴。not (或 never) as (或 so) much as = not (或 never) even；这个习语中的 much 是副词。

479 **by this time** 到这时候；不迟于这时候。

480 **shouting one another down** （两人）高声叫喊，彼此要（用更高的声音）压倒对方。 **one another** = each other. 不像旧说须用于三者或三者以上之间。 **Sh-sh-sh-sh!** 嘘——嘘！

484 **can get a word in edgeways** 能插进一句话；插得上嘴。

487 **when Eliza walked into Wimpole Street, something walked in with her** Eliza 走进 Wimpole 街（你们的住所）时，有什么跟着她进来了。 **something walked in** Mrs Higgins 说这话是比喻"问题发生"，而 Pickering 照字面去理解，所以回答说 Her father did (= walked in)。

489 **got rid of** 摆脱；打发掉；是习语；其中的 rid 是过去分词。

490 **It would have been more to the point if her mother had.** 如果她母亲来了，那才更对头。 **had** = had walked in. 这是与过去事实相反的虚拟语气；应该是母亲来而没有来，却来了父亲。 **to the point** 切中要害的；中肯的；是习语。

491 **as her mother didnt something else did** 既然她母亲不来，别的什么就要来了（问题就发生了）。两个 did 都 = walked in。

492 **what?** = what walked in?

MRS HIGGINS [*unconsciously dating herself by the word*] A problem.

PICKERING Oh, I see. The problem of how to pass her off as a lady.

HIGGINS I'll solve that problem. Ive half solved it already.

MRS HIGGINS No, you two infinitely stupid male creatures: the problem of what is to be done with her afterwards.

HIGGINS I dont see anything in that. She can go her own way, with all the advantages I have given her.

MRS HIGGINS The advantages of that poor woman who was here just now! The manners and habits that disqualify a fine lady from earning her own living without giving her a fine lady's income! Is that what you mean?

PICKERING [*indulgently, being rather bored*] Oh, that will be all right, Mrs Higgins. [*He rises to go.*]

HIGGINS [*rising also*] We'll find her some light employment.

PICKERING She's happy enough. Dont you worry about her. Goodbye. [*He shakes hands as if he were consoling a frightened child, and makes for the door.*]

HIGGINS Anyhow, theres no good bothering now. The thing's done. Goodbye, mother. [*He kissed her, and follows Pickering.*]

PICKERING [*turning for a final consolation*] There are plenty of openings. We'll do whats right. Goodbye.

---

493 **unconsciously dating herself by the word** 用了那个词（指后面的 A problem），无意中显示她是什么时代的人。十九世纪末英国奢谈各种社会问题（problem），此时已过时，Mrs Higgins 用这个词，显示她是属于旧时

代的人。

496 **you two infinitely** ['ɪnfɪnətli] **stupid male creatures** 你们这两个无限愚蠢的男人。you 是呼唤语，two ... creatures 是它的同位语；用 male creatures 而不用 men，含有可怜他们愚蠢的意思。 **the problem of what is to be done with her afterwards** 我是说今后把她怎么办的问题。前面省略 I mean。

498 **I dont see anything in that.** 在（今后把她怎么办的）那一点上我看不出有任何问题；我看那根本不是问题。 **go her own way** 走她自己的路；要怎样就怎样。her own way 是状语宾语。

499 **with all the advantages I have given her** 带着我给予她的一切有利条件。with 和 all 连用，常有"虽有"、"尽管"的意思，如 With all his attainments he never stops learning. 他尽管有学问，还是不断学习。但这里文中的 with 单纯是"有"的意思，advantages 后面省略 that。

500 **The advantages of that poor woman who was here just now!** = She can go her own way with the advantages of that poor woman ... ! 有了刚才在这里那个可怜的女人（指 Mrs Eynsford Hill）的条件，她能要怎样就怎样吗?

501 **The manners and habits that disqualify a fine lady from earning her own living without giving her a fine lady's income!** 有了不给她上等女人的收入、而又把她弄得不能自食其力的礼貌和习惯！（她能要怎样就怎样吗？）The manners and habits 和上句 The advantages 同位，进一步把 advantages 具体化。

503 **Is that what you mean?** 你说的是（上面）那个意思吗?

504 **indulgently, being rather bored** （不跟 Mrs Higgins 争辩）因为他已很厌烦，所以顺从地（对她说）。 **that will be all right** 那（今后 Liza 怎样）没问题。

506 **find her some light employment** 给她找某个轻松的职业。

507 **Dont you worry** ['wʌri] **about her.** 你不用为她担心。Dont you 比 Dont 的祈使语气重，前已屡见。 **worry** 这里是不及物动词；它也可作及物动词，因此也可说 Dont let her worry you.

510 **theres no good bothering now** 现在担心没用。there is (或 it is) no good 后面直接接动名词是一个惯用句型；这里的 good 是名词，作"好处"、"用处"解。**The thing's done.** 事情已经做了；木已成舟。比较：谚语 What is done cannot be undone. 覆水难收。

512 **turning for a final consolation** 回过身去（对 Mrs Higgins）作最后一次的安慰。

513 **openings** 空缺；就业的机会。

HIGGINS [*to Pickering as they go out together*] Lets take her to the Shakespear exhibition at Earls Court.

PICKERING Yes: lets. Her remarks will be delicious.

HIGGINS She'll mimic all the people for us when we get home.

PICKERING Ripping. [*Both are heard laughing as they go downstairs.*]

MRS HIGGINS [*rises with an impatient bounce, and returns to her work at the writing-table. She sweeps a litter of disarranged papers out of the way; snatches a sheet of paper from her stationery case, and tries resolutely to write. At the third line she gives it up; flings down her pen; grips the table angrily and exclaims.*] Oh, men! men!! men!!!

Clearly Eliza will not pass as a duchess yet; and Higgins's bet remains unwon. But the six months are not yet exhausted; and just in time Eliza does actually pass as a princess. For a glimpse of how she did it imagine an Embassy in London one summer evening after dark. The hall door has an awning and a carpet across the sidewalk to the kerb, because a grand reception is in progress. A small crowd is lined up to see the guests arrive.

---

514 **the Shakespear exhibition at Earls Court** 在 Earls Court 的莎士比亚展览会。Earls Court 在伦敦 Kensington 区。

516 **lets** = let's take her to the Shakespear exhibition at Earls Court. **Her remarks will be delicious.** 她的谈论将很有趣。Liza 参观了莎士比亚展览会定有许多妙论。

518 **mimic all the people for us** 模仿所有(在展览会上遇到的)人给我们看和听。

518 **Ripping.** 好极；妙极；英国俚语；是形容词。也作副词，作副词时还可作“非常”解，如 We had a ripping good time.

520 **sweeps a litter of disarranged papers out of the way** 把（写字台上）杂乱的一堆纸全推开，使不妨碍她（写字）。 **papers** 信件、文件等。

521 **stationery case** 文具匣。stationery 统称“文具”，也专指“信笺”；读音和 stationary（静止的）相同，两词不要混淆。

522 **At the third line she gives it up** 她写到第三行不写下去了。it 指写。

525 **remains unwon** [ʌnˈwʌn] 还没有赢得。unwon 是形容词，作表语。 **the six months are not yet exhausted** [ɪgˈzɔːstɪd] 这六个月还没有过完；（约定把 Eliza 训练得能冒充公爵夫人的）六个月限期还未满。

526 **just in time Eliza does actually pass as a princess** 赶在六个月到期之前 Eliza 真的被人当作是一位公主。**princess** 读 [prɪnˈses]，但用于名字前时，读 [ˈprɪnses]，如 Princess Elizabeth。 **For a glimpse of how she did it imagine ...** 想要看一看她是如何被当作公主的，请想像一下…… **did it** = passed as a princess.

527 **an Embassy in London** 驻伦敦的一个大使馆；某国的驻英大使馆。说“驻某国的大使馆”，习惯用 Embassy in + 某国的首都，而不用 Embassy in + 某国。

528 **after dark** 傍晚后。 **dark** 天暗下来；傍晚；不能用 darkness；在 after（或 before, at) dark 等短语中，dark 前面没有 the。 **The hall door has an awning** [ˈɔːnɪŋ] 门廊门口装有遮篷。 **hall** 可指“门廊”（在美国也指“大厦里的走廊”）；也可指“大厅”、“礼堂”；这里指前者。 **a carpet across the sidewalk to the kerb** 跨越人行道铺到路边镶边石的一条地毯。 **sidewalk** 主要是美国用语，即英国的 pavement。

529 **a grand reception is in progress** 正在举行盛大的招待会。

530 **A small crowd is lined up** 一小群人已排成了行。比较：A small crowd lines up. 前者着眼于状态，后者着眼于行动。

A Rolls-Royce car drives up. Pickering in evening dress, with medals and orders, alights, and hands out Eliza, in opera cloak, evening dress, diamonds, fan, flowers and all accessories. Higgins follows. The car drives off; and the three go up the steps and into the house, the door opening for them as they approach.

Inside the house they find themselves in a spacious hall from which the grand staircase rises. On the left are the arrangements for the gentlemen's cloaks. The male guests are depositing their hats and wraps there.

On the right is a door leading to the ladies' cloakroom. Ladies are going in cloaked and coming out in splendor. Pickering whispers to Eliza and points out the ladies' room. She goes into it. Higgins and Pickering take off their overcoats and take tickets for them from the attendant.

One of the guests, occupied in the same way, has his back turned. Having taken his ticket, he turns round and reveals himself as an important looking young man with an astonishingly hairy face. He has an enormous moustache, flowing out into luxuriant whiskers. Waves of hair cluster on his brow.

---

531 **A Rolls-Royce** [ˌrəʊlzˈrɔɪs] **car drives up**. 一辆 Rolls-Royce 汽车开来。Rolls-Royce 是 Charles Stewart（1877–1910）和 Sir Frederick Henry Royce（1863–

1933）两个英国工程师合设的汽车制造厂。

532 **medals and orders** medals 泛指各种“奖章”、“勋章”；orders 是“（某种勋位或骑士团等的）勋章”。 **alights, and hands out Eliza** 下车，并搀扶出 Eliza 来。 **opera cloak** 妇女看戏或参加晚会的礼服。

533 **diamonds, fan, flowers and all accessories** [əkˈsesərɪz] 按语法，diamonds 前面应有介词 with 或其他类似意义的词。 **fan** 可数名词单数前面应有限定词，但这里因与其他东西并列，所以省略了。 **accessories** 附属品；复数指妇女衣饰的配套用品，如手套、手提包等。

535 **the door opening for them as they approach** 他们（三人）走到门口时，门为他们打开。这是个独立结构，表示 the three go up the steps and into the house 时伴随发生的事。

536 **find themselves in ...** 见到自己在……之中；自己已在……之中。

537 **arrangements** [əˈreɪndʒmənts] **for the gentlemen's cloaks** 男宾存放外套的设施；男宾衣帽间。 **cloak** 斗篷；大氅；所以“衣帽间”称 cloakroom。（cloakroom 也指“行李寄放处”；在英国还作为“厕所”的委婉语。）

539 **wraps** [ræps] 指“外衣、围巾等”，常用复数。

541 **going in cloaked and coming out in splendor** 穿着外套进去，（脱去外套）穿着里面的华丽服装出来。cloaked 和 in splendor 都是表语（或称主语补足语）。

542 **ladies' room** 即上文的 ladies' cloakroom，参看下文 Eliza comes from the cloakroom. (p.206)

543 **take off their overcoats and take tickets for them from the attendant** 脱下大衣（交给侍者存放在衣帽间），从侍者那里拿了衣帽牌。

545 **occupied in the same way** 同样忙着（存放大衣）。 **has his back turned** 背回转着（背向台下观众）。一般 have (something 或 somebody) + 过去分词作“使（某物或某人）被……”的意思，如 I have my hair cut fortnightly. 我每两星期使头发被修剪一次；意译“我每两星期理发一次”，但这里并不是“使背被旋转”的意思；turned 也看作是形容词，作“回过去了的”解。

547 **important looking** 模样神气的；一般写作 important-looking。 **astonishingly hairy face** 须发浓密得惊人的脸。

548 **an enormous moustache** [məˈstɑːʃ], **flowing out into luxuriant** [lʌgˈʒʊərɪənt] **whiskers** 厚大的唇髭延伸出去和浓密的颊须连成一片；whiskers 常用复数。

549 **Waves of hair cluster on his brow.** 头发的波浪聚集在他前额上；额上堆满鬈发。

His hair is cropped closely at the back, and glows with oil. Otherwise he is very smart. He wears several worthless orders. He is evidently a foreigner, guessable as a whiskered Pandour from Hungary; but in spite of the ferocity of his moustache he is amiable and genially voluble.

Recognizing Higgins, he flings his arms wide apart and approaches him enthusiastically.

WHISKERS Maestro, maestro. [*He embraces Higgins and kisses him on both cheeks.*] You remember me?

HIGGINS No I dont. Who the devil are you?

WHISKERS I am your pupil: your first pupil, your best and greatest pupil. I am little Nepommuck, the marvellous boy. I have made your name famous throughout Europe. You teach me phonetic. You cannot forget ME.

HIGGINS Why dont you shave?

NEPOMMUCK I have not your imposing appearance, your chin, your brow. Nobody notice me when I shave. Now I am famous: they call me Hairy Faced Dick.

HIGGINS And what are you doing here among all these swells?

---

550 **His hair is cropped closely at the back** 他后面的头发修得很短。close-cropped (或 close-cut) hair，修得短短的头发。

551 **Otherwise** 否则；若不是须发浓密得惊人的话。 **worthless orders** 不足道

的勋章。

552 **guessable as a whiskered Pandour** [ˈpændʊə] **from Hungary** 可以猜想是个毛发浓密的匈牙利残暴军人。 **from Hungary** 说 He is from Hungary，有两种意思，一是“他是匈牙利来的”，一是“他是匈牙利人”。

553 **ferocity** [fəˈrɒsəti] 原义“凶暴”、“暴行”；这里作“凶相”解。

554 **genially voluble** [ˈvɒljʊbl] 和蔼地侃侃而谈。

555 **Recognizing Higgins** 认出是 Higgins。 **recognize** 是“认（得）出”，不是“认识”，所以 He recognized his father in the crowd 不是“他在人群中认识他父亲”，而是“他在人群中看到（而知道是）他父亲”。 **flings his arms wide apart** 猛地张开双臂。 **apart** 副词作宾语补足语；his arms 和 wide apart 在逻辑上有主谓关系，所以也称 his arms wide apart 为复合宾语。 **wide** 这里是副词，和 widely 略有不同。widely 表示“广阔地”。而 wide 则有“广阔到极限”的意思；所以 widely open 是“开得大”，而 wide open 则有“开足”之意。

557 **Whiskers** 大胡子，指上面介绍的那个有大胡子的人。**Maestro** [ˈmaɪstrəʊ] 大师，原指（音乐等）艺术大师；是意大利语，相当于英语 master；复数为 maestros 或 maestri。

561 **little Nepommuck** [ˈnepəmʌk] 小小的 Nepommuck。这里的 little 指年轻，也指资历浅、地位低等。Nepommuck，姓。

563 **phonetic** 语音（学）的；是形容词；这里说“语音学”，该用名词 phonetics（复数形式作单数）。这位“语音学家”的语言不高明，常有错误。 **ME** 用大写字母比用斜体更表示强调语气。

565 **imposing appearance** 堂堂的仪表。后面的 your chin, your brow 是它的同位语。imposing 原是“给人深刻印象的”意思。

566 **Nobody notice me when I shave** 我刮了胡子，就没有人注意我了。不是“我在刮胡子的时候没有人注意到我”的意思，表示这个意思该说“... when I am shaving.” **notice** 是 notices 之讹，shave 该作 am shaved。

567 **Hairy Faced Dick** 胡子狄克。

568 **swells** 时髦人物，既指名流，也指衣着花哨的人。

NEPOMMUCK I am interpreter. I speak 32 languages. I am indispensable at these international parties. You are great cockney specialist: you place a man anywhere in London the moment he open his mouth. I place any man in Europe.

A footman hurries down the grand staircase and comes to Nepommuck.

FOOTMAN You are wanted upstairs. Her Excellency cannot understand the Greek gentleman.

NEPOMMUCK Thank you, yes, immediately.

The footman goes and is lost in the crowd.

NEPOMMUCK [*to Higgins*] This Greek diplomatist pretends he cannot speak nor understand English. He cannot deceive me. He is the son of a Clerkenwell watchmaker. He speaks English so villainously that he dare not utter a word of it without betraying his origin. I help him to pretend; but I make him pay through the nose. I make them all pay. Ha ha! [*He hurries upstairs.*]

PICKERING Is this fellow really an expert? Can he find out Eliza and blackmail her?

HIGGINS We shall see. If he find her out I lose my bet.

---

569 **I am interpreter** [ɪnˈtɜːprɪtə] 我是翻译员。interpreter 前应有 an。比较：in-

terpret，口译；translate，笔译。 **indispensable at these international parties** 在这种国际性的聚会上不可少的。

570 **You are great cockney specialist** 你是著名的伦敦土音专家，又漏冠词。**cockney** 伦敦佬（尤指东区贫民）；伦敦土音。

571 **you place a man anywhere in London the moment he open his mouth** 只要他一开口，你就能确定他是伦敦什么地区的人。 **the moment** 有连词性质，= at the moment when / as soon as。

575 **You are wanted upstairs.** 楼上要你（去翻译）。 **Her Excellency** 大使夫人。 **Excellency** 对大使、总督等的尊称。如对面称"大使夫人"，则用 Your Excellency。

577 **immediately** = I'll come (或 be there) immediately.

578 **is lost in the crowd** （走到）人群中不见了。

579 **cannot speak nor understand** 现代英语中用 cannot speak or understand 较普遍。

580 **He cannot deceive me.** 他不可能骗过我；他骗不了我。在不同的上下文中，这句话也可作"他不可能骗我"解，即"他不会骗我"。还有，请注意：deceive 是"欺骗成功"的意思，欺骗但没有成功不能用 deceive。如不能说 He deceived me, but I was not so foolish as to believe in him. 这个 deceived 该改用 tried to deceive。

581 **a Clerkenwell** ['klɑːkənwəl] **watchmaker** Clerkenwell 的一个钟表匠。Clerkenwell 是伦敦北面的一个工业区。 **watchmaker** 兼指制造钟表或修理钟表的人。

582 **villainously** ['vɪlənəsli] 极坏的，讨厌的。它的形容词 villainous 原义是"坏人的"、"卑鄙的"；口语中可作"极坏的"、"讨厌的"解。 **he dare not utter a word of it without betraying his origin** 他不敢说出一个英语单词，怕暴露他出身（于钟表匠家庭）。在资本主义上层社会中，钟表匠被视为低贱的工种。句中 dare not 有误，该改作 cannot；要是保留 dare，则该把 without 改作 for fear of，否则原句不通。

583 **pretend** 假装（希腊人）。 **make him pay through the nose** 要他出大价钱；敲他竹杠。pay through the nose 是习语。

584 **pay** = pay through the nose.

586 **find out Eliza** 发现 Eliza（是假装成公主的）。

588 **We shall see.** 我们瞧着吧。

Eliza comes from the cloakroom and joins them.

PICKERING Well, Eliza, now for it. Are you ready?

LIZA Are you nervous, Colonel?

PICKERING Frightfully. I feel exactly as I felt before my first battle. It's the first time that frightens.

LIZA It is not the first time for me, Colonel. I have done this fifty times – hundreds of times – in my little piggery in Angel Court in my day-dreams. I am in a dream now. Promise me not to let Professor Higgins wake me; for if he does I shall forget everything and talk as I used to in Drury Lane.

PICKERING Not a word, Higgins. [*to Eliza*] Now, ready?

LIZA Ready.

PICKERING Go.

They mount the stairs, Higgins last. Pickering whispers to the footman on the first landing.

FIRST LANDING FOOTMAN Miss Doolittle, Colonel Pickering, Professor Higgins.

SECOND LANDING FOOTMAN Miss Doolittle, Colonel Pickering, Professor Higgins.

At the top of the staircase the Ambassador and his wife, with Nepommuck at her elbow, are receiving.

---

590 **now for it** 现在干起来吧；是习语；犹如汉语口语中说“上！”

591 **Are you nervous, Colonel?** Pickering 上校问 Eliza 准备好了吗，她反问上校“你紧张吗？”说明 Eliza 定心得很，且看下面 Eliza 自己说她当时的精神状态。

592 **Frightfully.** = I'm frightfully nervous. 我紧张得要命。frightfully 原义“可怕的”，口语作“非常”、“讨厌地”解。 **exactly as I felt before my first battle** 正如我第一次上战场前所感觉的一样（紧张）。

593 **It's the first time that frightens.** 叫人害怕的是第一次；因为是第一次，所以叫人害怕。这里 frighten 是及物动词，却没有宾语，有的语法家称此为及物动词的“绝对用法”（the absolute use of the transitive verb）。句中 that 是关系代词，It 是它的先行词。

594 **It is not the first time for me** 这对我来说不是第一次。这里的 It 指她以贵妇人身份出现一事。 **I have done this fifty times – hundreds of times – in my little piggery in Angel Court in my day-dreams** 我在 Angel Court 我的小猪圈里白日做梦的时候做过这个（以贵妇人身份出现）五十次——（不是五十次而是）几百次。 **my little piggery in Angel Court** 指 Liza 的家；她家住 Angel Court, Drury Lane，见第一幕。 **day-dreams** 白日梦；幻想。

596 **I am in a dream now.** 我现在就（像）是在梦幻中。

598 **talk as I used to in Drury Lane** 像我过去在 Drury Lane 时那样说话。 **used to** = used to talk. 过去经常说。

599 **Not a word** = Do not say a (single) word. **Now, ready?** = Now are you ready? 后面 Liza 回答说 Ready。Pickering 上校又说 Go。这势必使人联想到赛跑的号令：On your marks! Ready! Go!（各就各位！预备！跑！）因而造成了像起跑时一样的紧张气氛。

602 **They mount the stairs, Higgins last.** 他们（三人）上楼梯，Higgins 走在最后。**Higgins last** = with Higgins at the last 或 Higgins mounting last。

603 **landing** 每一段楼梯（flight）口的平台；楼梯平台。

604 **Miss Doolittle** 这里连叫 Miss Doolittle 等三人名字，不是招呼他们，而是通报他们到来。

609 **at her elbow** 在她臂肘旁边。即“就在身旁”的意思。 **receiving** 迎接。

HOSTESS [*taking Eliza's hand*] How d'ye do?

HOST [*same play*] How d'ye do? How d'ye do, Pickering?

LIZA [*with a beautiful gravity that awes her hostess*] How do you do? [*She passes on to the drawing room.*]

HOSTESS Is that your adopted daughter, Colonel Pickering? She will make a sensation.

PICKERING Most kind of you to invite her for me. [*He passes on.*]

HOSTESS [*to Nepommuck*] Find out all about her.

NEPOMMUCK [*bowing*] Excellency – [*He goes into the crowd.*]

HOST How d'ye do, Higgins? You have a rival here tonight. He introduced himself as your pupil. Is he any good?

HIGGINS He can learn a language in a fortnight – knows dozens of them. A sure mark of a fool. As a phonetician, no good whatever.

HOSTESS How d'ye do, Professor?

HIGGINS How do you do? Fearful bore for you this sort of thing. Forgive my part in it. [*He passes on.*]

In the drawing room and its suite of salons the reception is in full swing. Eliza passes through. She is so intent on her ordeal that she walks like a somnambulist in a desert instead of a

---

610 **Hostess** （聚会或宴会的）女主人，这里指大使夫人。下面 Host（主人）指大使。 **How d'ye do?** 语气比 How d'you (= do you) do? 随便。

611 **same play** 同样这样做。

612 **a beautiful gravity** [ˈɡrævəti] **that awes her hostess** 一种使她的女主人（大

使夫人）肃然起敬的优美的端庄。

614 **adopted daughter** 领养的女儿；养女。

615 **make a sensation** 引起轰动。

616 **Most kind of you to invite her for me.** = It is most kind of you to invite her for me. 非常感谢你替我邀请她来（参加你的招待会）。 **most** 非常；比较：作“最”解释时前面用 the。It is most kind of you 和 It is very considerate of you 等是常用客套语。

617 **Find out all about her.** 弄清关于她的一切情况；摸清她的底细。

618 **Excellency** = Your Excellency. 对大使夫人的尊称。

619 **You have a rival** 你有个对手。Higgins 是语音学家，大使告诉他今夜这里也有一个语音学家（指 Nepommuck）。 **He introduced himself as your pupil.** 他自称是你的学生。 **pupil** 原指“小学生”（大、中学生称 student）；但说某人的学生时，即使那个学生已经是专家、学者，也称 pupil，如：Our professor is a pupil of Einstein's. 我们的教授是爱因斯坦的学生。

620 **Is he any good?** 他行吗？ good 这里是名词，作“好处”、“用处”解。Is he any good? = Is he of any good?

622 **A sure mark of a fool.** = That's a sure mark of a fool. 那（两个星期能学会一种语言、懂得几十种语言）正是傻瓜的确实标志；说明必然是傻瓜。 **As a phonetician, no good whatever.** 作为一个语音学家，他什么用处也没有（一窍不通）。no good 前面省略 he is (of)。 **whatever** 这里是形容词，用于有否定意义的句子中 = at all。萧伯纳在这个剧本中以语音学家 Henry Sweet 作为 Higgins 的原型（见前注），Sweet 认为凡是不懂语音学的就是傻瓜。

625 **Fearful bore for you this sort of thing.** = This sort of thing is a fearful bore for you. 这种东西（指语音学）对你是非常讨厌的东西；语音学这玩意会把你烦厌得要死。一般 you 后应加逗号。 **fearful** 口语中作“非常”解。

626 **Forgive my part in it.** 恕我是搞这一行（语音学）的。

627 **In the drawing room and its suite of salons** [ˈsælɒnz] **the reception is in full swing.** 在客厅和它（旁边）的一套交谊室里，招待会正在热闹地进行着。

628 **She is so intent on her ordeal** [ɔːˈdiːl] **that she walks like a somnambulist** [sɒmˈnæmbjəlɪst] **in a desert instead of a débutante** [debjʊˈtɑːnt] **in a fashionable crowd.** 她是那么专心于她（正在经受）的考验，所以她像在沙漠中梦游的人，而不像一个初进社交界的女子在一群时髦人中间行走。 **débutante** 初进社交

débutante in a fashionable crowd. They stop talking to look at her, admiring her dress, her jewels, and her strangely attractive self. Some of the younger ones at the back stand on their chairs to see.

The Host and Hostess come in from the staircase and mingle with their guests. Higgins, gloomy and contemptuous of the whole business, comes into the group where they are chatting.

HOSTESS Ah, here is Professor Higgins: he will tell us. Tell us about the wonderful young lady, Professor.

HIGGINS [*almost morosely*] What wonderful young lady?

HOSTESS You know very well. They tell me there has been nothing like her in London since people stood on their chairs to look at Mrs Langtry.

Nepommuck joins the group, full of news.

HOSTESS Ah, here you are at last, Nepommuck. Have you found out all about the Doolittle lady?

NEPOMMUCK I have found out all about her. She is a fraud.

HOSTESS A fraud! Oh, no.

NEPOMMUCK YES, yes. She cannot deceive me. Her name cannot be Doolittle.

HIGGINS Why?

NEPOMMUCK Because Doolittle is an English name. And she is

界的女子；初次登台的女演员；这是法语；男性则用 débutant [debjʊˈtɑːŋ]。

630 **stop talking to look at her, admiring her dress** 停下谈话看她，欣赏她的衣着。talking 是动名词，作 stop 的宾语；admiring 是现在分词，修饰 to look。

631 **her strangely attractive self** 她那异常迷人、有魅力的本人。

632 **Some of the younger ones at the back** 有些在后面的比较年轻的人们。

635 **gloomy and contemptuous** [kənˈtemptʃʊəs] **of the whole business** 阴郁的，看不起整个招待会的活动。注意：contemptuous 后面的介词用 of。

636 **chatting** 闲谈。此词和 chatter（喋喋不休）含义不同，不要混淆。

639 **morosely** [məˈrəʊsli] 很不耐烦地；别扭地。

640 **there has been nothing like her in London since ...** 从……以来伦敦不曾有过一个像她这样的（美）人。这里的 nothing = none。

642 **Mrs Langtry** [ˈlæŋtri] Emily Charlotte Langtry（1852–1929），英国女演员，艺名 Lily Longtry，是著名的美人。

643 **full of news** = being full of news. 带着一肚子新闻。

646 **a fraud** 原义“欺骗”、“骗局”；这里是“使人上当的人”、“假冒的人”的意思。

648 **YES** 全部用大写字母拼写，比用斜体更表示强调，要加倍重读。 **She cannot deceive me**. 前面已见 He cannot deceive me，有译注，请参看 p.205。 **Her name cannot be Doolittle.** 她的姓氏不可能是 Doolittle。（因为他认为她不是英国人，所以不能姓 Doolittle 这个英国姓；见下文。）

not English.

HOSTESS Oh, nonsense! She speaks English perfectly.

NEPOMMUCK Too perfectly. Can you shew me any English woman who speaks English as it should be spoken? Only foreigners who have been taught to speak it well.

HOSTESS Certainly she terrified me by the way she said How d'ye do. I had a schoolmistress who talked like that; and I was mortally afraid of her. But if she is not English what is she?

NEPOMMUCK Hungarian.

ALL THE REST Hungarian!

NEPOMMUCK Hungarian. And of royal blood. I am Hungarian. My blood is royal.

HIGGINS Did you speak to her in Hungarian?

NEPOMMUCK I did. She was very clever. She said 'Please speak to me in English: I do not understand French.' French! She pretend not to know the difference between Hungarian and French. Impossible: she knows both.

HIGGINS And the blood royal? How did you find that out?

NEPOMMUCK Instinct, maestro, instinct. Only the Magyar races can produce that air of the divine right, those resolute eyes. She is a princess.

HOST What do you say, Professor?

HIGGINS I say an ordinary London girl out of the gutter and

---

655 **speaks English as it should be spoken** 照应该那么说英语那样地说英语；

说完全正确的英语。这话可以包括正确的语法和正确的发音两重意思。

657 **she terrified me by the way she said How d'ye do** 她说 How d'ye do 的发音和语调使我惊讶（正确到吓人的地步）。**by the way she said** = by the way in which she said.

658 **I was mortally afraid of her** 我对她吓得要死。萧伯纳讽刺英国女人读音不正确，所以听到读音太正确反而会致命地害怕（mortally afraid）。

659 **But if she is not English what is she?** 然而若说她不是英国人，那她是哪一国人呢？ **what is she** 问她是什么身份（职业、国籍等）用 what is she，不能用 who is she（她是谁）。

660 **Hungarian** [hʌŋˈgeərɪən] 匈牙利的，就是说"她是匈牙利人"，下文 speak to her in Hungarian 的 Hungarian 是指"匈牙利语"。**And of royal blood** = And she is Hungarian and of royal blood. 而且是王族血统。

665 **She was very clever** 她很机灵。（指她善于应变，假装不懂匈牙利语。其实不是假装，她原来就不懂英语以外的任何语言。）

666 **I do not understand French.** 我不懂法语。Nepommuck 以为她假装把匈牙利语误当法语。其实她确实分不清楚。

668 **Impossible: she knows both.** = It is impossible that she does not know the difference between Hungarian and French; she knows both Hungarian and French.

669 **the blood royal** 王族的统称。比较：上文 royal blood（没有 the）指王族的血统。**How did you find that out?** 你怎样发现（她是）王族的？

670 **Instinct** [ˈɪnstɪŋkt] = I find out that by instinct. 我凭直觉（本能地）发现她是王族。that 指 the blood royal。 **the Magyar** [ˈmægjɑː] **races** 马扎尔族的各氏族。马扎尔族是匈牙利的主要民族。

671 **produce that air of the divine right, those resolute** [ˈrezəluːt] **eyes** 表现出那种天赋王权的气度和那双坚定的眼睛。 **the divine right** 在英国史上，尤其十七世纪斯图亚特（Stuart）王朝时代，宣扬"天赋王权"（the divine right of kings）。

672 **princess** 公主；也指"王妃"、"亲王夫人"。

673 **What do you say** 你怎么说？你的意见如何？

674 **I say an ordinary London girl** = I say (that) she is an ordinary London girl. **out of the gutter** 从街头捡来的。 **gutter** 街沟；转指"街头"、"平民区（或窟）"。

taught to speak by an expert. I place her in Drury Lane.

NEPOMMUCK Ha ha ha! Oh, maestro, maestro, you are mad on the subject of cockney dialects. The London gutter is the whole world for you.

HIGGINS [*to the Hostess*] What does Your Excellency say?

HOSTESS Oh, of course I agree with Nepommuck. She must be a princess at least.

HOST Not necessarily legitimate, of course. Morganatic perhaps. But that is undoubtedly her class.

HIGGINS I stick to my opinion.

HOSTESS Oh, you are incorrigible.

The group breaks up, leaving Higgins isolated. Pickering joins him.

PICKERING Where is Eliza? We must keep an eye on her.

Eliza joins them.

LIZA I dont think I can bear much more. The people all stare so at me. An old lady has just told me that I speak exactly like Queen Victoria. I am sorry if I have lost your bet. I have done my best; but nothing can make me the same as these people.

PICKERING You have not lost it, my dear. You have won it ten times over.

675 **taught** 过去分词，由它组成的分词短语和 out of the gutter 并列。 **place her in Drury Lane** 确定她（生活）在 Drury Lane。见第一幕。

676 **mad on the subject of cockney dialects** 对伦敦各区方言这个课题（研究得）头脑发疯了；说什么都只知道伦敦方言。

677 **The London gutter is the whole world for you.** 伦敦街头对于你来说就是整个世界；只知伦敦街头。

680 **She must be a princess at least.** 我看她至少一定是位公主。（言下之意，是王后也不是不可能的。）

682 **Not necessarily**（[ˈnesəserəli]，加强语气时也读 [nesəˈserəli]）**legitimate** [lɪˈdʒɪtəmət] 不一定是正统的，参看下条注。 **Morganatic** [ˌmɔːgəˈnætɪk] **perhaps.** 也许是王族男子和低贱女子的婚姻关系的。在欧洲诸王国，除英国外，这种贵贱婚姻关系中的女子和她的子女都没有继承权。

683 **But that is undoubtedly her class.** 不管正统不正统，反正她的阶级是确定无疑的（总是属于王族的）。

684 **I stick to my opinion.** 我坚持我的意见，即她是经过专家语音训练的街头姑娘。

685 **incorrigible** [ɪnˈkɒrɪdʒəbl] 无法被改正的；固执己见的。

686 **breaks up** 散开。 **leaving Higgins isolated** [ˈaɪsəleɪtɪd] 留下 Higgins 孤单单一个人。 **isolated** 过去分词作宾语补足语，Higgins isolated 构成复合宾语。

688 **keep an eye on her** 盯着她（别让她出岔子）。

690 **bear much more** 忍受更多（的无聊和麻烦）。bear 是及物动词，more 是名词，作宾语，much 修饰 more。 **The people all stare so at me.** 人们全都那样盯着我。all 是代词；The people all 也可说 All the people。

692 **Queen Victoria** [vɪkˈtɔːrɪə] 英国维多利亚女王（1819–1901，1837–1901 在位）。 **I am sorry if I have lost your bet** 我要是使你打赌输了，很抱歉。Liza 冒充贵妇人的试验很成功，Higgins 打赌赢了，Pickering 输了。

694 **You have not lost it** 你没有使打赌输掉。it 指 bet。Liza 虽没有参加打赌，她当然是站在试验成功的一面，所以这句话 = You have not spoiled the experiment – you have succeeded in it. **won it ten times over** 超过十倍地赢了。ten times 修饰 over，over 有“超过原来要求”的意思。

HIGGINS Let us get out of this. I have had enough of chattering to these fools.

PICKERING Eliza is tired; and I am hungry. Let us clear out and have supper somewhere.

696 **get out of this** 摆脱这（无聊和烦扰）。 **chattering** 喋喋不休；饶舌；与 chat 含义不同，见前注。
698 **clear out** （赶快）离开。

第四幕
剧情提要

Higgins 教授、Pickering 上校和 Liza 从大使馆招待会回到 Higgins 的实验室，时已午夜。Liza 脸色苍白，疲惫不堪。Higgins 和 Pickering 尽是谈论着招待会的情景。Higgins 认为这些绅士淑女都是些糊涂虫，无聊之极，这整个一场把戏简直是活受罪，以后再也不搞这种教人冒充公爵夫人的把戏了。他们全不理会 Liza；Liza 怨恨之极，却强自抑制着。

临了，Higgins 回房睡觉去的时候，照例又差 Liza 做这做那，一会儿找不到拖鞋，又大叫大嚷。Liza 忍无可忍，抓起拖鞋猛力向他扔去。他们大吵起来。Liza 说：“我原来卖花，并不卖自己。现在你把我变成了个小姐，除了卖自己之外，还能卖什么？你把我变成了这个样子，叫我怎么办？我到哪里去？”

Liza 终于在深更半夜离开了这个家。

Liza 走出门口，看见 Freddy 在那里，很惊讶。他说：“我夜里多半都在这里，只有在这里我才快活。”她发现了真正尊重她、爱她的人。警察不许青年男女半夜三更在街头谈情说爱；正好来了一辆出租汽车，他俩就乘上汽车，准备兜到天明。Liza 说：“我一早去找 Higgins 太太，问她我该怎么办。”

ACT IV

The Wimpole Street laboratory. Midnight. Nobody in the room. The clock on the mantelpiece strikes twelve. The fire is not alight: it is a summer night.

Presently Higgins and Pickering are heard on the stairs.

HIGGINS [*calling down to Pickering*] I say, Pick: lock up, will you? I shant be going out again.

PICKERING Right. Can Mrs Pearce go to bed? We dont want anything more, do we?

HIGGINS Lord, no!

Eliza opens the door and is seen on the lighted landing in all the finery in which she has just won Higgins's bet for him. She comes to the hearth, and switches on the electric lights there. She is tired: her pallor contrasts strongly with her dark eyes and hair; and her expression is almost tragic. She takes off her cloak; puts her fan and gloves on the piano; and sits down on the bench, brooding and silent. Higgins, in the evening dress, with overcoat and hat, comes in, carrying a smoking jacket which he has picked up downstairs. He takes off the hat and overcoat; throws them carelessly on the newspaper stand; disposes of his coat in the same way; puts on the smoking jacket;

---

2 **strikes twelve** （钟）敲十二点。 **alight** 燃着的；形容词，常作表语。

4 **Presently** 一会儿；随即。 **Higgins and Pickering are heard on the stairs** 听到楼梯上 Higgins 和 Pickering 的声音；这里 on the stairs 是表语，或称主语补足语，不是修饰 are heard 的状语，因而不是"在楼梯上听见……"的意思。

5 **I say** 引起说话，或表示惊奇；在美国常用 Say。 **lock up**（把大门）锁好。

7 **Right** = All right. 英语口语中也说 Right oh。 **Can Mrs Pearce go to bed?** Pearce 太太可以去睡觉了吗？这里 Can 表示 Higgins 对 Mrs Pearce 的"允许"的意思。

9 **Lord** 老天爷；感叹语，也作 Good Lord、Lord God 等。

10 **is seen on the lighted landing** 看见（Eliza）在开着灯的楼梯口上。on the lighted landing 是表语，不是状语。 **landing** 楼梯平台。 **in all the finery in which she has just won Higgins's bet for him** 穿戴着刚才（在第三幕中）为 Higgins 赢得他的打赌的全套华丽的衣装首饰。

13 **her pallor contrasts strongly with her dark eyes and hair** 她（脸色的）苍白跟她黑色的眼睛和头发形成强烈的对比；黑色的眼睛和头发更显出她脸色苍白。contrast 此处是动词，读 [kənˈtrɑːst]，作名词时读 [ˈkɒntrɑːst]。

16 **brooding and silent** 抑郁地沉思，不声不响。silent = being silent. **evening dress** 晚礼服；是不可数名词，前面没有冠词。full dress（大礼服）前面也没有冠词。

17 **with overcoat and hat** 两个或两个以上名词并列时，习惯可省略冠词 a 或 the 或所有格代词。 **smoking jacket** 吸烟服（男子在家吸烟时穿的便服）。smoking 是动名词作定语。

18 **picked up** 随手拿起。

19 **newspaper stand** 报架。 **disposes of his coat in the same way** 同样处置他的外套；同样随随便便地扔在报架上。dispose of 是习语，有"处置"、"卖掉"、"去掉"、"解决"等多种意思。

and throws himself wearily into the easy-chair at the hearth. Pickering, similarly attired, comes in. He also takes off his hat and overcoat, and is about to throw them on Higgins's when he hesitates.

PICKERING I say: Mrs Pearce will row if we leave these thing lying about in the drawing room.

HIGGINS Oh, chuck them over the banisters into the hall. She'll find them there in the morning and put them away all right. She'll think we were drunk.

PICKERING We are, slightly. Are there any letters?

HIGGINS I didnt look. [*Pickering takes the overcoats and hats and goes downstairs. Higgins begins half singing half yawning an air from* La Fanciulla del West. *Suddenly he stops and exclaims.*] I wonder where the devil my slippers are!

Eliza looks at him darkly; then rises suddenly and leaves the room.

Higgins yawns again, and resumes his song.

Pickering returns, with the contents of the letter-box in his hand.

PICKERING Only circulars, and this coroneted billet-doux for you. [*He throws the circulars into the fender, and posts himself on*

21 **throws himself wearily** [ˈwɪərɪli] **into the easy-chair at the hearth** 疲乏地把身子往壁炉跟前的安乐椅上一倒。

22 **similarly attired** （同 Higgins）类似打扮。

23 **is about to throw them on Higgins's when he hesitates** 正要把它们（他的帽子和大衣）往 Higgins 的帽子、大衣上面扔时，犹豫了（没有扔上去）。

25 **row** [raʊ] 吵嚷；是口语；注意，作“（划）船”和“（一）排”解的 row 读 [rəʊ]。**leave these thing lying about** 把这些东西（大衣、帽子）到处乱放。**leave about** 乱放；是习语；about 是副词，是“到处”的意思。

27 **chuck them over the banisters** [ˈbænɪstəz] **into the hall** 把它们从楼梯扶手这边扔到下面门廊里去。**banisters** 楼梯扶手；栏杆；用复数。

28 **put them away all right** 收拾好（不会吵嚷）。

29 **She'll think we were drunk.** 她之后（在将来）想到我们两个人现在的情况，这情况已成过去，所以“醉”用过去时 were drunk。

30 **We are, slightly.** = We are slightly drunk. slight 前面用一逗号，有“虽然不大醉，也稍有些醉”的意味。

31 **I didn't look.** 我没看；没去看信箱，也没看是否有信放在桌子等处。

32 **half singing half yawning an air from *La Fanciulla del West*** 一边打呵欠，一边唱着《西部女郎》中的一支曲子。**half singing half yawning** 半似歌唱、半似打着呵欠在哼。**air** 歌曲，曲调。an air 是 singing 和 yawning 的共同宾语。***La Fanciulla del*** [The Girl of the] ***West*** 是意大利歌剧作曲家 Giacomo [ˈdʒɑːkɒmɒ] Puccini [puːˈtʃiːnɪ]（1858–1924）作曲的歌剧，著名的歌剧《蝴蝶夫人》（*Madame Butterfly*）也是由 Puccini 作曲的。

34 **the devil** 诅咒语，无具体意义，用在 where 后加重语气。

35 **darkly** 阴郁地；冷冷地。

38 **the contents** [ˈkɒntents] **of the letter-box** 信箱中的信件。

40 **circulars** 通函，指向多方分发的通知、广告信等。**coroneted** [ˈkɒrənetɪd] **billet-doux** [ˌbɪleɪˈduː] 印有冠冕花样的“情书”。**billet-doux** 法语，原义“情书”，它有作谑语的用法，指不受欢迎的信，如广告信等。

41 **into the fender** 往壁炉的围栏里边（扔）。**posts himself on the hearthrug** [ˈhɑːθrʌg]（使自己）站立在壁炉前的地毯上。

the hearthrug, with his back to the grate.]

HIGGINS [*glancing at the billet-doux*] Money-lender. [*He throws the letter after the circulars.*]

Eliza returns with a pair of large down-at-heel slippers. She places them on the carpet before Higgins, and sits as before without a word.

HIGGINS [*yawning again*] Oh Lord! What an evening! What a crew! What a silly tomfoolery! [*He raises his shoe to unlace it, and catches sight of the slippers. He stops unlacing and looks at them as if they had appeared there of their own accord.*] Oh! theyre there, are they?

PICKERING [*stretching himself*] Well, I feel a bit tired. It's been a long day. The garden party, a dinner party, and the reception! Rather too much of a good thing. But youve won your bet, Higgins. Eliza did the trick, and something to spare, eh?

HIGGINS [*fervently*] Thank God it's over!

Eliza flinches violently; but they take no notice of her; and she recovers herself and sits stonily as before.

PICKERING Were you nervous at the garden party? I was. Eliza didnt seem a bit nervous.

HIGGINS Oh, she wasnt nervous. I knew she'd be all right. No: it's the strain of putting the job through all these months

42 **with his back to the grate** 他背朝壁炉。 **grate** 原义“炉栅”，转指“有炉栅的炉子”、“壁炉”。

43 **Money-lender** 放债者。这里当指推销分期付款商品的广告信。分期付款等于放债；广告信甜言蜜语犹如情书，所以前面说是 billet-doux。

45 **down-at-heel slippers** 磨掉了后跟的拖鞋。down-at-heel 作表语时作 down at heel、down at the heel、或 down at heels。

48 **What an evening!** = What an evening it is! 可作“多好的一个夜晚!”解，也可作“多糟的一个夜晚!”解，这里指后者。 **a crew** 原义为“全体船员”，这里是贬义，作“一伙人”解。

49 **tomfoolery** [ˌtɒmˈfuːləri] 蠢事；蠢话。

51 **as if they had appeared there of their own accord** 仿佛它们（slippers）自动地出现在那里。 **of one's own accord** 自动地；主动地；是习语。

53 **stretching himself** 伸懒腰。

55 **too much of a good thing** 好事过了头；过犹不及；是习语。

56 **did the trick** 达到预期目的；成功（这里指冒充公爵夫人成功）；是俚语；也作 turn the trick。 **and something to spare** 而且有余。and to spare 或 enough and to spare 是习语；作“足足有余”解。

57 **Thank God** 谢天（谢地）；幸亏。

59 **recovers herself** 恢复正常不再畏缩了。 **sits stonily** 没有表情地坐着；呆坐。

62 **I knew she'd be all right.** 我早知道她（在招待会上）会安然无事的（不会出问题）。she'd = she would.

63 **it's the strain of putting the job through all these months that has told on me** 倒是这几个月来完成这项（训练她冒充公爵夫人的）工作的艰辛使我精疲力尽。 **put through** 完成；是习语。through 是副词。has told 这里是“发生影响”的意思。 **has told on me** 影响我；伤我元气。

that has told on me. It was interesting enough at first, while we were at the phonetics; but after that I got deadly sick of it. If I hadnt backed myself to do it I should have chucked the whole thing up two months ago. It was a silly notion: the whole thing has been a bore.

PICKERING Oh come! The garden part was frightfully exciting. My heart began beating like anything.

HIGGINS Yes, for the first three minutes. But when I saw we were going to win hands down, I felt like a bear in a cage, hanging about doing nothing. The dinner was worse: sitting gorging there for over an hour, with nobody but a damned fool of a fashionable woman to talk to! I tell you, Pickering, never again for me. No more artificial duchesses. The whole thing has been simple purgatory.

PICKERING Youve never been broken in properly to the social routine. [*strolling over to the piano*] I rather enjoy dipping into it occasionally myself: it makes me feel young again. Anyhow, it was a great success: an immense success. I was quite frightened once or twice because Eliza was doing it so well. You see, lots of the real people cant do it at all: theyre such fools that they think style comes by nature to people in their

---

64 **while we were at the phonetics** 在我们教她语音的那段时期里。

65 **I got deadly sick of it** 变得厌恶得要死。 **deadly** 非常。it 指 the job（训练 Eliza 冒充公爵夫人的工作）。 **sick of** 厌恶。

66 **If I hadnt backed myself to do it I should have chucked the whole thing up two months ago.** 要不是我拿自己打了赌要做这件事，我早在两个月前就把整件事丢下不干了。这是表示与过去事实相反的虚拟语气，实际上是“我打了赌，所以没有丢下不干”。back 是“在……上下赌注”的意思，如言 back a horse（赛马中把赌注下在某一匹马上）。**chuck up** 丢下；放弃。

69 **come** 感叹词，叫人注意或表示不耐烦等。 **frightfully** 非常地；是口语。

70 **like anything** 什么似地；猛烈地；是习语。

71 **for the first three minutes** = the garden party was frightfully exciting for the first three minutes.

72 **win hands down** 轻易取胜。 **hands down** 垂手而得地；轻而易举地。 **felt like a bear in a cage** 觉得像笼中的熊。注意：不要和习语 feel like（想要……）混淆，如：I feel like (having) a walk with you. **hanging about** 闲荡；是习语。

73 **The dinner was worse** 席面上更糟。这里 dinner 指进餐的情况，不是指菜肴。 **sitting gorging there** 坐在那儿大啖大嚼；这里 sitting 是动名词，与 dinner 同位；gorging 是分词，修饰 sitting。

74 **with nobody but a damned fool of a fashionable woman to talk to** 只能对着一个该死的傻子般的时髦女人说话。 **nobody but** 除……之外没有别人，只有（某人）。but = except. **a damned fool of ...** 该死的傻子般的……。与 of 的这种习惯用法类似的例子有 a palace of a house（王宫般的房屋）、his angel of a wife（他的天使般的妻子）。

75 **never again for me** 从此我不再干这种事。口语句中常不完整，有时也很难说省略了什么，这里这个例子很典型。

77 **has been simple purgatory** [ˈpɜːɡətəri] 简直是受罪。 **simple** 不折不扣的。purgatory 原义“炼狱”，转义“一时的磨难”。

78 **broken in properly to the social routine** [ruːˈtiːn] 好好习惯于社交应酬这一套。break in 是习语，有“训练”、“使适应”等多种意思。

79 **dipping into it** 参加一下社交应酬。dip，原义“浸一下”，引申为“涉猎”等意思。

83 **lots of the real people** 好多真正的绅士淑女（别于冒充公爵夫人的 Eliza）。lots of 和 a lot of 相同，后面可数名词或不可数名词都可用。

84 **style comes by nature to people in their position** 风度自然来到有地位的人面前；有地位自有风度。style 作“风度”、“气派”解时为不可数名词。

position; and so they never learn. Theres always something professional about doing a thing superlatively well.

HIGGINS Yes: thats what drives me mad: the silly people dont know their own silly business. [*rising*] However, it's over and done with; and now I can go to bed at last without dreading tomorrow.

Eliza's beauty becomes murderous.

PICKERING I think I shall turn in too. Still, it's been a great occasion: a triumph for you. Goodnight. [*He goes.*]

HIGGINS [*following him*] Goodnight. [*over his shoulder, at the door*] Put out the lights, Eliza; and tell Mrs Pearce not to make coffee for me in the morning: I'll take tea. [*He goes out.*]

Eliza tries to control herself and feel indifferent as she rises and walks across to the hearth to switch off the lights. By the time she gets there she is on the point of screaming. She sits down in Higgins's chair and holds on hard to the arms. Finally she gives way and flings herself furiously on the floor, raging.

HIGGINS [*in despairing wrath outside*] What the devil have I done with my slippers? [*He appears at the door.*]

LIZA [*snatching up the slippers, and hurling them at him one after the other with all her force*] There are your slippers. And there. Take your slippers; and may you never have a day's luck with

---

85 **something professional** 专门的东西；专门技术。

86 **superlatively** [sjuːˈpɜːlətɪvli] **well** 最好；特别好。

87 **drives me mad** 使我不得不恼火。 **mad** 作“狂怒”解，是口语。

88 **their own silly business** 他们自己的蠢事（指显示身份）。 **it's over and done with** 这件事已成过去，圆满了结。 **done with** 了结；口语。

91 **Eliza's beauty becomes murderous.** Eliza 的美（美丽的容貌）变得杀气腾腾。

92 **turn in** 上床睡觉；是习语。 **a great occasion** 一大盛事。

94 **over his shoulder** 回过头来。区别 over one's shoulder 和 over somebody's shoulder，前者是“回头”，后者“探头隔着别人的肩膀”，如：He is looking over your shoulder. 他在你肩后瞧着。

97 **control herself** 控制自己（的感情）。 **feel indifferent** 觉得无所谓；不介意。

98 **By the time she gets there** 当她走到（壁炉）那里的时候。 **By the time** 当……的时候；是习语，后面省略 when，因此它有近似 when 的连词的作用。

99 **on the point of screaming** 几乎要放声尖叫起来。 **on the point of** 即将；濒于；几乎；是习语。

100 **holds on hard to the arms** 紧紧抓住（椅子两边的）扶手。 **gives way** 坚持不住；是习语；这里有“情不自禁”的意思。

101 **flings herself furiously on the floor, raging** 猛然倒在地上，大发脾气。

102 **in despairing wrath** [rɒθ] **outside** 在门外冒着无可奈何的怒火。 **What the devil have I done with my slippers?** 我对我的拖鞋做了什么？我把拖鞋弄到哪儿去了？ the devil 加强 What 的口气，见前注。

104 **one after the other** 一只又一只地；是习语。

106 **may you never have a day's luck with them** 但愿你穿着它们（这双拖鞋）没有一天好运气（永无宁日）。 **may** 表示祈愿，常放在主语前，如 May you succeed!（愿你成功！）Long may she live!（愿她长寿！）

them!

HIGGINS [*astounded*] What on earth – ! [*He comes to her.*] Whats the matter? Get up. [*He pulls her up.*] Anything wrong?

LIZA [*breathless*] Nothing wrong – with *you*. Ive won your bet for you, havnt I? Thats enough for you. *I* dont matter, I suppose.

HIGGINS You won my bet! You! Presumptuous insect! *I* won it. What did you throw those slippers at me for?

LIZA Because I wanted to smash your face. I'd like to kill you, you selfish brute. Why didnt you leave me where you picked me out of – in the gutter? You thank God it's all over, and that now you can throw me back again there, do you? [*She crisps her fingers frantically.*]

HIGGINS [*looking at her in cool wonder*] The creature is nervous, after all.

LIZA [*gives a suffocated scream of fury, and instinctively darts her nails at his face*] !

HIGGINS [*catching her wrists*] Ah! Would you? Claws in, you cat. How dare you shew your temper to me? Sit down and be quiet. [*He throws her roughly into the easy-chair.*]

LIZA [*crushed by superior strength and weight*] Whats to become of me? Whats to become of me?

HIGGINS How the devil do I know whats to become of you? What does it matter what becomes of you?

LIZA You dont care. I know you dont care. You wouldnt care if I

---

108 **What on earth – !** 究竟怎么回事！ on earth，是习语，没有具体意义，用

以加强 What 的语气；破折号表示话未说完，未说出的话当是 is the matter。

110 **Nothing wrong – with *you*.** = There is nothing wrong – with you. 没有什么事——对你来说；没你的事。 **wrong** 出毛病；有问题；与 the matter 同义，后面用 with。

111 ***I* dont matter** 我无关紧要。matter 作“要紧”解，主要用于否定句或疑问句。

112 **You won my bet!** 你使我打赌赢了！这是反语，实际意思是“打赌赢关你什么事！” **Presumptuous** [prɪˈzʌmptʃʊəs] **insect** 妄自尊大的家伙。 **insect** 虫；转义“可鄙的人”、“卑微的人”；汉语中也有把糊涂人称“糊涂虫”的用例。

113 **What did you throw those slippers at me for?** = For what (= Why) did you throw those slippers at me? 但习惯上不用 For what ... ?

115 **leave me where you picked me out of – in the gutter** 让我留在你把我捡来的地方——马路旁边。in the gutter 和 where you picked me out of 同位；gutter，街沟，贫民区。这里的 where 是关系代词，作 out of 的宾语，同时在从句和主句间起连接作用。

117 **that** 这个 that 引起的原因状语从句，承接 thank God，与 it's all over 并列。 **do you?** 是附加疑问（a tag question），一般肯定的陈述用否定的附加疑问，这里用肯定的附加句，表示肯定上面的陈述部分。

118 **crisps her fingers** 扳弄指头。

119 **in cool wonder** 以冷静的诧异。

121 **instinctively darts her nails at his face** 本能地突然用指甲朝他脸上抓来。darts 原义“标枪”，这里是“把……像投标枪似地抓上来”的意思。

123 **Would you?** 你要（抓我的脸）吗？ **Claws in** 抓到肉里来吧。 **you cat** 你这泼妇。cat 原可作“恶毒的女人”解，这里 Eliza 要抓人，称她 cat 有双重意思。cat 和 you 同位，是呼语。

126 **crushed by superior** [sjuːˈpɪərɪə] **strength and weight** 被（Higgins 的）超过她的力量和重量所压倒。 **Whats to become of me?** 我将成为什么？我将怎么样？What is to (或 will, has) become of somebody (或 something)? 是惯用句型。

130 **You dont care.** 你不放在心上；你不关心。下文 You wouldnt care if I was dead 是“即使我死，你也不放在心上”的意思；if = even if（即使）；这一句是虚拟语气。

was dead. I'm nothing to you – not so much as them slippers.

HIGGINS [*thundering*] *Those* slippers.

LIZA [*with bitter submission*] Those slippers. I didnt think it made any difference now.

A pause. Eliza hopeless and crushed. Higgins a little uneasy.

HIGGINS [*in his loftiest manner*] Why have you begun going on like this? May I ask whether you complain of your treatment here?

LIZA No.

HIGGINS Has anybody behaved badly to you? Colonel Pickering? Mrs Pearce? Any of the servants?

LIZA No.

HIGGINS I presume you dont pretend that *I* have treated you badly?

LIZA No.

HIGGINS I am glad to hear it. [*He moderates his tone.*] Perhaps youre tired after the strain of the day. Will you have a glass of champagne? [*He moves towards the door.*]

LIZA No. [*recollecting her manners*] Thank you.

HIGGINS [*good-humored again*] This has been coming on you for some days. I suppose it was natural for you to be anxious about the garden party. But thats all over now. [*He pats her kindly on the shoulder. She writhes.*] Theres nothing more to worry about.

---

131 **not so much as them slippers** （我）还不如那双拖鞋；前面省略 I'm；them 是 those 之讹，所以 Higgins 随即加以纠正。

132 **thundering** 大发雷霆。

133 **bitter submission** 愤恨的屈服。 **I didnt think it made any difference now.** 现在我并不认为这（them slippers 和 those slippers 之类的语法正误）有什么关系。make some (any, no) difference 是习语。

135 **A pause** 停顿；稍顿（剧本说明词中常见）。 **Eliza hopeless and crushed.** Eliza 后省略连系动词 is 或 becomes；下句 Higgins a little uneasy 同例；说明词中常有这种省略。

136 **going on like this** 这样轻举妄动；这样乱说乱动。

137 **complain of your treatment here** 抱怨（不满）你在这里所受的待遇。complain 后面惯用 of。

140 **behaved badly to you** 对你态度不好；待你不好。behaved well (badly) 是"行为好（不好）"的意思。

143 **presume** 猜想；（没有根据地）相信。后面接宾语从句时，常不用连词 that。 **pretend** 假托；违心地说。

146 **moderates his tone** 缓和声调。

148 **champagne** [ʃæmˈpeɪn] 香槟酒。

149 **recollecting her manners** 记起了（Higgins 教）她的礼貌。 **manners** 礼貌；用复数。

150 **This has been coming on you for some days.** 这件事（指去参加招待会的事）已经侵袭了你几天；这件事几天来弄得你一直很紧张。

152 **pats her kindly on the shoulder** 亲切地拍拍她的肩膀；注意这里用 on the shoulder 而不用 on her shoulder；即使前面是 pat them（复数），后面也用 on the shoulder（单数）。

153 **Theres nothing more to worry about.** 不再有需要伤脑筋的事了；无需再操心了。 **to worry about** 习惯上用主动态形式表示被动态，即 to be worried about。

LIZA No. Nothing more for you to worry about. [*She suddenly rises and gets away from him by going to the piano bench, where she sits and hides her face.*] Oh God! I wish I was dead.

HIGGINS [*staring after her in sincere surprise*] Why? In heaven's name, why? [*reasonably, going to her*] Listen to me, Eliza. All this irritation is purely subjective.

LIZA I dont understand. I'm too ignorant.

HIGGINS It's only imagination. Low spirits and nothing else. Nobody's hurting you. Nothing's wrong. You go to bed like a good girl and sleep it off. Have a little cry and say your prayers: that will make you comfortable.

LIZA I heard your prayers. 'Thank God it's all over!'

HIGGINS [*impatiently*] Well, dont you thank God it's all over? Now you are free and can do what you like.

LIZA [*pulling herself together in desperation*] What am I fit for? What have you left me fit for? Where am I to go? What am I to do? Whats to become of me?

HIGGINS [*enlightened, but not at all impressed*] Oh, thats whats worrying you, is it? [*He thrusts his hands into his pockets, and walks about in his usual manner, rattling the contents of his pockets, as if condescending to a trivial subject out of pure kindness.*] I shouldnt bother about it if I were you. I should imagine you wont have much difficulty in settling yourself somewhere or other, though I hadnt quite realized that you were going away.

---

156 **Nothing more for you to worry about.** = There's nothing more for you to

worry about. 不再有你要伤脑筋的事了。这里 for you to worry about 是个带有逻辑主语的不定式短语；这个逻辑主语前面习惯用介词 for。

157 **hides her face** 以手掩面。 **I wish I was dead.** 我但愿死了；我死了多好。wish 后面的宾语从句用虚拟语气，这里的 was，传统语法认为应用 were，但现代英语中用 was 的很多。

158 **staring after her in sincere surprise** 真心诧异地从背后注视着她。 **In heaven's name, why?** 用上帝的名义（问你，到底）为什么？ in heaven's name 也作 in God's name 或 in the name of God，用以发誓，祈求，或加强疑问语气，如：What in heaven's name is the matter? 究竟出了什么事？

159 **All this irritation is purely subjective.** 这种暴躁纯粹全都是主观的；客观上并没有什么事，而是她自己在凭空地烦躁不安。

161 **I dont understand.** 我不懂（你说的话）；Eliza 不懂 Higgins 以学者口吻所说的什么"主观"、"客观"。

162 **Low spirits and nothing else** 低落的情绪，没有其他；情绪不好而已。 **spirits** 情绪；心情；用复数。 and nothing else 别的没有什么。

164 **sleep it off** 用睡眠消除它（指低落的情绪）。

169 **pulling herself together in desperation** 在绝望中镇定下来。 **pull oneself together** 振作起来，恢复镇定；是习语。 **What am I fit for?** 我适合做什么？我能做什么？

170 **left me fit for** 把我弄得适合做（什么）；让我去做（什么）。fit for (what) 是宾语补足语，me 和 fit for (what) 构成复合宾语。

172 **impressed** 被使有印象；有印象；受感动。

174 **rattling the contents of his pockets** 搅乱（裤）袋里放着的东西（硬币、钥匙之类）使叮当作响。 **as if condescending to a trivial** [ˈtrɪvɪəl] **subject out of pure kindness** 仿佛纯粹出于好意而屈尊考虑一个琐碎的问题；as if condescending = as if he was (或 were) condescending，虚拟语气。

176 **I should imagine** = I should think. 用 should imagine 比直接用 imagine 婉转而客气。

177 **settling yourself somewhere or other** 在什么地方安顿下来。 **somewhere or other** 不是某处，便是别处；some ... or other，表示不确定；某个……

178 **realized** 意识到；想到。

[*She looks quickly at him: he does not look at her, but examines the dessert stand on the piano and decides that he will eat an apple.*] You might marry, you know. [*He bites a large piece out of the apple and munches it noisily.*] You see, Eliza, all men are not confirmed old bachelors like me and the Colonel. Most men are the marrying sort (poor devils!); and youre not bad-looking: it's quite a pleasure to look at you sometimes – not now, of course, because youre crying and looking as ugly as the very devil; but when youre all right and quite yourself, youre what I should call attractive. That is, to the people in the marrying line, you understand. You go to bed and have a good nice rest; and then get up and look at yourself in the glass; and you wont feel so cheap.

Eliza again looks at him, speechless, and does not stir.

The look is quite lost on him: he eats his apple with a dreamy expression of happiness, as it is quite a good one.

HIGGINS [*a genial afterthought occurring to him*] I daresay my mother could find some chap or other who would do very well.

LIZA We were above that at the corner of Tottenham Court Road.

HIGGINS [*waking up*] What do you mean?

---

180 **dessert stand** 果盘。

181 **You might marry** 这是虚拟语气，省略 if you would like (to marry) 或 if you could do nothing else 之类的假定从句。

182 **all men are not confirmed old bachelors like me and the Colonel** 并不是所有的男人都像我和这位上校那样是坚定（不结婚）的老独生汉。注意：不作“所有男人都不是坚定的老独身汉”解。

183 **Most men are the marrying sort** 大多数男人都是想要结婚的一类人。**marrying** 想要结婚的；比较：married，结了婚的；married 又常用复数作名词，如 the young marrieds，已婚青年。

184 **poor devils** 可怜的家伙们。devil 原义“魔鬼”，常与 poor 连用，转义为“家伙”。

185 **not now** = it's not quite a pleasure to look at you now.

186 **the very devil** 真正的魔鬼；十足的魔鬼。这里 very 是形容词。

187 **when youre all right** 在你（不哭，不闹，不沮丧）好好的时候。**quite yourself** （身体、精神）完全正常的时候。

188 **what I should call attractive** 我该说是令人喜爱的。What one calls 和 what is called 都是“人家所说的”、“所谓”的意思，它们和 so-called 不同之处是后者往往含有“不配叫做”的意思。**That is** 那是说，那就是说。**to the people in the marrying line** 在想要结婚的一类（男）人看来是（令人喜爱的）。承接上句 attractive。

190 **look at yourself in the glass** 自己照镜子看看。glass = looking glass.

191 **feel so cheap** 觉得心情不好。feel cheap 是口语中常用的习语；除“身体不好”、“心情不好”外，也作“感到惭愧”解，如：He felt cheap about his failure.

193 **The look is quite lost on him** （Eliza 望着他的）眼神全是白费（他根本不在意）。**dreamy expression of happiness** 像在做梦似的快乐的表情；悠然自得。

195 **a genial afterthought occurring to him** 一个好心的事后想起的念头突然来到他（头脑里）；后来忽然想到一个好主意。

196 **some chap or other** 某个小伙子。**chap** 家伙；小伙子；是口语。**Some ... or other** 见前 somewhere or other 条注。**would do very well** 会非常合适。do 有“行”的意思。

197 **We were above that** 我们这种人(原来)不屑为此。Eliza 把嫁人看作是卖掉自己，所以这样说；见下文自明。

199 **waking up** 醒来；原先如在梦中（dreamy），现在听到 Eliza 说不屑嫁人，惊醒过来。

LIZA I sold flowers. I didnt sell myself. Now youve made a lady of me I'm not fit to sell anything else. I wish youd left me where you found me.

HIGGINS [*slinging the core of the apple decisively into the grate*] Tosh, Eliza. Dont you insult human relations by dragging all this cant about buying and selling into it. You neednt marry the fellow if you dont like him.

LIZA What else am I to do?

HIGGINS Oh, lots of things. What about your old idea of a florist's shop? Pickering could set you up in one: he has lots of money. [*chuckling*] He'll have to pay for all those togs you have been wearing today; and that, with the hire of the jewellery, will make a big hole in two hundred pounds. Why, six months ago you would have thought it the millennium to have a flower shop of your own. Come! Youll be all right. I must clear off to bed: I'm devilish sleepy. By the way, I came down for something: I forget what it was.

LIZA Your slippers.

HIGGINS Oh yes, of course. You shied them at me. [*He picks them up, and is going out when she rises and speaks to him.*]

LIZA Before you go, sir —

HIGGINS [*dropping the slippers in his surprise at her calling him Sir*] Eh?

---

200 **Now** = Now that. 既然；由于；是连词。 **made a lady of me** 把我（训练得）变成了个贵妇人。

201 **not fit to sell anything else** 不能卖任何其他东西（只好卖自己）。 **left me where you found me** 把我留在你遇到我的地方（原来卖花的街头）; where you found me 这个状语从句作宾语补足语 me 和 where you found me 构成复合宾语。

203 **Tosh** 英国俚语，= Nonsense，胡说，废话。

204 **Dont you insult human relations by dragging all this cant about buying and selling into it.** 你不要把买进卖出那一套话全拉扯来污蔑人与人之间的关系（指婚姻关系）。 **Dont you** 是加强 Dont 的语气的说法。 **cant** "行话"，也作"假话"等解；是总称；犹如 slang 是"俚语"的总称，都是不可数名词。

208 **lots of things** = you can do lots of things. 你能做的事情多了。 **What about** （征求意见或询问情况时用）……怎么样?

209 **set you up in one** 替你开个花铺。set up 是习语，这里 set 是及物动词，作"使……自立"解，如：He set up for himself. 他开始独立经营。one = a florist's shop.

210 **He'll have to pay for all those togs** 他（Pickering）得支付所有那些行头的钱（因为 Pickering 打赌输了）。 **togs** 衣服；是口语，只作复数形式。

211 **that, with the hire of the jewellery** [ˈdʒu:əlri] 那一笔（购买行头的钱）加上这些珠宝首饰的租金。hire 为"租用"；也作"租金"解。 **jewellery** 是珠宝首饰的总称。

212 **will make a big hole in two hundred pounds** make a hole in 是习语，意思是"在……中花去一大笔钱"，所以这句话按字面讲是"在两百英镑中花去一大部分"，实际指"差不多要花掉两百镑"。 **Why** 语助词，没有具体意义，犹言"哎"、"嘿"。

213 **would have thought it the millennium** [mɪˈlenɪəm] （过去）会把这件事（指自己开个花铺）看作是无上的幸福。 **would have thought** 表示与过去事实相反的虚拟语气，其实未必真这样想过。 **millennium** 从《圣经·启示录》所说耶稣将再临人间统治的"至福一千年"转义为"太平盛世"、"黄金时代"。

215 **clear off to bed** 走去床上睡觉。 **clear off** 走去；溜走；是习语。 **devilish** 作副词，作"非常"、"过分"解，是口语。 **By the way** 顺便说；是习语。

218 **shied** 投掷；是口语。

220 **Before you go, sir –** 在你走开之前，先生——（我还有话对你说）。这里 Eliza 忽用 sir 称 Higgins，他觉得突兀（见下文），因为 sir 是用以尊称陌生男子，或是仆人称主人、下属称上司用的。

LIZA Do my clothes belong to me or to Colonel Pickering?

HIGGINS [*coming back into the room as if her question were the very climax of unreason*] What the devil use would they be to Pickering?

LIZA He might want them for the next girl you pick up to experiment on.

HIGGINS [*shocked and hurt*] Is that the way you feel towards us?

LIZA I dont want to hear anything more about that. All I want to know is whether anything belongs to me. My own clothes were burnt.

HIGGINS But what does it matter? Why need you start bothering about that in the middle of the night?

LIZA I want to know what I may take away with me. I dont want to be accused of stealing.

HIGGINS [*now deeply wounded*] Stealing! You shouldnt have said that, Eliza. That shews a want of feeling.

LIZA I'm sorry. I'm only a common ignorant girl; and in my station I have to be careful. There cant be any feelings between the like of you and the like of me. Please will you tell me what belongs to me and what doesnt?

HIGGINS [*very sulky*] You may take the whole damned houseful if you like. Except the jewels. Theyre hired. Will that satisfy you? [*He turns on his heel and is about to go in extreme dudgeon.*]

---

224 **the very climax of unreason** [ʌnˈriːzn] 真正无理之极。 **climax** 逐步加强而

达到的顶点；（小说、戏剧）高潮。

225 **What the devil use** 是口语中 What use 的强调说法；What use 在这里等于 of what use。

227 **experiment on** 用……作试验。比较：experience in chemistry 做化学实验；experiment with drugs 试验药品。experiment 作动词时读 [ɪk'sperɪmənt]。

229 **shocked and hurt** 感到震惊且受了委屈。hurt 是过去分词，与原形动词同形。

230 **about that** 关于那个（指上文 the way you feel towards us，Eliza 看待 Higgins 和 Pickering 的态度）。 **All I want to know is whether anything belongs to me.** 我想知道的只是是否有什么东西是属于我的。注意：不作“是否一切东西都是属于我的”解。

231 **My own clothes were burnt** 我自己的衣服已经被烧掉了。见第二幕，Higgins 叫 Mrs Pearce 把 Eliza 原来破烂肮脏的衣服都扔进炉子里烧掉。

234 **about that** 关于那个（指 Eliza 问什么东西属于她的那件事情）。

236 **to be accused of stealing** 被指控偷窃。accused somebody of 后接表示罪过或错误的名词或动名词；介词用 of。

237 **wounded** ['wu:ndɪd] 感情上受到伤害。是过去分词。wound 比 hurt 正式且严重。

238 **That shews a want of feeling.** 那（指 Eliza 说不愿被指控偷窃的话）是一种缺乏体贴之情的表示。在 want of feeling/thought 之类的词组中，want 前面一般不用冠词，这里用 a，表示“某种”的意思。

239 **in my station** 处于我的地位。

240 **feelings** 指与理智相对的感情时，用复数。

241 **the like of you** 像你（们）这样的人；你（们）这种人；通常说 the likes of you，是口语。

243 **take the whole damned houseful** 把整个倒霉的屋里的东西都拿走。Damned 是诅咒语，Higgins 身为专家、教授，常出言粗鲁，已屡见前。

244 **Except the jewels.** 是上句的一部分；今独立成句，表示说话中间有停顿，是说了上句之后想起而补充的，称为 afterthought，同时也加强语气。

245 **turns on his heel** 急遽转身；是习语。 **in extreme dudgeon** ['dʌdʒən] 极其愤怒地。

LIZA [*drinking in his emotion like nectar, and nagging him to provoke a further supply*] Stop, please. [*She takes off her jewels.*] Will you take these to your room and keep them safe? I dont want to run the risk of their being missing.

HIGGINS [*furious*] Hand them over. [*She puts them into his hands.*] If these belonged to me instead of to the jeweller, I'd ram them down your ungrateful throat. [*He perfunctorily thrusts them into his pockets, unconsciously decorating himself with the protruding ends of the chains.*]

LIZA [*taking a ring off*] This ring isnt the jeweller's: it's the one you bought me in Brighton. I dont want it now. [*Higgins dashes the ring violently into the fireplace, and turns on her so threateningly that she crouches over the piano with her hands over her face, and exclaims.*] Dont you hit me.

HIGGINS Hit you! You infamous creature, how dare you accuse me of such a thing? It is you who have hit me. You have wounded me to the heart.

LIZA [*thrilling with hidden joy*] I'm glad. Ive got a little of my own back, anyhow.

HIGGINS [*with dignity, in his finest professional style*] You have caused me to lose my temper: a thing that has hardly ever happened

---

246 **drinking in his emotion like nectar** 喜看他激动的感情（Higgins 的盛怒），如饮甘露；（Eliza）看见他激动，得意之至。 **drink in** 急于吸收；陶醉于。in 是副词。 **nectar** 原指希腊神话中神饮的酒，转义为“美味的饮料”。 **nagging him to provoke a further supply** 困扰他，使他再发脾气。

Eliza 把 Higgins 的盛怒当作甘露，所以惹他再发一次脾气，等于再供应一份甘露（a further supply）。

248 **keep them safe** 把它们（珠宝首饰）收藏得安全妥当。safe 是形容词作宾语补足语，them 和 safe 构成复合宾语。

249 **run the risk of their being missing** 冒它们遗失的风险。missing 是由现在分词变成的形容词，并非和 being 构成进行式；miss 在现代英语中不能作“遗失”解的不及物动词用。

251 **belonged to me instead of to the jeweller** 属于我而不是属于珠宝商。这里 instead of 后面的 to 一般不可省略。 **ram them down your ungrateful throat** 把它们塞进你这不义（之人）的喉咙。不可说“不义的喉咙”，用“忘恩负义的喉咙”表示“忘恩负义的人的喉咙”。这里的 ungrateful 在修辞学上叫做 transferred epithet（转移修饰词）。

252 **perfunctorily** [pəˈfʌŋ*k*trəli] 马马虎虎地，草率地。注意这个词中即使不发 [k] 音，n 仍读作 [ŋ]。

253 **unconsciously decorating himself with the protruding ends of the chains** 不自觉地把拖出的链条的末端装饰着自己。首饰链条一部分拖出在口袋外，无意中成了“装饰”。

256 **Brighton** [ˈbraɪtn] 布莱顿，英格兰南部海滨城市，是游览胜地。

257 **turns on her** 转身向她；对她发怒。

258 **with her hands over her face** 双手掩面。

260 **Hit you!** 是反问句 Do I hit you? 的强调语气。 **You infamous** [ˈɪnfəməs] **creature** 你这不要脸的东西。You 和 infamous creature 同位，是呼语。 **infamous** 臭名昭著的；不名誉的；无耻的；注意重音在第一音节。

261 **such a thing** 指打人。

262 **wounded me to the heart** 伤透了我的心。

263 **thrilling with hidden joy** 因暗暗高兴而激动。 **got a little of my own back** 得回了一点；得到了一点报复，比较习语 come into one's own，得到自己应得的（名誉、利益等）。

265 **his finest professional style** 他的最优美的专家风度。

266 **lose my temper** 发脾气。 **a thing that has hardly ever happened to me before** 一件在我身上不太发生的事（指发脾气）。其实 Higgins 常发脾气。

to me before. I prefer to say nothing more tonight. I am going to bed.

LIZA [*pertly*] Youd better leave a note for Mrs pearce about the coffee; for she wont be told by me.

HIGGINS [*formally*] Damn Mrs Pearce; and damn the coffee; and damn you; and [*wildly*] damn my own folly in having lavished my hard-earned knowledge and the treasure of my regard and intimacy on a heartless guttersnipe. [*He goes out with impressive decorum, and spoils it by slamming the door savagely.*]

Eliza goes down on her knees on the hearthrug to look for the ring. When she finds it she considers for a moment what to do with it. Finally she flings it down on the dessert stand and goes upstairs in a tearing rage.

The furniture of Eliza's room has been increased by a big wardrobe and a sumptuous dressing-table. She comes in and switches on the electric light. She goes to the wardrobe; opens it; and pulls out a walking dress, a hat, and a pair of shoes, which she throws on the bed. She takes off her evening dress and shoes; then takes a padded hanger from the wardrobe; adjusts it carefully in the evening dress; and hangs it in the wardrobe, which she shuts with a slam. She puts on her walking shoes, her walking dress, and hat. She takes her wrist watch from the dressing-table and fastens it on. She pulls on her gloves; takes her vanity bag; and looks into it to see that her purse is there before

269 **pertly** 无礼地；泼辣地。 **leave a note** 留个条子。

270 **she wont be told by me** 她不会被我告诉；我不会告诉她（不替你传话）。

271 **formally** 一本正经地。 **Damn Mrs Pearce** Mrs Pearce 见鬼去。Higgins 刚说从来不大发脾气，这下又大发雷霆了。

272 **lavished my hard-earned knowledge and the treasure of my regard and intimacy** [ˈɪntɪməsi] **on a heartless guttersnipe** 把我辛苦得来的知识和我珍贵的关心及亲切浪费在一个没心肝的小叫花子身上。Higgins 在第二幕中就骂 Eliza 是 draggletailed guttersnipe。

275 **impressive decorum** [dɪˈkɔːrəm] 给人深刻印象的文雅仪态。 **spoils it by slamming the door savagely** 粗野地砰的一声猛力关门而破坏了这个（文雅的仪态）。

276 **Eliza goes down on her knees** 跪下；是习语。

277 **what to do with it** 如何处置它（戒指）。

279 **in a tearing** [ˈteərɪŋ] **rage** 愤怒欲裂地。 **tearing** 形容词，原义"撕裂的"，转义"强烈的"。

281 **sumptuous** [ˈsʌmptʃʊəs] **dressing-table** 豪华的梳妆台。

283 **walking dress** 妇女（平常出门穿的）便服。which 指 walking dress，hat 和 shoes。

285 **padded hanger** [ˈhæŋə] 有装垫的衣架。 **adjusts it carefully in the evening dress** 把它（衣架）小心地安放在晚礼服里；把晚礼服小心挂在衣架上。

287 **walking shoes** （平常出门穿的）轻便鞋。

289 **fastens it on** 把它（手表）带上。 **pulls on her gloves** 戴上手套。戴手套、穿袜子的动词用 pull on，这是习语。

290 **vanity bag** （妇女携带化妆品等用的）手提包。也称 vanity case，vanity box。**to see that her purse is there** 查看一下，确认她的钱包在那里（手提包里）；看看钱包是否在那里。习语 see (to it) that ... 表示"留心做到"、"务使"的意思。**before hanging** [ˈhæŋɪŋ] **it on her wrist** 在把它（手提包）挂在手腕上之前。这个状语短语修饰 looks。

hanging it on her wrist. She makes for the door. Every movement expresses her furious resolution.

She takes a last look at herself in the glass.

She suddenly puts out her tongue at herself; then leaves the room, switching off the electric light at the door.

Meanwhile, in the street outside, Freddy Eynsford Hill, lovelorn, is gazing up at the second floor, in which one of the windows is still lighted.

The light goes out.

FREDDY Goodnight, darling, darling, darling.

Eliza comes out, giving the door a considerable bang behind her.

LIZA Whatever are you doing here?

FREDDY Nothing. I spend most of my nights here. It's the only place where I'm happy. Dont laugh at me, Miss Doolittle.

LIZA Dont you call me Miss Doolittle, do you hear? Liza's good enough for me. [*She breaks down and grabs him by the shoulders.*] Freddy: you dont think I'm a heartless guttersnipe, do you?

FREDDY Oh no, no, darling: how can you imagine such a thing? You are the loveliest, dearest –

291 **makes for** 向……走去；是习语。

292 **furious resolution** 强烈的决心。furious 原义“盛怒的”，也作“狂暴的”、“喧闹的”解。

294 **puts out her tongue at herself** 对（在镜子里的）自己伸出舌头；做鬼脸自嘲。

296 **Freddy Eynsford Hill** 在第一幕开场就和他的母亲及妹妹一起在教堂廊下避雨和叫车的 Freddy。 **lovelorn** 失恋的；因相思而憔悴的。

297 **the second floor** 英国用法，指我国所说的“三楼”，美国用法指“二楼”；按第二幕场景说明，Higgins 的实验室在 the first floor，而 Eliza 住的当是实验室楼上一层。 **in which** which 当然代替 the second floor，这里指的是这一层的房间，所以前面介词用 in，表示“在房间里”。

301 **giving the door a considerable bang behind her** （走出房门）把背后的房门狠狠地砰的一声（关上）。

302 **Whatever are you doing here?** 你在这里到底干什么？这里的 whatever 严格应作 What ever，在口语中加强 what 的语气；通常 whatever 作“无论什么”解，例如：Read whatever you like. 你喜欢读什么就读什么。

303 **most of my nights** 我大多数的夜晚。

305 **Liza's good enough for me.** 叫我 Liza 就好了。

306 **breaks down** 失去自制；是习语。

309 **the loveliest, dearest –** 破折号表示话未说完，一时说不出是最亲爱的什么。

He loses all self-control and smothers her with kisses. She hungry for comfort, responds. They stand there in one another's arms.

An elderly police constable arrives.

CONSTABLE [*scandalized*] Now then! Now then!! Now then!!!

They release one another hastily.

FREDDY Sorry, constable. Weve only just become engaged.

They run away.

The constable shakes his head, reflecting on his own courtship and on the vanity of human hopes. He moves off in the opposite direction with slow professional steps.

The flight of the lovers takes them to Cavendish Square. There they halt to consider their next move.

LIZA [*out of breath*] He didnt half give me a fright, that copper. But you answered him proper.

FREDDY I hope I havent taken you out of your way. Where were you going?

LIZA To the river.

310 **smothers her with kisses** 连连吻她，弄得她透不过气来。

311 **hungry for comfort** 如饥似渴地需要安慰。 **responds** 作出反应；回应他的吻。 **in one another's arms** 互相拥抱。one another 和 each other 可以通用，虽然旧语法家认为 each other 用于两者之间，one another 用于两者以上之间。

313 **elderly** 上了年纪的；中年以上的；是形容词。 **police constable** [ˈkʌnstəbl] 警察；也单称 constable，见下文。

314 **scandalized** 被使感到震惊（或反感），即"震惊（或反感）"；是过去分词。 **Now then!** 比较缓和地向人抗议或叫人注意时用语，也作 Now now! 犹言"喂，喂！"

315 **release one another** 彼此松开。

316 **only just become engaged** 只是刚订了婚的；engaged 是表语，也称主语补足语。

317 **run away** 逃跑；潜逃；是习语。

318 **reflecting on his own courtship and on the vanity of human hopes** 想到自己追求情人的情况和人生希望的空虚。

319 **moves off in the opposite** [ˈɒpəzɪt] **direction with slow professional steps** 用缓慢的（警察的）职业（所习惯）的步子向（Eliza 和 Freddy 逃走的）相反方向走去。

321 **The flight of the lovers takes them to Cavendish** [ˈkævəndɪʃ] **Square.** 这对情人的逃跑把他们带到了 Cavendish 广场；他们一逃逃到了那个广场。

322 **next move** 下一步行动；也就是"再往哪里走"。

323 **out of breath** 喘不过气来；是习语。 **He didnt half give me a fright, that copper.** 那个警察，他让我吃了个不小的惊讶（把我吓得不轻）。not half 是习语，有两个相反的意思：一是"没有一半"、"一半也没有"、"极不"；一是"不止一半"、"极其"；这里是用作后一义；用作前一义的例如：That's not half bad. 那是好透了。 that copper 是 He 的同位语；copper 或 cop 作"警察"解是俚语。

324 **answered him proper** 回答得恰当；proper 是副词。

325 **taken you out of your way** 把你带到了离开你要去的路；使你走到了不是你原来要走的路上。

FREDDY What for?

LIZA To make a hole in it.

FREDDY [*horrified*] Eliza, darling. What do you mean? What's the matter?

LIZA Never mind. It doesnt matter now. There's nobody in the world now but you and me, is there?

FREDDY Not a soul.

They indulge in another embrace, and are again surprised by a much younger constable.

SECOND CONSTABLE Now then, you two! What's this? Where do you think you are? Move along here, double quick.

FREDDY As you say, sir, double quick.

They run away again, and are in Hanover Square before they stop for another conference.

FREDDY I had no idea the police were so devilishly prudish.

LIZA It's their business to hunt girls off the streets.

FREDDY We must go somewhere. We cant wander about the streets all night.

LIZA Cant we? I think it'd be lovely to wander about for ever.

FREDDY Oh, darling.

328 **What for?** = What are you going to the river for? 你去河边干什么?

329 **To make a hole in it.** = I'm going to the river to make a hole in it. "在河上打个窟窿"就是"跳入河中"。

332 **It doesnt matter now.** 现在（我跳不跳河）都不重要了。(因为她已打消这个念头。) **There's nobody in the world now but you and me** 现在除了你和我之外没有任何人。in the world 是习语，无具体意思，只是强调 nobody。**but** = except.

334 **Not a soul** 指"人"，一般用于 not a soul，a dear old soul，500 (大数) souls 等语中；原来用 soul (灵魂) 指人，在修辞学上称为 synecdoche (举偶法)，现在用得很普遍，可直接作"人"解。

337 **What's this?** 这是怎么回事？这算什么？

338 **Move along here** 从这里往前走；离开这里。 **along** 向前。 **double quick** 速度加倍地，迅速地。double 作副词，是口语，修饰 quick；quick 作副词，也是口语；常用在被修饰的动词后面，如 Come quick，不能说 Quick come。

339 **As you say** 依你所说的，指"(Move along here) double quick"。

340 **Hanover** [ˈhænəvə] **Square** 伦敦广场名。

341 **conference** 商量，此词也作"（正式）会议"解，这里当然不是。

342 **had no idea** 没想到过。 **devilishly prudish** [ˈpruːdɪʃ] 十分一本（假）正经的。**devilishly** 在口语中也用 devilish，是"非常"的意思。

343 **It's their business** 这是他们的职责。 **hunt girls off the streets** 在街上寻找女孩子，发现有女孩子就把她们赶走。

344 **wander about the streets all night** 整夜在各条街上游荡。这里 about 是介词；下文 wander about for ever 中的 about 是副词。all night 是习语，也作 all the night，all night long。

They embrace again, oblivious of the arrival of a crawling taxi. It stops.

TAXIMAN Can I drive you and the lady anywhere, sir?

They start asunder.

LIZA Oh, Freddy, a taxi. The very thing.

FREDDY But, damn it, I've no money.

LIZA I have plenty. The Colonel thinks you should never go out without ten pounds in your pocket. Listen. We'll drive about all night; and in the morning I'll call on old Mrs Higgins and ask her what I ought to do. I'll tell you all about it in the cab. And the police wont touch us there.

FREDDY Righto! Ripping. [*to the Taximan*] Wimbledon Common. [*They drive off.*]

348 **oblivious** [ə'blɪvɪəs] 不在意的；不觉；此词也作“忘却的”解；后面介词用 of。 **crawling taxi** 爬行（一般慢慢开着）的出租汽车；在街上慢慢开着当是在兜揽乘客。

350 **Can I drive you and the lady anywhere, sir?** 先生，要我把你和这位小姐开到什么地方去吗？决不是“我有没有能力把你们开到任何地方去”的意思，Can I = May I；anywhere 的用法也要体会，实际上等于 somewhere。

351 **They start asunder** 他们（原来拥抱着，听见声音）连忙分开。

352 **The very thing** = It's (A taxi is) the very thing. 正是（我）需要的东西。

353 **damn it** 见鬼去吧，这是个常用的诅咒语。it 并不是实指 taxi 的代词。

354 **plenty** = plenty of money. plenty of 后面可数名词和不可数名词都可以用。 **you should never go out without ten pounds in your pocket** 你决不该袋里不装十英镑出门。这里的 you 和 your 都是指任何人，不是指说话的对方 Freddy；“不带十镑不能出门”的说法反映 Pickering 上校的绅士派头。

355 **Listen.** 听我说（叫人注意用语）。 **drive about** 开来开去。drive 作不及物动词时可作“开车”解，也可如文中作“乘车”解；作及物动词时，可作“开(车)”解，也可作“开车送（人）”解，如：I'll drive you home. 我开车送你回家。

356 **in the morning** （第二天）早上。 **old Mrs Higgins** 指 Higgins 教授的母亲，见第三幕。

358 **the police wont touch us there** 那里（在汽车里）警察不会来碰我们（干涉我们）。 **the police** 警察局；警务人员的总称；前面往往有 the。

359 **Righto!** = Righto oh! 好！行！是英国俚语，表示赞同。 **Ripping** 好极的；是英国俚语。 **Wimbledon**['wɪmbldən] **Common** 伦敦西南郊有名的公地。“... Common（公地）”前面不用 the。

第五幕
剧情提要

Higgins 和 Pickering 来到 Higgins 母亲家，告诉她 Liza 在半夜里走掉了。其实 Liza 此刻就在 Higgins 太太家，Higgins 太太叫她躲在楼上。

Liza 的父亲 Doolittle 也来了。这回他不再是衣衫褴褛的垃圾工人，而是一个非常体面的绅士。他穿着漂亮的礼服，钮孔里还插着一朵花，又是大礼帽，又是漆皮皮鞋，完全是新郎的打扮。连自己的女儿下楼来，一看见都失声惊叫起来。

他有钱了，却埋怨 Higgins 害他陷入了他一向嫌恶的中产阶级。原来美国有个大富翁，捐巨款要在全世界建立道德改进会，曾请 Higgins 发明一种世界语，以利宣传，而 Higgins 在给他的回信中提到，英国有个独特的道德家，他就是倒垃圾的 Alfred Doolittle。那个富翁死了，遗赠给 Doolittle 一笔财产，每年可有四千镑收入。

现在 Doolittle 自己也不得不受中产阶级道德的束缚。他和他的“老伴”都无可奈何地只能正式结婚。这一天正是他结婚的日子。他邀请 Higgins 太太和大家一起去参加他的婚礼。

Liza 呢，她不要那对她呼幺喝六的 Higgins 教授，也不要那对她彬彬有礼的绅士 Pickering 上校。她挑中了和她真诚相爱的穷小子 Freddy。

ACT V

Mrs Higgins's drawing room. She is at her writing-table as before. The parlormaid comes in.

THE PARLORMAID [*at the door*] Mr Henry, maam, is downstairs with Colonel Pickering.

MRS HIGGINS Well, shew them up.

THE PARLORMAID Theyre using the telephone, maam. Telephoning to the police, I think.

MRS HIGGINS What!

THE PARLORMAID [*coming further in and lowering her voice*] Mr Henry is in a state, maam. I thought I'd better tell you.

MRS HIGGINS If you had told me that Mr Henry was not in a state it would have been more surprising. Tell them to come up when theyve finished with the police. I suppose he's lost something.

THE PARLORMAID Yes, maam [*going*].

MRS HIGGINS Go upstairs and tell Miss Doolittle that Mr Henry and the Colonel are here. Ask her not to come down til I send for her.

THE PARLORMAID Yes, maam.

Higgins bursts in. He is, as the parlormaid has said, in a state.

---

1 **as before** 和先前一样；和在第三幕时一样。

3 **Mr Henry** Henry 少爷，即 Henry Higgins。Mr 和 Miss 一般用在姓或者名和姓的前面；但仆人称呼男女小主人时，在 Mr 和 Miss 后用名而不是用姓，如男的小主人年纪很轻，则用 Master，同样用名不用姓。 **maam** = ma'am [məm]. madam 的缩略；太太；小姐；是仆人对女主人的称呼；用作对女王、公主等的称呼时读 [mæm, mɑːm]。

5 **shew them up** 领他们上楼来。

6 **using the telephone** 在（借）打电话。

9 **coming further in** 再走近些。further 和 farther 都是 far 的比较级形式，farther 常指本义，指更远；further 转义指“近一步”；这里 further 修饰 in。

10 **in a state** 处于激动的状态。 **state** 在口语中可作“激动”、“不安”解；也可作“不良状态”解，如：His business is in a state. 他生意很不好。in a state 和习语 in state 不要混淆，后者是“正式地”、“隆重地”、“堂皇地”的意思。 **I thought I'd better tell you.** 我想还是告诉你。在告诉之前先有这想法，所以“想”用过去时 thought。 **'d better** = had better. 最好……，还是……；是习语。如果这里主句中用 I think，从句中还是 had better；had better 在口语中也常用 better，如：You better go. 你还是去好。

11 **If you had told me that Mr Henry was not in a state it would have been more surprising.** 要是你告诉我 Henry 少爷并不激动，这倒是使人惊异的。这是与过去事实相反的虚拟语气；实际上是“你告诉我 Henry 少爷很激动，所以这事情一点不使人惊异。”

13 **finished with the police** 跟警察局通话完毕（打完交道）。

17 **send for her** 派人去叫她。send for 是习语；派人去叫（人）；派人去拿（东西）；派人叫商店送（货）来；反正都是“派人”或者“托人”，而不是亲自去。

20 **bursts in** 直冲进来；闯进来。

HIGGINS Look here, mother: heres a confounded thing!

MRS HIGGINS Yes, dear. Good morning. [*He checks his impatience and kisses her, whilst the parlormaid goes out.*] What is it?

HIGGINS Eliza's bolted.

MRS HIGGINS [*calmly continuing her writing*] You must have frightened her.

HIGGINS Frightened her! nonsense! She was left last night, as usual, to turn out the lights and all that; and instead of going to bed she changed her clothes and went right off: her bed wasnt slept in. She came in a cab for her things before seven this morning; and that fool Mrs Pearce let her have them without telling me a word about it. What am I to do?

MRS HIGGINS Do without, I'm afraid, Henry. The girl has a perfect right to leave if she chooses.

HIGGINS [*wandering distractedly across the room*] But I cant find anything. I dont know what appointments Ive got. I'm – [*Pickering comes in. Mrs Higgins puts down her pen and turns away from the writing-table.*]

PICKERING [*shaking hands*] Good morning, Mrs Higgins. Has Henry told you? [*He sits down on the ottoman.*]

HIGGINS What does that ass of an inspector say? Have you offered a reward?

MRS HIGGINS [*rising in indignant amazement*] You dont mean to say you have set the police after Eliza.

---

21 **Look here** 叫人注意的口头语，并不真叫人"看这里"。**confounded** 该死的；

诅咒语。 **confound** 原义“搅乱”、“挫败”的意思，用作诅咒语，作“使……毁灭”解，如 confound you（见你的鬼），confound it（该死）。

22 **checks his impatience** 抑止他的烦躁。

23 **whilst** 同时；是古旧英语，现在用 while。 **What is it?** 这是怎么回事？

24 **Eliza's bolted** [ˈbəʊltɪd] Eliza 逃跑了。bolted 在这里是不及物动词的过去分词作形容词，犹如 He is gone 中的 gone。

25 **must have frightened her** 准是吓着她了。must，这里是“谅必”的意思。

28 **to turn out the lights and all that** 关灯以及诸如此类（的工作）。

29 **went right off** 径自走掉了；溜掉了。 **right** 有“就这么”的意思，是副词，修饰 off。 **her bed wasnt slept in** 她的床没被睡过；没睡在床上。 **sleep** 原是不及物动词，后面用了介词，可以同及物动词一样构成被动式。

30 **for her things** 来拿她的东西。

31 **that fool Mrs Pearce** Pearce 太太那个笨蛋。Mrs Pearce 是 that fool 的同位语。 **let her have them without telling me a word about it.** 让她（Eliza）把它们（东西）拿走，而不把这（Eliza 来拿东西的）事情告诉我一声。

32 **What am I to do?** 我该怎么办？动词 be 后接不定式，表示“应该”、“安排”、“可能”等意思。

33 **Do without, I'm afraid.** 恐怕只好没有了。 **Do without** 没有也行；是习语；这里 without 是副词。这句话 = I'm afraid that you have to do without (Eliza). 倘用了 Eliza，without 便是介词。 **has a perfect right to leave if she chooses** 如果她要（离去），她完全有权利离去。 **if she chooses** = if she likes（或 pleases）。

35 **wandering distractedly across the room** 心烦意躁地在房间里走来走去。 **across** 从……的这一边到那一边。 **But I cant find anything.** 可是（没有 Eliza）我什么东西都找不到（本来 Higgins 要什么东西都由 Eliza 拿到他手里）。

36 **I dont know what appointments Ive got** （没有 Eliza 随时提醒）我不知道有什么约会。 **I'm –** 话没说完，被 Pickering 上校的进来打断了。

39 **Has Henry told you?** Henry（把 Eliza 走掉的事）告诉你了吗？

41 **that ass of an inspector** 那个蠢驴般的警长。 **a ... of a ...** 是“……般的……”的意思，见前注。 **offered a reward** 答应给奖金；悬奖。

43 **rising in indignant amazement** 在愤慨的惊讶中站起身来；愤慨而惊讶地站起。 **You dont mean to say** 你的意思总不会是说……；难道你是说……

44 **set the police after Eliza** 叫警察局捉拿她。

HIGGINS Of course. What are the police for? What else could we do? [*He sits in the Elizabethan chair.*]

PICKERING The inspector made a lot of difficulties. I really think he suspected us of some improper purpose.

MRS HIGGINS Well, of course he did. What right have you to go to the police and give the girl's name as if she were a thief, or a lost umbrella, or something? Really! [*She sits down again, deeply vexed.*]

HIGGINS But we want to find her.

PICKERING We cant let her go like this, you know, Mrs Higgins. What were we to do?

MRS HIGGINS You have no more sense, either of you, than two children. Why –

The parlormaid comes in and breaks off the conversation.

THE PARLORMAID Mr Henry: a gentleman wants to see you very particular. He's been sent on from Wimpole Street.

HIGGINS Oh, bother! I cant see anyone now. Who is it?

THE PARLORMAID A Mr Doolittle, sir.

PICKERING Doolittle! Do you mean the dustman?

THE PARLORMAID Dustman! Oh no, sir: a gentleman.

HIGGINS [*springing up excitedly*] By George, Pick, it's some relative of hers that she's gone to. Somebody we know nothing about.

---

45 **What are the police for?** 要警察做什么？（就为了要他们抓人。）

47 **made a lot of difficulties** 制造许多麻烦（或刁难）。

48 **suspected us of some improper purpose** 怀疑我们有什么不正当的企图。suspect 后面的介词用 of。

49 **he did** = he suspected you (of some improper purpose). **What right have you** 你们有什么权利（或理由）。

50 **give the girl's name as if she were a thief, or a lost umbrella, or something** 把她的名字报（警察局），仿佛她是个贼，或者是把被丢失的伞，或者是什么（别的东西）。or something，表示讲不确切，如：He is a writer or something. 他大概是作家。She turned dizzy or something. 她大概头晕了。

51 **Really!** 竟然（你们这样轻举妄动）岂有此理！

52 **deeply vexed** = being deeply vexed.

55 **What were we to do?** 我们本来该怎么办？

56 **sense** 常识（common sense）。 **either of you** 你们两个中的任何一个。与主语 You 同位。

58 **breaks off the conversation** 打断谈话。比较：The conversation breaks off. break off 是习语，作"打断"、"停止"解，其中的 break 作及物和不及物动词均可。

59 **very particular** 专诚地；非（见到）不可；是 very particularly 之讹。没受过教育的英美人常把形容词作副词用。

60 **He's been sent on from Wimpole Street.** 他是被 Wimpole Street（Higgins 的住所）转来的。他（Mr Doolittle）先到 Wimpole Street 去找 Higgins，那里的人（应是 Mrs Pearce）叫他到这里来找。

61 **cant see anyone** 不能接见任何人；任何人来都不接见。 **Who is it?**（来访者）是谁？注意：这里习惯用 it 而不用 he。

62 **A Mr Doolittle** 一位 Doolittle 先生；一个名叫 Doolittle 的先生。

64 **a gentleman** 垃圾工人已成为绅士。见下文。

65 **it's some relative of hers that she's gone to** （来者）是她去找的一位亲属。注意：这里的 it 和 that 并不呼应而构成强调语气的句型，并不强调 she's gone to some relative of hers。

66 **Somebody we know nothing about.** = It's somebody (whom/that) we know nothing about. 是一个我们一无所知的什么人。

[*to the parlormaid*] Send him up, quick.

THE PARLORMAID Yes, sir. [*She goes.*]

HIGGINS [*eagerly, going to his mother*] Genteel relatives! Now we shall hear something. [*He sits down in the Chippendale chair.*]

MRS HIGGINS Do you know any of her people?

PICKERING Only her father: the fellow we told you about.

THE PARLORMAID [*announcing*] Mr Doolittle. [*She withdraws.*]

Doolittle enters. He is resplendently dressed as for a fashionable wedding and might, in fact, be the bridegroom. A flower in his buttonhole, a dazzling silk hat, and patent leather shoes complete the effect. He is too concerned with the business he has come on to notice Mrs Higgins. He walks straight to Higgins, and accosts him with vehement reproach.

DOOLITTLE [*indicating his own person*] See here! Do you see this? You done this.

HIGGINS Done what, man?

DOOLITTLE This, I tell you. Look at it. Look at this hat. Look at this coat.

PICKERING Has Eliza been buying you clothes?

DOOLITTLE Eliza! Not she. Why would she buy me clothes?

MRS HIGGINS Good morning, Mr Doolittle. Wont you sit down?

---

67 **Send him up, quick.** 叫他上（楼）来，快。 **quick** 可以理解为 = be quick，

也可理解为 = quickly。

69 **Genteel** [dʒenˈtiːl] **relatives** 上流亲属。 **genteel** 上流社会的；有修养的；有时带讽刺，指“假斯文的”；因为 Parlormaid 说来访的是个绅士，所以 Higgins 这样说。

70 **hear something** = hear something about Eliza. 听到一些关于 Eliza 的消息。

71 **her people** 她的家属。

74 **He is resplendently dressed as for a fashionable wedding** 他穿得漂亮得好像要去参加上流社会的婚礼；as 后面省略 if he is dressed。

75 **might, in fact, be the bridegroom** 竟然好像就是（这个婚礼中的）新郎。

76 **patent** [ˈpeɪtnt] **leather shoes** 漆皮皮鞋。 **complete the effect** 使（新郎打扮的）效果完备；complete 的主语是 flower、silk hat 和 patent leather shoes，有此三者，完全像个出席时髦婚礼的人或者新郎了。

77 **He is too concerned with the business he has come on to notice Mrs Higgins.** 他太专心于他来此所为的事情，所以没注意到 Mrs Higgins。concerned 后面介词用 with。 **the business he has come on** = the business on which he has come. **on business** 因事；是习语。

78 **walks straight to Higgins** 径直向 Higgins 走去；straight，是副词，习惯上不用 straightly。

79 **accosts** [əˈkɒst] **him with vehement** [ˈviːəmənt] **reproach** 走到他面前就破口大骂。 **accosts** 走上前向（人）说话；招呼。

80 **indicating his own person** 指着他自己身上（这副样子）。

81 **You done this.** 该说 You did (或 have done) this。是你造成（我现在）这个（样子）的。

82 **Done what, man?** （我）干了什么呢，朋友？ Done what 是承接前言而问的，= what did I do? 或 What have I done, man? 是对男子极不客气的称呼，常有亲切或戏谑的意味，犹如我们称“朋友”、“老兄”。

83 **This, I tell you.** = I tell you that it is this that you have done: 我告诉你，这（我现在这样子）就是你造成的。 **Look at it.** 瞧这个（我现在的样子）就是你造成的。

85 **Has Eliza been buying you clothes?** Eliza 一直在买衣服给你吗？

86 **Eliza! Not she.** Eliza 吗，她才不（买衣服给我）呢！ not she 是 she has not been buying me clothes 的强调语气的说法。

DOOLITTLE [*taken aback as he becomes conscious that he has forgotten his hostess*] Asking your pardon, maam. [*He approaches her and shakes her proffered hand.*] Thank you. [*He sits down on the ottoman, on Pickering's right.*] I am that full of what has happened to me that I cant think of anything else.

HIGGINS What the dickens has happened to you?

DOOLITTLE I shouldnt mind if it had only happened to me. Anything might happened to anybody and nobody to blame but Providence, as you might say. But this is something that you done to me: yes, you, Enry Iggins.

HIGGINS Have you found Eliza?

DOOLITTLE Have you lost her?

HIGGINS Yes.

DOOLITTLE You have all the luck, you have. I aint found her; but she'll find me quick enough now after what you done to me.

MRS HIGGINS But what has my son done to you, Mr Doolittle?

DOOLITTLE Done to me! Ruined me. Destroyed my happiness. Tied me up and delivered me into the hands of middle class morality.

HIGGINS [*rising intolerantly and standing over Doolittle*] Youre raving. Youre drunk. Youre mad. I gave you five pounds.

---

88 **taken aback** 吃了一惊；是习语。 **becomes conscious that he has forgotten his hostess** 开始觉察他忘记了（招呼）女主人。

89 **Asking your pardon** 一般说 (I) Beg your pardon. 请你原谅。

90 **her proffered hand** 她已经伸出的手。 **Thank you.** 因 Mrs Higgins 伸手向他握手而致谢。

91 **I am that full of what has happened to me that I cant think of anything else.** 我是满脑子尽想着发生在我头上的事情，弄得任何其他的事情都顾不到了。**that full** 口语，= so full；和后面的 that 呼应 full，（思想中）充满着……，后面介词用 of。

93 **What the dickens** 究竟什么。 **the dickens** 是诅咒语 the devil 的委婉语，用以加强疑问词的语气，没有具体意思。

94 **I shouldnt mind if it had only happened to me.** 要是这事情只是（自然地）发生在我身上，那我也不介意。这是与事实相反的虚拟语气，实际上这事情不是自然发生，而是 Higgins 造成的，所以他恼恨。

95 **nobody to blame but Providence** [ˈprɒvɪdəns], **as you might say** 犹如你们会说，除了老天爷，谁也怪不了。 **nobody to blame** = nobody is (/ might be) to blame. **to blame** 主动态形式的不定式表示被动的意思，习惯不用 to be blamed。**Providence** 首字母大写，指“天公”、“上帝”。 **as you might say** （如果你们谈起来）你们会这样说。

97 **yes, you** 重复强调肯定句中前面的 you。

101 **You have all the luck, you have.** 你真有完全的（极度的）运气；你真是运气好极了（否则你要供养她）；句末重复用 you have，强调句首的 You have。 **aint found** 是俚语用法，= have not found；aint（正常写作 ain't），除表示 have/has not 外，也表示 are/am/is not。

102 **she'll find me quick enough now** 现在她会够快地找到我。

104 **Done to me!** 是“你问我他对我做了什么吗？”的意思。 **Ruined me.** = Your son has ruined me.（你儿子）毁了我；下面 destroyed 等都是过去分词，省略 Your son has。

105 **Tied me up** 把我束缚了起来。 **delivered me into the hands of middle class morality** [məˈræləti] 把我交到了中产阶级道德的手中。萧伯纳在许多剧本和论文中严厉抨击中产阶级道德的虚伪、庸俗。

107 **intolerantly** 不容（异说）地；偏执地。区别：intolerant，不容异说的；尤指在宗教、政治方面；intolerable，使人无可忍受的。如：The intolerant religious fanatics are intolerable. 那些偏执的宗教狂热分子令人无可容忍。

108 **raving** 狂乱地说话；激昂地说话。

After that I had two conversations with you, at half-a-crown an hour. Ive never seen you since.

DOOLITTLE Oh! Drunk am I? Mad am I? Tell me this. Did you or did you not write a letter to an old blighter in America that was giving five millions to found Moral Reform Societies all over the world, and that wanted you to invent a universal language for him?

HIGGINS What! Ezra D. Wannafeller! He's dead. [*He sits down again carelessly.*]

DOOLITTLE Yes: he's dead; and I'm done for. Now did you or did you not write a letter to him to say that the most original moralist at present in England, to the best of your knowledge, was Alfred Doolittle, a common dustman?

HIGGINS Oh, after your first visit I remember making some silly joke of the kind.

DOOLITTLE Ah! You may well call it a silly joke. It put the lid on me right enough. Just give him the chance he wanted to shew that Americans is not like us: that they reckonize and respect merit in every class of life, however humble. Them words is in his blooming will, in which, Henry Higgins, thanks to

---

109 **After that I had two conversations with you, at half-a-crown an hour.** 在那回（给过你五镑）之后，我跟你谈过两次话，每小时（支付给你）半个克朗；Higgins 为研究 Doolittle 的语言特意付了钱和他谈话。 **crown** 英国旧币制的五先令硬币。

110 **since** （两次谈话）以后。

111 **Drunk am I?** = Am I drunk? 倒装句强调句首的 Drunk。旧本作 Drunk! Am I? 下句 Mad am I? 同。 **Tell me this.** 回答我这个（问题）；你说我醉了、疯了吗？ **Did you or did you not** 这是雄辩家的强调口吻；Doolittle 说话常是这种口气，所以在第二幕中 Higgins 说他大可当个内阁阁员或威尔士传教士。

112 **old blighter** 老家伙；blighter，英俚，是对人的鄙称。 **that was giving five millions to found Moral Reform Societies all over the world** 他要捐出五百万，在全世界各地建立道德改进会。 **was giving** 这里用过去进行时表示过去未来时，= would give。

114 **that wanted you to invent a universal language for him** 他要你给他创造一种全世界通用的语言（当为便于宣传道德改进）。

116 **Ezra** [ˈezrə] **D. Wannafeller** [ˈwɒnəfelə] 虚伪的美国富翁名；这个姓氏当是取美国 Wannamaker 和 Rockfeller 两个豪门的姓氏的首尾拼合而成。

118 **I'm done for.** 我完蛋了。 **be done for** 完了；不中用了；是习语。

119 **original moralist** 独创一格的德育家。

120 **to the best of your knowledge** = to your knowledge = as far as you know. 据你自己所能知道的，三者都是习语。

122 **remember making some silly joke of the kind** 记得开过一个这一类的无聊的玩笑。

124 **may well** 满可以；尽可。 **well** 有充分理由地。 **put the lid on me right enough** 够彻底地毁了我。 **put the lid on** 制止；破坏；使到顶；是口语中的习语。 **right** 副词；有“正好”、“立刻”、“完全”等意思。

125 **Just give him the chance he wanted to shew** （你）正好给了他所需要的机会以显示…… shew 后面接两个并列的 that 从句。Just give，应作 You just gave。

127 **merit** [ˈmerɪt] 长处；才能。 **every class of life, however humble** 生活中的每一个等级（的人），不管是怎么低微的。 **however humble** = however humble it is. **Them words is** 应该是 These words are。

128 **his blooming will** 他的该死的遗嘱。 **blooming** 原义“开着花的”；这里是诅咒语 bloody（该死的）的委婉语；有时只是加强语气，没有具体意义。 **thanks to** 幸亏；由于（由于某种原因，其结果可以是好的，也可以是坏的）。这是个习语。

your silly joking, he leaves me a share in his Pre-digested Cheese Trust worth four thousand a year on condition that I lecture for his Wannafeller Moral Reform World Lecture as often as they ask me up to six times a year.

HIGGINS The devil he does! Whew! [*brightening suddenly*] What a lark!

PICKERING A safe thing for you, Doolittle. They wont ask you twice.

DOOLITTLE It aint the lecturing I mind. I'll lecture them blue in the face, I will, and not turn a hair. It's making a gentleman of me that I object to. Who asked him to make a gentleman of me? I was happy. I was free. I touched pretty nigh everybody for money when I wanted it, same as I touched you, Enry Iggins. Now I am worrited; tied neck and heels; and everybody touches me for money. It's a fine thing for you, says my solicitor. Is it? says I. You mean it's a good thing for you, I says. When I was a poor man and had a solicitor once when

---

129 **he leaves me a share in his Pre-digested Cheese Trust** 把他在消化干酪托拉斯的股份遗赠给我。 **leaves** 遗赠。因遗嘱的文字在 Doolittle 说话时还是存在的，所以用现在时。**a share** 可有两种解释，一是股份公司的"一股"，如：He holds 500 shares in the trust. 他持有这托拉斯的五百股股票；一是"一份"，如文中，这个份额可能有许多"股"。**Pre-digested** 预先消化好的。digest，动词读作 [daɪˈdʒest] 或 [dɪˈdʒest]，名词读 [ˈdaɪdʒest]。

130 **worth four thousand a year** 值每年四千（镑）。这里的"值"是"可得红利（若干）"的意思；worth，是形容词，只作表语用，后面接的作为它的宾语。 **on condition that ...** 以……为条件；如果。

131 **Wannafeller Moral Reform World Lecture** Wannafeller 道德改进世界同盟。这和上面的 Moral Reform Societies 都是虚构的团体名称。 **as often as they ask me up to six times a year** 次数多到他们每年叫我(演讲)六次。they 指那 League(中的人们)；up to 是习语。

133 **The devil he does!** 他竟然如此。The devil 是诅咒语，无意义，并不与 he 同位语主语。he does 代替 he leaves you a share ... on condition that you lecture ... as often as they ask you up to six times a year。 **Whew!** 呦！表示惊讶、失望等，常含诙谐意；读作 [hwu:]。 **brightening** 面露喜色；快活起来。 **What a lark!** 多么有趣！ **lark** 嬉戏；开心事。

135 **A safe thing** 安全的事；无害的事。 **They wont ask you twice.** 他们（League 中人）不会请你（讲演）两次的。这可能有两个解释：一是他们听了 Doolittle 一次演讲就“不敢领教”，一是那些 League 不会认真地组织一次次的演讲会；似以前为是。

137 **It aint the lecturing I mind.** 我所介意的倒不是演说（这件事）。lecturing 后省略 that。 **lecture them blue in the face** 对他们演说得使他们脸上发青；讲得他们脸色发青。

138 **and not turn a hair** = and I'll not turn a hair. 而我将不动声色。not turn a hair 是习语。 **It's making a gentleman of me that I object to.** 这是 I object to making a gentleman of me 的强调句型。这里 object 是不及物动词，后面用介词 to，作“反对”解；object 作及物动词，后接 that 从句时，是“提出……作为反对的理由”的意思，不作“反对”解。

140 **touched pretty nigh everybody for money** 很接近于(几乎)向每个人弄到钱(讨钱或借钱)。 **pretty** = very. **nigh** = nearly.

141 **same as** = the same as. same 是副词。

142 **worrited** = worried.（被使）感到烦恼。把 worry 说成 worrit 是俚语。 **tied neck and heels** 颈项和脚跟都被缚住。tied 承接 I am，与 worrited 并列；类似的说法如 be tied hand and foot（缚手缚脚；不得自由行动）。

144 **says I** 是 said I 的俚语说法。前面 says my solicitor 的 says 也该作 said。 **You mean it's a good thing for you** 你的意思是说这对你是件好事(对你有好处)吧？资本主义社会中律师处理遗产有利可得。

145 **had a solicitor** 请到了律师；找到了律师。

they found a pram in the dust cart, he got me off, and got shut of me and got me shut of him as quick as he could. Same with the doctors: used to shove me out of the hospital before I could hardly stand on my legs, and nothing to pay. Now they finds out that I'm not a healthy man and cant live unless they looks after me twice a day. In the house I'm not let do a hand's turn for myself: somebody else must do it and touch me for it. A year ago I hadnt a relative in the world except two or three that wouldnt speak to me. Now Ive fifty, and not a decent week's wages among the lot of them. I have to live for others and not for myself: thats middle class morality. You talk of losing Eliza. Dont you be anxious: I bet she's on my doorstep by this: she that could support herself easy by selling flowers if I wasnt respectable. And the next one to touch me will be you, Enry Iggins. I'll have to learn to speak middle class language from you, instead of speaking proper English. Thats where youll come in; and I daresay thats what you done it for.

MRS HIGGINS But, my dear Mr Doolittle, you need not suffer all this if you are really in earnest. Nobody can force you to accept this bequest. You can repudiate it. Isnt that so, Colonel Pickering?

PICKERING I believe so.

---

146 **they found a pram in the dust cart** 人家在我垃圾车里发现一辆童车（因而指控他偷窃或向他要还）。pram 是 perambulator [pəˈræmbjʊleɪtə] 的简称，

主要是英国语。 **got me off, and got shut of me and got me shut of him** 三个并列的谓语实际上都是“把我摆脱掉”的意思。Doolittle 惯于用这雄辩式的说法。shut（过去分词）在方言和俚语中等于 rid，因此 got shut of = got rid of（摆脱；去掉）；got me shut of him 直解是“使我摆脱掉他”，意谓“律师使我不需要他为我辩护”。

147 **Same with the doctors** = It is the same with the doctors. 关于医生的情况也是如此（同样不理睬穷人）。the doctors 中的 the 指“（医生）这般（人物）”。

148 **used to shove** [ʃʌv] **me out of the hospital before I could hardly stand on my legs, and nothing to pay** （医生们）在我还不能站得稳（病尚未愈），因为没钱支付（医药费），就把我推出医院。used to 前面省略 they (the doctors)。and nothing to pay 按语法该说 because I had nothing to pay。

151 **In the house** 该说 At home。 **I'm not let do a hand's turn** 不让我动一动手。**not do a hand's turn** 一点也不动手；一点也不帮忙；是习语。let 的宾语后面的不定式不用 to，用被动式时用 to 或不用 to 均可，但通常不用 be let (to) 而用 be allowed to。

154 **not a decent week's wages among the lot of them** = there is not a decent week's wages among the lot of them = none among the lot of them (或 none of them) get a decent week's wage. 他们全都没有像样的星期工资。 **the lot** 全部；全体。

155 **I have to live for others** 我必须为别人而生活（意谓许多人向他要钱，他得拿钱给他们用）。这里的 live for others 显然不是我们所说的“我为人人”的意思。

157 **I bet** 我打赌；我可以断定。

158 **by this** = by now.（至迟）在此刻。 **she** 与前面 she's on my doorstep 的 she 同位。 **easy** 应作 easily。

161 **proper English** 正当的英语；Doolittle 认为他原来说的土语、俚语是正当的英语，而中产阶级说的是不正当的英语。

162 **Thats where youll come in** 那就有你的份儿。 **come in** 是习语，有许多意思，这里作“起作用”、“有份儿”解。**I daresay** 我敢说；我认为；大概。**daresay** 也作 dare say，后面接 that 从句时常省去 that。 **thats what you done it for** 你做这事情就为此。

165 **if you are really in earnest** 你要是真正认真的话；要是真的认为得到遗赠使你倒霉的话。 in earnest 是习语，作“认真地”解。really in earnest 也可说 in real earnest。

DOOLITTLE [*softening his manner in deference to her sex*] Thats the tragedy of it, maam. It's easy to say chuck it; but I havnt the nerve. Which of us has? We're all intimidated. Intimidated, maam: thats what we are. What is there for me if I chuck it but the workhouse in my old age? I have to dye my hair already to keep my job as a dustman. If I was one of the deserving poor, and had put by a bit, I could chuck it; but then why should I, acause the deserving poor might as well be millionaires for all the happiness they ever has. They dont know what happiness is. But I, as one of the undeserving poor, have nothing between me and the pauper's uniform but this here blasted four thousand a year that shoves me into the middle class. (Excuse the expression, maam; youd use it yourself if you had my provocation.) Theyve got you every way you turn: it's a choice between the Skilly of the workhouse and the Char Bydis of the middle class; and I havnt the nerve for the

---

169 **in deference** ['defərəns] **to her sex** 以示尊重女性。 **in deference to** 尊重；服从；是习语。 **Thats the tragedy of it** 这就是事情的悲剧性（所在）；it，泛指接受遗赠的事；可悲的是受也不是、不受也不是，见下文。

170 **say chuck it** = say "chuck it." **chuck it** 放弃它（指遗赠）；在英国俚语中 chuck it（it 无所实指）作"停止"、"不干"解。 **havnt the nerve** 没有这胆量（或坚强意志）；不敢。

171 **has** = has the nerve. **intimidated** [ɪn'tɪmɪdeɪtɪd] 被威胁（而使服从），被胁迫。

172 **What is there for me if I chuck it but the workhouse in my old age?** 我要是放弃遗赠，老来除孤老院之外还有什么依傍？ **What is there for me but ...** 除……之外我还有什么出路。 **if I chuck it ...** 插入的条件从句，可移在句

首或句末。

173 **I have to dye my hair already** = I have already to dye my hair. 我已经必须染黑头发（使雇主不嫌我老）。

174 **the deserving poor** 值得救济的穷人们；符合救济条件的贫民们。

175 **put by a bit** 积蓄一些钱。 **put by** 储存；是习语。 **but then** 但是另一方面；是习语。

176 **acause** 应作 because。 **the deserving poor might as well be millionaires for all the happiness they ever has** 值得救济的穷人们，尽管他们有得欢乐，也不妨成为百万富翁。这是萧伯纳借 Doolittle 之口所说的俏皮话，说穷人自由自在，可以向人要钱，而富翁有所拘束，又有各方面来向他要钱——犹如 Eliza 说她贫困可以卖花，变成贵妇人只能卖她自己，同样是尖刻的讽刺。 **might as well** 大可；不妨；是习语。 **for all ...** 尽管有了……；也是习语。has 该作 have。

177 **They dont know what happiness is.** 他们（指 the deserving poor）不知幸福是什么。说他们不知贫穷的自由自在。这句话和上句是同样意义的俏皮话。

178 **the undeserving** [ˌʌndɪˈzɜːvɪŋ] **poor** 不值得救济（不符受救济）的穷人们。 **have nothing between me and the pauper's uniform but ...** 除……之外，在我和救济所贫民的制服之间一无所有（别无选择，只有进救济所）。 **pauper** 乞丐；受救济的贫民。

179 **this here blasted four thousand a year** 这里的该死的一年四千镑（所遗赠的股份的红利）。 **this here** 是俚语用法。this here man = this man here.

181 **Excuse the expression** 原谅（我用）这个词（指 blasted）。这句话也可说成 Excuse me for using the expression 和 Excuse my using the expression。 **if you had my provocation** [ˌprɒvəˈkeɪʃən] 要是你有像我那样恼火的事；要是你碰到我这样恼火的情况。这是与事实相反的虚拟语气，事实上你并没有。

182 **Theyve got you every way you turn** 无论你走向哪边，他们都抓住你；他们已使人走头无路。every way 有连词的作用，= wherever。you 这里泛指任何人。

183 **a choice between the Skilly of the workhouse and the Char Bydis** 习语 between Scylla [ˈsɪlə] and Charybdis [kəˈrɪbdɪs] 是"进退维谷"的意思。Scylla（Doolittle 误作 Skilly）是意大利本土和西西里之间墨西拿（Messina）海峡中的岩礁，希腊罗马神话中说这岩礁为妖魔所居，它对面是 Charybdis（Doolittle 误作 Char Bydis）大漩涡，因此这两者之间的选择是在妖魔和漩涡之间的选择，总是死路一条。

workhouse. Intimidated: thats what I am. Broke. Bought up. Happier men than me will call for my dust, and touch me for their tip; and I'll look on helpless, and envy them. And thats what your son has brought me to. [*He is overcome by emotion.*]

MRS HIGGINS Well, I'm very glad youre not going to anything foolish, Mr Doolittle. For this solves the problem of Eliza's future. You can provide for her now.

DOOLITTLE [*with melancholy resignation*] Yes, maam: I'm expected to provide for everyone now, out of four thousand a year.

HIGGINS [*jumping up*] Nonsense! He cant provide for her. He shant provide for her. She doesnt belong to him. I paid him five pounds for her. Doolittle: either youre an honest man or a rogue.

DOOLITTLE [*tolerantly*] A little of both, Henry, like the rest of us: a little of both.

HIGGINS Well, you took that money for the girl; and you have no right to take her as well.

MRS HIGGINS Henry: dont be absurd. If you want to know where Eliza is, she is upstairs.

HIGGINS [*amazed*] Upstairs!!! Then I shall jolly soon fetch her downstairs. [*He makes resolutely for the door.*]

MRS HIGGINS [*rising and following him*] Be quiet, Henry. Sit down.

HIGGINS I –

MRS HIGGINS Sit down, dear; and listen to me.

HIGGINS Oh very well, very well, very well. [*He throws himself ungraciously on the ottoman, with his face towards the windows.*] But I

---

185 **Broke** = I'm broke. broke 俚语中作表语用的形容词，是“一文不名的”、“破产了的”意思，这里作“被弄垮了”、“完蛋了”解。 **Bought up** = I am (或 have been) bought up. 我整个儿被人买去了。

186 **Happier men than me will call for my dust** 比我快乐的人要来倒我的垃圾；than me 应作 that I (am)。

187 **tip** 小费；小账。 **look on helpless** 只好眼看着。 **look on** 旁观；是习语。 **helpless** 无可奈何的。

188 **is overcome by emotion** 被感情压倒；不胜伤感。

189 **youre not going to anything foolish** 你不准备做什么蠢事（蠢事指放弃遗赠）。

190 **this** 指接受遗赠。

192 **melancholy** [ˈmelənkli] **resignation** [ˌrezɪɡˈneɪʃən] 忧郁的屈从；无可奈何。melancholy 是名词，也是形容词，作形容词时，可作“忧郁的”解，也可作“令人忧郁的”解。 **I'm expected to provide for everyone** 我被指望供养每个人；人人都要我供养。

193 **out of four thousand a year** 从一年四千镑（的红利收入）中（拿出钱来）。原本 three thousand，今据上文改正。

194 **He cant provide for her** 他不能养她。这里的 cant 表示说话人的意志，所以是“不得”的意思。 **He shant** 在第二、第三人称后用 shall 或 shant 表示说话人的意志，有“我不准他”、即“他不得”的意思。

196 **either youre an honest man or a rogue** 要么你是个老实人，不然你就是个流氓；你要做老实人，还是做流氓。either 和 or 连结的成分应该是相同的，但这里 either 后面接的是个从句，而 or 后接的是个名字，所以最好改作 either youre an honest man or youre a rogue，或者 youre either an honest man or a rogue。

198 **A little of both** = I'm a little of both. 我两者（老实人和流氓）都有一点；我既有点是老实人，也有点是流氓。

200 **you have no right to take her as well** 你（把 Eliza 交给我们已拿了钱去，）没有权利（或理由）又要把她带去。 **as well** 也；又；是习语。

204 **jolly** 在英国口语中作副词，等于 very。

209 **throws himself ungraciously on the ottoman** 粗鲁地猛力地往软垫长凳上坐下。

think you might have told us this half an hour ago.

MRS HIGGINS Eliza came to me this morning. She told me of the brutal way you two treated her.

HIGGINS [*bounding up again*] What!

PICKERING [*rising also*] My dear Mrs Higgins, she's been telling you stories. We didnt treat her brutally. We hardly said a word to her; and we parted on particularly good terms. [*turning on Higgins*] Higgins: did you bully her after I went to bed?

HIGGINS Just the other way about. She threw my slippers in my face. She behaved in the most outrageous way. I never gave her the slightest provocation. The slippers came bang into may face the moment I entered the room – before I had uttered a word. And used perfectly awful language.

PICKERING [*astonished*] But why? What did we do to her?

MRS HIGGINS I think I know pretty well what you did. The girl is naturally rather affectionate, I think. Isnt she, Mr Doolittle?

DOOLITTLE Very tender-hearted, maam. Takes after me.

MRS HIGGINS Just so. She had become attached to you both. She worked very hard for you, Henry. I dont think you quite realize what anything in the nature of brain work means to a girl of her class. Well, it seems that when the great day of trial came, and she did this wonderful thing for you without

---

211 **you might have told us this half an hour ago** 你原可以（早该）在半小时前告诉我们（Eliza 在楼上）这个情况。这是表示与过去事实相反的虚拟语气，实际上并没有告诉。

212 **the brutal way you two treated her** 你们俩对待她的粗暴态度。the brutal way 后面省略 in which（in which 也可简略用 that）。brutal 原义“畜生（brute）般的”，转义为“横蛮的”、“粗暴的”。two 是 you 的同位语。

215 **telling you stories** 对你说谎。 **tell a story** 作为习语有“说谎”的意思，所以 story-teller 除“讲故事的人”、“小说作家”之外，口语中可作“说谎的人”解。

216 **hardly said a word to her** 几乎没对她说一句话；几乎没说过她一句话。**word** 话；这里指责骂的话。事实上是骂过她的，见上一幕。

217 **parted on particularly good terms** 特别友好地分手（各自回房睡觉）。**on ... terms** 处于……（好或坏）的关系。

219 **Just the other way about** 恰恰相反。about 是副词，是“（转向）相反方向”的意思，如“向后转！”说 About turn!

220 **never gave her the slightest provocation** 决没有给她一点（即使是）最微小的惹犯；一点没去激怒她。

221 **The slippers came bang into may face** 拖鞋砰地（掷）到了我脸上来。 **bang** 砰地，突然，作副词；口语中也作“正好”解，所以这句话也可作“拖鞋正朝我脸上（掷）来”。

222 **the moment** 相当于连词 as soon as，由 at the moment when 衍化而来。

223 **used perfectly awful language** 用了非常难听的语言；used 前面省略 she。perfectly（十足地），它与 perfect 一样，不一定用于褒义作“十全十美”解，也可用于贬义，如 a perfect fool（十足的傻瓜）。

226 **naturally rather affectionate** 本性很温柔。注意：affectionate 是“爱（人）的”；dear 是“被爱的”；因此 He is affectionate to her 和 She is dear to him 都是“他爱她”的意思。

227 **Takes after me** = She takes after me. 她像我。 **take after** （在面貌、性格等方面）像（自己的父亲或母亲或祖父或祖母）；是习语。

228 **Just so.** 正是如此；是习语。 **become attached to you both** 对你们两个都变得有了感情。 **attached** 是过去分词作表语。 **attached to** 依恋；喜爱。

230 **what anything in the nature of brain work means to a girl of her class** 任何脑力劳动性质的工作对她这个阶级的姑娘意味着什么（对她有多大的困难）。

231 **the great day of trial** 重大的试验的日子（指 Eliza 冒充公爵夫人参加大使馆招待会的那一天）。

232 **did this wonderful thing** 做了这件了不起的事情（指冒充公爵夫人）。

making a single mistake, you two sat there and never said a word to her, but talked together of how glad you were that it was all over and how you had been bored with the whole thing. And then you were surprised because she threw your slippers at you! I should have thrown the fire-irons at you.

HIGGINS We said nothing except that we were tired and wanted to go to bed. Did we, Pick?

PICKERING [*shrugging his shoulders*] That was all.

MRS HIGGINS [*ironically*] Quite sure?

PICKERING Absolutely. Really, that was all.

MRS HIGGINS You didnt thank her, or pet her, or admire her, or tell her how splendid she'd been.

HIGGINS [*impatiently*] But she knew all about that. We didnt make speeches to her, if thats what you mean.

PICKERING [*conscience stricken*] Perhaps we were a little inconsiderate. Is she very angry?

MRS HIGGINS [*returning to her place at the writing-table*] Well, I'm afraid she wont go back to Wimpole Street, especially now that Mr Doolittle is able to keep up the position you have thrust on her; but she says she is quite willing to meet you on friendly terms and to let bygones be bygones.

HIGGINS [*furious*] Is she, by George? Ho!

MRS HIGGINS If you promise to behave yourself, Henry, I'll ask her to come down. If not, go home; for you have taken up quite enough of my time.

HIGGINS Oh, all right. Very well. Pick: you behave yourself. Let

233 **you two sat there and never said a word to her** 你们俩坐在那里，一句话也不对她说。这里的 there 并不是指在招待会上，而是指回家后和 Eliza 一起在房间里。**said a word to her** 对她说一句话（或者是安慰，或者是赞扬她，反正不是上面 Higgins 所说的 gave her the slightest provocation 之有"责骂"之意）。

235 **had been bored with the whole thing** 已经对整个这件事（从训练 Eliza 到带她去冒充公爵夫人）感到厌烦了。

237 **I should have thrown the fire-irons** [ˈfaɪərˌaɪənz] **at you** （换了我）我准要用火钳扔你。这是表示与过去事实相反的虚拟语气，省略条件从句 if I were she 或 if it had been I。

241 **Quite sure?** = Are you sure (that) that was all?

242 **Absolutely** 一般读 [ˈæbsəlu:tli]，在加强语气或作 Certainly（当然）的意义时，也读作 [ˌæbsəˈlu:tli]。

244 **splendid** 出色的；令人非常满意的；是口语。

245 **about that** that 指 how splendid she'd been。 **We didnt make speeches to her, if thats what you mean.** 要么你的意思是说我们没有对她发表演说（一般地长篇大论地赞扬她表现得如何出色）。

247 **conscience** [ˈkɒnʃəns] **stricken** 良心受到打击，感到内疚。

251 **Mr Doolittle is able to keep up the position you have thrust on her**（Eliza 的父亲）Doolittle 先生（现在有钱了，）能够维持你（们）强加于她的（贵妇人的）身份。**keep up** 维持；继续；是习语。

253 **let bygones be bygones** 让过去的事情过去（算了）。

254 **Is she** = Is she willing to meet us on friendly terms and let bygones be bygones. **Ho!** 呵！感叹词，表示惊讶，赞美，嘲笑等，常与其他感叹词合用，如 heigh-ho [ˈheɪˈhəʊ]、what ho。

255 **behave yourself** 举止规矩；不胡闹。

256 **If not** = If you do not promise to behave yourself. **taken up quite enough of my time** 占用了我够多的时间。

258 **you behave yourself** Higgins 自己最不讲规矩，却叫 Pickering 要规矩；这是萧伯纳的幽默之处。

us put on our best Sunday manners for this creature that we picked out of the mud. [*He flings himself sulkily into the Elizabethan chair.*]

DOOLITTLE [*remonstrating*] Now, now, Enry Iggins! Have some consideration for my feelings as a middle class man.

MRS HIGGINS Remember your promise, Henry. [*She presses the bell-button on the writing-table.*] Mr Doolittle: will you be so good as to step out on the balcony for a moment. I dont want Eliza to have the shock of your news until she has made it up with these two gentlemen. Would you mind?

DOOLITTLE As you wish, lady. Anything to help Henry to keep her off my hands. [*He disappears through the window.*]

The parlormaid answers the bell. Pickering sits down in Doolittle's place.

MRS HIGGINS Ask Miss Doolittle to come down, please.

THE PARLORMAID Yes, maam. [*She goes out.*]

MRS HIGGINS Now, Henry: be good.

HIGGINS I am behaving myself perfectly.

PICKERING He is doing his best, Mrs Higgins.

A pause. Higgins throws back his head; stretches out his legs; and begins to whistle.

MRS HIGGINS Henry, dearest, you dont look at all nice in that

259 **put on our best Sunday manners** 拿出我们最好的礼拜日的礼貌来。基督徒礼拜天上礼拜堂，需要衣冠整齐、举止文雅，所以有 a Sunday suit 和 in one's Sunday best（穿最好的节日服装）等语。 **manners** 礼貌；用复数。 **for this creature that we picked out of the mud** 为了我们这个从泥潭里捡出来的东西。**creature** 用以指"人"，含怜爱或轻蔑之意。

262 **Now, now** = Now then. 见前注。 **Have some consideration for my feelings as a middle class man.** 稍为我作为一个中产阶级中人的感情着想。feelings（复数）所说的"感情"是指"感受性"、"心里反应"的意思。

265 **will you be so good as to step out** 请你走出去。倒装的疑问句形式表示祈使的意思。be so good as to 也作 be good enough to。 **step out** 走开；（短时间或短距离地）离开。

267 **have the shock of your news** 受到你的新闻的震动；突然听到你有了钱而震惊。**until** 用在否定句中作"不到……（不）"、"到……才……"的意思。如 Dont go until he comes（在他到来之前你不要走；到他来了你才走）。 **made it up with** 和（某人）和解；是习语。这里的 it 没有具体意义，有人称为"空泛的 it"（vague 'it'）。

268 **Would you mind?** 你介意吗？好吗？注意在这个常用语中现在习惯用 would 而不用其他助动词。**mind** 作"反对"、"介意"解是及物动词，这里没有宾语，是及物动词的一种特殊用法，有人称为"绝对用法"（absolute use）。

269 **As you wish** 你要我怎样做就怎样做。前面省略 I'll do。 **Anything to help Henry to keep her off my hands.** 我愿做任何事情，以帮助 Henry (Higgins) 使她不再要我照管；只要 Henry 让我摆脱她，我什么都愿意效劳；前面也省略 I'll do。help 的宾语后面接不定式时，英国人常用不定式记号 to，美国人一般不用。**keep ... off one's hands** 不管；不负责；摆脱掉；是习语。

270 **disappears through the window** 从落地长窗（french window）的窗门口隐退。

271 **answers the bell** 应铃声（而来）。

273 **Ask Miss Doolittle to come down, please.** 请你请 Doolittle 小姐（Eliza）下楼来。

275 **be good** 好好的；乖乖的；这是习语。

278 **throws back his head** （倏地）把头往后仰。

280 **dont look at all nice** = dont look nice at all. 看上去一点不好看；太难看。

attitude.

HIGGINS [*pulling himself together*] I was not trying to look nice, mother.

MRS HIGGINS It doesnt matter, dear. I only wanted to make you speak.

HIGGINS Why?

MRS HIGGINS Because you cant speak and whistle at the same time.

Higgins groans. Another very trying pause.

HIGGINS [*springing up, out of patience*] Where the devil is that girl? Are we to wait here all day?

Eliza enters, sunny, self-possessed, and giving a staggeringly convincing exhibition of ease of manner. She carries a little work-basket, and is very much at home. Pickering is too much taken aback to rise.

LIZA How do you do, Professor Higgins? Are you quite well?

HIGGINS [*chocking*] Am I – [*He can say no more.*]

LIZA But of course you are: you are never ill. So glad to see you again, Colonel Pickering. [*He rises hastily; and they shake hands.*] Quite chilly this morning, isnt it? [*She sits down on his left. He sits beside her.*]

HIGGINS Dont you dare try this game on me. I taught it to you;

284 **It doesnt matter** 这倒无关紧要；it 指 Higgins 不求好看。

289 **trying** 令人难堪的。

290 **out of patience** 耐不住；不耐烦。这是个形容词性质的习语作表语用；不能用作状语短语。

292 **sunny, self-possessed** = being sunny, self-possessed. 喜形于色，从容自若；与下面 giving 加宾语的分词短语并列。 **giving a staggeringly convincing exhibition** [ˌeksɪˈbɪʃən] **of ease of manner** 作出一副惊人地令人信服的悠闲的姿态。

294 **work-basket** 针线篮。 **very much at home** 非常自由自在。at home 是习语。**is too much taken aback to rise** 过分惊讶而忘了站起来。Pickering 一向很有礼貌，这回看见 Eliza 突然以雍容自在的姿态出现在面前，竟忘了应该起立的礼貌。

297 **Am I –** Higgins 对 Eliza 装腔作势向他敷衍客套气得话也说不出了。

302 **Dont you dare try this game on me.** 你不要胆敢向我要这一套把戏（指敷衍客套）。 **Dont you** 比单用 Dont 语气重。 **dare** 现在时形式的 dare 用在否定句或有否定意思的句子里，往往后面接没有 to 的不定式。

and it doesnt take me in. Get up and come home; and dont be a fool.

Eliza takes a piece of needlework from her basket, and begins to stitch at it, without taking the least notice of this outburst.

MRS HIGGINS Very nicely put, indeed, Henry. No woman could resist such an invitation.

HIGGINS You let her alone, mother. Let her speak for herself. You will jolly soon see whether she has an idea that I havnt put into her head or a word that I havnt put into her mouth. I tell you I have created this thing out of the squashed cabbage leaves of Covent Garden; and now she pretends to play the fine lady with me.

MRS HIGGINS [*placidly*] Yes, dear; but youll sit down wont you?

Higgins sits down again, savagely.

LIZA [*to Pickering, talking no apparent notice of Higgins, and working away deftly*] Will you drop me altogether now that the experiment is over, Colonel Pickering?

PICKERING Oh dont. You mustnt think of it as an experiment.

---

303 **take me in** 使我上当；骗到我。take in 作“欺骗”解，是这个习语的许多意思之一。 **Get up and come home** 站起身来，回家去。这里的“家”是指 Higgins 在 Wimpole Street 的家。 **dont be a fool** 别做傻瓜；不要愚蠢

地装腔作势做这一套。

306 **without taking the least notice of this outburst**[ˈaʊtbɜːst] 对（Higgins 的）这突然发作的吵闹一点不理睬。 **take notice** 注意；理会；是习语；后面介词用 of。

307 **Very nicely put** = That's (指 Higgins 说的话) very nicely put. 说得真好（真得体，客气）。显然是讽刺 Higgins 的无礼。 **No woman could resist such an invitation.** 没有一个女人抵制得了这样一个邀请；任何女人都乐于接受这样的邀请呢。这是反语，强烈讽刺 Higgins 的无礼。

309 **You let her alone** 你由她去，不要管她。 **let alone** 是习语；它另有一个特殊的用法，作"更不用说"解，如：He cannot read, let alone write. 他不会读，更不用说写了。 **speak for herself** 自己说（发表自己的意见、讲自己的事情或者为自己辩解）；是习语。 **You will jolly soon see** 你很快就会看到；你马上就会知道。

310 **whether she has an idea that I havnt put into her head or a word that I havnt put into her mouth** 她可有点滴不是我灌输给她的思想，可有一个不是我教她说的字；她所想的、说的全都是我教给她的。

311 **I tell you I have created** [krɪˈeɪtɪd] **this thing out of the squashed** [skwɒʃt] **cabbage leaves of Covent Garden** 我告诉你，我用 Covent Garden 那里的压扁的白菜叶子制造出了这个东西（指 Eliza）。Higgins 自恃清高，任性之至，经常使用粗野的语言辱骂 Eliza。I tell you 有"相信我的话"的意思。**out of** 用……（制成）；是习语。

313 **pretends to play the fine lady with me** 现在她倒装腔作势对我作出高雅的贵妇人的样子来。**play the fine lady** play 作"摆出……的架势"、"扮演……的角色"解时，常用 play the ...，如 play the man（显示丈夫气概），play the hero（逞英雄）。

315 **placidly** [ˈplæsɪdli] 平静地；心平气和地。

317 **talking no apparent notice of Higgins** 表面上好像不理会 Higgins。 **apparent** [əˈpærənt] 含有"表面上明明如此而实际上并非如此"的意思。 **working away** 继续（做针线）工作。 away 表示"继续不停"。

318 **Will you drop me altogether** 可否请你把我整个儿丢开。这里 will you 是说话人祈求的口气，而不是表示纯粹的未来或主语 you 的意向。

320 **think of it as an experiment** 把这件事情看作是一个试验。 **think of ... as ...** 把……当作……；是习语。it 指把 Eliza 训练成一个贵妇人；这在 Pickering 看来是完成了一件大事，决不只是什么随便的"试验"。

It shocks me, somehow.

LIZA Oh, I'm only a squashed cabbage leaf –

PICKERING [*impulsively*] No.

LIZA [*continuing quietly*] – but I owe so much to you that I should be very unhappy if you forgot me.

PICKERING It's very kind of you to say so, Miss Doolittle.

LIZA It's not because you paid for my dresses. I know you are generous to everybody with money. But it was from you that I learnt really nice manners; and that is what makes one a lady, isnt it? You see it was so very difficult for me with the example of Professor Higgins always before me. I was brought up to be just like him, unable to control myself, and using bad language on the slightest provocation. And I should never have known that ladies and gentlemen didnt behave like that if you hadnt been there.

HIGGINS Well!!

PICKERING Oh, thats only his way, you know. He doesnt mean it.

LIZA Oh, *I* didnt mean it either, when I was a flower girl. It was only my way. But you see I did it; and thats what makes the difference after all.

PICKERING No doubt. Still, he taught you to speak; and I couldnt have done that, you know.

LIZA [*trivially*] Of course: that is his profession.

HIGGINS Damnation!

LIZA [*continuing*] It was just like learning to dance in the fashion-

321 **It shocks me, somehow.** 这话（不知怎么）总觉得刺耳；it 指这件事只是个试验的说法。 **shock** 除“使震惊”外，还可作“使愤慨”、“使厌恶”等解。

324 **owe so much to you** 受惠（或得益）于你（Pickering），而该报答你的有那么多。

327 **are generous to everybody with money** 对每个人都慷慨解囊。注意 generous with money 一语中介词用 with。

328 **it was from you that I learnt really nice manners** 我是从你这里（而不是从 Higgins 或其他人那里）学得真正好的礼貌的。

329 **that is what makes one a lady** 那（指礼貌）是使一个人成为上等女人的东西。that 指 really nice manners；manners 虽是复数形式，却具有抽象名词的性质，被看作为单数。what 是关系代词，= that which。

330 **so very difficult for me with the example of Professor Higgins always before me** 一直有 Higgins 教授的榜样在我面前，我（要学习好礼貌）有那么大的困难（因为 Higgins 一向不讲礼貌，他的榜样实在太坏）。

331 **I was brought up to be just like him** 我从小被培养成正像是他这个样子。 **bring up** 培养，是习语。

332 **unable to control myself, and using bad language on the slightest provocation** 不能控制自己，碰到了即使极小的冒犯就恶言相向。在语法结构上，由 and 连接的两个词组都是修饰 just like him 的那种人（虽然上文并没有“人”）。

333 **I should never have known that ladies and gentlemen didnt behave like that if you hadnt been there** 要是没有你在那里（在 Wimpole Street）我决不会知道贵妇绅士不是（像 Higgins）那样（粗野无礼）的。这是与过去事实相反的虚拟语气，事实上是因为看到了你（彬彬有礼的 Pickering），我才知道贵妇绅士不是那样（粗野无礼）的。

337 **thats only his way** 那只是他的与众不同的习惯。**doesnt mean it**（天生如此而）并非故意如此。it 指 his way。

339 **I did it; and thats what makes the difference after all.** 过去我就是那样做的，那毕竟（使上等人和下等人）有区别。

341 **I couldnt have done that** 我（要教你说也）教不来。 **done that** = taught you to speak.

343 **trivially** 不作为奇地；口气轻飘飘地。

344 **Damnation!** 作感叹词，是诅咒语，= Damn! 该死。

able way: there was nothing more than that in it. But do you know what began may real education?

PICKERING What?

LIZA [*stopping her work for a moment*] Your calling me Miss Doolittle that day when I first came to Wimpole Street. That was the beginning of self-respect for me. [*She resumes her stitching.*] And there were a hundred little things you never noticed, because they came naturally to you. Things about standing up and taking off your hat and opening doors –

PICKERING Oh, that was nothing.

LIZA Yes: things that shewed you thought and felt about me as if I were something better than a scullery-maid; though of course I know you would have been just the same to a scullery-maid if she had been let into the drawing room. You never took off your boots in the dining room when I was there.

PICKERING You mustnt mind that. Higgins takes off his boots all over the place.

LIZA I know. I am not blaming him. It is his way, isnt it? But it made such a difference to me that you didnt do it. You see, really and truly, apart from the things anyone can pick up (the dressing and the proper way of speaking, and so on), the

---

346 **there was nothing more than that in it** 这（学上等人的语言）里面没有比那（学时髦的舞蹈）有更多的东西；不过如此而已。

349 **Your calling me Miss Doolittle** 你称呼我 Doolittle 小姐（见第二幕）。 **calling** 是动名词，既作名词，又有动词的性质，所以后面可有状语短语 that day 和状语从句 when I first came to Wimpole Street 修饰它，而 calling 的谓语 began my education 却省略了，全句成了只有主语的单部句。

350 **That** = Your calling me Miss Doolittle.

352 **there were a hundred little things you never noticed** 有许多你全没注意到的小事情。**a hundred** 喻其多，并不实指“一百”。**little things** 指生活细节、小节；后面省略 which 或 that。

353 **they came naturally to you** 它们（这些小事情）自然地在你身上表现出来（你的一举一动都出于自然）。 **Things** 承接上句，与上句中 a hundred little things 并列，进一步列举具体事例。 **standing up and taking off your hat and opening doors –** （见人进来时）起立，（进屋内时）脱帽，以及（为人）开门等等；这都是西方礼仪。

355 **that was nothing** 那不算什么。上文讲 things，且一件件列举，但总的概念是礼仪，所以代词可用单数 that。

356 **things that shewed you thought and felt about me as if I were something better than a scullery-maid** 这些事情显出你把我想作、看作仿佛是高于后厨女仆的某类人；说明你不把我当低三下四的人。things 指上面列举的那些细节；前面省略 these（或 the）。

358 **you would have been just the same to a scullery-maid if she had been let into the drawing room** 要是后厨女仆被允许进入会客室，你也会（像对待我那样）同样（有礼貌）的。这是与过去事实相反的虚拟语气，实际并非曾有这样的事。

360 **took off your boots in the dining room when I was there** 在餐厅里当着我脱靴子。在餐室里脱靴子已经够不文雅，还要当着女人的面，更是粗野无礼，而 Higgins 习以为常。

362 **mind that** 介意那个（指上述脱靴事）。mind 作“反对”解时，后面常接动名词（不可接不定式），也接名词、代词，间或还接 that 从句。 **all over the place** 遍地；到处；随地。

366 **really and truly** 真正地；千真万确地。 **apart from the things anyone can pick up** 除了任何人能随便学会的那些东西之外。apart from 和 pick 都是习语。

367 **the dressing** 衣装打扮。

difference between a lady and a flower girl is not how she behaves, but how she's treated. I shall always be a flower girl to Professor Higgins, because he always treats me as a flower girl, and always will; but I know I can be a lady to you, because you always treat me as a lady, and always will.

MRS HIGGINS Please dont grind your teeth, Henry.

PICKERING Well, this is really very nice of you, Miss Doolittle.

LIZA I should like you to call me Eliza, now, if you would.

PICKERING Thank you. Eliza, of course.

LIZA And I should like Professor Higgins to call me Miss Doolittle.

HIGGINS I'll see you damned first.

MRS HIGGINS Henry! Henry!

PICKERING [*laughing*] Why dont you slang back at him? Dont stand it. It would do him a lot of good.

LIZA I cant. I could have done it once; but now I cant go back to it. You told me, you know, that when a child is brought to a foreign country, it picks up the language in a few weeks, and forgets its own. Well, I am a child in your country. I have forgotten my own language, and can speak nothing but yours. Thats the real break-off with the corner of Tottenham Court Road. Leaving Wimpole Street finishes it.

---

369 **how she's treated** 她是怎样被对待的；人家怎么对待她。

371 **and always will** = and will always treat me as a flower girl. always 一般放在助动词后面，但像这里省略了助动词后面的部分时，always 放在助动词前面。

373 **grind your teeth** 咬牙切齿；是习语。

375 **I should like you to call me Eliza, now** 现在我倒喜欢你叫我 Eliza（叫 Eliza 比叫 Miss Doolittle 亲切）。

376 **Thank you.** 感谢 Eliza 叫他更随意地称呼她的亲切表示。

377 **And I should like Professor Higgins to call me Miss Doolittle.** 而我希望 Higgins 教授叫我 Doolittle 小姐（要 Higgins 尊重她些）。

379 **I'll see you damned first.** 我要先看你被打入了地狱(才叫你 Doolittle 小姐)；我才不叫你 Doolittle 小姐呢。see somebody damned first 是习语；这里的 damned 也作 blowed，hanged 等，都是诅咒语。

380 **Henry! Henry!** Mrs Higgins 喝住她儿子不要粗野地口出诅咒语。

381 **slang back at him** 用粗话骂还他。Pickering 是个文雅的绅士，并不真要叫 Eliza 骂人，他说这话是开玩笑的。**Dont stand it.** 不要忍受它；不要听受他吆五喝六。it，泛指 Higgins 的诅咒。stand 作"忍受"解时，宾语除用名词、代词、动名词外，美国人也用不定式。

382 **It would do him a lot of good.** 这（用粗话骂还他）对他有很大好处。**do somebody good** 对（某人）起好作用（有益）。good 是名词，作 do 的直接宾语，somebody 是间接宾语。

383 **I cant** = I cant slang back at him. **go back to it** 回头再这样做；（学了文雅的语言之后）重又说粗话。

385 **it picks up the language in a few weeks** 他（这孩子）几个星期就自然学会了那种（外国的）语言。英语中常用 it 指婴儿和幼年的孩子，相反常用 he、she 指喜爱的小动物。

386 **I am a child in your country** 我是在你们国家里的一个孩子。Eliza 把 Higgins 和 Pickering 看作是属于另一个国家的，把他们的语言看作是外国语（跟她自己原来所用的语言不同）。

387 **can speak nothing but yours** 除了你们的语言，说不来任何其他的语言；只会说你们的话。

388 **break-off** 脱离关系。 **the corner of Tottenham Court Road** Eliza 原来卖花处，见第二幕（p.62）。

389 **Leaving Wimpole Street finishes it.** 离开 Wimpole Street（Higgins 的实验室），便完成了这件事。犹言"离校毕业"。it 指 break-off，即 Eliza 从卖花女变成了贵妇人。

PICKERING [*much alarmed*] Oh! But youre coming back to Wimpole Street, arent you? Youll forgive Higgins?

HIGGINS [*rising*] Forgive! Will she, by George! Let her go. Let her find out how she can get on without us. She will relapse into the gutter in three weeks without me at her elbow.

Doolittle appears at the centre window. With a look of dignified reproach at Higgins, he comes slowly and silently to his daughter, who, with her back to the window, is unconscious of his approach.

PICKERING He's incorrigible, Eliza. You wont relapse, will you?

LIZA No: not now. Never again. I have learnt my lesson. I dont believe I could utter one of the old sounds if I tried. [*Doolittle touches her on her left shoulder. She drops her work, losing her self-possession utterly at the spectacle of her father's splendor*]. A-a-a-a-a-ah-ow-ooh!

HIGGINS [*with a crow of triumph*] Aha! Just so. A-a-a-a-ahowooh! A-a-a-a-ahowooh! A-a-a-a-ahowooh! Victory! Victory! [*He throws himself on the divan, folding his arms, and spraddling arrogantly.*]

DOOLITTLE Can you blame the girl? Dont look at me like that, Eliza. It aint my fault. Ive come into some money.

---

390 **much alarmed** 大为震动；大惊小怪；这里 alarmed 没有“惊吓”的意思。

392 **Forgive!** 要她饶恕！

393 **get on without us** 没有我们而过下去；不靠我们过活。 **get on** 是习语，作“过活”解时，也作 get along。 **relapse into the gutter in three weeks without me at her elbow** （倘）没有我在她身旁，三个星期后就又流落街头。 in three weeks 修饰一时的动作 relapse，是“三星期后”的意思；倘若修饰持续的动作，则 in 是“……之内”的意思，如 see him several times in a week、learn another language in three years。 **at one's elbow** 在手边；是习语。

395 **With a look of dignified reproach at Higgins** 用严肃的责备的眼光瞧着 Higgins。

399 **He's incorrigible** [ɪnˈkɒrɪdʒəbl] 他（Higgins）是改不好的（指 Higgins 的口出恶言）。

400 **not now** = I shall not relapse now. 现在我不会又流落街头了。 **learnt my lesson** 领教了。这里指“学好了（语音）课业”，兼含“得到教训”的双关意思，即学了上流社会的语音，弄得不尴不尬，得到了痛苦的教训。（汉语中“领教”也有正面和反面的两个意思。）

401 **if I tried** 即使我想要这样做。这是虚拟语气，if = even if；tried 后面省略 to utter one of the old sounds。

402 **She drops her work** 她丢下针线活。drop 这里是“无意地掉落”的意思。work 指 needlework，可指抽象的工作，也可指具体的工作物。 **losing her self-possession utterly at the spectacle of her father's splendor** （看见）她父亲华贵的景象，完全失去了自制。因为失去自制，所以原先的 A-a-a-a-a-ah-ow-ooh 的怪叫声又脱口而出。

405 **a crow** [krəʊ] **of triumph** [ˈtraɪʌmf] 胜利的欢呼。（因为 Higgins 听见 Eliza 果然又发出原来的土音了。） **Just so** 正是如此；是习语。这里的意思是“原先就是这样怪叫的”。

407 **spraddling arrogantly** [ˈærəgəntli] 傲慢地张开双腿。 **spraddle** 是方言，作“摆开”、“展开”解。

409 **Dont look at me like that** 别那样瞧着我。Eliza 看见她父亲神气的样子，定然目光里露出惊讶的表情。

410 **It aint my fault.** 这（变了神气的样子）不是我的过错；怪不得我。 **come into some money** 得到一些钱。 **come into** 得到；继承（财产等）；是习语。

LIZA You must have touched a millionaire this time, dad.

DOOLITTLE I have. But I'm dressed something special today. I'm going to St George's, Hanover Square. Your stepmother is going to marry me.

LIZA [*angrily*] Youre going to let yourself down to marry that low common woman!

PICKERING [*quietly*] He ought to, Eliza. [*to Doolittle*] Why has she changed her mind?

DOOLITTLE [*sadly*] Intimidated, Governor. Intimidated. Middle class morality claims its victim. Wont you put on your hat, Liza, and come and see me turned off?

LIZA If the Colonel says I must, I – I'll [*almost sobbing*] I'll demean myself. And get insulted for my pains, like enough.

DOOLITTLE Dont be afraid: she never comes to words with anyone now, poor woman! Respectability has broke all the spirit out of her.

PICKERING [*squeezing Eliza's elbow gently*] Be kind to them, Eliza. Make the best of it.

LIZA [*forcing a little smile for him through her vexation*] Oh well, just to shew theres no ill feeling. I'll be back in a moment. [*She goes out.*]

DOOLITTLE [*sitting down beside Pickering*] I feel uncommon nerv-

---

411 **You must have touched a millionaire** [ˌmɪljəˈneər] **this time** 这回你一定从一个百万富翁那里弄到了钱。 **dad** 爹，口语中常用 dad 或 daddy 称父亲。

412 **I'm dressed something special today** 今天我穿得特别（漂亮）了些。

something 这里是副词；意为“多少”、“几分”，等于 somewhat。 **special** 这里该用 specially 修饰 am dressed。

413 **St George's, Hanover** [ˈhænəvə] **Square** Hanover 广场的 St George 教堂。 **Your stepmother is going to marry me.** 你的后娘将嫁给我（和我正式结婚）。所谓“后娘”实则是 Doolittle 的姘妇，过去一直不肯跟他正式结婚，见第二幕（p.130）。

415 **let yourself down to marry that low common woman** 降低你自己的身份去娶那个下流的低贱女人。 **low** 下等的；低贱的。 **common** 粗俗的；低贱的。

417 **ought to** = ought to marry her. 不能硬扣上文理解为 ought to marry that low common woman，更不该理解为 ought to let himself down to marry that low common woman。 **Why has she changed her mind?** 为什么她（原来不肯结婚而）现在改变宗旨（愿意结婚）了？

419 **Governor** 英国口语用以尊称男子，见前注。

420 **claims its victim** （把我们）作为它（中产阶级道德）的理所应当的牺牲品。

421 **come and see me turned off** 来看我结婚。 **come and see** = come to see. **turn off** 俚语里有“绞死”、“使结婚”等意思，这里 turned off 是宾语补足语，me 和 turned off（使被迫结婚）有逻辑上的主谓关系，构成复合宾语。

422 **demean myself** 降低自己身份。区别：另一词源相当于 behave 的 demean，如 demean oneself well/ill，表现良好（或不好）。

423 **get insulted for my pains** 费了心（去参加婚礼）还要受（后娘的）气。and 首字母小写，紧接上句，这里另起一句，表示说话时稍顿的口气。 **for (all) one's pains** 尽管费（尽）力气（或心思）；是习语。 **like enough** 很可能；大概，常用作插入语，也可作 very like，等于 very likely。

424 **comes to words with** 跟……吵起嘴来。 **words** 口角；用复数。

425 **Respectability has broke all the spirit out of her** （中产阶级的）体面身份使她完全丧气了。这里的 respectability 含有贬义，讽刺一本正经的市侩习俗。broke 应作 broken。

428 **Make the best of it** 随遇而安。 **make the best of** （在不幸等情况中）求最大的幸运（或结果）；是习语。it 泛指面临的情况。

429 **forcing a little smile for him through her vexation** 从她的烦躁中勉强对他作出微笑。 **just to shew theres no ill feeling** 即以表示没有恶感。这句话在意义上连接下一句，可以看作是个状语短语。

432 **uncommon** 应作 uncommonly，异常地。

ous about the ceremony, Colonel. I wish youd come and see me through it.

PICKERING But youve been through it before, man. You were married to Eliza's mother.

DOOLITTLE Who told you that, Colonel?

PICKERING Well, nobody told me. But I concluded – naturally –

DOOLITTLE No: that aint the natural way, Colonel: it's only the middle class way. My way was always the undeserving way. But dont say nothing to Eliza. She dont know: I always had a delicacy about telling her.

PICKERING Quite right. We'll leave it so, if you dont mind.

DOOLITTLE And youll come to the church, Colonel, and put me through straight?

PICKERING With pleasure. As far as a bachelor can.

MRS HIGGINS May I come, Mr Doolittle? I should be very sorry to miss your wedding.

DOOLITTLE I should indeed be honored by your condescension, maam; and my poor old woman would take it as a tremenjous compliment. She's been very low, thinking of the happy days that are no more.

MRS HIGGINS [*rising*] I'll order the carriage and get ready. [*The men rise, except Higgins.*] I shant be more than fifteen minutes. [*As she goes to the door Eliza comes in, hatted and buttoning her gloves.*]

---

433 **see me through it** 看看我经历这个（结婚仪式）。 **see somebody through** 帮某人渡过（难关）（或维持过……）；是习语。

435 **man** 用 man 作为对男子的称呼，有亲密或轻蔑的意思。 **You were married to Eliza's mother.** 你跟 Eliza 的母亲已经是结了婚的。Pickering 以为孩子也生下了，当然早已是夫妇。

438 **I concluded – naturally –** 我自然地得出结论（你们已经结了婚）；或者我得出的结论是（你们）自然（已经结了婚）。两个解释实际的意义是相同的。

439 **that aint the natural way** 那（结婚）不是自然的做法。 **it's only the middle class way** 那（结婚）只是中产阶级的做法；中产阶级才讲究结婚。

440 **the undeserving way** = the way of the undeserving poor.

441 **dont say nothing to Eliza** 这是不正当的“双重否定”，应作 dont say anything to Eliza 或 say nothing to Eliza。 **She dont know** 应作 She doesnt know。 **had a delicacy** [ˈdelɪkəsi] **about telling her** 告诉她有所不便；不便告诉她（我和她妈妈没有结过婚）。

443 **leave it so** 让它这样（指不说穿）。 **if you dont mind** 如果你不反对。这是常用口语，实际是“好吗？”的意思。

444 **put me through straight** 帮我从头到底地完成婚礼。 **put through** 使做完；使经受；是习语；straight，是副词。

446 **With pleasure.** 很高兴；好的。是常用应答语。 **As far as a bachelor can.** 尽一个单身汉所能地（帮你完成婚礼）。Pickering 自己不曾有举行婚礼的经验，故作此语。

447 **I should be very sorry to miss your wedding.** 这是虚拟语气，= I should be very sorry if I missed your wedding.（如果）我错过你的婚礼，我将十分遗憾；我真想参加你的婚礼。

449 **your condescension** 你屈尊（参加我的婚礼）。

450 **take it as a tremenjous compliment** 把它（你屈尊来临）看作是极大的褒奖（赏光）。tremenjous [trəˈmendʒəs] 是 tremendous [trəˈmendəs] 的误读。

451 **low** 意气消沉；沮丧。 **the happy days that are no more** 不再有的（一去不返的）快活的日子。Doolittle 总把过去的穷日子说成是快活的，因为不受中产阶级道德的束缚。

453 **carriage** 四轮马车。

454 **I shant be more than fifteen minutes.** 我不会超过十五分钟（就来）。

455 **hatted and buttoning her gloves** 戴着帽子和正在扣上手套的钮子。过去分词 hatted 和现在分词 buttoning 同样作修饰词。

I'm going to the church to see your father married, Eliza. You had better come in the brougham with me. Colonel Pickering can go on with the bridegroom.

Mrs Higgins goes out. Eliza comes to the middle of the room between the centre window and the ottoman. pickering joins her.

DOOLITTLE Bridegroom! What a word! It makes a man realize his position, somehow. [*He takes up his hat and goes towards the door.*]

PICKERING Before I go, Eliza, do forgive Higgins and come back to us.

LIZA I dont think dad would allow me. Would you, dad?

DOOLITTLE [*sad but magnanimous*] They played you off very cunning, Eliza, them two sportsmen. If it had been only one of them, you could have nailed him. But you see, there was two; and one of them chaperoned the other, as you might say. [*to Pickering*] It was artful of you, Colonel; but I bear no malice: I should have done the same myself. I been the victim of one woman after another all my life, and I dont grudge you two getting the better of Liza. I shant interfere. It's time for us to

457 **brougham** [ˈbruːəm] 一匹马拉的四轮轿车。上面所说的 carriage 即指此车。
458 **go on with the bridegroom** 和新郎同行（上教堂去）。

460 **joins her** 到她那里，和她在一起。

462 **It makes a man realize his position, somehow.** 它（bridegroom 这个词）总会使人意识到自己所处的地位。somehow，修饰 makes。

465 **do forgive** 是 forgive 的强势式；do 重读。

467 **allow me** = allow me to come back to you. **Would you, dad?** = Would you allow me to come back to them, dad? Eliza 以为她父亲有了钱，不会允许她再回到 Higgins 和 Pickering 那里，而要她一起回家去的。

468 **sad but magnanimous** [mæg'nænɪməs] 抑郁而宽大。Doolittle 以为 Higgins 和 Pickering 两个人占了 Eliza 的便宜，所以他抑郁；但是他不责怪他们，也不领她回家，还是愿意把她交给这两个人，所以他是“宽大”的。 **played you off very cunning** 很巧妙地把你对付过去。play off 是习语。

469 **them two sportsmen** 应作 these two sportsmen，是主语 They 的同位语；sportsman，原义“运动家”，运动比赛中有规则、要正大光明，所以引伸为“有（运动家的）正大光明的道德、风格的人”；同时 sport 原是“娱乐”、“游戏”的意思，所以这里称他们“正人君子”，又含有“（拿 Eliza）开玩笑的人”的意思，是双关语。 **If it had been only one of them, you could have nailed him.** 要是有关这事情的是他们（two sportsmen）中的一个，你就可以钉住他。**nail**，口语中作“抓住”、“捕获”解；这句子是虚拟语气，事实上，正因为是两个而不是一个，所以没法抓住哪一个，见下文 Doolittle 自己对这话的解释。

470 **there was two** 应作 there were two。

471 **one of them chaperoned the other, as you might say** 犹如你（们）说的，他们两个相互伴随着，社交场中未婚少女常有年长妇女伴随监护，称为 chaperone，这个词也作及物动词用。

472 **It was artful of you** 你们真乖巧。这个句型和 It is kind/nice/good of you to come 的句型同，这里 of you 省略 to do so；有许多形容词可用这句型，但并不是所有形容词都可用此句型。 **bear no malice** ['mælɪs] 不怀恶意。 **bear malice to/towards somebody** 对某人怀有恶意；是习语。

473 **I been** 应作 I have been。 **the victim of one woman after another** 一个又一个女人的牺牲品；吃过许多女人的亏。

474 **dont grudge you two getting the better of Liza** 不抱怨你们两个占 Eliza 的便宜。**get the better of** 占……的上风；智胜；是习语。

go, Colonel. So long, Henry. See you in St George's, Eliza. [*He goes out.*]

PICKERING [*coaxing*] Do stay with us, Eliza. [*He follows Doolittle.*]

Eliza goes out on the balcony to avoid being alone with Higgins. He rises and joins her there. She immediately comes back into the room and makes for the door; but he goes along the balcony quickly and gets his back to the door before she reaches it.

HIGGINS Well, Eliza, youve had a bit of your own back, as you call it. Have you had enough? And are you going to be reasonable? Or do you want any more?

LIZA You want me back only to pick up your slippers and put up with your tempers and fetch and carry for you.

HIGGINS I havnt said I wanted you back at all.

LIZA Oh, indeed. Then what are we talking about?

HIGGINS About you, not about me. If you come back I shall treat you just as I have always treated you. I cant change my nature; and I dont intend to change my manners. My manners are exactly the same as Colonel Pickering's.

LIZA Thats not true. He treats a flower girl as if she was a duchess.

HIGGINS And I treat a duchess as if she was a flower girl.

LIZA I see. [*She turns away composedly, and sits on the ottoman, facing the window.*] The same to everybody.

HIGGINS Just so.

LIZA Like father.

---

476 **So long** 再见；是口语，多用于熟人间。Doolittle 用此语，以及用教名 Henry 称 Higgins，都表示他对 Higgins 已经谬托知己，熟不拘礼。 **See you in St George's** 在 St George's 教堂和你见面。See 前面省略 I'll。

481 **goes along the balcony** 顺着阳台走去（兜来兜去追逐 Eliza）。

483 **had a bit of your own back** 报复到了一点。习语 get one's own back (on somebody) 是"（对某人）进行报复"的意思。back 是副词。 **as you call it** 如你所说的；所谓。指上面 had a bit of your own back 这说法。

484 **had enough** 可理解为 had enough of your own back。 **reasonable** 合情合理的；不过分的。

486 **want me back** 要我回（到你那里）去。这里 back 是宾语补足语，me 和 back 有逻辑上的主谓关系，构成复合宾语。 **put up with your tempers** 忍受你的发脾气；受你的气。 **put up with** 忍受；是习语。tempers 指一次次的发脾气，= fits of temper。

487 **fetch and carry** 打杂；当听差；是习语。

490 **About you** = I'm talking about you.

491 **change my nature** 改变我的本性。

494 **Thats not true.** 那（你说的话）不真实（不符实际）。 **He treats a flower girl as if she was a duchess.** 他对待一个卖花女，仿佛她是个公爵夫人。这里的 as if 引起的虚拟语气的从句中，有些语法家认为该用 were，但实际上用 was 很普遍。

496 **composedly** [kəmˈpəʊzdli] 镇定自若。它的相应的形容词 composed 读 [kəmˈpəʊzd]；同样的例子如 marked [mɑːkt]，markedly [ˈmɑːktli]（显著）；resigned [rɪˈzaɪnd]，resignedly [rɪˈzaɪnɪdli]（无可奈何）；但 determinedly 读 [dɪˈtɜːmɪndli]，不读 [-ɪdli]。

497 **The same to everybody.** = You are the same to everybody. = You treat everybody in the same way.

499 **Like father.** = You are the same to everybody, like father. father = my (Eliza's) father. 口语中谈到自己的父、母等亲人时，常省略 my、our。

HIGGINS [*grinning, a little taken down*] Without accepting the comparison at all points, Eliza, it's quite true that your father is not a snob, and that he will be quite at home in any station of life to which his eccentric destiny may call him. [*seriously*] The great secret, Eliza, is not having bad manners or good manners or any other particular sort of manners, but having the same manner for all human souls: in short, behaving as if you were in Heaven, where there are no third-class carriages, and one soul is as good as another.

LIZA Amen. You are a born preacher.

HIGGINS [*irritated*] The question is not whether I treat you rudely, but whether you ever heard me treat anyone else better.

LIZA [*with sudden sincerity*] I dont care how you treat me. I dont mind your swearing at me. I shouldnt mind a black eye: Ive had one before this. But [*standing up and facing him*] I wont be passed over.

HIGGINS Then get out of my way; for I wont stop for you. You talk

---

500 **grinning, a little taken down** 露齿而笑，傲慢的气焰被压下了些。 **take down** 压下……的气焰；是习语。 **without accepting the comparison at all points** 不是在每一点上都接受这个比较。注意：不作“在所有各点上都不接受这个比较”解。the comparison 指 Eliza 拿 Higgins 比作她的父亲 Doolittle。

502 **any station of life to which his eccentric destiny may call him** 他的怪癖的命运可能使他达到的任何生活地位。 **his eccentric destiny** 他的古怪的命运（指垃圾工人莫名其妙地变成富人）。 **call sombody to** 使（某人）处于（某

种处境）或做（某事）。

503 **seriously** 严肃地；认真地。Higgins 喜怒无常，（雅俗无常），俗起来什么粗野的话都说，雅起来俨然专家教授；这里的一段话就完全是讲台上的口气。

504 **The great secret, Eliza, is not having bad manners or good manners** Eliza，重大的秘密（关键）不在无礼或有礼（礼貌好不好）。 **having** 是动名词，和它的宾语 bad manners or good manners 组成的动名词短语，作主语补足语，也称表语；having 并不和 is 构成进行时。

505 **having the same manner for all human souls** 对所有的人抱同样的态度。 **human souls** 人。

506 **in short** 简而言之；总之；是习语。 **behaving as if you were in Heaven** 仿佛你（死后）在天国里那样地待人接物。you 泛指任何人。Heaven 作“天堂”解，用单数，前面没有 the，首字母一般不用大写；指“上帝”时，也用单数，不用 the，但首字母用大写。

507 **carriages** （客车的）车厢（在美国称 car）。

508 **one soul is as good as another** 一个个灵魂彼此平等。 **as good as** 和……一样；同……一般；是习语。

509 **Amen.** 阿门（基督教徒祷告或唱赞美诗结束时用语）意思是“心愿如此”。Eliza 讽刺 Higgins 说这一番话像在教堂里讲道，所以用了教会的用语。 **a born preacher** 天生的传教士（或鼓吹家）。

511 **whether you ever heard me treat anyone else better** 可曾听见过我对待任何别人（比对待你）较好（或更好）的。better 后面省略 than I treat you。

512 **I dont care how you treat me.** 我不在乎你怎样对待我。 **I dont care** 我不介意；但在后面接不定式时，便作“我不愿”、“我不肯”解，如 I dont care to go（我不高兴去）。

513 **I shouldnt mind a black eye** 我不在乎（被打成）青眼眶。 **mind** 作“反对”、“介意”解时，除动名词（如上句 swearing）外，后面也可接名词。这里用虚拟语气，表示“即使你打青我的眼眶也没关系”之意，省略了条件从句。

514 **I wont be passed over.** 我不愿被人走过面前（而不理睬我）；我不愿人家不把我放在眼里。 **pass over** 忽略；省略；是习语。

516 **get out of my way** 不要挡我的路；给我让路。 **I wont stop for you** 我不会为你停（车）。Higgins 故意把 Eliza 所说的 be passed away 误解为“被（车）轧过”，故作此语；下句说 Eliza 把他当作了公共汽车，意思更清楚。

about me as if I were a motor bus.

LIZA So you are a motor bus: all bounce and go, and no consideration for anyone. But I can do without you: dont think I cant.

HIGGINS I know you can. I told you you could.

LIZA [*wounded, getting away from him to the other side of the ottoman with her face to the hearth*] I know you did, you brute. You wanted to get rid of me.

HIGGINS Liar.

LIZA Thank you. [*She sits down with dignity.*]

HIGGINS You never asked yourself, I suppose, whether *I* could do without you.

LIZA [*earnestly*] Dont you try to get round me. Youll have to do without me.

HIGGINS [*arrogant*] I can do without anybody. I have my own soul: my own spark of divine fire. But [*with sudden humility*] I shall miss you, Eliza. [*He sits down near her on the ottoman.*] I have learnt something from your idiotic notions: I confess that humbly and gratefully. And I have grown accustomed to your voice and appearance. I like them, rather.

LIZA Well, you have both of them on your gramophone and in your book of photographs. When you feel lonely without me, you can turn the machine on. It's got no feelings to hurt.

HIGGINS I cant turn your soul on. Leave me those feelings; and

518 **So** 有"就是这样"、"这么看来"的意思。 **all bounce and go, and no consideration for anyone** 一味横冲直撞，而不顾任何人。 **all ... and ...** 只有……而没有…… bounce 和 go 都是名词，作表语；类似的用例如：I'm all attention. 我全神贯注着。The sentence is simplicity itself. 这句句子简洁之极。

519 **do without** 没有……也行；不用；是习语。 **dont think I cant** = (you) dont think I cant do without you.

521 **I told you you could.** 我对你说过，你没有我也行（是尽可不必留在这里的）。后面省略 do without you。

523 **you did** = you told me I could (do without you).

524 **get rid of** 摆脱；去掉；是习语；中间 rid 是过去分词，作表语。

525 **Liar** 说谎的人；这里是"你胡说"的意思。

526 **Thank you.** Eliza 说 Higgins 要摆脱她，他说"胡说"，那就是说 Higgins 需要她，所以她说 thank you，犹如我们说"承情"；这话实际是讽刺，因为 Eliza 已经决定离去。

527 **I suppose** = I think. 这里是插入语。

529 **get round** 使回心转意；说服；智胜；是习语。

532 **my own spark of divine fire** 我自己的神圣的火焰之花（比喻自己的才智）；与 soul 同位。 **I shall miss you** 我将感到缺少了你；我将想念你。

534 **learnt something from your idiotic** [ˌɪdɪˈɒtɪk] **notions** 从你白痴般的观念中学到了些东西。

535 **grown accustomed to** 已经对……习惯了；习惯于……

536 **I like them, rather** 我倒（不是讨厌而是）喜欢它们（your voice and appearance）。rather 放在句末，比放在 like 前面的语气重。

537 **both of them** 指 my voice and appearance。

539 **turn the machine** [məˈʃiːn] **on** 开（留声）机器。 **turn on** 开（机器、电灯、自来水等）；是习语。 **It's got no feelings to hurt.** 它（留声机）没有会被刺伤的感情；没有伤留声机感情的事。to hurt，主动态不定式表示被动态的意思。

540 **cant turn your soul on** （我可以开留声机，可是）不能开你的灵魂。 **Leave me those feelings; and you can take away the voice and the face.** 把（你的）那些感情留下给我，而声音和面貌你都可以拿走；留声机和照片我都不要，我所要的正是你的感情。

you can take away the voice and the face. They are not you.

LIZA Oh, you are a devil. You can twist the heart in a girl as easy as some could twist her arms to hurt her. Mrs Pearce warned me. Time and again she has wanted to leave you; and you always got round her at the last minute. And you dont care a bit for her. And you dont care a bit for me.

HIGGINS I care for life, for humanity; and you are a part of it that has come my way and been built into my house. What more can you or anyone ask?

LIZA I wont care for anybody that doesnt care for me.

HIGGINS Commercial principles, Eliza. Like [*reproducing her Covent Garden pronunciation with professional exactness*] s'yollin voylets [selling violets], isnt it?

LIZA Dont sneer at me. It's mean to sneer at me.

HIGGINS I have never sneered in my life. Sneering doesnt become either the human face or the human soul. I am expressing my righteous contempt for Commercialism. I dont and wont trade in affection. You call me a brute because you couldnt buy a claim on me by fetching my slippers and finding my spectacles. You were a fool: I think a woman fetching a man's slippers is a disgusting sight: did I ever fetch your slippers? I think a good deal more of you for throwing them in my face. No use slaving for me and then saying you want to be cared

---

541 **They are not you.** 它们（留声机里声音和照片上的面貌）不是你（自己）（而

我要的是你）。

542 **you are a devil** Eliza 认为 Higgins 是在用甜言蜜语哄骗她，使她不要走，所以称他“魔鬼”。**twist the heart in a girl** 搅乱一个少女的心；使她糊涂。**twist** 原义“扭弯”；这里用 twist the heart 和下面 twist her arms（拗她的臂膀）相映成趣。 **as easy as** 应作 as easily as。

543 **warned** 警告；也作“预先使（人）注意”解。

544 **Time and again** 屡次地；时常；是习语。

545 **at the last minute** 在最后一分钟；到最后时刻；在 Mrs Pearce 即将离去的时候。

547 **I care for life, for humanity** 我关心生命，关心人类。 **you are a part of it that has come my way and been built into my house** 你是它（兼指生命和人类）的一部分，碰上了我，并融入我家中。that 的先行词是 part 或 part of it，不是 it。

548 **What more can you or anyone ask?** 你或者任何人（如你父亲）还能要求什么更多的呢?

551 **Commercial principles** （你说的是）商业原则。指“既然你不关心我，我也不关心你”，有如对等的买卖关系。 **reproducing her Covent Garden pronunciation with professional exactness** 用专家的准确性照样发出（模仿）她（在第一幕中）在 Covent Garden 的发音。

554 **mean** 卑鄙的；讨厌的。

555 **I have never sneered in my life.** 我一生没有嗤笑过人。其实 Higgins 经常嗤笑人，只是并不有心，并不自觉。 **Sneering doesnt become either the human face or the human soul.** 嗤笑对人的面貌和人的灵魂都不合适。

557 **righteous** [ˈraɪtʃəs] **contempt** [kənˈtempt] **for Commercialism** 对商业主义（买卖原则）的正当鄙视。

558 **trade in affection** 用感情做交易。说“做……买卖”用 trade in。

559 **buy a claim on me** 买到受我喜爱的权利；买到我的情感；要我对你感恩。

561 **a disgusting sight** 令人作呕的景象；极难看的行为。 **I think a good deal more of you for throwing them in my face.** 你拿它们（拖鞋）向我脸上扔，我倒认为你好得多（对你尊重得多）。 **think much (little) of** 看重（看轻）；是习语。

563 **No use slaving for me and then saying you want to be cared for** 为我做奴隶，又说要人家关心你，这是徒然的。 **No use slaving ...** = It is no use slaving ... It is no use = It is of no use. slaving ... 与 it 同位。

for: who cares for a slave? If you come back, come back for the sake of good fellowship; for youll get nothing else. Youve had a thousand times as much out of me as I have out of you; and if you dare to set up your little dog's tricks of fetching and carrying slippers against my creation of a Duchess Eliza, I'll slam the door in your silly face.

LIZA What did you do it for if you didnt care for me?

HIGGINS [*heartily*] Why, because it was my job.

LIZA You never thought of the trouble it would make for me.

HIGGINS Would the world ever have been made if its maker had been afraid of making trouble. Making life means making trouble. Theres only one way of escaping trouble; and thats killing things. Cowards, you notice, are always shrieking to have troublesome people killed.

LIZA I'm no preacher: I dont notice things like that. I notice that you dont notice me.

HIGGINS [*jumping up and walking about intolerantly*] Eliza: youre an idiot. I waste the treasures of my Miltonic mind by spreading them before you. Once for all, understand that I go my way and do my work without caring twopence what happens to either of us. I am not intimidated, like your father and your

---

564 **come back for the sake of good fellowship** 为良好的伙伴关系而回来；来做好朋友。

565 **youll get nothing else** 你（除了 good fellowship 之外）得不到其他任何东西。**Youve had a thousand times as much out of me as I have out of you** 你从我

这里得到的好处是我从你那里得到的好处的一千倍。 **a thousand** 喻其多。

567 **if you dare to set up your little dog's tricks of fetching and carrying slippers against my creation of a Duchess Eliza** 要是你敢拿出把拖鞋搬来搬去的小狗的把戏，来和我创造出的 Eliza 公爵夫人相对立；我把你训练成了 Eliza 公爵夫人，而你敢像小狗那样耍些搬搬拖鞋的把戏的话。Higgins 不许 Eliza 做那样的蠢事，所以下文用 silly 这个词。

569 **slam the door in your silly face** 朝着你的蠢脸把门砰地关上；把你这蠢货关出门外。注意这里介词用 in。

570 **do it** 把 Eliza 训练成公爵夫人。it，指 creation of a Duchess Eliza。

572 **the trouble it would make for me** 它（把我训练成了公爵夫人）会给我造成的麻烦（弄得我不能再去卖花，自食其力）。

573 **Would the world ever have been made if its maker had been afraid of making trouble?** 如果世界的创造者（“创世主”，即上帝）害怕制造麻烦，世界会被创造出来吗？这是表示与过去事实相反的虚拟语气的反问句，意思是：上帝创造世界，不怕制造麻烦。

574 **Making life means making trouble.** 创造生命就意味着制造麻烦，有生命就有麻烦。

576 **killing things** 扼杀事物；把一切毁掉（以逃避麻烦）。 **you notice** 你注意吧；你看；是插入语。 **shrieking to have troublesome people killed** 叫嚷着要使制造麻烦的人都被杀掉。

578 **I notice that you dont notice me.** 我只注意到你不注意我（你心目中没有我这个人）。

581 **I waste the treasures of my Miltonic mind by spreading them before you.** 我将我弥尔顿般的心灵的宝藏展现在你面前，全是白费；你全不理解我崇高的心意。前注中已说过，萧伯纳拿语言学家 Henry Sweet 作 Higgins 的原型，Sweet 是 Milton 的崇拜者；Milton 有崇高的心灵。

582 **Once for all** 只此一次不再重复；一次解决地；是习语。 **go my way** 走我的路；做我要做的事。 **my way** 有些语法家称为是“状语宾语”。

583 **without caring twopence** [ˈtʌpəns] **what happens to either of us** 全不管会有什么发生到我们两人中任何一个的身上；不管对你或我有什么影响。 **twopence** 二便士，喻其价值微小。 **do not care twopence** 是“毫不在乎”的意思。

stepmother. So you can come back or go to the devil: which you please.

LIZA What am I to come back for?

HIGGINS [*bouncing up on his knees on the ottoman and leaning over it to her*] For the fun of it. Thats why I took you on.

LIZA [*with averted face*] And you may throw me out tomorrow if I dont do everything you want me to?

HIGGINS Yes; and you may walk out tomorrow if I dont do everything you want me to.

LIZA And live with my stepmother?

HIGGINS Yes, or sell flowers.

LIZA Oh! If I only could go back to my flower basket! I should be independent of both you and father and all the world! Why did you take my independence from me? Why did I give it up? I'm a slave now, for all my fine clothes.

HIGGINS Not a bit. I'll adopt you as my daughter and settle money on you if you like. Or would you rather marry Pickering?

LIZA [*looking fiercely round at him*] I wouldnt marry you if you asked me; and youre nearer my age than what he is.

HIGGINS [*gently*] Than he is: not 'than what he is.'

LIZA [*losing her temper and rising*] I'll talk as I like. Youre not my teacher now.

---

585 **go to the devil** 见鬼去；滚开；也作 go to hell；都是习语。 **which you please** = whichever you please = whichever please you. 无论你喜欢哪一个；随你选择。

588 **bouncing up on his knees on the ottoman and leaning over it to her** 跳起来，跪在长榻上。在榻上倾斜着身子对着她。 **on one's knees** 跪下；是习语。

589 **For the fun of it** = You are to come back for the fun of it. 你回（到我这儿）来，为了好玩嘛。of it 的 it 没有具体意义，被称为 vague 'it'。 **took you on** 收留你。take on，是习语。

590 **with averted face** 转过脸去（避而不朝 Higgins 看）。 **throw me out** 把我撵走；赶我出去。

591 **you want me to** = you want me to do.

592 **walk out** 走出去；离去；作习语，也作"罢工"解。

596 **If I only could go back to my flower basket!** 只要假如我能回到我的（提着）花篮（卖花的生活，该多好啊）。这是虚拟语气表示与现在事实相反的愿望；即但愿我能重新去卖花！ **if only** 只要……（就好）；是习语；注意不是 only if。 **I should be independent of both you and father and all the world!** 我就既不靠你，也不靠爹和所有（其他）的人。independent，后面介词用 of。这里的 both ... and ... 以说话的对方（you）为一面，第三者（father and all the world）为另一面。这句也是虚拟语气；承接上句 if I only could go back to my flower basket。

598 **take my independence from me** 从我身上拿去了我的独立；剥夺我的独立。

599 **for all my fine clothes** 尽管（有）我这些华美的衣裳；纵然穿得漂亮。

600 **Not a bit.** 一点也不；是习语，口语中常用以否定对方的说法，如甲说 Sorry to have bothered you. 乙说 Not a bit (of it). **adopt you as my daughter** 领养你作为我的女儿；认你作养女。

601 **would you rather** 你宁愿…… **would rather** 宁可；是习语；= would sooner；但是 would rather 有它特殊的用法，它后面可接一般省略 that 的 that 从句，从句用表示与事实相反的虚拟语气，如：I would rather you didn't go. 我认为你最好不去。

602 **looking fiercely round at him** 凶狠地回眸瞧着他。 **I wouldnt marry you if you asked me** 假如你要我嫁你，我也不肯（更不要说嫁 Pickering 了）。Higgins 和她年龄的差距比 Pickering 和她的年龄差距接近些；Pickering 和 Eliza 年龄相差更大，见下文。

603 **than what he is** 应作 than he is。Higgins 接着就给她改正。

605 **losing her temper** 发脾气；是习语。

HIGGINS [*reflectively*] I dont suppose Pickering would, though. He's as confirmed an old bachelor as I am.

LIZA Thats not what I want; and dont you think it. Ive always had chaps enough wanting me that way. Freddy Hill writes to me twice and three times a day, sheets and sheets.

HIGGINS [*disagreeably surprised*] Damn his impudence! [*He recoils and finds himself sitting on his heels.*]

LIZA He has a right to if he likes, poor lad. And he does love me.

HIGGINS [*getting off the ottoman*] You have no right to encourage him.

LIZA Every girl has a right to be loved.

HIGGINS What! By fools like that?

LIZA Freddy's not a fool. And if he's weak and poor and wants me, may be he'd make me happier than my betters that bully me and dont want me.

HIGGINS Can he make anything of you? Thats the point.

LIZA Perhaps I could make something of him. But I never thought of us making anything of one another; and you never think of anything else. I only want to be natural.

HIGGINS In short, you want me to be as infatuated about you as Freddy? Is that it?

---

607 **I dont suppose Pickering would, though.** 然而我想 Pickering 不会（娶你）。would 后面省略 marry you。 **though** 是副词，用在句末，相当于 however 然而；不过。

609 **Thats not what I want** 那不是我所要的；我不要那个。that 指嫁人。 **dont you think it** 你别这么想。 **dont you** 加强 dont 的语气。it = that that's what I want. **had chaps enough wanting me that way** 有够多的人要我那样（嫁给他们）。**chap** 家伙；小伙子。

610 **Freddy Hill** Freddy 的姓是 Eynsford Hill，这是双姓（double-barrelled surname），这里可能是 Eliza 随便叫的。

611 **twice and three times** 两三次；一般说 twice or three times，但这里说 twice and three times 绝非“五次”的意思。 **sheets and sheets** 几张几张；表示数量多；可作为 writes 的宾语，也可看作是状语短语。

612 **disagreeably surprised** 不高兴地感到惊异。 **Damn his impudence** [ˈɪmpjədəns]! 他的厚颜无耻该死！ **recoils and finds himself sitting on his heels** （Higgins 原来跪在长榻上）往后一缩，发现自己坐在脚跟上（不觉屈膝而坐着）。

614 **He has a right to if he likes** = He has the right to write to me twice and three times a day, sheets and sheets if he likes. likes 后面实际上也省略 to write ... sheets and sheets. **poor lad** 可怜的家伙；与 He 同位。Freddy 是个破落人家的穷小子，可这里 poor 是“可怜的”意思。 **lad** 原义“男孩子”，这里亲切地称“家伙”。

615 **You have no right to encourage him.** 你没有权利去鼓励他；不该怂恿他（爱你）。

618 **By fools like that?** = Every girl has a right to be loved by fools like that?

619 **if he's weak and poor and wants me** 如果说，他软弱贫穷而要我的话。注意这里 if 的用法。

620 **may be** 也许。一般写作 maybe。 **he'd make me happier than my betters that bully** [ˈbʊli] **me and dont want me** 他会比欺侮我而不要我的那些比我身份高的人使我更快活些。 **one's betters** 高于或胜过自己的人们。

622 **Can he make anything of you?** （我能使你成为贵妇人，）他（Freddy）能使你成为什么吗？ **Thats the point.** 那（上句所提出的问题）是要点；关键在此。

623 **I could make something of him** （如果我要那样做的话）我能使他成为什么。这是虚拟语气，省略条件从句 if I would。

624 **you never think of anything else** 你（除使人成为什么之外）其他什么也不想；你只知道把人改变成什么。

625 **only want to be natural** 只要自然（是什么就什么）。

626 **infatuated** [ɪnˈfætʃʊeɪtɪd] 变得昏头昏脑的；着迷；痴恋；这是过去分词变成的形容词。

LIZA No I dont. Thats not the sort of feeling I want from you. And dont you be too sure of yourself or of me. I could have been a bad girl if I'd liked. Ive seen more of some things than you, for all your learning. Girls like me can drag gentlemen down to make love to them easy enough. And they wish each other dead the next minute.

HIGGINS Of course they do. Then what in thunder are we quarrelling about?

LIZA [*much troubled*] I want a little kindness. I know I'm a common ignorant girl, and you a book-learned gentleman; but I'm not dirt under your feet. What I done [*correcting herself*] what I did was not for the dresses and the taxis: I did it because we were pleasant together and I come – came – to care for you; not to want you to make love to me, and not forgetting the difference between us, but more friendly like.

HIGGINS Well, of course. Thats just how I feel. And how Pickering feels. Eliza: youre a fool.

LIZA Thats not a proper answer to give me. [*She sinks on the chair*

---

628 **Thats not the sort of feeling I want from you.** 那（infatuation）不是我要从你那里得到的那种感情；我不要你迷恋我。

629 **dont you be too sure of yourself or of me** 你不要太肯定自己（一定不会迷恋我），或者太肯定我（准要你迷恋）。 **I could have been a bad girl if I'd liked.** 倘若我要做坏女孩子的话，我早就可能做坏女孩子了。这是表示与过去事实相反的虚拟语气。

630 **seen more of some things than you** 关于有些事情比你看得多；有些方面见

识比你广。

631 **for all your learning** 尽管你有学问。 **Girls like me can drag gentlemen down to make love to them easy enough.** 像我这样的女孩子们要使上流社会的先生们降低身份来向她们求爱，是很容易的。 **make love (to)** （向……）求爱；这个习语现在含有色情的意思。easy 应作 easily，修饰 can drag。

632 **And they wish each other dead the next minute.** 不过他们（像我这样的姑娘和上流社会的先生）在下一分钟（过了一会儿）就彼此但愿对方死掉；相恋不久就成为势不两立的冤家了。each other 是 wish 的宾语，dead 是宾语补足语，each other dead 称为复合宾语。

634 **they do** = they wish each other dead the next minute. **Then what in thunder are we quarrelling about?** （你既没有让我向你求爱，因而我们也没有成为冤家，）那么，我们到底在争吵些什么呢？ **in thunder** 究竟；到底；口语中还有 Thunder! 或 By thunder! 表示愤怒、感叹和强调等意思。

637 **book-learned** [ˈbʊklɜːnd] 有书本知识的（常含有“缺乏实际知识”的意思）。

638 **What I done** Eliza 说错了，随即自己改正为 what I did；我所做的，指接受 Higgins 的语言训练和冒充公爵夫人出席招待会。

639 **dresses** dress 统指“服装”时，是不可数名词；作可数名词时，a dress 指一件女服或童装。

640 **we were pleasant together** 我们（俩）互相认为对方是可爱的。不是“互爱”，也不是“一起感到愉快”。 **come – came – to care for you** 渐渐关心起你来。先误用 come，随即改正为 came; come 后接不定式，表示“渐渐开始……”、“终于……”。

641 **not to want you to make love to me** （关心你）可不是要你向我求爱。 **and not forgetting the difference between us** 没忘记我们之间的（阶级）不同。**and ... ing** 是爱尔兰用法，表示伴随的动作或情况，如：She was adsorbed in her needlework, and minding her baby. 她一边做针线活，一边当心着她的婴儿。

642 **but more friendly like** 只是可以说比较友好些。but 后面可理解为省略了 getting；这样，not forgetting 和 but getting 相呼应。 **like** 用在形容词等后面作副词的俚语用法已屡见前。

643 **Thats just how I feel.** 我正是那样感觉；我正是觉得你就像是你自己说的那样。

645 **Thats not a proper answer to give me** 那（说我是傻瓜）不是你应该给我的回答；你应该好好回答我的话，不该没头没脑地说我是傻瓜。

at the writing-table in tears.]

HIGGINS It's all youll get until you stop being a common idiot. If youre going to be a lady, youll have to give up feeling neglected if the men you know dont spend half their time snivelling over you and the other half giving you black eyes. If you cant stand the coldness of my sort of life, and the strain of it, go back to the gutter. Work til youre more a brute than a human being; and then cuddle and squabble and drink til you fall asleep. Oh, it's a fine life, the life of the gutter. It's real: it's warm: it's violent: you can feel it through the thickest skin: you can taste it and smell it without any training or any work. Not like Science and Literature and Classical Music and Philosophy and Art. You find me cold, unfeeling, selfish, dont you? Very well: be off with you to the sort of people you like. Marry some sentimental hog or other with lots of money, and a thick pair of lips to kiss you with and a thick pair of boots to kick you with. If you cant appreciate what youve got,

---

646 **in tears** 流着泪；含泪；是习语。

647 **It's all youll get** 这（说你是傻瓜的这个回答）是你所能得到的一切；你只能得到这个（回答）。 **If youre going to be a lady, youll have to give up feeling neglected** 如果你想要做一个上流社会的女人，你不得不放弃（务必不要）感到被忽视（冷淡）。 **If youre going to be...** 要是你想做……；neglected 是表语。

649 **if the men you know dont spend half their time snivelling** [ˈsnɪvəlɪŋ] **over you and the other half giving you black eyes** 如果你认识的那些男人不是用一半的时间向你啼啼哭哭、假作多情，另一半的时间把你的眼睛打得发

青。 **snivel** 抽鼻子；啜泣；假作悲伤；假作多情。

651 **stand the coldness of my sort of life** 忍受我这种生活的冷酷（指冷冰冰的生活）。 **and the strain of it** 和它（我这种生活）的紧张。承接 stand，同 the coldness of my sort of life 并列。and 连接两个词或词组一般不用逗号，这里 and 前用逗号，表示说话顿一下，强调语气，或表示是补充的话。 **go back to the gutter** （你）回到贫民区去。这是主句。

652 **Work til youre more a brute than a human being** 工作到你更（像）是畜生而不（像）是人。

653 **cuddle and squabble and drink til you fall asleep** 拥抱、吵闹、喝酒，直到昏昏睡去。 **cuddle** 紧贴着拥抱。 **squabble** 为琐事而吵闹。

654 **it's a fine life, the life of the gutter** 这种贫民窟的生活真是美好的生活。the life of the gutter 是 it 的同位语。这是反话；fine 常用以讽刺，类似的例子如：What a fine state of affairs! 情况好极（实谓"糟透"）！ **It's real: it's warm: it's violent** 它（那种生活）真实，它温暖，它强烈。正和上文 Higgins 所说的他的生活是冷冰冰的（coldness）相对照。

655 **feel it through the thickest skin** 透过（即使）最厚的皮肤也感觉得到它（那种生活）。

656 **can taste it and smell it without any training or any work** 无需任何训练、任何努力就能够尝到它和嗅到它。这和 Higgins 所说他的生活的紧张（strain）相对照。taste 和 smell 是比喻的说法，犹如我们所说"尝到甜头"、"政治嗅觉"中的"尝"和"嗅"。

657 **Not like** 不像（科学、文学等需要训练、努力学习和钻研）。

658 **unfeeling** 缺乏感情的；无情的；冷酷的。

659 **be off with you** 你去吧；去你的吧；这是惯用语。

660 **some sentimental hog or other** 某一个易动感情的蠢猪。 **some ... or other** 某一个（不肯定哪一个）。 **hog** 原义"猪"，口语中用以鄙称"人"。

661 **a thick pair of lips** 一双厚嘴唇。实际是 a pair of thick lips，但文中的说法极普遍。 **a thick pair of boots to kick you with** 一双用以踢你的厚皮靴。to kick you with = with which to kick you. 但后者在口语中不用。

662 **cant appreciate** [əˈpriːʃieɪt] **what youve got** 不能欣赏你得到了的（指在 Higgins 家学会了上流社会的语言而可以成为个贵妇人）。 **appreciate** 认识到……的好处；欣赏。

youd better get what you can appreciate.

LIZA [*desperate*] Oh, you are a cruel tyrant. I cant talk to you: you turn everything against me: I'm always in the wrong. But you know very well all the time that youre nothing but a bully. You know I cant go back to the gutter, as you call it, and that I have no real friends in the world but you and the Colonel. You know well I couldnt bear to live with a low common man after you two; and it's wicked and cruel of you to insult me by pretending I could. You think I must go back to Wimpole Street because I have nowhere else to go but father's. But dont you be too sure that you have me under your feet to be trampled on and talked down. I'll marry Freddy, I will, as soon as I'm able to support him.

HIGGINS [*thunderstruck*] Freddy!!! That young fool! That poor devil who couldnt get a job as an errand boy even if he had the guts to try for it! Woman: do you not understand that I have made you a consort for a King?

LIZA Freddy loves me: that makes him king enough for me. I dont want him to work: he wasnt brought up to it as I was. I'll go and be a teacher.

HIGGINS Whatll you teach, in heaven's name?

LIZA What you taught me. I'll teach phonetics.

---

663 **youd better get what you can appreciate** 你还是去过你能够欣赏的（指Higgins所描绘的“贫民窟生活”）。

665 **turn everything against me** 谈到一切事总是反对我；样样都说我不是。 **I'm always in the wrong.** 我总是错的。 **be in the wrong** 错；理亏；是习语。

666 **youre nothing but a bully** 你只是个强凶霸道的人。 **nothing but** 除……之外不是任何其他；只是；是习语。

668 **but you and the Colonel** 除了你和上校之外。 **but** = except. 上条 nothing but 中的 but 也是这个意思。

669 **I couldnt bear to live with a low common man after you two** 在（和）你们两个（生活在一起）之后，我没法忍受和一个下等的普通男人生活在一起。这里用虚拟语气 couldnt，表示要想这样做也不能。

670 **it's wicked** [ˈwɪkɪd] **and cruel of you to insult me by pretending I could** 你假装以为我能（忍受和下等普通男人一起生活）来侮辱我，你这是恶毒、狠心的。 **insult** 动词读 [ɪnˈsʌlt]，名词读 [ˈɪnsʌlt]。

672 **but father's** = except my father's home.

673 **have me under your feet to be trampled on and talked down** 把我放在脚底下被践踏和被吆五喝六地压倒。 **talked down** 被用大声压倒；被用语言鄙薄；承接 to be。

676 **thunderstruck** 如遭雷击；大为震惊。 **That poor devil who couldnt get a job as an errand boy even if he had the guts to try for it!** 即使他胆敢想要找个工作，连个跑腿的工作也找不到的那个可怜虫！这是个只有名词词组（没有谓语）的单部句。 **guts** 胆量；力量；用复数；是俚语。

678 **I have made you a consort** [ˈkɒnsɔːt] **for a King** 我已经使你成为（可以做）一个国王的配偶（这里并非说已成国王的配偶）。

680 **that makes him king enough for me** 那（指爱我）使他成为对于我是足够的国王；爱我的人足以抵得上国王。这里 king 前面没有冠词，是因为后面用 enough（enough 修饰 king），又如 He is scholar enough to take up the editorship (/ for the editorship). 他有足够的学问担任这编辑工作。

681 **he wasnt brought up to it as I was** 他不像我这样从小需要干活。 **it** 指工作、劳动。 **as I was** 后面省略 brought up to it。

682 **go and be a teacher** 设法做教师。

683 **in heaven's name** 用上帝的名字；这是发誓用语，在疑问句中用以加强语气，有"究竟"、"到底"的意思。

684 **What you taught me.** = I'll teach what you taught me.

HIGGINS Ha! Ha! Ha!

LIZA I'll offer myself as an assistant to that hairy faced Hungarian.

HIGGINS [*rising in a fury*] What! That impostor! That humbug! That toadying ignoramus! Teach him my methods! my discoveries! You take one step in his direction and I'll wring your neck. [*He lays hands on her.*] Do you hear?

LIZA [*defiantly non-resistant*] Wring away. What do I care? I knew youd strike me some day. [*He lets her go, stamping with rage at having forgotten himself, and recoils so hastily that he stumbles back into his seat on the ottoman.*] Aha! Now I know how to deal with you. What a fool I was not to think of it before! You cant take away the knowledge you gave me. You said I had a finer ear than you. And I can be civil and kind to people, which is more than you can. Aha! [*purposely dropping her aitches to annoy him*] Thats done you, Enry Iggins, it az. Now I dont care that [*snapping her fingers*] for your bullying and your big talk. I'll advertize it in the papers that your duchess is only a flower girl that you taught, and that she'll teach anybody to be a duchess just the same in six months for a thousand guineas. Oh, when I think of myself crawling under your feet and

686 **offer myself** 自荐。 **hairy faced Hungarian** 须发浓密的匈牙利人，即 Nepommuck，见第三幕（p.200）。

689 **toadying ignoramus** [ˌɪgnəˈreɪməs] 奉承拍马的无知无识的人。 **Teach him my methods! my discoveries!** 把我的方法和我的发现去教给他吗？惊叹号代替疑问号，加强反问的语气。

690 **You take one step in his direction and I'll wring your neck.** 要是你向他的方向走一步（接近一步），那我就扭断你的脖子（要你的命）。 **and** （要是……）那么……

691 **lays hands on** 对……动手；抓住；是习语。

692 **defiantly** [dɪˈfaɪəntli] **non-resistant** 倔强地不抵抗；虽不抵抗但态度倔强地。**Wring away** 尽情扭吧。away 表示"继续"。 **What do I care?** 我介意什么？这是反问，意即 I dont care（我不介意）。 **I knew youd strike me some day** 我早知道你有一天会打我。

693 **lets her go** （Higgins 原来动手抓住她，现在）松手将她放开。**let go** 松手放开；是习语；这个习语中的 go 是没有 to 的不定式。 **stamping with rage at having forgotten himself** 对刚才自己失态（做出了不恰当的举动，指动手抓住 Eliza）愤怒得顿着脚。 **forget oneself** 忘了自己；忘乎所以；失去理智；是习语。

696 **think of it** 想到这一点（指 how to deal with you，如何对付你）。

697 **had a finer ear than you** 有比你更好的耳朵；（辨别语音的）听觉比你灵敏。

698 **And I can** 可改为 and that I could 而并入上句。这种在 You said 后面先用过去时 had，后用现在时 can，也可以，因为所说的状态不只存在于说话当时。**which is more than you can** 那（指有礼、和善）是比你更能够；我比你更能待人有礼、和善。 **which** 代替整个主句所包含的意义。

699 **dropping her aitches** [ˈeɪtʃez] 脱落 [h] 音，如下文把 Henry Higgins 读作 [ˈenri ˈɪgɪnz]。

700 **Thats done you** 那使你瘪掉了；这可使你没有办法了。 **That** 统指上面 Eliza 已经学会本领，且有比 Higgins 更多的优点。 **it az** = it has (done you). 重复以加强语气。 **I dont care that [*snapping her fingers*] for your bullying and your big talk** 我这么一点（弹指头）也不在乎你的强凶霸道和说大话了。 **not care a snap of one's finger** 原是口语中的习语，意思是"毫不介意"；这里口说 that 而弹指，即以 that 代替 a snap of my fingers。

702 **advertize it in the papers that ...** 在报纸上登广告说；it 后面有两个 that 从句作为它的同位语。

704 **just the same** 完全一样；同样地；是习语。

being trampled on and called names, when all the time I had only to lift up my finger to be as good as you, I could just kick myself.

HIGGINS [*wondering at her*] You damned impudent slut, you! But it's better than snivelling; better than fetching slippers and finding spectacles, isnt it? [*rising*] By George, Eliza, I said I'd make a woman of you; and I have. I like you like this.

LIZA Yes: you turn round and make up to me now that I'm not afraid of you, and can do without you.

HIGGINS Of course I do, you little fool. Five minutes ago you were like a millstone round my neck. Now youre a tower of strength: a consort battleship. You and I and Pickering will be three old bachelors instead of only two men and a silly girl.

Mrs Higgins returns, dressed for the wedding. Eliza instantly becomes cool and elegant.

MRS HIGGINS The carriage is waiting, Eliza. Are you ready?

LIZA Quite. Is the Professor coming?

MRS HIGGINS Certainly not. He cant behave himself in church. He makes remarks out loud all the time on the clergyman's pronunciation.

---

706 **called names** （被）辱骂；与 trampled on 并列，都和 being 构成被动式分词。 **when all the time I had only to lift up my finger to be as good as you** 在（受你凌辱的）整个那段时间里，我只要一举手（轻易地）就可以和

你一样（地位平等）。注意；这个 when 引起的状语从句修饰 crawling under your feet and being trampled on and called names，前面一个 when 引起的状语从句修饰主句 I could just kick myself。

707 **I could just kick myself** 我正会踢自己；Eliza 想到当初本可以和 Higgins 处于平等地位而偏要听任他凌辱，不胜怨恨，所以她要“踢自己”，犹如我们说“打自己的耳光”。这是这句的主句。

709 **slut** 贱妇；懒妇；这是对女人极粗野的用语。

710 **it's better than snivelling** 这（这样理直气壮地和他争论）比哭哭啼啼好。Higgins 宁愿 Eliza 和他分庭抗礼，见下文。

711 **I said I'd make a woman of you** 我早说要使你成为一个（真正的）女人（而不是脓包、奴隶）。

712 **I have** = I have made a woman of you. **I like you like this** 我喜欢你这个样子。like this 是宾语补足语，you 和 like this 构成复合宾语。

713 **turn round** 转身；转变；是习语。 **make up to me** 讨好我。 **make up to** 原义“接近”，转义“巴结”、“向（女人）求爱”、“补偿”；是习语。 **now that** 既然；由于；是连接词；有时单用 now。

715 **I do** = I turn round and make up to you.

716 **a millstone round my neck** 挂在我脖子上的磨石；我的沉重负担。 **a tower of strength** 力量之塔。比喻“坚强的形象”。这是很正常的比喻，但接下来说 a consort battleship（护航军舰），那是萧伯纳的诙谐笔墨罢了。

718 **bachelors** 独身汉，指男性。独身女子称 spinster 或 old maid；也可用 bachelor girl（或 woman）称未婚职业妇女；但这里作者用 three old bachelors 把 Eliza 也包括在内，显然又是诙谐。

719 **dressed for the wedding** 穿着参加（Doolittle 的）婚礼的服装；dressed 是过去分词。

722 **Is the Professor coming?** （Higgins）教授去（参加婚礼）吗？注意：这里用 coming 而不用 going，是因为 Eliza 就要去参加她父亲的婚礼，好像已经到了那里似的。

723 **behave himself in church** 在教堂里守规矩。 **behave oneself** 举动好；守规矩；是习语。 **in church** 和 at home、school 等语同例，可数名词前面不用限定词。

724 **makes remarks out loud all the time on the clergyman's pronunciation** （在牧师讲道时）只会大声地评论牧师的发音。

LIZA Then I shall not see you again, Professor. Goodbye. [*She goes to the door.*]

MRS HIGGINS [*coming to Higgins*] Goodbye, dear.

HIGGINS Goodbye, mother. [*He is about to kiss her, when he recollects something.*] Oh, by the way, Eliza, order a ham and a Stilton cheese, will you? And buy me a pair of reindeer gloves, number eights, and a tie to match that new suit of mine. You can choose the color. [*His cheerful, careless, vigorous voice shews that he is incorrigible.*]

LIZA [*disdainfully*] Number eights are too small for you if you want them lined with lamb's wool. You have three new ties that you have forgotten in the drawer of your washstand. Colonel Pickering prefers double Gloucester to Stilton; and you dont notice the difference. I telephoned Mrs Pearce this morning not to forget the ham. What you are to do without me I cannot imagine. [*She sweeps out.*]

MRS HIGGINS I'm afraid youve spoilt that girl, Henry. I should be uneasy about you and her if she were less fond of Colonel Pickering.

HIGGINS Pickering! Nonsense: she's going to marry Freddy. Ha ha! Freddy! Freddy!! Ha ha ha ha ha!!!!! [*He roars with laughter as the play ends.*]

---

729 **is about to ...** 即将；正要……；是习语。 **when** = and at that time. 这个

when 引起的从句有同主语并列的性质。

730 **by the way** 顺便说起；附带说；是习语。 **order a ham and a Stilton** [ˈstɪltən] **cheese** 叫店里送一只火腿和一块 Stilton 干酪来。 **ham** 作“火腿肉”解时为不可数名词，作“一只火腿”解，是可数名词。 **Stilton cheese** 英国中东部 Huntingdonshire（郡）Stilton 村所制的干酪，味道浓厚；简称 Stilton。

731 **a pair of reindeer** [ˈreɪndɪə] **gloves, number eights** 一双鹿皮手套，（尺码）八号的。 **reindeer** 驯鹿。

732 **match that new suit of mine** （颜色、花纹等方面）配我的那套新衣服。一套西装称 a suit。 **You can choose the color.** 你可以挑选颜色；颜色由你挑好了。这里 can 表示说话人对对方的“允许”；所以这句不作“你能够（有能力）挑选颜色”解。

733 **careless** 漫不经心的；随随便便的。这里不是“粗心”、“疏忽”的意思。

735 **Number eights** 八号（尺码的手套）。数码指手套，所以可以用复数。

736 **lined with lamb's wool** 用羔羊毛绒衬里。

737 **that you have forgotten in the drawer of your washstand** 你把这（三条新领带）忘记在你洗脸台的抽屉里。in the drawer of your washstand 是宾语补足语，和 forgotten 的宾语 that 构成复合宾语。

738 **double Gloucester** ([ˈglɒstə], 也读 [ˈglɔːstə]) 全脂 Gloucester（干酪）。 **Gloucester** 英国西南部 Gloucestershire（郡）的首府；这里是 Gloucester cheese 的简称。脱脂的 Gloucester 干酪称 single Gloucester。

739 **you dont notice the difference** 你没有注意到（你和 Pickering 的口味）不同。

740 **What you are to do without me I cannot imagine.** = I cannot imagine what you are to do without me. 我没法想象你没有我怎么办。

741 **sweeps out** 飘然走出。 **sweep** 原义“扫”、“掠过”；转义“急速移动”。

742 **youve spoilt that girl** 你（Higgins）把那个女孩子纵坏了。Spoil 的过去时和过去分词也作 spoiled，读作 [spɔɪlt] 或 [spɔɪld]。 **I should be uneasy about you and her if she were less fond of Colonel Pickering.** 要不是她更喜欢 Pickering 上校，我准要为你（Higgins）和她不安。Higgins 太太还以为 Eliza 喜欢 Pickering，会嫁给 Pickering，所以她以为 Eliza 倘和 Higgins 结了婚，他们俩准会搞得很糟。

745 **Pickering!** （你说 Eliza 喜欢）Pickering 吗?

746 **roars with laughter** 笑声如吼；大声狂笑。

图书在版编目(CIP)数据

卖花女：五幕传奇剧 /（爱尔兰）萧伯纳（Bernard Shaw）著；
葛传椝，俞亢咏注解．—上海：上海译文出版社，2018.1（2024.8重印）
书名原文：Pygmalion
ISBN 978－7－5327－7332－9

Ⅰ.①卖…　Ⅱ.①萧…②葛…③俞…　Ⅲ.①传奇剧（话剧）—
剧本—英国—中世纪　Ⅳ.①I562.33

中国版本图书馆 CIP 数据核字(2016)第 209190 号

Bernard Shaw
Pygmalion

卖花女(五幕传奇剧)
[爱尔兰]萧伯纳　著　葛传椝　俞亢咏　注解
责任编辑/陆亚平　封面设计/张志全工作室　版式设计/ideaforma工作室

上海译文出版社有限公司出版、发行
网址：www.yiwen.com.cn
201101　上海市闵行区号景路159弄B座
上海新华印刷有限公司印刷

开本 787×1092　1/32　印张 10.75　插页 5　字数 217,000
2018年1月第1版　2024年8月第5次印刷
印数：9,001–10,000 册

ISBN 978－7－5327－7332－9/H·1318
定价：55.00元